RAZOR-TIPPED ARROWS, A SWORD OF TEMPERED STEEL AND AN UNSHAKABLE COURAGE WERE HIS WEAPONS . . .

ROBERT PARKER—Naval chopper pilot whose crash in the frigid Antarctic catapults him into a mysterious future world where he must fight to survive.

KAETHA—the lovely, statuesque Relori woman who could hold Parker a prisoner to her love, but would risk her life to help him find his way back in time.

VOULA—an exotic young beauty from the fabulous land of Par'z, her magic samra seeds had the power to rob Parker of all desire to escape.

CAPTAIN BYERYAS—a Terasian with a twisted soul, who took Parker prisoner and set a monstrous price on his freedom.

NISSRAL—dreaded high priest of the evil Terasians, he planned a gruesome death for Parker and for all who befriended him.

how reached such a world. Whatever thing was
progress and prosp ity   e the Terasians, whoever they were. And   iads whom these

Books edited by Richard A. Lupoff

What If? Volume 1
What If? Volume 2

Forthcoming

What If? Volume 3
What If? Volume 4

Published by TIMESCAPE/POCKET BOOKS

RICHARD A. LUPOFF

ONE MILLION CENTURIES

A TIMESCAPE BOOK
PUBLISHED BY POCKET BOOKS NEW YORK

A Timescape Book published by
POCKET BOOKS, a Simon & Schuster division of
GULF & WESTERN CORPORATION
1230 Avenue of the Americas, New York, N.Y. 10020

ISBN: 0-671-83226-3

First Timescape Books printing April, 1981

10 9 8 7 6 5 4 3 2 1

POCKET and colophon are trademarks of Simon & Schuster.

Printed in the U.S.A.

CHAPTER

1

A touch so light it was hardly there was the first evidence of returning consciousness. A touch, a feeling of cold through every bone and fiber, a gurgling, trickling sound, a sense of motion passing over his body, the touch. It moved from Parker's hip toward one knee, a tiny pressure, tiny, incredibly delicate, yet it held the full consciousness of the man as he lay on his left side.

Parker concentrated on the feeling, ignoring the sound, ignoring other tactile responses. The touch resolved itself into a pattern of separate contacts, coming and going on the surface of his naked leg. After a time the pressure, almost imperceptible to begin with, grew momentarily greater by the smallest degree, then was removed, leaving behind a ghost of a shadow of a sensation.

Parker sprang upward, fully aware in the instant of the occurrence, saw a butterfly—surely it was a butterfly—soaring gracefully upward from his leg which it had been inspecting. It was by far the largest flying insect Parker had ever seen, its wings spanning fully eight inches of velvety black trimmed with an intricate pattern of vivid yellow.

The insect hovered, seemingly without fear, a few feet over the man's head, then flew off into the woods nearby, woods so lush as to suggest near-tropical growth. Parker shook himself, trying to grasp his surroundings. He was drenched with frigid water, standing on the bank of a fast-flowing stream from which he had leaped in that first moment of vivid awareness. Now he stood, slowly ceasing to tremble as the sun and warm air relieved the cold of his body. He had to orient himself to the situation.

But—what was the situation? And what were these surroundings? He must have dozed in his pilot's seat as Logan handled the chopper controls. No, Parker remembered the storm, the crash. Logan was dead. He had felt

Logan's corpse, known he was dead. Parker remembered climbing from the wrecked helicopter, becoming lost in the blackness, and then . . . butterflies? Woods? What had happened?

Parker looked about him at a thick forest of tall trees, a wealth of saplings and smaller bushes between the trunks and a carpet of fallen vegetation covering the ground. He looked at his own body, feeling for the injured ribs he had suffered the day before. Except for a general feeling of soreness and a particular tenderness of his skin, Parker seemed uninjured.

Certainly he was *not* blind, and that was a gigantic relief. Unless the whole experience was an hallucination and he really lay still in the polar storm, his life being frozen from his body . . . If that was the case . . . If that was the case, he could just forget everything, lie back and enjoy the final dream-moments of his existence. But if it was not, he'd better try to take charge of himself and figure a way out of the puzzle.

And being uncertain, Parker chose to assume that this new world was real. Whatever, wherever, this world was, it was real.

And Parker's injuries seemed to have healed. The blow to his head—he must have had at least a fractured cheekbone—no longer made tender his face, nor did his neck ache. His side seemed well. Healthy, naked, puzzled, Parker took one reassuring look at the blue sky, lowered his gaze to the level of the surrounding forest, and set out to find some sign of habitation. Lacking that he would settle happily for a sign of food.

He must have made three-quarters of a mile before he saw the cat, or what must have been a cat. It was walking apparently parallel to him, and at a break between two heavily boled trees the cat and Parker caught each other's eye at the same moment. Parker saw a parti-colored beast the size of a large shepherd dog. Parti-colored! The cat was a geneticist's nightmare: orange, black and white, it had the mad markings of a perfect calico, with solid patches, stripes, splotches interspersed among salt-and-pepper patches of orange on black. A white muzzle, the rest of its face black except for an exclamation point of brilliant yellow-orange reaching from the top of the skull to a point between and below the eyes. The cat must have weighed easily eighty pounds, and carried every ounce of it with muscular grace that spoke of speed and strength in equal portions. The animal's head, somehow proportionately larger than the head of any cat Parker could recall, seemed also oddly shaped, as if the cat's skull had been modified to accommodate more brain than was proper for a cat. The ears were pointed and alert, and from that strangely intelligent-appearing face two eyes of brilliant green-blue gazed enigmatically at the man.

Parker stopped in his tracks, glancing at the nearest tree and thinking about limbs for climbing, but the cat merely surveyed him, pausing momentarily in its progress, and then continued.

Shortly, so did Parker, altering course to the left to avoid the path of his newest acquaintance. In the next mile or so he noticed several more of the giant black and yellow butterflies, some settled on fruit trees that bore egg-sized fruit resembling slightly enlarged kumquats. He was tempted to try one of them, but before he could reach a tree his attention leaped to a new sound in the previously still woods. Voices.

For a moment Parker thought of hiding in the trees, attempting to spy out the nature of the owners of the voices, but his own curiosity and a sudden, desperate need for human companionship were more powerful than caution. He faced the direction from which the voices had come and shouted, "Hello!"

The voices ceased abruptly and Parker shouted again. There was a quick, indistinguishable conversation, then Parker heard the sounds of underbrush snapping, several pairs of booted feet advancing toward him.

Four figures stepped into view. Before Parker could register any reaction or say anything, one of the men spoke.

"January hayrick slant funnerway?" he asked.

Parker looked blank. Gibberish, a big portion of his mind told him. No, a smaller corner replied, not gibberish. That's a foreign language. It sounded like gibberish and I made myself hear it as English words, but it doesn't mean anything. "English," said Parker. "Do any of you speak English?"

The four men looked at one another, exchanged a few sentences Parker could not understand, then addressed more slant funnerway at him. "Habla Español?" Parker tried. Blank looks from the four.

More January hayrick.

"Deutsch?"

Hayrick slant funnerzip trapshoot.

"Russian? Chinese?" asked Parker, thinking that it *would* be some language that he didn't understand himself.

More slant January. That was hopeless. Parker and the four surveyed one another. To the four, Parker realized, he must be a naked brown figure. Himself seemingly much the better for wear since the accident with Logan, standing ready to talk, flee or fight as the occasion demanded, Parker saw four men of varied stature, ranging in age by some ten years over or under his own thirty.

At first he thought that they were all Negroes. Their color was much the same as his own, and varied little from one to another. The hair of all was black, the build varying. There was the small, sharp-featured man. He had spoken first. There was a huge, muscular fellow who must have stood close to seven feet and weighed 300 at least, who wore an incongruous handlebar mustache. There was another tall man, but built with a rangy, long-muscled shape, and there was the slim, well-proportioned fellow with the darting eyes and ever-mobile features.

But all four had the distinctive eye-folds and high cheekbones of the Chinese, and their hair was slack rather than curly. Chinese Negroes, thought Parker. Descendants of American GIs? And whom? Koreans? Vietnamese?

He let go of that puzzle in favor of the immediate one of getting some food and establishing communication with the four. They were all armed, apparently hunters. The two taller men each carried a longbow. Each of the four had a cutting weapon. The sharp-featured man held his in his hand. It had the look of hand workmanship on it. Twenty inches long, Parker guessed, shaped like a . . . like a combination of a scimitar and a meat cleaver. Broad, heavy blade. Curved, pointed, sharpened along the sweep edge and for about five inches on the back edge. An improved machete.

You could stab with it, flick backhanded if you missed and give an adversary a nice wound, or slash with the long side. A pretty sticker with a basket handle to protect the wielder.

Not as handy as a gravity knife, the American thought. But a good weapon. But not as handy. For a moment he felt dizzy, closed his eyes. He was back at home, thirteen again, and carrying his own first good knife. Seven inches of wicked, pointed blade, ready to drop out of a white pearl handle at the touch of the catch . . .

"Butchy" Parker was cold with fright. He could feel the perspiration running off his face, his hands were clammy, and in the right he clutched his new knife. Bought with money stolen from his mother's purse, honed and polished as he'd long since learned from older boys.

Now he was in the street and Carlos, the local bully, appeared out of a bunch of kids loitering on a stoop. Carlos was fifteen and big. He'd been away to reform school, and since his return no kid crossed him.

"Whatcha got there, Butchy?" Carlos asked.

"Nothing," the young Parker replied, trying to slide the white-pearl knife unobtrusively into his jeans.

"Not a pretty knife, is it?"

"Nothing, Carlos, just let me go to the store, I have to go the store and get something."

"Let's see the knife, Butchy. That looks like too big a knife for a little kid like you." Carlos took a step toward Parker. Parker backed, and suddenly realized that the two boys were surrounded by a ring, an impenetrable ring of expressionless brown faces, black faces.

"Just let me go, Carlos, I don't want no trouble!" But Carlos lunged forward. Butchy dodged to one side, slid the knife back out of his jeans. He looked at the older boy in terror, held the folded knife out in mute offering, wordlessly begging to buy free of the circle of faces, of the confrontation.

Carlos's hand made an astonishingly rapid move to his own trousers, in a flash was back at waist-height, his own knife held forward. His hand made a rapid flicking motion and with a sharp click the knife's gleaming blade flew into position, the twin of the steel sliver still concealed in Parker's knife handle.

A strange grin appeared on Carlos's face, a look of anticipation. He began the slow, classic circling of the knife fighter, his blade before him, his left hand held out for balance as he rolled his weight forward onto the sole of his feet. "Aren't you going to open your knife, Butchy?"

"I don't want to fight you, Carlos. You can have my knife."

The bigger boy only laughed, and Parker clutched at

his own weapon, depressing the catch that released the blade. It swung downward, out of the handle, and Parker clumsily imitated Carlos's wrist motion to lock the blade in position. "I don't want to fight you, Carlos," the boy repeated. His voice broke and tears of fright began to force their way past his efforts to contain them.

Carlos feinted with his knife, Parker backed and tried to run but the boys surrounding the two refused to open, their serious faces telling him that there was no escape from the fight. Desperately Parker ran at his larger opponent, holding his knife directly before him, trying to spear the bigger boy. Carlos sidestepped nimbly, poked his knife gently into Parker's shoulder as he blundered past. Blood began to run from the wound.

Parker turned, terror weakening his knees so that he could barely stand. He raced again at Carlos, took another small cut as the other boy dodged and poked, playing a game of blood and fright with the smaller boy. Parker sat down on the sidewalk and began to cry.

Carlos danced over, tauting him for cowardice. He kicked at the smaller boy who sat weeping and trembling as he bled from a half dozen petty wounds. He sat on the edge of the curb, his knees raised, head down, left arm across his face, right hand hanging in the gutter with his knife lying across the inside of the first joint of his fingers.

Carlos danced, kicked at Parker's left thigh, taunted, danced, kicked, danced, the pain coming to Parker as an inevitable part of the icy rhythm, the sound of Carlos's voice, taunting, dancing, the thud and pain of another kick, Carlos's voice, his shoes on the dirty sidewalk, kick. Parker's right hand came up from the gutter bringing his knife with it in a sudden arc over his own upraised knees, over Carlos's moving leg, disappearing into the older boy's colored shirt, passing from sight into the dark belly flesh of the bully, coming back dripping dark red held in a now dark red hand as Carlos's blood spurted over Parker's hand, his knees, the sidewalk, the gutter. . . .

Parker shuddered, squeezed his eyes shut for a moment, opened them again in the small clearing where he had faced the four Chinese-Negro hunters. He was still sitting with his knees upraised. He was covered with sweat. His forearms were bound behind his back and the biggest hunter was standing near, cleaver-scimitar in hand, watching him. The other three stood a few yards away.

"What happened?" Parker asked.

"Monday Alberta raceway slinkers," the big hunter answered. "Afterthoughts proxyboo highway." Oh God, thought Parker, more of that.

"January hayrick," he said.

A surprised look from the big hunter was his reward, and the other three spun about where they stood, regarding him also with startled expressions.

"It's all a gag. I don't understand your January talk. I just imitated you," said Parker.

The four clustered, jabbered for a few moments. Then their little sharp-featured leader said something that sounded imperative to the big man guarding Parker. The leader looked down at the bound aviator and gestured for him to rise, simultaneously issuing a command that Parker interpreted as obviously meaning "Get up!"

He did. The sharp-faced man allowed himself a look of slight gratification. So did Parker. At least it was communication of a sort, however simple it was.

He repeated the nonsense syllable that he knew meant *get up,* mimicking the hunter's voice and accompanying the sound with a body pantomime of his own just completed movement.

The hunter nodded and said, "Gibblegabble, get up."

Obvious again, the nonsense sound that came to Parker as *gibblegabble* was the local equivalent of *that's right.* His January hayrick vocabulary now stood at four words. At this rate he wouldn't be discussing technical aerodynamics with the local aviation crowd for a while, but he expected to be able to carry on simple conversations before very long.

How he had got to be tied up on the ground was another matter, as was the totally unexpected and totally realistic flashback to his fight with Carlos almost two decades before. Unless the sight of the four hunters with their cleaver-scimitars had triggered a fear-reaction. Then he might not only have hallucinated but re-enacted the street fight, wielding an imaginary gravity knife against one or more of the hunters and their nearly two-foot-long blades.

If so, he was lucky they had subdued him instead of simply dispatching him. Four armed hunters against one naked berserker was odds he did not care to face again, and if he had already faced them unknowingly he was grateful for his opponents' care for his life.

Once more the lead hunter issued instructions in the local tongue, accompanying them with gestures chiefly for Parker's sake. The small hunter led the way into the woods, using a trail so lightly marked that Parker could detect no sign of it, if it was marked at all.

Parker followed along stolidly, surrounded by the other hunters, pondering upon his situation.

First of all, the four must regard him as some sort of fantastic savage. They had come across him alone in the forest, naked and with no implements at hand. He had spoken to them in what was to them necessarily a non-sense language, just as theirs had been at first to him. After a brief, futile conversation he had probably lunged at them in savage and unprovoked attack. . . .

He would have to convince his captors somehow that he was *not* a wild man but a bewildered stranger. Probably compliance with their wishes and the fastest possible progress in the local language would serve that purpose.

Less immediate but of more staggering importance was the basic question of what had happened to him. He had passed out in the Antarctic snow following a helicopter crash, he knew. And awakened in a strange land of lush vegetation, giant butterflies, somehow wrong-looking wild cats and Chinese Negroes—again the idea stopped him for a moment—Chinese Negroes forming a hunting party and speaking a completely alien language!

That puzzle, and his own strange behavior. A flash-back, a mental fugue; all right, write it off. He'd very simply skipped a track under the impact of the accident and awakening in new surroundings. But—could he be sure he wouldn't find himself doing it again, losing touch with the moment, reliving an old incident . . . and maybe next time not coming out of the experience as easily as he had this time?

His mind flashed momentarily to the hackneyed dramatic moment in ten thousand grade-B movies. The brainless heroine recoiled in horror from the menace of monstrous murder and asked the even stupider hero: *What does it all mean?*

CHAPTER

2

They reached the hunters' camp in less than an hour's march. Passing through the woods Parker had time to study his surroundings and his captors a bit more than the hectic scene of their first meeting had permitted.

The woods looked perfectly normal. Parker eyed the growth appraisingly, searching for some clue, some familiarity or some notable unfamiliarity, some wrongness like that of the cat, that might present a clue as to where he was. The floor of the forest was partially covered with green shafts, a few inches long and as broad as a bloated needle—they were pine needles.

Not bad for a city boy. Pines. That would be . . . Parker dredged the term from some long-unused corner of of his memory . . . conifers. Right. Pine cones? A few were scattered among the needles, more could be seen hanging from dark green branches. Other trees: maples, oaks, palms? How do I know? A tree grew in Bedford-Stuyvesant, not on Lenox Avenue. Central Park was not for botany lessons.

No palms, though, he would surely recognize the bare trunks and the fronds at the peak. No palms, no pineapples. No, make that coconuts. No coconut palms.

Parker watched more of the big black-and-yellow butterflies gliding among the trees, but they seemed to ignore the party of men. Few birds were to be seen, those nondescript. The prisoner heard an occasional rustle of some animal, but he saw none. He caught an occasional glimpse of the stream in which he had awakened, heard its sound when it was hidden by trunks, occasional rocks, or its own course's vagaries.

Parker's four captors strode along silently for the most part, exchanging occasional words in their own language. There seemed no special effort at silence, and Parker was

cheered when the biggest of his captors rumbled a tune in
the same tongue. *Roll me over.* Natural rhythm.

The four hunters were dressed similarly to one another.
Parker studied the obvious leader of the group, pacing
along ahead of him. He wore a shirt and baggy trousers
of plain cloth—homespun?—and a jacket that looked like
buckskin. Boots, apparently of good quality but also obviously hand made. Parker dropped his glance to the trail
he strode, gave an inward sigh for a pair of those boots.
Well, pine needles were better than rocks.

Coming to a turn in the trail, Parker saw that they had
reached their goal, the hunters' camp. It was in a clearing
Parker estimated at about twenty feet across. The ground
was clear. The hunt must be nearly over, and successful,
for sides of meat hung over a slowly smoldering pit, the
flesh being preserved as the smoke rose steadily.

Some yards from the smoking pit lay heaped the cloths
and skins and implements that Parker surmised made up
the hunters' packs. Atop the pile lay another—or was it
the same?—of the huge cats. It barely twitched as the five
men stepped into the clearing. The leader spoke to the
animal as the other hunters went to various duties.

"Clarg, Longa, Longa," said the thin hunter. "Better
buy bird's-eye."

The cat rose haughtily from its appointed nest, strode
slowly to the hunter and Parker. "Here, kitty, kitty," the
American translated for himself. I wonder what the com-
mercial meant.

The cat approached the hunter, walked once around
him rubbing against his thighs, stretched and exhibited its
inch-long, wicked fangs in a friendly yawn. The hunter
scratched the cat under its pale chin. The cat switched its
tail.

Again the hunter spoke to the cat, pointing to Parker as
he did so. The beast took two steps to the American, sniffed
his naked legs, looked into his face. Those eyes! That expression! Once more, Parker wondered what manner of
cat this was. It looked like a common alley calico
grown to mountain-lion size. It must weigh as much as a
boy or a small woman.

But the expression on its face, the oversized head,
pointed to—what? A mutation? Was it as intelligent as it
looked, or was Parker reading mentality into the same

dumb cat stare that had spooked the Egyptians into making the ordinary mouser a god?

The cat stalked around the man, stopped to sniff at his hands, continued and sat on its haunches, looking up at him. Parker worried about the level of the cat's head and wished that he had some clothes on.

The lead hunter turned to Parker, jabbered at length, gesturing alternately at Parker and the cat. He took time out to point to himself, his blade, and his three fellows. The giant stood near Parker and the leader, apparently back on guard duty. The rangily built man was at the smoke-pit, cutting steak-sized slices from a side of meat. The slim hunter with the restless features had got a separate fire started away from the pit.

The leader, hands on his hips, stood before the American. Still speaking gibberish he concluded on a rising note with the local equivalent of *that's right*.

Parker shrugged.

The short man went through the routine again, slowly, his impatience obvious in his face and voice. This time he added gestures—to the big cat—Longa, was that its, her, name?—to the giant. He made sawing motions with his oversized knife, indicating Parker's bonds.

Parole, thought the prisoner. American POW accept no parole. Duty to organize escape attempts. Who said anything about any war, Parker grumbled to himself. He nodded his affirmative and added a definite *that's right* in the local tongue.

The leader spoke briefly to the giant who did not slash Parker's bonds after all, but painstakingly untied the knots after handing his own cleaver-scimitar to the small hunter. When Parker was untied he watched the big hunter carefully loop the rope—Parker noticed that it was of plaited rough leather, not vegetable fibres—and hang it at his belt.

Recovering his weapon the big hunter shepherded Parker around the camp, outfitting him with a loose shirt and a pair of buckskin trousers. As Parker clambered into the pants he shot a quick glance at the cat, Longa, who seemed, incredibly, to return a silent laugh.

There seemed to be no extra boots in the camp, at least Parker could see none as he and the giant hunter completed their circuit. Most of Parker's new raiment had come from the pack, now separated, of the rangy man.

The donor's grumbles seemed good-natured to the American, but he was not at all certain that the man was unannoyed. The man called something angry to the chief hunter, gestured at his pack and at Parker. The leader returned his comment. The rangy man stumped angrily away as the giant handed Parker a pair of moccasins from the pile.

A whiff of broiling meat brought Parker's attention from his surroundings to his interior. He had not eaten since his awakening, and before that for—how long? Hours? Eons?

With a rush he realized that he was ravenously hungry. He saw that five slabs of meat had been cooked over the wood fire and each of the hunters took a slab on a pointed stick, hunkered down and began to gorge. Parker wondered only briefly about local etiquette, grabbed the remaining steak and joined the others. Apparently he'd made no error. And the meat was delicious; rare broiled, unseasoned except for the smoky flavor, it seemed a similitude of beef but stronger in flavor and richer in texture. Marvelous!

There seemed to be considerable mealtime conversation, the big cat Longa now alertly circling the camp, her eyes reflecting the firelight now and then, showing the aquamarine tint Parker had never seen in another feline.

Talk among the hunters, to judge by their gestures, must center on Parker. The prisoner could imagine their meaning when he could not understand the words of the hunters. Who was this stranger? Where was he from? What strange language did he speak? For his part the American speculated back, pondering the same questions about himself and about the hunters, lacking only the companionship of someone with whom to discuss the puzzle.

The hunters had their meat on sticks in one hand, cutting off chunks with their big knives held in the other, holding the gobbets against the blade with their thumbs and conveying the food to their mouths still on the blade. Parker grunted, forced to tear his food with his teeth, wondered what it was. Beef? Venison? He looked at the sides hanging over the smoke pit, could not identify their source.

Parker looked up from his food between mouthfuls, but saw nothing new. He did notice more of the kumquat-fruit growing on rather small trees, and a number of the big butterflies.

By the time Parker finished his venison-like slab of meat the four hunters had completed their meal as well and the tall, rangy member of the party uncovered a large jug among the remaining pile of tools and clothes, offered it to the small leader.

Watching the leader swig at the jug Parker narrowly repressed a laugh—mountain dew, he thought. The jug was passed among the four hunters, ending with the giant who seemed determined to guzzle its remaining contents but finally lowered the big jug—it looked to Parker like glazed-clay, nicely made but again a hand product—and offered it to Parker.

The American took the jug. Certainly can't be drugged, he thought, and, taking the weight of the pottery on his biceps, he sipped a careful mouthful of its contents. The liquid stung his mouth with a pleasant fire, warmed his throat as he swallowed. He took a bigger swig, held it in his mouth a few seconds to savor the pleasure-pain of its feel as well as the odd flavor, swallowed, passed the jug back to the rangy hunter who looked annoyed as he took the jug, stoppered it and returned it to its place. Apparently one quick round after dinner was the rule.

Even after one, Parker felt slightly light-headed, but he was not certain that the drink was intoxicating. After the shocks of his day and with a good portion of meat in his stomach, it might not take alcohol to have this effect.

Night had fallen now, and the lead hunter was jabbering and gesturing again at Parker. He indicated a spot on the ground halfway between the cooking fire and the edge of the clearing, and motioned Parker to lie down. Before the American could comply the hunter went to the pile of material, fished out a rough skin blanket, and threw it to the prisoner. Parker caught it, lay on one edge, folded the blanket over himself to make an impromptu sleeping bag of it.

He watched three of the hunters stretch themselves about the clearing and cover themselves for sleep while the fourth, the man with the restless features, sat near the fire. The cat continued to prowl at the perimeter of the clearing.

Guards, thought Parker. For the camp . . . or for me?

He lay back, gazing at the starry, moonless sky, and

quickly fell asleep. He did not dream. Once during the night he awoke briefly, watched a change of guards, thought briefly that it was damned considerate of his captors to post guards instead of just tying him up for the night, then dozed again.

When Parker next woke the camp was already active. He felt the pleasant warmth of the sun's rays streaming through the trees, recalled a submerged memory of chill during the night. Apparently these people travel light and live rough, he mused. Rather sleep in their clothes with just a blanket on the ground than carry tents or sleeping bags. Must be rough when it rains. Did it ever snow here?

Where was *here*, anyway? By the climate and vegetation, certainly not Antarctica, although Parker *had* heard stories of oases in the ice, where submerged hot springs and quiescent volcanoes melted away the ground-covering ice and vegetation and animals throve. And some of the coastal islands were supposedly volcanic. If they'd heated up again . . .

But those were old wives' tales, fancy stories to spin for new arrivals, a polar equivalent of the snipe hunt. Or were they? There were penguins and some flying birds on the ice continent. Had they evolved in the polar environment? Migrated from elsewhere? The flying birds might have, but how could penguins? Or were they the degenerate descendants of flying birds?

Parker found it all going around in his mind, leading nowhere. He saw the hunters strip, all but one, the leader himself, who motioned to Parker to take off his borrowed clothing. Then the four naked men filed through the woods to the nearby stream and bathed while the fifth stood guard with bow and nocked arrow. Again Parker wondered whether he was merely being protected, along with the others, or whether the hunter leader was guarding against his escape.

Refreshed, Parker and the others breakfasted on smaller steaks, briefly cooked over a small fire. Then the camp was struck. Light work mainly, consisting of little more than each hunter's making up his pack. Parker was allowed to keep his clothes and blanket, and when the sides of meat were assigned, he got a heavy one.

Criminals would not be maintained in idleness at *these* taxpayers' expense!

The two fires, the smoke-fire in the shallow pit and the

smaller cooking fire, were doused with water brought from the stream in a rough hide bag. The jug of the night before was passed once again—no light-headedness this time—and the day's march commenced.

They walked for three days, setting up light camps in clearings the hunters obviously knew. They got by on two meals a day—Parker's stomach growled menacingly at the absence of lunch the first day out, quickly reconciled itself to doing without. The meat was supplemented by fruit picked from trees between campsites. Parker recognized none of the varieties. One, rather like a peach but with a citrus-like tone to its flavor, was Parker's guess for the base of the morning-and-evening drink. The kumquats were ignored.

The jug they had been using since he joined the party seemed to be the hunters' only one . . . either this had been a short expedition or the hunters must have discarded some empties, he decided.

The American was picking up a vocabulary in the local language as they marched. The method used was elementary: a hunter would use a word, Parker would say "What's that?" The question in English might mean nothing to the hunter but the message was obvious. If the word was a noun, the hunter pointed. If it was an easy verb, he pantomimed. Parker followed suit, repeated the word.

When he wanted a name for something, *he* pointed or pantomimed and the hunter replied. Before the end of the trek Parker was able to carry on a rudimentary conversation with any of his companions. He had learned their names, rendered them in his mind into English equivalents that he found easy to convert as he spoke or heard them spoken.

Fletcher, the little leader. A sharp, aggressive man, a good leader, conscientious, Parker decided.

The man with the restless features was called Scenter. He was known for his sharp senses, his acute ability to detect odors and sounds. He was the party's scout.

Broadarm was the giant. Ready with a grin and a helping hand, often with a song rumbling in his bass undertone, a companion if ever Parker needed one, he thought.

And the rawboned, rangy Fleet, a strong man of sorts. Parker remained uncertain whether Fleet was serious in his objections to contributing clothes to the newcomer. His conversation seemed polite if curt, at least to the extent that Parker could judge through the unfamiliar language and unknown customs of his captor-hosts, but hardly friendly, to say the least.

Parker managed to pronounce their names with the proper intonation, a slightly singsong effect with strong tonal qualities adding to the meaning of everything that was said. The same word with a different intonation had a different meaning. One sentence could derive endless meaning from its pronunciation, without changing a word.

As they broke camp the third morning and started through the woods, Parker noticed a kumquat tree near the path. He started toward it to pick some fruit, felt his hand struck down by Fletcher.

"Don't touch that!" grated the leader.

"What's wrong, isn't it edible?" asked Parker.

"The kissers, the kissers."

"What?"

The little hunter held his hands before him, made a flapping motion, repeated, "The kissers."

Parker watched, knew Fletcher must mean some flying creature. A bird? Insect? The black and yellow butterflies, that must be it! Were they the kissers? If so, why should they stop him from picking the fruit? Were they sacred creatures, the kumquats taboo?

Clumsily, searching for words, he tried to ask what the butterflies—they *must* be the kissers—had to do with eating the fruit. The best he could get back was the name of the kumquats—roughly, *jellyfruit*—and the information that if he picked any the kissers were likely to kiss him.

Parker gave up on the jellyfruit. The interrupted march continued. Near noon Fleet disappeared ahead of the party. Parker learned from the giant that Fleet had gone ahead to check in with outposts near their home base. The three remaining hunters and the American continued through the woods for another two hours or so, then broke through to a sight that made Parker exclaim:

"Abe Lincoln!"

Before him was a community of a few dozen log cabins. Around the town a wooden palisade had been erected, a single swinging gate now open. A guard stood at the gate, bow slung over one shoulder, arrows in a quiver-like pouch on his right hip, cleaver-scimitar—Parker had learned that this was called ironically a *friendmaker*—on the left.

Fleet had obviously got there well ahead of the four. The guard gave Fletcher, Broadarm and Scenter only a cursory glance; gazed in open curiosity at Parker as they passed through the palisade.

The big cat, Longa, had curvetted off into the woods during each day's march, but always turned up at dinner time. She never took food with the hunters—must have caught her own during the day—but stayed faithfully each night.

As they approached the palisade she had appeared briefly at the edge of the woods, then disappeared again.

CHAPTER

3

Still half distrustful of his companions, Parker hesitated momentarily at the palisade, reluctant to follow Fletcher into the apparent pioneer community. Before he could act he felt himself swept from the ground by a hugely muscular arm and deposited within the wooden wall.

"Don't worry, Parker," came the bass rumble of Broadarm, "you'll be all right in our town. You're a little old to play Founder."

Parker laughed weakly, trying to take the situation in his already shaken stride. "I hope you're right, Broadarm, and I hope you mean it. All I need now is unfriendly neighbors!

"And what do you mean by playing Founder?"

Broadarm looked surprised now, then looked down from his immense height to mutter, "That's right, you don't know anything about this place, do you? Well, don't worry, you'll learn it fast enough. It won't surprise me if you're ready to speak up yourself by Founder's Day."

"Founder's Day? You're kidding."

"No. It's the big thing in town, coming up pretty soon. You'll see. But look . . ." The little company— Fletcher in the lead, Parker and Broadarm, then (a quick glance over Parker's shoulder showed him) Scenter bringing up the rear—seemed headed for the center of the wooden community.

"Look at what?" asked Parker. If anything there was *too much* for the aviator to look at. The log cabins of the town—but they weren't quite the log cabins he'd seen in his school books two decades before in Harlem. Some differences in the architecture he'd have to study to pin down. And even the logs themselves. . . . Again Parker found himself wishing he'd known more about different kinds of plant life. The logs *looked* discomfortingly strange, not wholly alien but somehow subtly different from any he'd ever seen. But—Parker thought in discouragement—they might be perfectly ordinary trunks of perfectly ordinary trees, of a variety he'd never happened to come across before.

And the people! Trust a stranger to draw stares in a small town, in America or in Vietnam or in a polar research outpost. Any place where everybody knows everybody else . . . introduce a new face and you'd think it was a five-eyed freak, the way the locals flocked around for a look. And this town, so far nameless to Robert Parker, built to a strange architecture of a strange timber, inhabited by a race whose identity he could only guess speaking a language he had to pick up totally from scratch . . . How could it possibly be an exception? How could the American be less a curiosity to the townsmen than they were to him?

Yet Parker found himself responding to the villagers' interest in a way that surprised him. They seemed, for the most part, an attractive people. Their appearance gave the same odd feeling of the familiar mixed with the strange that so much else here caused. The brown skins everywhere made it so like a home community for Parker that he felt more comfortable, in a way, than he ever had in many parts of his own home country.

And the common garb of homespun shirts and trousers, leather boots or moccasins, and occasional buckskin garments, made the town seem like a western movie set come to life. Except for the Negro-Chinese pioneers.

Maybe they were Indians! The thought struck Parker like a bolt. American Indians. Weren't all the aborigines of the new world supposedly Asians who had crossed from Siberia to Alaska thousands of years ago, and then drifted southward? Darkly pigmented, black straight hair, vaguely Oriental features. Parker's mind whirled briefly to an incident, how many years before, on a Fifth Avenue bus.

There was a brown girl, two seats ahead of him, half stoned on something, pleading to every other passenger and to no one, "I'm a Indian, that's what I am, I'm a Indian." And briefly there returned to Parker the wave of mixed sympathy and disgust he had felt for her, obviously little past twenty, not unattractive, utterly beaten and destroyed by her life.

"I'm a Negro, that's what I am, I'm a Negro," Parker paraphrased his ancient non-acquaintance, half aloud in his brief reverie, using the English noun in his new-language sentence.

"You're a what?" asked Broadarm.

"A Negro."

"What's that?"

Now it was Parker's turn at incredulity. "A Negro," he repeated yet again, "a colored man. Look, can't you see," he demanded, holding his hand upraised before Broadarm's face.

"Sure," replied the giant. "You're a man and that's the color you are. Isn't everybody? But I will admit," Broadarm broke stride for a moment to look closely into Parker's face, "that your eyes have a funny slant to them."

Parker merely grunted.

Or maybe they were Indian Indians at that, mixed with Chinese from over the Himalayas in one of those endless border wars. Where the hell was he, Nepal?

The chain of thought was dropped as they took a turn between two, dammit, that's what they *were,* log cabins, and into a primitive sort of plaza that must be the town square. From one of the buildings Parker heard voices, one that he thought he recognized as Fleet's, and a woman's, and a third that must be that of a frightened, crying child. Fleet's voice and that of the woman sounded angry.

Without warning Parker felt his arm grasped by his giant companion, found himself hustled across the simple plaza, quickly following Fletcher into an open cabin.

Within the structure Parker stood, Broadarm still beside him, Scenter now on the other side. A few paces across the room Fletcher stood facing an older man, the hunter still armed with his friendmaker, bow and hip-quiver. The older man too wore the large cleaver-scimitar at his belt; it seemed the custom to go armed with these personal tool-weapons although bows were carried chiefly outside the confines of the town.

Fletcher began his report to the other man, but before he could get into the story the other gestured him, Parker, Broadarm and Scenter to sit on the pelt-covered floor of the cabin. Gratefully Parker complied, with the others, and partook with enthusiasm when their—host?—produced a jug of the ubiquitous local home brew and passed it around.

The jug went around the circle of Fletcher, Scenter, Parker, Broadarm, and back to its owner, twice. The first time, Parker observed, each took only the smallest sip, as if of a ceremonial or sacramental drink. The second time, to the American's great relief, each took a hearty swig of the tangy fluid. As the jug was passed a few drops splashed from its neck and Parker realized with a start that this was the first time he had ever *seen* the liquid. Still, its brilliantly bright but still clear pink seemed entirely appropriate to the tart flavor of the drink.

"Now," announced the middle-aged host, putting the re-stoppered jug aside, "you will tell me what happened, Fletcher, and who this fellow is."

Fletcher, obviously responding to authority, began to narrate the events of the hunting trip. The part up to their discovering Parker in the woods was new to him, of course, but contained no startling news to the American. Fletcher told the older man—Parker noted that he called him Olduncle, though whether that was the man's name or a title the aviator could not tell—of the party's progress through the woods, of the game they bagged. The animals were not described, but Parker inferred that the larger animals were indeed deer or some deerlike game.

When Fletcher got to the part about capturing the stranger—Parker—the American paid close attention to the narrative.

"First we thought he might be a Terasian," Fletcher told Olduncle. Parker logged *that* away for later reference. What was a Terasian? "Then when he attacked us —can you imagine, one barehanded man against four friendmakers?—we thought he must be crazy rather than hostile. That was the only reason we exercised care not to injure him when we subdued him.

"So we don't really know *who* he is," the lead hunter concluded. "Except that he spoke some language none of us had ever heard before. He's learned enough of ours to tell us that his name is Parker. He's wearing mostly Fleet's clothes. And here he is."

Parker's attention went from Fletcher to Olduncle, eager to see the reaction of the—village chief? mayor? —to the hunter's tale. Parker thought Olduncle's first question odd: "What did Fleet think of giving up a set of clothes to this fellow?" Olduncle asked Fletcher.

"He wasn't too happy," the hunter replied.

"Not surprising. He doesn't like to give anything up. I'm a little worried about Fleet and, well . . ." Olduncle let the statement trail off, and neither Fletcher nor the others present pressed him further.

Olduncle looked closely at Parker, rubbed his head as if to stimulate his own brain, then began to question him.

"You call yourself Parker?"

"Right."

"Okay, Parker, that's your name. Now, who are you?"

Parker pondered that one a moment. Well, let's work it out together, he thought. Let's start with this: "Parker, Robert Leroy, lieutenant United States Navy, serial number NO46366."

"I got the name part all right," said Olduncle. "Your name is Parker Robert Leroy but we'll call you Parker, agreed?"

Parker grinned. That's where backwards navy jargon gets you. But: "All right, Parker will do fine."

"The rest of it though . . . must be that queer language of yours. And what do all the numbers mean? Broadarm, you seem to have become chums with this fellow. Do you understand what he said?"

The giant grunted and shook his head, No. Another similarity, Parker noted; the locals nodded agreement, shook their heads for a negative. Just like us, thought the American. Or the Indians who greeted Columbus.

Olduncle spoke again to the aviator. "Parker, where did you come from, and where were you headed when you ran into Fletcher's hunting party?"

"As for where I was headed, I have no idea. I woke

up in that stream completely lost. Before I could get my
bearings I heard your pals and figured they could tell
me the way."

"Then why did you attack them?"

Parker looked about him, at the three of his captors
who were present in Olduncle's cabin. Fletcher, the
leader, now obviously reduced to the number two position by Olduncle's presence, leaned forward to hear his
answer. Big Broadarm, too, attended, in his expression
as much interest and more sympathy than in that of the
lead hunter. Scenter, alert, curious, seemed surprisingly
aloof.

"I'm not sure," Parker said. "Look, the last thing I
know *before* the stream was a violent crash. Then I wandered in some snow until I . . ." The word *snow,* he
realized, he'd spoken in English. Was there a local equivalent? "Do you know what I mean? Very cold water,
turned white and solid, falls like rain?"

The four natives—Parker was disturbed for a moment
at the word, even in thought, but could find none he liked
better—exchanged a few sentences, then, "It never falls
here but we have seen it."

"Okay, I was lost and blinded in a snow storm. I'm
not sure what happened next but I'm sure I must have
been frozen. I can only guess why it didn't kill me. My
whole body must have been in shock from the crash and
the injuries I suffered. If all my body processes were
slowed down and my temprature dropped too, from the
shock, and the wind and snow helped send down my
temperature fast enough, I must have been quick-frozen!

"Then how I thawed, and how my injuries healed—
that's another problem. I'm sure the stream helped somehow, maybe there's some impurity in the water that was
just lucky for me. And only chance kept me from drown-
ing before I could get out of the stream, chance that it
wasn't too deep and chance that I wasn't lying face
down when I thawed.

"And I still don't know where I am."

Parker stopped and waited for a reply. Olduncle and
Fletcher exchanged glances. Then Olduncle passed the
jug once more, and again spoke to Parker.

"You still haven't told us where you came from,
Parker. But let that wait. I cannot see any harm in telling
you that you are in the forest community of Relore. You

know who these men are. I am the Olduncle of the community. The people have chosen each Olduncle in turn since the Founder died longer ago than anyone can remember."

"But where is Relore?" the American demanded.

"If you were from Teras, which I'm fairly certain you're not, Parker, you would already know that. If you're from Par'z you won't be any menace and if you're from somewhere else this may prove very useful." The older man turned to Scenter. "Go over to Kaetha's for me, would you. Tell Fleet, if he's there, that he could at least have waited for the rest of the party to arrive before he ran off to his girl's house. And ask Kaetha to come back with you and bring her map of the Country with her."

The mobile-featured scout disappeared from the room. Olduncle swigged at the pottery jug, then told the American, "Parker, you interest me greatly. You attack four armed men and just fortunately escape with your life. I ask you why you did it and you say you don't know, you were in a state of puzzlement and shock."

"That's the truth," Parker rejoined. "If you think I'm a madman I can't even say you're wrong. This whole thing is so fantastic I'm tempted to say it's just a dream and curl up till it all goes away."

"Well, don't try it."

"Don't worry, I won't. Just in case it *is* real. Are you?"

"Don't be silly. This is all real and I have to take care of this community. They chose me and I'm the Olduncle. Now whoever you are, you didn't spring into being just as you are. You came from some place and there must be a people there. Should we turn you loose? Should we try to contact your people?"

"I wish you would," Parker interrupted.

Olduncle frowned and Broadarm gave Parker a gentle shove in the ribs that nearly sent him sprawling, but as the American recovered himself he saw a suppressed smile working around the giant's mouth.

"I was saying," Olduncle resumed, "should we just do away with you and hope that you were a mere stray? Your people might prove to be helpful allies or dangerous enemies. I want to know all that before I decide what to do with you."

Out came the jug again, and Parker asked what the

pink drink was called. "Qrart," said Olduncle, "have some."

Parker took the jug and swallowed a liberal mouthful of the pleasant stuff. Thou preparest a table before me, he thought. But is it in the presence of mine enemies? But all he said was thanks.

Before Olduncle could continued his lecture Scenter returned, ushering before him Nancy Wilson, Diahann Carroll and the three Supremes all rolled into one beautiful woman. She was tall and slim, with beautiful soft brown skin, long jet hair plaited into a glossy stream that caressed her cheek and flowed over the front of her left shoulder almost to her gracefully rising breast.

She was a woman, no mere girl. She wore dark tight trousers that could have passed at a quick glance as blue jeans, and a lighter, faded shirt tucked snugly at the waist. And she was annoyed.

"Kaetha," Olduncle greeted her without rising. She knelt beside the leader, kissed his cheek and then sat back on her heels, a newspaper-sized map she had carried in lying on the floor beside her. "What's the trouble?" Olduncle asked her.

She shook her head.

"Fleet again?" he asked.

Kaetha nodded. "Trili was almost asleep when he arrived, and . . ."

"Well, we'll see about that," Olduncle interjected. "Now, this strange fellow"—he indicated Parker who noticed only because Olduncle sat beside Kaetha—"says his name is Parker. Says he doesn't know where he is. Says he isn't from Teras or Par'z. Says he can't tell us where he is from. Never heard of Relore.

"So I asked Scenter to bring you and your map. You know the Country as well as anyone in Relore, and if you can teach it to small fry too young to go on hunting parties, maybe you and Parker can figure out where his home is. If you do, then maybe we can figure out what to do with him. So!"

The last word seemed to serve as a command, and as Olduncle, Broadarm and Scenter looked on, Kaetha explained the map to Parker.

CHAPTER

4

The map was drawn on a rough sort of paper. One more for the, ah, Relori, thought Parker, they have paper and they write. And one more problem for me: the writing resembles nothing I've ever seen.

Kaetha leaned over the map, drew a writing instrument from some unseen pocket in her simple garb. It was a crude-looking but obviously effective cross between a stylus and a grease-pencil, obviously hand-made, as was everything Parker had seen since awaking in the stream and coming to Relore.

The pilot followed as the stylus was pointed at the chart. Parker saw an elementary outline map of a body of land, high ground indicated by curving parallel hash lines, a few streams shown running from the high ground, feeding small lakes which gave birth to new running water, or flowing directly to seas. Most of the map was taken up by a peninsula, broad at the base, tapering quickly as it curved first one way, then another into the great body of water surrounding the land mass. A few islands were shown near the peninsula, but they were drawn in rough, broad strokes, as if to indicate that they were seldom if ever visited by the mapmaker or anyone who could contribute to the making of the chart.

Inland from the peninsula the map became similarly vague, features becoming fewer and fewer as the drawing faded into an undefined highland region.

There must be a way of telling the scale of the map, but until he found it out, Parker could not place the region. It could be anything from Baja California to the whole Indian subcontinent to some crummy little spit of land sticking into the Mediterranean off the coast of North Africa.

Or . . . it looked a damned lot like the Palmer Peninsula that pointed like a Fieldsian warped pool cue from the Antarctic toward Cape Horn and all of South America. If Relore and the rest of the Country were located on the Palmer Peninsula, at least Parker was still on the right continent. There was no indication on the map of the Larsen ice shelf, but whatever crazy occurence had warmed the polar climate and charged the long Antartic days and nights to something like the intermediate norm would probably melt the Larsen shelf too.

Parker still had a long trip to account for. The crash with Logan—poor Logan, no super-quick-freeze treatment would repair *his* injuries—must have taken place hundreds of miles away, on the other side of the Pole. They had set out in the copter from McMurdo headed toward the Pole. They ran into the storm after passing Mount McClintock. Then they must have crashed somewhere around the Markhams.

If the Country *was* the Palmer Peninsula, then, Parker had somehow traveled across country without knowing it. How? And if it wasn't that body of land separating the Weddell Sea from the Bellinghausen, then where was Parker and how had he got to wherever he was? Could the Country be on another continent? Or another planet?

Parker heaved a small sigh, looked up from the map, said to Olduncle, "It might look familiar to me, I'm not sure. But even if it shows the place I think, it's not where I'm from and I don't know how I got here. Did you ever hear of the Palmer Peninsula?"

Olduncle had not.

Fletcher pointed a brown finger at a spot on the map alongside an apparently small stream flowing into the peninsula from the highland region beyond the Country. "Here is where we found Parker," he told Olduncle and the others. "We'd made our camp near the stream so we would have running water when we returned to it, and we were headed back to our camp from the day's work when we, ah, ran into him."

Kaetha now used her stylus to point to a mark on the map. It looked like a conventionalized drawing of a wooden palisade—of course, that must be Relore! "Here we are," Kaetha said. "It took you . . ."

Fletcher filled in the answer, "Three days."

". . . to get to Relore."

Parker did a quick calculation. About sixty miles from

the spot Fletcher had indicated to the little drawing of Relore. That gave the map a scale of only about twenty miles to the inch. If this was all that the Relori knew of their world, they had a lot to learn!

"Here," Kaetha said, pointing to a blacked-in area far out on the peninsula, "is Teras." Parker looked up to see the expressions on the faces about him at the mention of the word. He was unable to read their meaning.

"And here," the graceful hand swung the stylus to a small island off the western coast of the peninsula, "is Par'z."

Parker asked: "Are those villages like Relore?"

Kaetha paused, then told him: "More or less. Each has its own way of living. We don't know very much about Par'z. It's almost impossible to get there. You have to cross the sea to do it, you know."

"So what?"

"So Teras controls the sea! Don't you know anything?" Her annoyance of arrival seemed transferred now to Parker.

"No I don't! Kaetha, don't you understand, I am a U.S. naval helicopter pilot." The girl looked blank. "You don't even know what that is. Black man come from sky in great silver bird, baby!" He was angry now himself, angry not at any mistreatment he had received, but at the total frustration of not knowing what had happened, where—or even when!—he was, angry all the more because these people, these strange-faced, intelligent, attractive people seemed as eager as he to understand what had happened. And they were getting nowhere.

As Parker and the Relori Kaetha exchanged seething glances over the map, Olduncle broke the impasse. "That's enough," he said. "We won't work this out by shouting at each other. Kaetha, I know you are upset because of Trili and Fleet. Parker, you are clearly tired and annoyed. Fletcher, suppose we put this fellow in the custody of Broadarm. Broadarm can handle him if he tries anything, and if he can't Janna will."

Even the usually stoic Fletcher and the aloof Scenter grinned at the remark, and Broadarm gave a whoop and pounded Parker on the back so hard that he nearly collided with Kaetha who was bent over, gathering her map. As he shot his hands forward to avoid cracking skulls with the slim Relori, Parker instinctively grasped Kaetha's shoulders; as he straightened again their eyes met and instantly the anger was gone, replaced in Parker with a new interest in the beautiful, independent young woman; and in her eyes, as Parker saw, with a curiosity different from that of the local girl for the stranger. In Kaetha's eyes Parker could swear that he saw an interest in himself as a man.

"Come along with me, Parker." Again it was the giant Broadarm whose great voice sounded more an invitation than a command. "It's about time for a good feed. You'll see that my little Janna spreads the best table in all of Relore, maybe in the whole Country. Maybe they can do better in Par'z but I know she cooks better than any of those Terasian pigs."

"Fine," answered the American. "I guess I could use a meal. But what do you mean by Terasian pigs?"

"By the Founder, Parker, I keep forgetting you're a stranger around here. The Terasians are our parents. You'll learn about them, don't worry."

"They must be some interesting people. Kaetha says that Relore avoids the sea because Teras controls it. You call the Terasians pigs. And yet they're your parents?"

"Don't worry, Parker, you'll learn."

The meeting, as Parker now thought of it, was breaking up. Olduncle brought out the qrart jug again for one more round, but this time Parker noticed that it was the mere ceremonial sip, not the hearty round of drink. The jug circled the room quickly, almost perfunctorily, and even before it had reached the village leader's hands again Fletcher and Scenter were out the door, headed, Parker assumed, to their respective homes. Close in tow behind Broadarm, Parker now left. Kaetha, he observed, stayed behind with Olduncle.

As Parker and Broadarm started diagonally across the plaza outside Olduncle's wooden house, far fewer Relori gathered to stare curiously at the stranger. A few wide-eyed children gaped out windows or doors of the simple buildings, but were pulled away by mothers or called away by their stronger-voiced fathers. For a moment Parker almost imagined that he was visiting his cousins again in a small Florida town near the Georgia line. . . .

King's Ferry, Florida, population a hundred or fewer whites, a couple of hundred Negroes, mingling freely in

the drowsy daily activities that were hardly worthy of
the name commerce, yet rigidly separated in their homes.
The whites lived in plain wooden frame houses, most of
them showing vainly a coat of whitewash sorely in need
of renewal. And the blacks in their own quarter, their
homes resembling those of the whites but mostly lacking
that symbolic coat of whitening.

Ramshackle buildings, barefoot children in dusty streets,
happy and carefree under the benevolent care of the
kindly white man. Except when a Negro forgot his
place and failed to step aside for his social better on a
narrow sidewalk. And except when times were hard and
jobs became fewer. And except when a Negro became
dissatisfied with work as a field hand or a helper in one
of King's Ferry few stores. Then, God help him! The
sheriff of Nassau County, Florida, would not.

Then the King's Ferry Negro had better get out of
town, and make for the state line and St. Mary's, Georgia, or head the other way for Yulee, Callahan, or Mon-
crief. To the King's Ferry Negro Jacksonville was the
big city personified.

Yet that hot summer in King's Ferry had meant something to Butchy Parker. Helping his cousins in the fields,
sitting with them in the evenings he had thought a
thought that had never come to him in the teeming
streets or tenements of Harlem. What would it be like, the
boy had thought, if everyone were the same color?

Not a new Africa as Fard advocated, or the latter-day
black nationalists, not a new black racism, but what if
somehow there were just no longer such a thing as black
men and yellow and white, just . . . people? To his boy's
mind it seemed a solution of all the problems of man,
none of the conflicts of economics or religion or nation-
alism, or ideology seemed to matter, or perhaps, as a
boy, he had been simply unaware of them, all other differences merged and muted before the overwhelming
force of the *one* difference that made any difference to
him.

And now twenty years later—or maybe a number so
great as to bear no resemblance to twenty—he had somehow reached such a world. Where everything was peace,
progress and prosperity. Except for those pigs the Terasians, whoever they were. And the Par'zians whom these

Relori know so little of. And the suspicions of Old-uncle that a stranger might be an enemy.

"Here we are," exclaimed Broadarm, breaking into Parker's new reverie. "Here's my house and inside it waits little Janna, by the Founder the finest woman in the Country."

The two men entered the log building, Broadarm throwing his bow and waist-quiver into a corner of the main room. "Broadarm!" came a booming contralto from a back room. A huge woman swept through the doorway, threw herself into the giant's arms. To Parker she looked a giantess, a fitting mate for the great-statured Broad-arm. She must have stood several inches over six feet—she was easily taller than Parker—and weighed 200 pounds or more, yet the towering Broadarm swept her into the air and swung her about as any grown man would toss a crowing, delighted child.

"Janna," said Broadarm as he put her down, not even winded by his exertion, "this is my new friend Parker. He's a stranger we met in the woods a few days ago. No-body knows who he is and even with Kaetha's help he couldn't tell us where he comes from so Olduncle gave him to me to take care of until it's time to question him some more."

Parker met the gaze of the giantess squarely. Her ex-pression was one of open curiosity. "Yes, I'd heard," Janna said. "Everyone knows that you brought in a stranger and the whole town is talking about who he could be." That to Broadarm. Then, to Parker: "Are you sure you're not a spy from Teras? No, you couldn't pos-sibly be, you look like a nice man. Besides, never mind, if you were a spy I'm sure you wouldn't tell us, would you? Of course not, you'd have to be stupid to tell everybody you were a spy if you really were one and I'm sure you're not stupid, are you, Parker?"

The dazed newcomer began to reply but Janna cut him off by turning again to her husband: "I'm so silly, Broadarm, you've brought us a visitor and I haven't even offered him a drink of qrart, what will he think of us or of Relore if we don't even observe common hos-pitality. You'd like a sip of qrart, wouldn't you, Parker? Here, make yourself at home."

She swept a thick fur from a place where it hung on a wall-peg, spread it on the floor beside Parker and placed her hand gently on his shoulder, all but dislocating it as she spun him to a sitting position on the fur. Then she swirled from the room, more words of welcome trailing from behind her.

Parker turned to Broadarm who had also seated himself on a fur-covered hide. Before Parker could speak Broadarm exclaimed, "A fine woman, eh, Parker? The finest in Relore, the finest in the whole Country, I'll warrant. By the Founder, I'll bet she's gone to fetch us her special qrart. No ordinary table drink tonight. Parker, I'll tell you you're a lucky fellow, Janna's taken a shine to you already, I can tell that. You'll probably get the first ribs for dinner, too." Parker barely dodged the giant's good-natured palm as the latter swung yet another pat on the back at him.

Janna returned carrying another of the clay jugs that were becoming familiar to Parker and handed it to Broadarm for the first formal sip. Once around the circle, then back to the giant who held it to his mouth so long that Parker wondered again at his capacity. "Ah, that's the good stuff," Broadarm gasped as he handed the partially emptied jug to Parker. "Here, have a good swallow of some first-rate qrart. Soon Janna will have some food for us and we can just have a good relaxing evening after the hunt."

"I appreciate your sharing your food and drink with me," said the American. "But I'm not just a wanderer. I've got to find out where this place is and how I can get back to McMurdo. . . ."

"To where?"

"Oh, McMurdo," Parker explained, "that's a place in my world where my country has a weather post. I was flying out of there when the accident happened. If Relore is where I think it is, then McMurdo lies in the oposite direction from Teras."

"You mean it's in the uplands? Olduncle says that we sent some people into the uplands once to found a new Relore. Never heard from them again. But if we keep growing, we'll send another batch."

Parker looked at Broadarm. "You people have colonized the uplands?"

"I suppose you could call it that, Parker. Between births and finds, our population keeps going up. Every time we start to have a food problem hereabouts we just select a second Olduncle and about half the people in Relore, load 'em up with food and tools and supplies and send out some advance parties to help them make way, and then they're on their own. Come to think of it, maybe we've done it a few times. Olduncle would know. Or maybe Kaetha. She's his own find, he tells her everything."

"What do you mean by finds?" Parker asked.

"By the Founder, Parker, Kaetha was right, you don't know anything! She was a find, Janna was a find, Fletcher was a find. I'd guess that about a third of the people in Relore are finds. Anybody here who isn't a find, his mother or father was, or some of his grandparents were, or somewhere along the line his ancestors were. All Relori are finds or descended from finds, back to the Founder himself."

A great bustling sound entered the room along with the returning Janna, carrying a wooden tray loaded with platters of mouthwatering roast venison and fruits. Before the aviator could speak Janna had begun twittering again in her great voice, "Here it is, Broadarm, Parker. This is from your own hunt and the fruits are from the orchard. Now no more talk about mysteries and problems. We're going to have a nice family dinner and worry about everything else tomorrow. Parker, I hope you won't mind sleeping out here. There are plenty of pelts. Broadarm and I would give you our own room but you know he's been away." Her words gave way to a girlish giggle that astonished Parker coming from the amazonian Janna.

But, "That's fine with me," Parker replied. "A good meal in my belly and I'll happily roll over and play dead for about the next twelve hours. I promise I won't even run away."

"Don't worry about that," rumbled Broadarm. "The palisade is there to keep people we don't want out, but it will keep you in!"

CHAPTER

5

A massive hand shook Robert Parker out of swirling dreams of beating snow, freezing blackness, water and waking and black and yellow butterflies of giant proportions that drifted upward and down again and lit and lifted, a strange great cat, a mocking black bully's face and a foot that kicked and kicked and a hand that shook him awake.

"Come on, Parker, it's time to get going. By the Founder, you're a sound sleeper, I've been shaking you for an age. We'd best get ready for the day before Janna decides we don't want breakfast and eats it all herself!"

Parker allowed himself to be steered by the elbow, out of Broadarm's cabin, through bare-earth streets between rows of similar buildings to an open area near the wooden palisade where a stream—the same one he'd first found himself in?—ran beneath the village wall. The day's activities in Relore were already well under way, and Parker noted that a clear-cut area where the stream first brought its clean water to the village was set aside for drinking, and for the women of the settlement to draw off water for cooking. Next came portions of the stream clearly reserved for laundry, then bathing, finally what amounted to an open-air latrine.

"Straight out of the manual," he exclaimed, then, to Broadarm's questioning expression, "never mind, Broadarm, just another thing that we do at home too. At my home, that is, if I can ever find it again."

"You'll find it, Parker, or at least you will if we can help you find it. I could tell from Olduncle yesterday. He'll do everything he can to figure you out—that's one place where your wishes and his are the same."

The two men bathed—Relorians seemed thoroughly unconcerned at coeducational public bathing—and then Broadarm shaved using a kind of crude soap and his ubiquitous friendmaker, carefully trimming his heavy mustache with the glittering blade.

Parker rubbed his own chin, thought of the roughness of a four-days growth of stubble, asked Broadarm if he might also use the cleaver-scimitar.

"Why not?" asked the giant. Parker merely looked at him. "Oh, I see," Broadarm said. "I don't know what Olduncle is going to say about it, but I don't see how we can keep you disarmed, Parker. Everybody carries a friendmaker, and especially if you're going outside the village you can never tell when you might need a weapon badly—and fast!"

"If I'd had a knife that first day in the woods . . ."

"I know, Parker. Look, let me tell you something. I don't know what you do with madmen in your home . . ."

"Mostly we confine them," Parker interrupted. "We consider them sick people and keep them locked up for safety's sake until they're improved enough to be let out."

"Well, we can't do that. We don't have any way of keeping people confined for long periods. We can't just leave them loose in the village, they'd be a menace to everyone, and we can't just put them outside the wall—they'd probably get themselves killed in the forest if they didn't starve first, and they'd be a menace to hunting parties until they did."

"So . . . what do you do with them?"

"That's what I've been trying to tell you, my friend. If they're harmless eccentrics—and we have a *very* generous interpretation of that category—we leave 'em alone. But if they're dangerous madmen, they get a special drink, and they just go to sleep, and that's the end. Then they get outside the wall all right, but they never know it."

"Then I . . ." The American asked his question in two words.

Broadarm remained silent for a moment, nodded, then spoke. "That's right. Olduncle decided yesterday. If he hadn't decided you were all right, you would never have seen this morning's sun. As for the forest, that's past.

"I think you're still under a little suspicion, Parker, but how else could that be, until we figure you out?"

The American sank to a sitting position beside the stream. He stared into the reflective waters, saw the huge Relori lean over him, the great knife in his hand, then extend it, grip first, over Parker's shoulder.

"You surely do need a shave," Broadarm rumbled.

When Parker had finished, Broadarm retrieved the weapon, slid it into his waistband, and the two men returned to Broadarm's cabin to the tuneless rhythmic growling of the great Relori.

Janna was bustling about a back room at the cabin, as obviously a wife in a kitchen as if she were not a giantess in a strange land. And the odor that reached Parker's nostrils was, incredibly, that of frying bacon and eggs over a wood fire.

Bacon and eggs it was, the meat cut in thick slabs, fried to a sizzling tenderness of gold and brown-black, each slice calling for the juices of Parker's appetite, already stimulated by the clear morning and the cold waters of the stream. The eggs—hardly chicken eggs, but eggs without question or doubt—were huge, the whites done to a firm, satisfying texture matched fully by their fine, mouth-filling flavor, the yolks yellow suns floating in the brilliant white sky of albumin, turning the rough bread Janna served with the meal into a treat more delicious than any ward room viands Parker had ever eaten.

Chattering ceaselessly the giantess moved with surprising grace, bringing new servings of the marvelous food from a simple iron stove, clearing remnants, babying her mammoth husband, creating in the stranger's mind a flashing illusion of himself as a half-grown child breakfasting with two great brown parents as he had done so seldom and envied his cousins for being always able to do in King's Ferry uncounted decades of macromillenia before.

"I didn't know you had this kind of food," Parker managed to squeeze into a momentary gap in Janna's talk. "I thought all you ate was venison and fruit."

Janna began to answer, was beaten, for once, by her husband's words: "On the trail that's true, Parker. We like to travel light and live off our own game. That helps keep us mobile, and it also gives us a good reason to keep after our work. No kill no dinner will make any man a pretty attentive hunter."

"But that's all different at home," Janna took up the

thread. "The fowl are kept penned beyond the palisade. We keep them for eggs. We eat birds too but not the ones we keep, all the men think that wouldn't be fair, so we just get fowl to eat when someone brings down a wild bird. Broadarm is a wonderful archer. The bacon is from wild boars. I don't suppose you saw any this time, did you, Broadarm?"

The hunter shook his head, No.

"Well," Janna went on, "we don't get a boar very often but when we do it's a real treat. I just love bacon. So does Broadarm. Don't you, dear?" she asked the giant, then, without waiting for his reply, "Of course he does, Parker, and I'm so pleased to see that you do too. I'm so glad to see you have a good appetite, Parker,"—she refilled the American's wooden plate with eggs and with the smoky, salty meat, then her husband's and her own —"as soon as Broadarm brought you through the door I could tell that you were a hearty eater." The American choked back a sentence, gave up and returned to his food as the amazon rattled on. "I always like a person who eats a good meal, like my Broadarm. You can trust a man who sits down and really eats a meal. I never like a person who just picks at his food and leaves half a portion on his plate, no, Parker, that's why I like you, you're a good eater."

Then she was off again, into the kitchen for more clattering.

Parker looked at Broadarm. Broadarm returned the look. "She's the finest woman in the Country, my Janna is," he said with a sigh.

Breakfast completed, Broadarm told Parker, "Olduncle wants to talk to you and Kaetha again this morning. Janna and I will both be working in the fields today. Most of the people are there already but men just in from the hunt get to rest the next morning, and besides, the job of taking care of you is something out of the ordinary. But look, Parker, whatever you and Olduncle work out, if you're going to stay in Relore you'd better learn to use our weapons or you'll be useless in the hunt and helpless in a fight. I'll get some time off and give you some archery lessons, and teach you how to use the friend-maker."

Parker looked seriously at Broadarm. "I have no intention of staying in Relore," he said. "You seem to be a decent people here and I wish you well." Parker saw a nonplussed look cross the giant's face.

"But, look, Broadarm, I'm an American. I don't know how I can explain that to you. My country—what *I* call a *country*—is bigger than your whole Country. A little city-state like Relore wouldn't make one little corner of one little subdivision of one section of my country. I was born and raised and educated in America and I'm a professional officer in my country's military service.

"We have terrific problems in the world—in my world —and problems just as bad inside my own country. Look, you remember I said something about being a colored man and you said, 'Well, sure, isn't everybody?' " Broadarm nodded and grunted in agreement.

"Well, in my world everybody *isn't* the same color. In my own country most of the people aren't black or brown as they are here, and our whole people is struggling over that!"

"I don't see why," the giant interrupted. "If a fellow turned up in Relore with blue skin or speckles like a cat —what color did you say these other folk were in America? Well, no matter"—he did not wait for Parker to answer—"so what? I mean, a blue man might look pretty odd, and people might stare at him for a little while until they got accustomed to seeing blue skin, but why would it make any other difference?"

Parker allowed his laugh to come through loud. Then, "You make sense, Broadarm. Really you do. In fact, if you'll lend me your own expression, by the Founder you make sense, and that's one of the things that makes me like you Relori. All I can say about America is that she has her problems, sensible or not, and they're my problems, foreign or domestic, and I won't run out on them if I can help it.

"But I'll take you up on the archery lessons. And I think once I get the feel of a friendmaker I might surprise you with it. Meanwhile, if you'll show me over to Olduncle's cabin once more, I think I'll be able to find my own way after this."

Broadarm showing the way, the two men made their way between the rows of cabins. Most were deserted, their owners, Parker drew from Broadarm's statement, at work tending chickens or planted fields. A picture of Relore's economy was beginning to form for Parker.

There seemed to be both a hunting and an agricultural side to the villagers' life, the fields tended by the women and by those men home from the trail. Who owned the fields, whether they belonged to individual families or to the community, he could not tell.

The prize of the hunt seemed to be split, part going to the community, but first pick to the hunters and their families. The husbandman, Parker quoted to himself, shall be the first. . . .

Government, if you could call it that, seemed to be by an elected chief, almost a monarch, the Olduncle. But the post *was* elective, not hereditary and apparently not to be seized by force either . . . and there were laws, as shown by Broadarm's little lecture on the care and disposition of the insane. Execution, euthanasia, social murder, call it what you would, was a brutal way of dealing with a morally innocent madman, even if he was a danger to society. But a people on a subsistence economy with no means of caring for mentally ill . . .

"What do you with criminals, Broadarm," Parker asked.

"Huh? By the Founder, Parker, you ask sudden questions. Well, if somebody is found out stealing he has to indemnify his victim. That's really about all, the first time. Somebody beats a child or a helpless person, he'll get a thrashing himself.

"Anybody keeps it up, Olduncle gives the word and he gets a drink, like it or not. Anybody kills, same thing. But that's very rare, Parker. Very rare. Where the good of the community is at stake, we all work together. Rest of the time, people leave each other alone. That's all."

They crossed the town plaza, and Parker watched for a moment as a group of children played under the eye of a crone in the open area between the buildings. Two boys fought a great duel with razor-edged friendmakers made of unfamiliar sticks. A little circle of girls chattered and handed a cracked pottery jug from one to another, and Parker smiled in recognition of a bright day in the park and a little girl's tea party—or qrart party, as this surely was.

Inside Olduncle's cabin the village leader stood engaged in conversation with Kaetha, her slim figure,

Parker noted, again gracefully held in the simple home-spun shirt and trousers of the previous afternoon.

Broadarm, as the two men reached the doorway, told Parker, "I wish you luck," turned away and recrossed the plaza.

"Come in here," Olduncle commanded. In his belt was the familiar cleaver-scimitar.

Parker obeyed, began to speak but had to wait during the ceremonial sharing of qrart. Then, before either Relorian again broke silence, Parker turned to the young woman and said, "Kaetha, I was angry with you yesterday. I apologize."

Kaetha returned his look. "You were in a difficult situation, Parker. For that matter, you still are. Let's both promise to concentrate on the problem and not pick on each other. Agreed?"

"Agreed."

Parker's contemplation of the young woman's eyes was interrupted by a peremptory clearing of Olduncle's throat. "I'm pleased to see you two have decided not to be at each other's necks this morning," he said. "We will make another attempt to find out where you've come from, Parker. If that fails, we will try another approach."

Parker asked merely, "What other approach?"

"We will see in due course, Parker. For now, let us get to Kaetha's map again."

Again the map was set out, again the three sat about it on the fur-covered hides that overlay the floor of the village leader's home.

"You are sure you never were in Teras?" said Olduncle, indicating the area marked on the long neck of land that Parker had mentally labelled the Palmer Peninsula.

"Never," the American replied.

"Or Par'z?" Olduncle indicated an island that Parker thought he recalled as Adelaide.

"No, absolutely. If the Country is on the continent I suspect, Antarctica in my world, then the last place I was is the other way . . . not my home, that's farther than I think you can conceive, but the place I last remember before I found myself in the woods. Across the highlands, beyond where Broadarm says you send your colonies."

"Broadarm told you that?"

"He did. And I wish you would explain a good many things to me. You don't seem to have an excessive birth rate in Relore, at least I haven't seen awfully many pregnant women since I arrived. But there *do* seem to be plenty of children."

"That's because of the finds," answered Olduncle.

"Swell. I was going to ask about that next. Olduncle, you can clear up two mysteries for me then, if you'll explain what the finds are and how come you have a population problem without a high birth rate."

Olduncle looked at Kaetha, said, "You tell him. You teach the children, you can explain it better than I."

For an instant an insanely funny thought flashed through Parker's mind: she's the schoolmarm, that's what Kaetha is. All she needs is somebody to take her glasses off and say, why, do you know, without your glasses, you're . . . you're beautiful. Only she doesn't wear glasses.

"Our knowledge of Teras is largely limited to our observations of the city made by hunting expeditions which have penetrated the forest near to the Teras escarpment, plus a very occasional contact between Relori hunters or fishermen and Terasian military scouts or ships, also near Teras." The young woman's voice had taken on the intonation of a teacher lecturing a class with long-memorized lessons.

"As far as we know the Terasians are a thoroughly regimented people with a military organization tinctured by highly orthodox religious overtones." Parker wondered for a moment what religion, if any, the Relori had. "The Terasians are dedicated to the concept of a completely planned society, with population levels kept in careful balance with planned norms. Surplus infants cannot simply be killed because of Terasian religious attitudes, so they are exposed beyond the city. The Terasians consider this returning these infants to nature, leaving their fate in the hands of God rather than harming them in any way. This has been their practice for longer than any of us know. How many infants were exposed to die of starvation or be eaten by beasts we cannot even guess.

"But at some remote time one exposed infant somehow survived. We can only guess it was adopted and suckled by a wild animal. The child grew up as an animal; somehow, through warily observing Terasian parties near the city, the child realized that it was not a beast but a human being, even learned to speak the Terasian tongue.

"That child was the Founder. Eventually, watching the animals care for their young, seeing the babies abandoned by the Terasians to die, the Founder in turn adopted another abandoned baby, then another and another. How they survived, how the Founder, a mere child, was able to care for almost newborn infants, we can only guess. Many must have died.

"But in time there were enough of them, and they were old enough, to start a village. That was the beginning of Relore. The Founder and the other first Relori came far enough away, into the woods, to avoid seeming a challenge to Teras, or they would have been destroyed. But Relore has always kept the policy of taking in the abandoned infants of Teras. They are the finds. And between a normal birth rate and finds, Relore's population constantly grows, so that, not more than once in several generations, we split ourselves up and send a colonizing party into the high country."

As the young woman finished her statement silence fell on the cabin. In a far part of town Parker could hear a clear *tink-tink-tink* of metal on metal, the sound, he thought, of a village smithy. Under the spreading whatnut tree . . . Of course, the Relori could not *all* be farmers and hunters, they were obviously past that. There must be a few specialists: a smith, and Olduncle who seemed to be a full-time village leader and administrator, and Kaetha a teacher, probably a handful of others.

"Do you know what Teras itself is like?" Parker asked.

"We know little of Teras," answered Olduncle. "None of us has ever been in that city since infancy. Teras *looks* to our hunters as if it is built of black stone. There is a wall that stretches from sea to sea at the boundary of Teras; the Country is very narrow there. Kaetha's map beyond that point is based only on guesswork and our very few sea voyages."

"But why don't they attack you?" the American wanted to know. "I would think that Teras would be afraid of Relore's growing too powerful, and moving in on them."

Now Olduncle laughed bitterly. "Teras is not afraid of us. To us they may be our parents, but to them, what is Relore? We are their dumpings, their garbage. We are vermin. Do you make war on vermin, Parker, in your country? On the disgusting, dirty little creatures that live on your table scraps and your waste?"

"Well . . ."

"Don't be absurd. If vermin become a nuisance you kill a few and you feel better afterwards. If they ever become numerous enough to worry you, maybe you organize a hunt, you exterminate them. Even then you hardly dignify them with the status of equals that enmity carries.

"We stay out of sight, out of the Terasians' way. When scout meets hunter they sometimes even talk to us. I remember one time long before I was selected as Olduncle. There was another Olduncle then, and I was little more than a boy."

The older man paused for a moment, shrugged almost imperceptibly. "Well, never mind," he said. "Some day I may tell that tale, but not now. More likely it will go with me to the grave. Anyway, Parker, you see how it is with Teras and Relore. We share the land of the Country, we share our language, our very blood. But Teras despises Relore, her own child, scorns us beneath even hatred. But we do not hold Teras beneath hatred. No, we can hate Teras as the scorned and abandoned child hates the parent it would rather love. We can hate."

"But, Olduncle," Kaetha spoke. "This tells us nothing of Parker's origin. Unless you think he is a Terasian spy."

"No, Kaetha, I do not think that. I think he may help us if we ever have to fight Teras. I am sure he is not Terasian."

"I have sympathy for your people, Olduncle," Parker said. "But I'm interested in getting back to my own. I'm not even certain that this is the right planet. Look, Olduncle, Kaetha, what do you know of the world beyond the Country? Do you know what a . . ." he hesitated, could find no Relori word to express the concept, had to use English: "Do you know what a *planet* is? What the solar system is?" An incredible, trashy motion picture seen half a lifetime before sent a chilling image across the years to Robert Parker: "Is this Venus, am I in the fourth dimension, is it time travel? Isn't there any way I can find out?"

He saw Olduncle and Kaetha look at each other, seem to nod. Olduncle said, "Parker, I had hoped you would cast your lot with us. Perhaps you eventually will anyway. But for now I think you will go away.

"We are a busy people in Relore. We do not have an easy life and we do not have time for theories and philosophies. You speak of planets, we think of crops. You ask of the fourth dimension, we worry about enough rainfall. You talk about solar systems, we are occupied with the hunt. You think you travel in time, we travel the sea for fish when we must, when the hunt goes poorly or the crop fails.

"I will do this for you. You may settle with us if you wish, become one of Relore. At next Founder's Day you will become a citizen, take a wife, live out your life with us. What say you?"

"No," said Parker. "Thank you, but I can't settle for that. I have to know what's happened, to get home if I can or to know at least that I can't."

"Or," Olduncle continued, "you must seek your philospher and solve your riddle with some other people. Relore cannot unravel you mystery. I will do this if you wish. Stay with us while you may. When you are ready to go I will send a man to help you. Broadarm would be your choice, would he not?"

Parker nodded solemnly.

"And I will send with you our best guide. One person in all of Relore knows the country better even than Scenter or Fleet. That one is present now."

Again Parker saw a new look in Kaetha's eyes and again wondered at its message. "Broadarm and Kaetha to go with me? But where? Surely not Teras."

"I would think not, Parker, although if that were your choice, so it would be. No, I think you would go to Par'z. Of the Par'zians we know but little, and that from hardly reliable legend. But they are said to be a people of artists and philosophers, musicians to shame our crude huntsman's ditties, mystics and workers of marvels.

"To reach the Par'zians on their island you will have to cross the forest. You will have to come to the sea near Teras and avoid Terasians unless you would risk an uncertain treatment. You will have to cross the sea, which has perils of its own, not to mention Terasian craft again.

"And then you will have to get into the city of Par'z. That is something few men have done. Our legends do not tell of the danger you will face in entering Par'z. They tell only that few, few of those who try succeed. Once at least, some Relori must have reached Par'z and left again, to tell the tale. Where else come the legends? But no Relori living, nor any who lived in my lifetime, nor any who could be remembered by any who lived in my time, could tell of Par'z by the sight of his own eyes or the telling of his own deeds.

"But still, we have the legends.

"If you would visit Par'z, we will help you prepare, and you will arm you with bow and with friendmaker, and Broadarm and Kaetha will go with you as far as they can and then return to Relore. Then you will have to fare for yourself."

The cabin was silent after Olduncle finished making his offer. They offer me a good life, Parker thought. The Relori are an attractive people, vigorous and busy. I can be one of them, with a good home forever here. Or . . . There was no point in delaying or in trying to sell himself on staying. His new friend Broadarm, the gregarious Janna, Olduncle, even beautiful Kaetha, if he had ever had any thought of her except as a tutor and guide, must be given up. Parker could not quit now, not when Par'z beckoned.

"I'm sorry, Olduncle. Sincerely and deeply, I cannot express it beyond that. I have to go. I will go to Par'z."

"As you choose," the elder Relori said. "Kaetha, you see about getting Parker outfitted with a friendmaker. His good companion Broadarm can see to his training in its use, and it will do the three of you well to handle weapons together.

"Also, get him over to the house of Fletcher. See if he is at home this morning. Get Parker a bow and a quiver of arrows from Fletcher and look after his training as an archer. I imagine he will not stay with us long enough to become expert with the bow, but he should learn quickly enough to bring down his dinner at the least."

CHAPTER

6

In the plaza outside Olduncle's quarters Parker and Kaetha walked past the playing children. As they came opposite the chattering girls' qrart party a tiny child threw down her broken pottery jug and ran toward Kaetha.

"Mother, Mother," cried the child in a shrill voice. Parker stood as Kaetha stooped to gather the child into her arms. She rose again with the little girl riding proudly at one elbow, the woman beaming with no less pride and love than the child.

"This is my daughter Trili, Parker. Trili, this man is our new friend. His name is Parker and he will be staying in Relore for a little while."

The American swallowed as he felt a quick cold surprise. The schoolmarm was *always* a *spinster!* How could Kaetha have a child? Still: "Hello, Trili. Are you having a nice party with your friends?"

The child buried her face in her mother's neck, clung to two fistfuls of the glossy black hair Parker had admired the day before. Parker envied her. "You aren't afraid of me, are you, Trili?"

"You shouldn't even bring up the topic, Parker," Kaetha said. "Don't give her that idea. She's just being shy of a stranger." Kaetha squatted on the grassy earth, lowered the girl to stand between her knees. "Now, Trili, Parker is our friend. He lives with Broadarm and Janna. He is really a very nice man." The two Relori, mother and daughter, looked at the American. In Kaetha's face Parker read, he thought, a degree of confidence; in Trili's, doubt.

Parker watched the little girl as she retrieved her broken jug and ran to rejoin her friends. The two adults walked onward, leaving the plaza in the direction of the *ting*ing hammering sound Parker had heard. "I guess I just came into this Western about fifteen minutes too late," he mused.

45

"I don't understand," Kaetha said.

"Never mind. Where are we headed now?"

"To get you a friendmaker at . . ."

"Smith's?" Parker interrupted her.

"How did you know?" Kaetha asked, a look of puzzlement that delighted the American playing on her face.

"Ah, that can be my secret," Parker answered her. That's one advantage, he thought, of the language of the Country. Once you caught on to the use of names to describe as well as to identify—at least in some cases—you could half-guess a good deal. It should have been obvious, he told himself, that Fletcher would be the town archery expert and armorer. He was, indeed, the fletcher. And what better name for a smith could there be?

As the sounds of the smithy grew nearer Parker began to ask Kaetha "How do I—?" He stopped. How do I pay for my weapons, he had meant to find out. But he could think of no Relori word for pay or payment or money. He tried again: "Will I give something to Smith for the friendmaker? Will he expect something in exchange?"

"Nothing. Most of us in Relore take care of our own needs by farming and hunting but a few Relori—Fletcher and Smith and Olduncle of course—are supported by the community. Everyone contributes a share of food or cloth or leather to take care of them. Some of the hunters even bring Smith the iron rocks from the highlands when he needs a fresh supply, and they help him to make the iron from the rocks.

"Then Smith makes us all friendmakers, and makes metal tips for Fletcher's arrows and other metal things. The same way, Fletcher makes the best bows and arrows in Relore, although a few of the hunters would rather make their own."

They reached the blacksmith's workshop, an open-sided shed built onto the front of a typical Relori cabin. The logs used were both of the unfamiliar type common to many of the wooden buildings, and of other, more familiar woods. At the approach of Parker and Kaetha the blacksmith lay down the white-hot, glowing metal blank he had been hammering. He was a giant, Parker saw, nearly as tall as Broadarm, and built even more massively. He wore the homespun trousers common in the settlement, and over them a heavy leather apron to hold off the flying sparks that darted about as he worked. The bare arms of the workman rippled with great muscles beneath the skin scarred by countless cinders.

"Kaetha," he called, "is this the stranger of whom I have heard?"

"This is Parker, Smith," said the Relori woman.

Immediately the blacksmith disappeared into the cabin behind his workshop, reappeared in a moment with the inevitable jug of tart pink qrart. He handed it to Parker first. The aviator took a small ceremonial sip, passed the jug to Kaetha who did the same. When the qrart had finished its round with Smith the Relori worker returned it to its sanctum.

No social drinking here, thought Parker.

As the blacksmith emerged again from the cabin he asked, "Well, Kaetha, what can I do for you and, um, Parker here?"

"Nothing for me," Kaetha replied. "Olduncle wants you to provide a friendmaker for Parker. He'll be going on a difficult journey very soon, and Olduncle wants him well armed."

"That will take quite a wait. You see this blade is hardly even formed yet." He indicated the crude rod of iron he had laid aside at their approach.

"Don't you have one more nearly ready?" asked Kaetha.

"Um . . ." The smith hesitated. "—why, no."

"I thought you did. I was certain."

"Well," the blacksmith admitted, "there is one that really needs only the taste of the whetstone to be finished. But it is promised. Parker will have to wait."

"Olduncle does not want him to wait. You had best give Parker the blade that is ready, and save the other you were working on."

"Are you sure that is Olduncle's word?" asked the smith.

Kaetha nodded.

"Very well, then. But the man who was to have this blade will be angry, Kaetha. It was for Fleet."

Parker watched Kaetha's face for a reaction to the smith's words, but the Relori woman showed no feeling, whatever she might have felt within herself.

Turning once more to the dark recesses of his home the blacksmith produced the weapon. He extended it hilt-first toward the American who grasped eagerly at the ridged handle. Turning the cleaver-scimitar slowly Parker watched the play of sunlight on the metal bands of the basket hilt and the as-yet dull blade.

"A fine weapon, I think," Parker said to the smith. "I think I had better leave the blade dull for a day or so, until I have the feel and the balance of it." Shaving with Broadarm's friendmaker is hardly a thorough training in the weapon, he thought. "May I then use your whet-stone for it?"

"Use ahead," the blacksmith answered. "You'll have no ill will from me. Others may speak for themselves."

Stepping into the sunlight fully, Parker hefted the blade, trying for its balance. An unfamiliar weapon, yes, but one he thought he could use well with little practice, one he had admired since the first day of awakening in the forest. He tucked the weapon in his waistband, drew it, parried an imaginary foe, lunged, then, whirling the friendmaker in the air pirate fashion let out a joyous whoop for the first time in this new country.

As Parker half leaped back into the blacksmith shop he saw the smith scowl at his exhibition, was delighted then to see and hear Kaetha laugh indulgently at his antics. Parker joined her laughter, then, seizing her two hands in his own said, "Kaetha, I feel better now than I have since I came to the Country. Until now I've been an unarmed man in an armed society, and I haven't liked that way of going along since I was a kid. Come on now, let's go on to Fletcher's."

And behind, as he walked again with Kaetha, his heart thumping all but audibly now that he felt on his way at last, Parker heard the smith's *tink-tink-tink* resume its steady beat.

Fletcher had no separate shop. He made his bows and arrows and quivers in his own log home not far from the smithy. As Kaetha and Parker entered Fletcher's house he rose quickly from his work, exchanged a greeting with Kaetha, then spoke to the American. "Ah, Parker, you seem to be adjusting quickly to life in Relore. I see you've got yourself a guide."

Parker turned to Kaetha, saw—did he?—a blush emerge beneath the smooth brown skin of her face. At any rate, she did not appear displeased at Fletcher's remark . . . which puzzled Parker. The Relori view on marriage, at least judging by Broadarm and Janna, was not substantially different from the one Parker was accustomed to. And Kaetha was obviously a married woman. She had a daughter, Trili, and from remarks of Olduncle and Smith, Fleet was apparently her husband. One thing that Parker emphatically did not need, upon entering a new community, was to set up in business as a home wrecker. Still . . . he looked once more at the slim form of Kaetha standing beside him. Still . . .

Kaetha told Fletcher of Olduncle's instructions. Fletcher did not balk as had the blacksmith, but instead told Parker: "I've got a little ahead for once. People are taking good care of their equipment. You had better try a few sizes before you pick a bow."

He omitted the qrart ceremony. Parker decided that Fletcher meant no insult by the act, but was showing the informality that his friendship with Kaetha would permit. The hunter and weapon-maker went to a rack that hung upon one wall of the simple structure, took down a bow, selected a thong from a crude boxful and strung the bow. He handed it to Parker.

The bow was a beautiful thing, Parker observed. Unfamiliar as he was with this form of weapon, still the aviator admired the graceful curve, the fine quality of the long-grained, light wood of which the bow was made. The wood tapered from cloth-wrapped grip to the pointed tips of the arching shape. The wood was smoothed, worked to a fine finish, rubbed and waxed and polished as if it were a piece of fine furniture. The thong that joined the ends of the bow, drawn taut by Fletcher, was of tough but equally fine hide.

"Have you ever used a bow?" Fletcher asked him.

Parker replied: "Only at Coney Island."

"I do not know that island," Fletcher responded. "Is it near the Country? Were you stalking game there?"

"No, no," Parker laughed, "Coney Island is far away, and the game you stalk there you don't stalk with bow and arrows. I think you'd better teach me how to use this from the start."

"All right. First, we must see if this is a good bow for you. You will want the heaviest bow you can draw comfortably, but not a heavier one or you will miss your targets. Hold the bow at the grip there, arm straight out from your shoulder. Good. Now, draw the string back with two fingers, keep your thumb at a level with your eye."

Parker did as he was told. The thong pulled back to form a slightly flattened V, and the bow itself deepened its arch close to a semi-circle.

"No good," said Fletcher, taking the bow back from the American. "You are stronger than you look, Parker. Here, try a heavier bow." He replaced the weapon on its rack, loosed one end of the thong from the wood, removed a longer, thicker-bodied bow from the rack and again fixed a thong.

Once more Parker took the proffered weapon and tested it. The V this time was much shallower, the increase in the arc of the wood far less.

"That one looks right," Fletcher said. "Now to get you some arrows."

"Do arrows come in different sizes too?" the American asked in astonishment.

"Of course," Fletcher replied. "If you use too short an arrow you will be unable to get your full draw on the bow and you will lose range. Use too long an arrow, your balance will be off and you will lose accuracy. Here now." He grabbed up a roughly marked measuring stick, took the distance from Parker's right elbow to his fingertips, then from his eye to the end of his left arm, threw down the stick, handed Parker an arrow. "Now try drawing that on your bow. You'd better point it at the solid wall there in case it slips."

Parker fitted the arrow to the bow's thong, grasped it at the butt, drew back once more.

"All right, Parker, that is the right length arrow for you. But you are doing it all wrong. First of all, you should not hold the arrow as you draw. You'll never hit anything you shot at that way. Nock the arrow, draw back the string, that's the only way to shoot. Is that how you used your bow in Coney Island?"

"Well—" Parker began to explain.

"No, never mind," Fletcher interrupted him. "I am sure that someone will see to it that you get archery lessons. Here now, take a few practice arrows. Kaetha or Broadarm or Fleet can teach you to care for the equipment. When you are ready for some better arrows come back again. And now, you will excuse me."

Fletcher went back to work. Parker and Kaetha left his

cabin, the flier thinking how like boot camp this was, sizing, getting practice ammunition to use, learning new weapons. But, thinking of Kaetha at his side, and of his temporary home with Broadarm and Janna, there were important differences too.

In the days that followed Parker worked and learned. He continued to make his home with Broadarm and Janna, became even faster friends with the muscular giant, developed an equally admiring affection for Broadarm's slightly overwhelming mate.

Mornings were spent tending crops: fruit, vegetables, the grain of which the Relori made their rough, nourishing loaves. The ownership of land and crops and the working of the farmlands beyond the palisade of Relore were handled on a complex basis, neither private nor public but a combination of the two. A Relori family would speak of a field as theirs, yet others would share the burden of working the field, sometimes while the apparent owners were engaged in working land that belonged to others.

The working day in Relore began early—most Relori rose at dawn—and lasted until dusk. But Parker did not spend his full days in the fields, much as they reminded him of distant days in King's Ferry. Often he would stop work after noon and draft Broadarm for weapons drill. Parker mastered the friendmaker quickly, mock-dueling Broadarm with a still-dull blade.

If anything, Parker found the Relori cleaver-scimitar too versatile a weapon. It could be swung in the manner of a broadsword, used for a jabbing, fencing kind of offense, held close and utilized as a knife, or carried to the side and used as a hook. In his early drills, while still getting the balance of the weapon, Parker often hesitated a fraction of a second too long deciding whether to attack or defend, whether to swing, hook or jab with the weapon— fighting with the friendmaker was not unlike boxing from that angle—and wound up a mock-casualty.

Soon, however, he was holding his own with the giant, getting in as many simulated cuts and jabs as he received. At last, feeling fully competent to wield the friendmaker in battle—lacking only the final test of live combat— Parker visited the blacksmith, had the blade of the weapon finished to a glittering scalpel's edge.

Archery was another matter.

Either Broadarm or Kaetha might have taught him the use of the bow and arrow, but Parker hesitated to approach the Relori woman in the field, where Fleet was also present and obviously, increasingly, resentful of Parker.

A visit to Kaetha's home was equally unsatisfactory. Here too Fleet was present. When Parker hesitated in the open doorway of the building, Fleet demanded his business. Parker told him; Fleet, withholding even the formal hospitality of qrart, spat out, "Kaetha is busy caring for Trili. Get your lessons from somebody else!"

Before Parker could reply, Kaetha had sprung to her feet, shouted at Fleet: "I will answer for myself. If Trili can play with the other children while I work in the fields or teach she can play while I teach Parker to use his bow!"

"Wait a minute, Fleet—" Parker began.

Fleet cut him off: "Stay out, Parker. This is between Kaetha and me. You are less than a Teras find, you are not even of the Country. You've meant nothing but trouble since we found you in the forest. Why don't you go back where you came from!"

"That's exactly what I want to do," Parker exclaimed. "If Kaetha helps me I hope to get out of Relore and find somebody who can point me home. Nobody here can!"

Tears of rage in her eyes, Kaetha knotted her fists in frustration, told Parker: "Perhaps it would be best if you learned with Broadarm. Soon we will be on our way." Parker watched her stride furiously from the room. He looked at Fleet.

"Get out," said the Relori again.

Parker did. That night he asked Broadarm for archery lessons; the giant responded that he would teach Parker with pleasure, beginning with the next dawn. Janna could get help in the fields.

Next morning Parker and Broadarm went outside the palisade toward the wood where Parker had been found. Each wore friendmaker, quiver and bow. Broadarm suggested that they aim at a huge tree hole, shooting back toward the palisade to aid in recovering any arrows that missed and went beyond the target.

"Fair enough," the American told him. Broadarm

pointed to a tree of a type unknown to Parker. "What kind of tree is it?" the American asked.

"That's a bonewood," said Broadarm. "They grow hundreds of feet high. They bear a tasty nut and drop them when they're just fine for munching. The bark is useful too."

The two men had reached a point about twenty yards beyond the tree, faced back now toward the palisaded settlement. "Here's how!" cried the giant, loosing an arrow. It landed solidly, penetrated straight and deep into the trunk of the tree. "Give it a try," suggested Broadarm.

Parker pulled one of Fletcher's practice arrows from his quiver. It was the first time he had actually examined one closely, and he was surprised to see that instead of feathers the Relori used carved blades, almost ailerons of wood. They were as thin, nearly, as feathers, and as light. "Bonewood?" Parker asked.

Broadarm nodded.

The American nocked an arrow, nervously drew the thong on his bow, careful to pull the string, not the arrow. He sighted carefully down the shaft, held his left hand steady, released the right, and watched his arrow wobble fifteen yards through the air and fall to earth.

Broadarm threw his head back and laughed until Parker, ashamed, joined him. Then Broadarm said, "Try another."

Parker's second shot flew farther than the first, wobbling a bit less, and fell near the tree. On the third attempt Parker's bowstring rasped the skin inside his left forearm, leaving a burning pain and an angry red patch inches long. The arrow flew into the air, somersaulted and landed ten feet from the archers.

Parker dropped his bow disgustedly and sat on the cool ground.

"Now one important lesson, friend," said Broadarm, "is to keep your bow off the ground. The dampness will get into it and it will become warped and lose its resilience."

"Broadarm," the aviator blurted, "you can't imagine a place ten thousand miles from the Country and God knows how far separated in time or dimension or some other subtle way that I can't guess either." The giant looked puzzled at Parker's statement. Parker went on: "But I'll tell you something. You drill masters and weapons instructors are all alike. All alike.

"Okay," he said, springing back to his feet. "I'll get my arrows back, then maybe you can tell me what I'm doing wrong."

And they worked, and Parker learned. Set your feet, just *so*. No, farther apart. Yes. And your grip. Hold the bow just *so*. You must control it. Not too tightly, it will tremble, not too loosely, it will move when you draw. Just *so*, Parker. Right.

Your left arm, *so*, draw, *so*, sight, *so*, release, *so*.

The first time Parker hit the tree—it was still a wobbling, veering shot that caromed off the side of the trunk —they celebrated with a quick round of qrart. The second time he hit the tree his arrow actually penetrated the rough bark and hung there, high off the ground. Broadarm had to boost Parker on his shoulders to get it back. The third time Parker hit the tree his arrow struck with a gratifying *thunk* and stood rigidly out from the tree bole, its head well embedded in the strong, porous wood. By the tenth time, Parker was loosing his arrows from an increased distance, hits were outnumbering misses by a growing margin, and Broadarm was praising his pupil's progress and his own instruction in equally extravagant language.

Within another week, Parker was accompanying short hunting expeditions into the Country around Relore. The first deer he brought down was excuse for a celebration in in the Broadarm household as if a favorite son had brought home a promotion on his first job. The overflowing Janna gave Parker a hug that threatened to dislocate half his vertabrae while Broadarm enthusiastically pounded the bones back into place with great friendly slams on the back.

Only the absence of Kaetha from the celebration made the night less than perfect for Parker. After an uncounted number of rounds of qrart he told his hosts as much.

Next morning Parker pleaded a hangover—an ailment not unknown in Relore—to stay in the cabin after Broadarm and Kaetha were gone. Then he went to the cabin of Olduncle.

The elder man greeted him formally with qrart. Parker blanched at the prospect of even a ceremonial sip but managed to touch the jug to his lips before returning it to the leader. "I have had reports of your progress, Parker," the Relori said. "You farm, you hunt, you have become expert with our weapons. You have learned our language and many of our customs. You have friends now in Relore. Do you wish to reconsider your decision about going to Par'z?"

Parker sat down facing the other man as Olduncle signed him to do so. He said: "Thank you, Olduncle. Again, I feel flattered that you wish me to become one of your community, and the offer has its appeal, believe me. But I must go, and I think now, the sooner the better.

"I have come to ask you—I have not spoken with Broadarm or Kaetha about this yet—will you send them with me now? As quickly as may be. Tomorrow morning, if possible."

Olduncle nodded. "Very well. You are ready to go, and if you are decided, there is nothing to be gained by delay. Tomrorow, then."

"What will happen to Trili?" Parker asked. "Should she just stay with Fleet?"

"Oh, you are concerned?" said Olduncle. Parker said nothing. "Well, Fleet may be off on the hunt at any time. I am sure that Janna will be willing to take her until Kaetha returns, and Trili likes Janna."

"Fine," said Parker. "I will prepare to go."

CHAPTER

7

Packing for a Relori expedition into the Country was a small task. Parker would travel with Broadarm and Kaetha: that meant traveling on Relori terms. He checked his clothing—homespun dark trousers, lighter shirt, a warm hide garment that would serve as a jacket by day or a sleeping bag by night—and strong, heavy boots, that had long since replaced his borrowed raiment, returned to an unhospitable Fleet.

The flier's weapons were carefully examined. His friendmaker, spotlessly polished and honed to a fine edge, and a whetstone carried in Parker's quiver to keep the

sword-knife at the ready. Arrows, the product of Fletcher's prideful craft, and the heavy, polished bow he had
learned so well to use. Spare thongs with which to re-
string the bow, should need arise.

Other supplies were almost nil. A few small jugs of
qrart, the rosy fluid one of the few pleasures of home
that the Relori permitted themselves on the trail. One of
Janna's roughly baked loaves—even that wasn't quite ko-
sher, Parker thought—to get them started. Beyond that,
the three would live off the countryside. Such fruit as
they could find, such game as they could bag, and the
waters of the Country's streams that Kaetha and Broadarm knew well, these would be the provisions of the journey.

By noon Parker had set aside his supplies for the trip,
trudged through the quiet streets of Relore and beyond
the palisade to the field where Janna and Broadarm were
at work. Parker joined them, weeded perfunctorily for a
few minutes, then spoke to the two Relori.

"I have been with Olduncle," he said.

"That is no surprise," said Broadarm. Janna, for once,
held her silence.

"Will you be ready, Broadarm, to leave in the morning? If you and Kaetha are ready, then we will go to
Par'z."

"I will come in early today, Parker. Tomorrow we will
go."

Parker walked to the field worked by Kaetha and
Fleet. The man dropped his work and came to meet him.
"What do you want now, foreigner?" he demanded.

"I want to speak with Kaetha," Parker told him.

"You can see that she is busy," said Fleet. Parker
looked. Kaetha stood, some hundred yards away, watching the two men. To make an open break now, he wondered, or to let one more incident pass? Fleet stood, fists
balled, resting on his hips, as if waiting for Parker to challenge his authority over the slim Relori woman.

"Would you tell her for me that I have spoken with
Olduncle this morning," Parker spoke loudly to Fleet,
watching the more distant Kaetha to see if his voice carried to her. "Broadarm, Kaetha and I leave for Par'z tomorrow. Trili to stay with Janna." Before Fleet could
answer, Parker was able to see a look of pleasure and
relief in Kaetha's face. Parker felt that he had chosen

rightly, to avoid the open clash with Fleet. Time enough for that if he should, by any happening, decide to settle in Relore later on. But there was no point in it now.

Parker watched Kaetha return to her work. Fleet said: "You took my clothing on the trail. You took my friend-maker from Smith—yes, I have heard of that. Now you would take this woman from me. Well, Parker, if you never return to this community consider yourself fortu-nate. If you ever return, we will see about a few things!" The Relori turned away furiously, leaving Parker to stand a long moment, watching Fleet and Kaetha both at work, wondering and sad at the sight. Then he went back to rid himself of the rest of the day working with Janna and Broadarm.

That night after dinner Parker and Broadarm and Janna sat long, talking of many things. Of Relore, and of Par'z and the legends of her mysteried inhabitants, of the trip that lay ahead, of the Relori fishermen's shell in which they would cross to the Island of Par'z. After a while Parker excused himself and went for a walk in the cool, quiet streets of Relore.

From some of the wooden buildings the lights of small tallow lamps shone. Families were with families, friend visited friend. It's all here, Parker thought. Mankind, the whole thing in microcosm. Children warm in bed, youth with its dreams, companions at song, lovers in each other's arms, aged dozing in their corners content to watch their line go on in sons and daughters and grandsons and granddaughters.

And for me, the American thought, goodbye. Goodbye to New York, goodbye to King's Ferry. Goodbye even to McMurdo. And now, goodbye to Relore.

Beyond the last cabins, near the village palisade, he stood still looking at the sky. Strange, he thought, this is the first time I've really looked at the sky since I've been here. A bright gibbous moon lit the still night, a moon at which Parker looked, thought perhaps that it looked larger and showed more markings than he remembered. And the stars, twinkling with a cold, distant beauty, were they ranged in the standard constellations of the southern sky?

Parker could not be sure. He thought: Damn, I wish I'd paid more attention to celestial navigation. Who ever thought that a Huey jockey would ever have to worry about the stars? Maybe the high-altitude jet boys might be up at night and fly by the sky. In a copter you lived by your maps, your compass, and the terrain. If you ever had to fly blind it was more maps and more instruments. But the stars?

He looked up again. If the Country was where he guessed it was, running from the Ellsworth Highland down onto the Palmer Peninsula, then the Weddell Sea was to the east and the Southern Cross should be. . . . No, it was hopeless. If I had it all to do over, Parker thought . . . no, no, that kind of thinking was totally futile.

He headed back toward the house of Janna and Broadarm, deliberately gave wide berth to the one where lay Kaetha and Fleet and Trili. When Parker reached his destination the cabin lay dark and quiet. He slipped in, covered himself with pelts in the outer room, and slept little until sunrise came.

With dawn Janna and Broadarm emerged from their room, stretching and yawning. The huge Janna joined the men this day, chattering as they made their way to the stream, bathed, and as Parker and Broadarm shaved made her way back to the cabin to prepare breakfast. When the two men returned they found Kaetha and Trili already there, Kaetha's light pack thrown with Parker's and Broadarm's in the front room.

Kaetha stood with Janna, helping her prepare food for them all, interjecting only an occasional monosyllable into Janna's incessant talk of food and cooking, the giantess's concerned solicitude with the diet of the two boys —Broadarm and Parker, who between them weighed some five hundred pounds and, with Parker standing on Broadarm's massive shoulders, could reach thirteen feet into the air—during the rigorous trip.

Trili chattered gaily, with as few pauses as Janna and even less apparent concern over whether she was understood or even heard. She scuttled between the two women, bringing them implements and food and frequently getting underfoot.

As they all sat down to a light breakfast of eggs, bacon, juice, venison steak, qrart, bread, and fruit, Parker let his hearing go out of focus, could hear Janna's constant voice sounding nearly like his mother's—how long since he had thought of *her?*—as he would leave home on a chilly, rainy morning: Are you sure you have enough sweaters to keep you warm (he could hardly move in the layers of clothing she had piled on him), and make sure you wear your rubbers, and don't forget to take an umbrella, and will you have enough to eat, and. . . . That, to go to a Saturday movie with a skinny friend.

Parker and the Relori finished their meal. Then the three who would travel—two would return—gathered their light traveling gear, the flimsy packs, the bows and quivers and friendmakers. Janna hugged each in turn, clung to her husband and wept for a moment. The child Trili, her hair in two pigtails that flew behind her as she leaped into Broadarm's giant embrace. She permitted even Parker an instantaneous hug, accepted her mother's kiss, and stood holding Janna's huge hand as Kaetha, Broadarm and Parker trooped from the cabin.

At the palisade—a pleasant surprise—they were met by Fletcher and Scenter. "I saw you into Relore," the sharp-eyed scout said to Parker, "I now see you out. Good luck, stranger."

Fletcher, the community's chief hunter, armorer, and —Parker guessed—heir apparent to become Olduncle when the present village leader could no longer serve, was less taciturn. "You're a good man, Parker. I regret that you have decided not to stay with us. If you change your mind, come back. You'll be welcome."

Then, turning to the others, "Be careful, Broadarm and Kaetha. Steer clear of Teras and don't let the torzzi get you."

With that the three were beyond the gate, striding toward the woods with the long, easy pace of the far walker. The trees were spaced widely as yet, the ground clear of brush permitting the three to stride abreast, Kaetha in the center, Broadarm and Parker on either side.

They went along silently and easily at first. The sun was fully clear of the horizon, the night's chill dissipated from the forest air. A pleasant brightness filtered down through the leaves and branches of the towering forest growth, turning the moist, pleasant greenery into a magical evocation of Sherwood Forest.

For all the world, thought Parker, I could be a new Errol Flynn, and Broadarm Alan Hale, and Kaetha . . . who was it played Maid Marian? No matter, the game

was so pleasant he could keep it up for a longer while
than he'd thought, running ahead a few dozen yards,
waiting for the two Relori to catch up, shouting to Broadarm and Kaetha that they had better hurry or face the
wrath of the Sheriff of Nottingham.

And Broadarm and Kaetha, obviously at a total loss
as to what Parker was talking about, yet played along,
passing the time happily as they penetrated farther and
farther north, toward the black wall of Teras, and ever
tending slightly to the left, to the west. To the Island of
Par'z, according to the Relori, and to Adelaide Island in
the Bellinghausen Sea if Parker remembered his geography correctly, and if they were still on the same continent
where he had crashed with Logan an untold time before.

By mid-afternoon the long marches and short rests
were beginning to tell on Parker. Before he had time to
complain, however, he saw the giant Broadarm reach a
massive hand across Kaetha's and his own chest to bring
the party to a quick, silent halt. With astounding speed
the huge Relori had slipped his bow from his shoulder,
pulled a yard-long arrow from his quiver, nocked and
aimed the missile.

Parker's own sight darted ahead, caught a glimpse of
a tawny form fully sixty yards ahead, between a towering pine and a massive bonewood tree. Broadarm's
bladed shaft flew from the giant's bow, streaked between
forest trees; the tawny animal bounded once into the air,
jerked convulsively and fell. The three travelers ran to
see Broadarm's prey.

It was a huge buck, fixed by a single shaft in the
heart. Broadarm's aim, Parker thought, could not have
been better, his shot truer to the mark. The deer was so
large that the three of them could hardly lift it.

"We've made a good day's march already," Kaetha
said, "why don't we make camp here and clean the buck.
We can have it partly smoked by tomorrow, and carry
away enough venison to last us just about to the sea."

Parker and Broadarm agreed and the three set to work
plaiting a rope of spare bow thongs, tossing it over a low
tree limb, hoisting the carcass, cleaning, skinning, digging
out a pit beneath and building the smoke fire.

The work occupied the full attention of the two men
and the Relori woman until after dusk. Then Parker and
Kaetha built a second fire for cooking, and cut pointed

sticks to hold venison steaks, while Broadarm cut them all portions of the fresh meat. Before Parker and Kaetha rejoined Broadarm the American asked the Relori woman, "Kaetha, as we left Relore this morning Fletcher warned us to watch for torzzi. What are torzzi?"

"Maybe nothing, Parker," she replied. "Or maybe . . . They are said to be wild creatures, fierce man-like things but not men, that live in these woods. Many think that they are the descendents of a people who lived here before there was a Relore or even a Teras. That something terrible happened to them, that they began to lose their human character, and eventually turned into wild, hairy sub-men."

"Do you believe in them, Kaetha? Have you ever seen a torzz?"

"I have not, Parker. As for believing, I do not know."

The Yeti, the wild man of Borneo, the priests of Opar, thought Parker. The beast-man and the man-beast, part of every culture he had ever known of. And was the torzz another nightmare, a racial Mr. Hyde of the Relori . . . or was he, too, an inhabitant of this new world, whom Robert Parker had yet to meet?

The three travelers speared their venison steaks, roasted them over their fire, squatted or sat to slice the rich, smoking meat with friendmaker and wash down the hearty food with swigs of qrart. The discipline of Fletcher was missing from this camp, the sparkling drink was not reserved for after dinner but served as a mouth-cleansing counter to the heavy-textured meat.

At the end of the meal a quick rinse in an icy brook made Parker gasp at the frigid feel of the water.

"Plenty of streams coming from the highlands," Broadarm remarked. "We're lucky about that, Parker. There are little brooks and lakes all over the peninsula, and we have plenty of water for our crops at Relore unless there's a drought in the Country and the highlands at the same time. Not that that never happens, but it's rare."

When they returned to the opening between trees where the two fires burned, Parker was filled with a delicious weariness. A good day's travel, fresh dinner, a generous portion of qrart and the company of a good friend and a beautiful woman . . . if he could only close his mind to other considerations, it would seem an idyll.

But the woman was Fleet's, much as the Relori hunter abused her and much as she seemed to resent his treatment and favor Parker. And Parker's great friend Broadarm would be with him only to the sea, or perhaps to cross its narrow arm that separated Par'z from the mainland of the Country, and then would be back to Relore, taking Kaetha with him, back to Fleet.

Parker was tempted to ask Kaetha to abandon Relore, to turn her back on the people who had taken her in as an infant and made her one of themselves, but even that he could not do. He could not ask her to abandon her daughter Trili, Trili who so resembled her mother in appearance and character, and seemed so little like Fleet.

Broadarm stood near the dying cook-fire, said to Parker: "I do not know whether I believe in Fletcher's torzzi or not. But you remember, Parker, that we kept guard on the hunt when we found you, and I think I'll just stay up and watch tonight. If I feel too sleepy I'll wake you to take over."

Parker answered: "Fair enough," and lapsed into silence.

The night air was growing chilly now, and as Parker interrupted his own musings, staring into the dying fire, to pull his warm pelt about him, he felt a gentle touch on one side of his face. He looked up into the thin, smooth-skinned brown face of Kaetha; the twin flickering fires of the encampment weaving faint patterns of shadows on the planes of her face and dancing orange points in her darkly sad eyes.

He took the hand which she left on his, held it to his face with his own, surprised to find his hands unsteady.

"Parker, I . . ." she began.

"Sit with me, Kaetha," the American interrupted, pulling her gently to the ground beside him. He flung the warm, furred pelt so that it swung about Kaetha's shoulders as well as his own. The hand which held the hide he kept on her shoulder, with the other Parker held the Relori's slim hand, as a child holds the hand of a companion.

"I'm sorry you are leaving, Parker," Kaetha said in a voice little more than a whisper.

"And I," he answered. "But I cannot just give up. As long as there is any chance of solving this mystery in Par'z, I must go. Do you understand why?"

She did not speak in answer, but Parker felt Kaetha's head nod on his shoulder. He took her face into his hand, her plait of hair falling across his forearm, his fingers on her cheek, his thumb beside her mouth.

A tear welled in Kaetha's eye, trembled, about to roll down her dark cheek. Parker kissed her closed eye, tasted the salt of the tear. He traced with his lips the course it would have followed down her cheek. As he kissed her mouth the American felt her arm tighten about his own shoulders; they slid to the ground so that they lay facing each other, their arms about each other, bodies pressing tightly beneath the warm buckskin pelt.

Again he kissed her mouth, her face, felt many warm tears on her cheeks, her own lips on his mouth, his neck. "Oh, Parker," he half-heard, half-felt her mouth as she whispered to him, "please, stay, if you will not stay in Relore, at least stay with me this night, this journey."

"I will, Kaetha." His hands caressed her shoulders, her neck, her back beneath the flimsy shirt she wore. She did not speak as he moved to open its front, bent his head to kiss her on the shoulder, the breast. She held her two hands on his back, pulling him to her, whispering words. . . .

A huge weight smashed into Parker's back, dashing him and the Relori woman over. "Torzzi!" he cried, "Broadarm!" Parker tried to struggle to his feet, at the same time to hold himself between the still-sprawling form of the Relori woman and the heavily furred, growling animal form that had pounced on them.

"I come!" Broadarm's great voice preceded his even greater form as the giant pounded across the encampment, between the two fires, friendmaker glinting orange in Broadarm's upraised arm. "Where, Parker?" he shouted.

The American had no time to answer, grappling with the snarling, clawing beast that rolled and thrashed on the ground, mouthing his shoulders and neck with great pointed fangs yet strangely holding back from harming the aviator, seemingly unwilling to do any harm, pulling the punches of massive padded paws and the clash of those terrible teeth equally.

Even before Broadarm had arrived, great sword-knife in hand, Parker had subdued the animal, pinned its form to the ground, only the furious lashings of a heavy, powerful tail telling of the strength strangely restrained in the animal's attack.

Parker looked at the pinned beast in the flickering twin fires. "Kitty," he said, all but dumbfounded in amazement, "Kitty, Longa." Again an expression in the great cat's face, in her startlingly colored eye, reminded Parker of a fey, mocking laughter. From the form of the great variegated cat came a loud rumbling, rippling sound that Parker knew must be this canine's purr.

Parker turned to look at Kaetha, saw her slowly re-doing her shirt, but the American saw that she met his eyes evenly, steadily, with a look of still-welcome on her face.

He turned back to the gigantic cat, saw that she had rolled onto her back exposing a great patch of purest soft white fur on her belly, deckled with splotches of orange stripes and black. The super-calico waggled her paws, looked again into Parker's eyes with her own intelligent-seeming eyes. "Oh, all right, Kitty," he snorted, "I'll rub your belly."

And he did, and as he did so he felt Kaetha huddle down beside him with their warming-pelt. He felt her place an arm familiarly about his shoulders, saw in her face a look of warm familiarity and affection, as though their love had been consummated.

Parker watched Broadarm bend, pat Longa once familiarly on the head, then walk softly back to his watch-place on the other side of the cleared space. The giant fed new green wood to the fire which burned beneath the venison carcass; the rising smoke increased, obscuring his massive form.

Broadarm, Parker thought, is the most discreet man I have every known.

He turned to Kaetha now, took her confidently in his arms, whispered to her with a quiet chuckle: "Here we find our love. To the tune of a calico cat, guarded by the jolly brown giant."

She put her head on his chest, and Parker felt her relax as she gave herself to him wholly. He lay with her, and kissed her many times, pulled the furs about them for warmth, and removed her clothing, and loved her long and gladly, and slept, Kaetha's head upon his arm, and both his hands upon her.

In the morning they set out again. The deer brought

down by Broadarm's shaft had made dinner for the three marchers, and breakfast. Longa, contrary to her behavior when Parker had first seen her on his first trek into Relore, shared a hearty portion of the newly smoked venison for her breakfast, and seemed, during the day, pleased to accompany the three marchers, now running ahead, now doubling back to rejoin them, now dashing into the denser woods on some unknown mission of her own.

As the sun reached its high point and the heat of the day began to wear on the three, they called a halt to drink at an icy pond, then rest a few minutes in the shade. The black and yellow kissers floated from dazzling shaft of sunlight pouring between leafy heights and misty shadow, the many varieties of fruit Parker had seen in his first days were again in evidence. The kissers, as ever, favored the kumquat-like jelly fruit that grew in scattered grove-like concentrations.

The three travelers sat resting, Kaetha close beside Parker as new lover beside her lover. Broadarm, cheery, willingly carrying the heaviest share of the half-smoked venison, rested with them, making no mention of the previous night's events. The cat Longa prowled in and out of the trees of the forest.

To while the time they sang the hearty, lusty songs of the Relori people, songs to which Parker had first been introduced on his first trip to the village, when their words had been to him a senseless gabble. He followed them now as first Broadarm would lead the singing, then with equal energy Kaetha would give the tune.

Roll me over was not far wrong, although rather tame in comparison with the Relori trail songs. Finally Kaetha, her hand comfortably in Parker's, demanded: "Have your people no songs, Parker?"

"None that I know that can quite compare with your 'Ladies of the Vale'," he admitted. "There's the one about the sailor and the Wave if I can remember it. Or 'The Whore of Jerusalem.' Or . . ." He finally settled for "Old Man Mulligan"; by the time he had run out of verses Broadarm and Kaetha were competing to devise verses of their own.

At last, fully rested and ready to go on, the three shrugged into their light packs. Kaetha briefly consulted her seldom-used map and they set out. Heading down the towering ranks of irregular tree trunks, their only companions the ever-present floating butterflies and the unpredictable Longa, they set a good pace toward the wall of Teras and the sea.

Parker jogged a few paces off their chosen trail, reached into a patch of foliage and pulled back his hand triumphantly holding a beautifully rounded kumquat-fruit. Before he could more than start to call to Broad-arm and Kaetha they both shouted at him, "No, drop it!" And, "Parker, throw it away!"

Too late! Seemingly from nowhere a huge kisser lit on Parker's hand. He watched it in frozen fascination as the insect moved softly to reach his palm. A needle of flame seemed jabbing into his hand, into his flesh; in an instant it turned into a sheet of agony, a river of unbearable torment tearing up through the veins of his arm, even to his shoulder and his chest. Parker writhed, flailed his hand madly in an effort to dislodge the butterfly; it clung as, screaming, he sank toward the ground, felt strong hands grasp him, saw a blade glint as it swept past his tormented hand taking the blurring yellow and black object with it.

Parker felt himself flung, dragged insanely through brush, thrown down, his searing, flaming arm plunged into flowing water. Through half-seeing eyes he watched Broadarm's great blade flashing, moving on the palm of his swollen hand, watched a gout of red turn the clear moving water of the stream to an ugly ruddy tone.

The American was lifted, felt Broadarm holding him still despite convulsive twitches that now racked his body as the entire affected area from pectoral to fingertip continued to swell and pulse with waves of heat and pain, saw Kaetha, a ghastly look to her, pressing downward, downward on the flesh of his forearm, making the blood flow from the new wound Broadarm had inflicted on his hand.

He tried to speak, to ask what had happened, could force out only a gasping "What—whu" and fell silent again. At last a calm came slowly to replace the panicked confusion of the frantic minutes since he had picked the fruit. The shudders in Parker's frame were fewer. His vision cleared. He tried again to speak, succeeded in asking what had happened.

"You got yourself kissed," said Broadarm succinctly.

"But . . . I was . . . I . . ." He could not go on.

The rest of the afternoon was a blur to the American. Kaetha and Broadarm seemed to come and go, he felt himself rubbed and turned, tasted draughts of qrart forced through his lips. When his head rolled to the side he could see only a terrible bloated caricature of an arm and hand.

Through the night he slept and woke fitfully, grateful each time to find Kaetha still with him. Other figures drifted in and out of his vision: the giant Broadarm, the madly patterned cat Longa, fur and hide and a flickering flame, hands touching him, working somehow at the swollen limb, brown faces filled with concern.

In the morning he lay propped against a tree, too weak to more than whisper to Broadarm, as Kaetha at last slept nearby: "What kissed me, Broadarm? What happened to me?"

The great hunter squatted beside Parker, peered into his face. A faint smile of relief appeared on Broadarm's lips. "You got just one kiss, Parker. You were lucky. You'll be better today and walking tomorrow. Without help, you'd have been *very* lucky to survive. You would have been kissed to death."

"I don't understand," whispered the American. "The fruit. I picked the fruit, that's all. Then the butterfly came."

"It was my fault," Broadarm said. "Mine and Kaetha's too, but we must have assumed you knew about the kissers. But they don't come into Relore often, and they're harmless when they come because their food is not there."

Parker only looked at the Relori, his eyes holding his question.

"These butterflies," Broadarm said, "the kissers. They live on the juice and pulp of the fruit you picked. They can see well enough to fly but still not very well. They are guided to their food by the odor. And they have to get at the pulp to get the juice to live on, but they have no hard parts, no sharp parts to get through the rind."

The giant shifted his weight, shuffled himself to a more comfortable position on the ground beside Parker. Then he went on: "So they have a special part. Did you ever

wonder how creatures get the parts they need, Parker?
I sometimes wonder. But the kisser has a tube that drops
from his abdomen. When he lights on the fruit the end
of the tube rests on the rind. The kisser secretes a drop
of fluid through the tube. That fluid burns. It burns fast,
it dissolves the rind in an instant, and then the tube pene-
trates into the pulp of the fruit, and the kisser sucks the
citrus juice through the tube.

"But a kisser doesn't see very well. He finds his meals
by odor. That's why we never touch the kumquat-fruit.
When you picked the fruit you had to squeeze it, a little.
The odor went out. When the kisser came, the oil of the
fruit, the odor, was on your hand. You got the drop of
fluid through the kisser's proboscis. You saw what happened.

"You leave the kisser's food alone, he won't harm you.
Not even if you kill him. Relori children learn that before they ever pass the palisade. But you nearly lost your
life to learn it."

By the next day Parker was on his feet, as Broadarm
had promised. Weak, sick, leaning on either the Relori
man or woman, still he was able to move about the tiny
encampment a few steps at a time. The swelling and pain,
too, were subsiding in his arm. The deep, tiny hole inflicted by the kisser and the wounds around it made by
Broadarm to force bleeding were covered by an herb
poultice. Careful examination each time the dressing was
changed showed no infection developing.

Before dawn on the fifth morning after the nearly fatal
"kiss" Parker and Broadarm again woke early. Kaetha,
who had sat with Parker's head in her lap through the
night, slept in exhaustion.

The two men worked about the camp, cutting down
the now well-smoked venison, thoroughly dousing the
two fires that had burned, assembling their meagre packs.
The giant Broadarm, in Parker's eyes, worked with the
same tireless vigor as ever. Parker himself, recovered entirely from the kisser's sting except for a slight soreness
and the quickly healing cuts on the stung hand, was able
to do nearly his normal work.

The black and yellow butterflies floated about the
camp, fragile and harmless creatures now and, Parker

knew, as long as he did not trespass on their supply of nourishment.

As their work brought them together at the edge of the encampment farthest from the sleeping Kaetha, Parker laid his hand on Broadarm's shoulder, "Before Kaetha wakens, Broadarm, I want to talk with you," he said.

The giant looked at him, obviously waiting for Parker to speak.

"We will go on today," the American said.

The Relori nodded.

"And we will reach the sea—when?" Parker asked.

"We can camp tonight withing an hour's march of the shore," Broadarm said. "We will start early tomorrow and reach the edge of water before dawn. We cannot sail to Par'z in the dark—we would likely miss the island entirely and be lost in the sea—so we will start as soon as the sky begins to lighten. The Terasians sail these waters but keep no regular patrol. Our fishermen who have crossed their paths say that they do not always bother with Relori fishers. Still, we like to avoid them. But they seem to hate the Par'zians most bitterly. We do not know why."

"And to sail to Par'z," Parker asked, "where will we get a boat?"

"Our fishers leave their craft hidden on the shore. We will use a fishing craft to take you to Par'z. But how you will get back, Parker, if you do not come with us . . ."

The American looked seriously at the Relori. He said, "Don't worry about that, Broadarm. If I can find a way home in Par'z, you will never see me again. If Par'z cannot help me . . ." He paused, repeated, "if Par'z cannot help me, then the future will just have to take care of itself.

"And you, my friend, will take Kaetha back to Relore. That is my great regret. You will take her back to her child and her husband."

The giant reacted with surprise. "Her what?"

"Her child and husband," Parker said. "Trili and Fleet."

"Parker," Broadarm said incredulously, "Kaetha's husband is dead. Fleet is his brother, that is why he has taken the woman and the child. That is our way in Relore. The family is as one, but Fleet is no husband to Kaetha. Fleet is a bachelor. Everyone knows he wants to marry her, but she will not have him, and who can blame her! Fleet is a good hunter but a sour man."

Parker stepped back from his friend, sat on the ground. He was speechless. He looked at the sleeping Kaetha, back then to Broadarm, his mind a seething whirl of new ideas and fantastic speculation of Broadarm's revelation. After minutes of reeling, racing thought, he said to the giant: "I must still go on. I will go to Par'z. You must take her back with you as if nothing had been said between us. Will you promise me that, Broadarm?"

The giant nodded assent.

Parker went on. "But listen, Broadarm. You are my best friend in this new world. I tell you that if I find a way home, I will not take it until I have returned to Relore and I will take Kaetha and Trili with me, back to my world. And if I cannot find a way, I will come back to Relore for them anyway. I will become a Relori myself if I must, or I will take them elsewhere in this world. But whatever happens, I will come for them. Tell me, Broadarm, would there be any obstacle in Relore to my . . . to my marrying Kaetha?"

"Of course not, Parker. You must do what any other couple does."

"And that is . . . what?"

"Why, you must live together for one year, to prove you get along with each other. Or have a child, or take in a find. Then on Founder's Day, if you still wish it, you announce your marriage. It is very simple."

Parker said, "Very well, Broadarm. Somehow I will be back for them. Until then, I will entrust them to you. Will you take that care upon yourself?"

Parker had no wait for Broadarm's answer: "I will do it."

They resumed their work in silence. Soon Kaetha woke, and after the three had breakfasted on fruit and qrart they were on their way once more to the sea.

CHAPTER

8

For the first time since the three had started their trek from Relore the morning was not marked by clear sunlight. Instead, this day the dawn was dismal and late, and the light of the morning was a gloomy gray in place of the gold and green of the usual forest light. Robert Leroy Parker looked at the sky, at a patch visible through the almost continuous growth of tall trees. He saw clouds racing over the woods, darkening the sky. A damp wind moved through the forest.

"It looks like we're in for something," he said to the two Relori.

"Don't be so sure," Broadarm replied. "The rainy season is just about due, but this early in the year the storm might just pass over us. If it does hit it won't be very soon, I think. We might get our day's march in before it hits."

The wind was rising, its keening making conversation difficult. Still, Parker could hear Kaetha's voice as she called over the sound of the wind, "Broadarm is right, Parker. If you feel all right we should still use the day."

"All right," the American gave in. He squeezed the Relori woman's hand. The three figures continued through the woods in silence. Somehow, the American thought, I don't feel like songs today, funny, dirty, or any other kind. Neither, obviously, did Broadarm or Kaetha. Parker did ask, "Where's Longa this morning?"

"I haven't seen her," said Broadarm, "but I think she will be around. The big cats are very independent creatures, but once one joins a party she isn't likely to quit. They usually stay with us until we get back to Relore."

Well, the American thought, then Kaetha and Broadarm would have the cat with them after he himself was gone. Unless . . . "What happens when we get to Par'z?" he asked. "I suppose she'll go with you."

"I told you, Parker," said the giant, "they are very independent beasts. She might just decide to stay on the island with you. Unless she refuses to go at all. There's no telling what one of these big cats will do. If one feels like it, she can act practically like a human being. You remember how Longa stood guard over you?"

"I won't forget that very soon," Parker said ruefully.

"But this time she's been here and gone all the time," Broadarm continued. "That's cats!"

On and on the three went through the forest. Through the dark, gray day there was no sight of the calico cat. Conversation was sporadic, song totally absent. Parker's mind dwelt less and less on the promise of Par'z, more and more, sadly, on his imminent parting from Broadarm and from Kaetha. While the three had been tramping, hunting, camping on their way from Relore to the sea, it seemed as if Parker had taken a bit of Relore with him. The friendliness of Relore's brown people, the quiet and beauty of the Country, the mystery of who the Relori were and how Parker had come among them, all spun through Parker's mind.

And the love that he had found only on this trek. Now all seemed fading, drawing away from the American as his every step brought him closer to the sea, and to Par'z. With one hand he took Kaetha's hand, with the other, unashamedly, Broadarm's. Like schoolchildren the three walked abreast until a narrowing between pine tree and bonewood forced them to single file.

Parker could not tell when dusk fell that night. The sky was black with clouds, the first drops beginning to fall when Kaetha said: "This is far enough. We should camp here tonight. We don't want to be too close to the sea during the storm. There may be water where the land is low."

"You didn't even check the map," Parker protested.

"I know this land," Kaetha replied.

Broadarm nodded his agreement. "She does, Parker. I could not have got us here so well, but I recognize the place. We can reach the sea quickly in the morning. And I think we would do well to rig shelters tonight, if we want to sleep dry."

Without a word of discussion Parker and Kaetha set about tying their warm pelts into a crude lean-to. There was enough leathern material over to make a flap for the open side. Parker saw Broadarm walk a distance way, begin work on a one-man shelter.

They made a cooking fire, roasted steaks for their final dinner together. When the food was ready each sat, silently watching the flames rise from the cook fire, hearing the crackle of the flaming wood and hiss of the widely spaced, heavy raindrops as they spattered onto the fire and the heated rocks circled about it.

Parker was the first to turn to his flimsy pack, return to the fireside with a small jug of qrart. Holding the jug he spoke. "Kaetha," he paused, his eyes on the woman's sad, beautiful face, "Broadarm," he looked at his titanic friend, "in all my time in the Country I have never heard a toast. I never thought to ask, but I suppose the Relori just don't have that custom that my people have, although you do use qrart in ceremonial courtesy.

"In America when we drink to something, drink to honor someone or something, it makes that moment . . . I guess, sacred." A word he could not recall using before in his life.

"A good custom, Parker," the giant rumbled. "To what would you have us make our drink sacred?"

"I'm not sure," said the American. "Or . . . I am sure, but how can I say it? It's also our custom that the toast is proposed in elegant language. All right. To friends present and to friends absent. To the living and to the dead." He looked at the other two, saw them look back, Broadarm with a penetrating expression in his eyes, Kaetha with a split second of startlement followed by a looked of deepening understanding.

Parker drank, passed the liquor to Kaetha. As the jug was passed their hands touched, her slim hand transmitted a tremor to that of the American. She drank—no polite sip, Parker observed—then passed the jug to Broadarm. "Is that the elegant language of the toast?" he asked. "I would call it simple language bearing much meaning. I will drink to what you wish, but I will add friends as yet unborn."

He tilted the jug, emptied it, and from his own pack brought a replacement. Long the jugs made their rounds, empties replaced by new jugs, qrart replaced by more qrart. At last the three rose slowly from their places by the fire. The rain was increasing now. As Broadarm, Kaetha and Parker started toward their shelters the big cat Longa strode into their camp, brushed condescendingly against each in turn, and sat down by the fire.

"There is our torzzi-watcher," Broadarm said, his tones sounding thick to Parker. Hey, you've had enough friend, the American almost said aloud, you're starting to look fuzzy. "Up early," Broadarm concluded, and crawled into his animal-pelt rain cover.

Parker and Kaetha walked unsteadily to the lean-to they had set up, crawled inside it and lay silently, their arms about each other, watching the fire slowly lose its battle with the increasing rain. The aviator could not tell whether the Relori woman was awake or not. For himself, he felt only a sense of anticlimax and mild distaste.

This last night with the Relori, this last night with Kaetha, should be some kind of drama, some kind of climax to their relationship. Instead Parker felt only sadness, a disappointment. He listened to Kaetha's breathing, realized that she was sleeping now. Our last night. Well, she's been up with me ever since that damned kisser got me on the hand. She's entitled to sleep.

Parker lay back, the woman's head still resting on his chest as he watched the rain pounding to the earth inches away. Maybe the torzzi will come, Parker thought. Maybe they're all around us now and their leader is sitting just beyond the camp, waiting for me to close my eyes, and that will be the signal for them to attack. He thought of scores of torzzi, vague forms in the dark, ill-shaped horrible subhuman things covered with shaggy hair, their eyes gleaming red in the night, their fierce fangs ready to pierce, dripping fetid saliva onto their coats. He closed his eyes and slept.

Dawn awakened Parker. The rain had stopped, leaving behind a sky—the airman in him revived—of blue so brilliant that Parker blinked at its beauty. The forest, as far as he could see from the lean-to, was still wet, trees dripping their night's burden of rain to the leaves of lower branches, of smaller trees, and to the earth itself. Perhaps the long night's half-drunken sleep or perhaps the passing of the storm had carried away Parker's melancholy of the evening.

He looked at Kaetha still lying beside him, kissed her softly on the forehead and temple until she opened her eyes. "I'm sorry about last night, Kaetha," he said quietly.

She looked up at him, touched him on the face. "It wasn't your fault," she said. "And it's over. Don't let it spoil this morning."

The two climbed out of their lean-to, quickly tore it down, working together, and packed the heavy pelts they had used. Parker looked to see Broadarm up also and busily working to get a fire going again. "We'll have a good breakfast today," the giant greeted Kaetha and Parker. "We've a busy morning ahead."

"How are you going to get wet wood to burn?" Parker asked.

"No need to do that," Broadarm replied. "You may have had pleasanter company last night but I had no companion so I took in some wood out of the storm. One must look ahead, you know!"

"You big boy scout!" said Parker.

"What's that?"

"Never mind. But you take your time, Broadarm. Kaetha and I will take a little walk while you get breakfast."

Parker took Kaetha's hand, led her from the encampment. They walked together in silence until they came to a rippling stream, then sat on its embankment while the rays of the rising sun warmed them both. In Parker's chest his heart pounded. Like a goddamn schoolboy, he thought, scared to try for a little grab on a date.

He put his arm about Kaetha's shoulder, drew her to him for one kiss. Then he pressed her face to his cheek, said quietly to her: "Kaetha, when I go I will have the scent of you in my nostrils. I will carry the taste of your mouth in my mouth."

"I will hold the sense of your flesh in my flesh," she whispered her reply.

It was a wedding, Parker thought, a wedding at parting. Their time together, their love-making, their days and nights were past, and yet, he thought, that was what it was. He eased her back in the sunlight, and there made love to her, this time not with a night passion, nor longer with excitement, but simply as a man in sunlight.

At the end they bathed in chill moving water, and embraced naked in the water, then dressed and went back to their encampment.

Parker saw that Broadarm had roasted four venison steaks. One was being sniffed by Longa, then batted by the huge cat's paw; she seized the meat, worried it, flipped it into the air and then began the process again.

Broadarm was well into a second slab of meat. The other two sizzled on sticks. Parker took one and handed it to Kaetha, kept the second for himself. He attacked it ravenously, looked up to see Kaetha doing the same with hers.

"By the Founder, you two are eating this day," roared Broadarm. "I've always said there's nothing like a good walk before breakfast to give you an appetite!"

Parker grinned at the giant who returned the expression. Somehow, the American thought, the tension of yesterday is gone. Not just between Kaetha and me, but Broadarm too. And just as well that it is, on this day of all days!

At the end of the meal they cleaned up the traces of their camp and set out on the last leg of the trek from Relore. This morning the cat stayed close as if sensing that this was not merely another day of tramping through woodlands. As the two Relori had predicted, within an hour after breaking camp they saw the end of the woods.

Parker stepped beyond the last trees onto a narrow strip of grass and low shrubbery to survey the new scene. Far off to the right—to the north, he thought, the morning sun shining from behind him—he could see the edge of the forest running parallel to a gray and rocky shoreline. The trees seemed to grow smaller and smaller as they stretched into the distance; the parallel lines of forest and water's edge drawing closer and closer to each other as they became more distant from the eye.

Far off to the north, almost at the limit of the American's vision through the clear morning air, he saw a line of black jutting outward from the green of the forest to the edge of the sea. At the distance from which Parker saw the black line it was impossible to judge its height; it might have been a low black fence at a few hundred yards or . . . Parker tried to judge the distance from himself and the two Relori to the black line. If it was as far off as it seemed, it must be of almost unbelievable height.

Turning back to the sea Parker saw stretches of clearest dark blue-green. The surface of—was this Marguerite Bay, with the Bellinghausen Sea stretching far off beyond the black wall to Bransfield Strait?—the surface of the sea was nearly smooth, a steady succession of little choppy peaks rising and falling in the soft morning breeze, giving back glints of the orange-gold sun that shone from behind the three travelers, rising over the tops of the forest growth.

The small wind, coming from the westward over the water, brought to Parker an unmistakable tangy odor. That much, at least, was no different in this world, the salty, fecund smell of the sea-edge, where submarine vegetation struggles to grip its way onto exposed earth and amphibious life creeps eternally from sea to land and from land to sea, searching for its proper home.

Distant across the sea Parker could see a point of land rising, not the edge of another major body but a patch of sea-bottom raised above the waters, defying their slow appetite to bring it down. The American spoke: "Is that Par'z?"

Kaetha answered simply, "Yes."

"Then it isn't the island I thought it was. It's much too small." He thought: if it isn't Adelaide it might be Briscoe Island, or even one of the others lying out toward the South Shetlands. But only if this is really the Palmer Peninsula. Only if this is Antarctica. Only if this is Earth.

A voice broke in on his thoughts: "We have a boat hidden in the trees, Parker. We keep them at fishing points along the sea, each time they are used the fishermen check them over and leave them in the appointed place." It was Broadarm. The giant led the party back a short distance into the woods. There, racked in the lowest branches of a young bonewood, Parker saw a dugout.

Broadarm unslung his bow and handed it to Parker to hold for him. He reached into the branches, grasped the dugout by its gunwales and swung it to the ground. While the American watched, Broadarm and Kaetha swarmed over the wooden craft checking it for the condition of the wood. Carefully racked inside the dugout hull were half a dozen paddles; like all the artifacts of the Relori, Parker observed, they were hand-crafted but made with care and skill.

"These dugouts usually hold six to eight men," Broadarm explained to Parker, "three or four paddlers, the others to handle nets and the catch. Can you handle a paddle?"

The American replied, "I think I can."

"Good," said the giant. "That will make things much easier on the way out to Par'z. Coming back, Kaetha and I should be able to manage." He stood up to look around in the woods, then said, "I wonder if the cat will want to come along." He called first in one direction, then another: "Longa, Longa. Come on kitty, want a nice boat ride?"

For an instant there was no sound, then a graceful shape of black splotched insanely with orange and white plunged from the branches above the three startled travelers. There was a resounding *thunk!* as the great cat landed in the bottom of the dugout. She began curiously sniffing the wood, curling and rubbing herself about the inside of the boat.

"There's your answer," Parker laughed. "I would guess that she can still smell fish on the wood."

Leaving Longa in the dugout craft Parker, Broadarm and Kaetha squatted in a triangle beneath the trees. "Kaetha has planned this journey so far," Broadarm rumbled, "what do you want to do now?" Both he and Parker looked at Kaetha.

"I do not see anything to be gained by delay," she said. But she looked at the Relori giant as she spoke. "The sea is calm enough, there is little wind and we can see clearly where we go. We can take a good look for Terasians before we set out but once we are on the water we will just have to take our chance if we meet some. Do you agree?"

Broadarm said, "I agree." Parker chose to let the giant's answer serve for him as well.

Parker handed Broadarm's bow and his own to Kaetha, who slung them both with her own weapon; then the two men walked to the dugout to carry it to the water. The big cat was snuggled contentedly into the bottom of the craft.

Broadarm said, "All right, Longa, out." The cat did not move. "Out, kitty," the giant repeated, "this thing is heavy enough without carrying you too." The cat looked contemptuously at the Relori, then settled down more firmly onto the wood.

"Oh, come on, you dumb cat!" he roared. As Parker watched amazed the giant picked up the cat by the scruff of her neck and deposited her on the ground beside the dugout. She immediately slipped back over the edge and

settled upon the bottom of the boat. As Parker and
Kaetha watched in laughter the giant seized the cat
again, whirled twice about and hurled the parti-colored
beast into the air. The graceful animal performed an incredible twist in the air, extended her legs with their
needle claws unsheathed, arrested her own flight by arriving with a *thump!* high up on the bonewood, and,
clinging there, head downward, gave a single piercing
offended wail, spat at the Relori giant, and stayed still,
flat against the bonewood trunk.

"Okay!" said Broadarm. He and Parker lifted the dugout and carried it through the last rank of trees, across
the narrow stretch of grass, the rocky sea-edge, and deposited the boat in the shallow water.

Parker looked back into the woods but could no longer
see the big cat. "I'll miss her," he said. He picked up a
paddle, asked, "Where shall I sit?"

"I will take stroke at the stern," said Broadarm. "You
get in the middle of the boat, Parker. You are inexperi-
enced and you will do best there. Kaetha will take the
bow."

The three stood beside the dugout, each with his hands
grasping the gunwales. At Broadarm's shout of "Now!"
they ran forward into the water. First Kaetha jumped
into her position, began paddling, then Parker, then
Broadarm, with a final great shove, vaulted into the rear
of the boat. Except for the Island of Par'z rising ahead
of them to the west the horizon was clear. To the north
as far as the Wall of Teras and beyond and to the south
as far as Parker could see the water stretched glistening.
No other object stood above its surface.

Within a few dozen strokes the three paddlers settled
into a steady pace, Kaetha stroking on the left of the
dugout, Parker on the right, Broadarm shifting from time
to time to keep the open craft headed straight for Par'z.
The American watched the horizon ahead, waiting for the
speck that was Par'z to grow into a visible shape. Then
too he let his eyes fall on Kaetha, watching the play of
long muscles in her arms and her back, thinking of their
times together, the angry, frustrating sessions with Olduncle in Relore, the nights together in the woods, the joy
of their morning beside the brook and their sharing of
food with Broadarm. Was it only this morning, only hours
ago, Parker wondered. Already the golden time seemed

ancient, distant, like a memory of events in the far un-
forgotten past, or things that had happened to someone
else.

"Time for a little rest," came Broadarm's voice from
behind Parker. He shipped his paddle gratefully. He did
not want Kaetha to see his face now so Parker turned
toward the stern of the dugout, looked past Broadarm
toward the now distant shoreline of the Country. A hundred yards or more behind the dugout an object bobbed
on the surface of the sea, glistening dark and wet in the
bright sunlight.

It looked to Parker about the size of a football. As the
three travelers rested the object moved closer behind
their craft. Soon Parker could make out two pointed pro-
jections atop the object—ears, he thought, clearly they
were ears. Then two great, glittering spots, then a mad
mottling of golden and white specks on the black, glistening wet fur, and one long exclamation point of streaking
orange running from forehead, between the eyes, nearly
to the white-spotted nose of the cat.

"I almost forgot," Parker said to Broadarm, "that
these cats don't mind water."

"Don't mind it?" the giant exclaimed. "Don't your
countrymen have the expression 'Like a cat to water'?"

"I'm afraid not," Parker answered.,

"Well," said Broadarm, "they're natural swimmers. And
Longa's a good girl."

"She is that," Parker agreed. He faced about toward
Kaetha. She managed a smile for him. Then Parker said,
"Let's go on," and they began again to stroke, changing
sides now to ease their muscles. Parker's wounded hand,
although still somewhat tender, was otherwise close to
normal. The puncture wound of the kisser seemed almost cauterized by the very acid that had caused all
Parker's pain. The long cuts inflicted by Broadarm to
cause bleeding had been spectacular in appearance but
not deep, and the herb poultices applied by the Relori
during Parker's fever seemed not only to prevent infection but to aid in healing.

That was another thing Parker did not know about the
Relori, he thought. Despite his time with them, had he
really got to understand their society? Their government
—well, maybe. Apparently it was pretty much of a free-
wheeling arrangement in which everybody did what he

liked as long as he minded his business, the whole thing presided over by a sort of elected monarch with vaguely defined but not too extensive powers.

Economics? Apparently simple but actually not nearly so. The people of Relore seemed to own their own homes and land, but the working of the land was done on a co-operative basis that didn't look as if it could work, but somehow did. Hunters brought home part of their prize, the rest went to the community. And the few specialists in Relore—the smith, Fletcher when he was playing armorer rather than chief hunter, and a few more—were supported by the community in return for their special services.

The palisade itself seemed common property, as did the sporadically used fishing boats. Palisade guard duty seemed to rotate but Parker had never seen a duty roster.

But Parker had seen no sign of religion in Relore, no money, no literature beyond oral tradition, no art, a knowledge of the world limited to Kaetha's map of the Country. . . . But not seeing these things did not prove that they did not exist in Relore. He had seen no evidence of medicine either, until he had needed it. Then Broadarm and Kaetha had demonstrated an understanding of poisons and their treatment, and use of herbs for antisepsis. What else had Parker simply not been exposed to? What was it that the big Relori had said one day when they were practicing archery?

Without ceasing to stroke, Parker called the question back over his shoulder: "Broadarm, you once told me that the bark of the bonewood was useful. What is it used for?"

Broadarm answered: "The women brew a hot drink of it when they do not wish to conceive children. As long as they drink it frequently they cannot conceive. When they stop, they can."

Birth control too, thought Parker! Are these really a nearly primitive people with no more civilization than they show? Or do they just have all the civilization they want? Or—does it matter to me now that I am leaving them, maybe for good?

He dropped the train of thought, looked ahead again, past the brown woman he loved. Par'z was close now; a few more minutes of paddling would bring the three travelers to the shore of the island. Parker could see now that Par'z was nothing but a volcanic cone pushed out of the sea. Vegetation a good part of the way up showed that the volcano had been long dormant, if not extinct; only the last few hundred feet of its height, where the steepness of the sides would keep even the most hardy plant from taking root, showed bare and gray in the morning.

Over the lip of the crater, silhouetted against the sparkling clear sky, Parker saw a tiny speck. Before he could tell its shape the black dot dropped from sight below the rim. Breathlessly holding his paddle out of the water, Parker stared at the spot on the volcano rim where the object had fallen. Seconds passed without any movement in the sky as Broadarm and Kaetha continued to propel the dugout craft toward the shore of the island.

Parker had almost convinced himself that the speck was a bird when it appeared again, the same speck or another like it, an object long and roughly cylindrical, not unlike the shape of a human body. Straight upward it shot, upward above the edge of the crater, then, poised for an instant at the apex of its path, the figure seemed to squirm briefly, alter its form. Vanes appeared over the upper end of the cylinder, began to rotate as the figure fell slowly from sight, back behind the lip of the volcano.

"Broadarm, Kaetha!" Parker shouted, "did you see that? It looks like a helicopter! Who are the Par'zians? What do you know about them? Tell me!"

Kaetha was the first to respond to his excited query. "A heli-what?" she asked.

"It's a . . ." Damn! they didn't even have a word for machine!" . . . thing that you make that flies. In my country my work was to control one of them. But—what do you know about the Par'zians?"

"Very little," Kaetha said. "What you have already been told, that they are said to be wonder-workers, but we know almost nothing about them in detail."

The two Relori were silent, as if waiting for Parker to speak again, but he did not. As they resumed stroking the dugout through the last few dozen yards of water he kept his eyes fixed on the rim of the volcanic peak, but the whirling speck did not reappear; as the dugout arrived at the island's shore treetops blocked his view of the peak.

Kaetha dropped her paddle into the craft, jumped into

the shallow water alongside and began pulling in order to beach the dugout; a few feet more and Parker, and then Broadarm, duplicated her act. The three travelers pulled the boat up onto the rocky shore of the island. To both left and right Parker saw a rocky shoreline curving away, dropping off to the westward with the general outline of the island. Ahead of the travelers heavy greenery marched up the gently sloping foot of the crater. It was obvious to Parker that the island, whether truly the Biscoe of uncertainly recollected naval charts or not, was nothing more than a submarine volcano that had, at some ancient time, reared its way up through the waters into the air above.

And if the little aircraft he had seen had actually emerged from the crater and then fallen back within it, then the storied City of Par'z must actually be located inside the volcano. Looking around at the shoreline and the forest ahead, Parker saw no sign of habitation. That did not prove anything in itself, but it fit in with the idea that the city was inside the crater.

Parker and the two Relori walked up and down on the shore, stretching cramped and tired muscles after their chore of paddling. The American looked back toward the peninsula from which they had come. The sun was now directly overhead and back across the blue-green expanse of sea the Country could be seen as a dark line stretching from horizon to horizon. A hundred yards or more out in the water Parker still saw the black spot that had followed the dugout, moving steadily toward the shore.

In a few minutes the football-sized object emerged from the water, followed by a crazily marked but powerful torso, legs, and madly patterned tail. Longa rushed from the water to Broadarm, halted at the giant's feet with her hair bristling, gave a vengeful hiss and doglike, shook herself, spraying onto the Relori the brine from her coat. Then she walked to where Parker and Kaetha stood close, circled them once brushing her long tail about their thighs, and sat between them, glaring at Broadarm.

Parker brushed his fingers through the fur on top of the cat's head, told her, "I'll miss you, you big kitty." Longa turned to look at his face and made a sound that seemed to Parker somewhere between the wail of a hungry infant and the coo of a pigeon blown to incredible size. Parker gave the great cat a playful poke to the jaw, she responded with a cuffing blow with one forepaw, her claws held in their sheathes, that all but knocked the wind from Parker.

Seriously then the American asked the two Relori: "Do you really think that the city is inside the crater there?" To Kaetha's nod and Broadarm's grunt of assent he continued: "The crater looks unscalable to me, but there must be a way in, either over the top or by some other route."

"How can you be certain?" Kaetha asked.

"If there are people there they must have got in there somehow. I can't believe that a whole separate evolution took place in that crater and produced a human race all its own. The Par'zians must have come to this island from somewhere, and they must have got into that crater somehow, and if they could do it so can I!"

"Then let us help you find the way, Parker," Kaetha said.

He held her with one arm, looked at her brown face now drawn with an expression of loss. Parker thought: she didn't really believe I was going, all along. Now she does. He said: "Yes, please help me, Kaetha."

They carried the dugout farther from the water, securing it to a trunk at the edge of the forest with thongs so that a rising tide would not carry it away and strand them on the island. Parker and the others checked their packs, initially small, now further shrunken with the use of supplies on their trek. Each checked his bow, his supply of arrows, the condition of his friendmaker. The big cat in tow, they set off through the forest.

At first the going was easy. At times in file, at times abreast depending on the thickness of the growth, they worked forward through the trees toward the center of the island. The plant life seemed identical to that in the Country, conifers and other trees mixed with the bonewoods and other types Parker had first encountered since his awaking in the Country.

Animal life, relatively sparse in the forest of the Country, followed the same pattern here on the Island of Par'z, down to the presence of citrus-dependent butterflies. Parker caught an occasional glimpse of some shy forest animal, and one weird creature, looking like a cross between a goat and an antelope, that stared unafraid at the humans but fled at sight of Longa.

As the three travelers toiled through the woods the gently sloping forest floor began to climb at a steeper and steeper angle. They had to work harder to make progress, at first simply laboring their pace somewhat, then stopping for increasingly frequent rests, finally hauling each other, hand to hand, from a rest clinging to one tree trunk to a higher spot clutching another.

The trees too were spread farther apart as the slope became more steep, and at last, where a few hardy, scrubby plants gave way to bare rock, the climbers could progress no farther. Parker looked upward toward the peak of the volcanic hillside. Ahead there still lay hundreds of feet of smooth-surfaced lava rock. At whatever ancient time Par'z—or Biscoe—had been an active volcano, lesser lava flows must have followed behind greater ones. The outlines of the later flows were still visible on the hillside above the travelers, in the form of broad bulges that overhung the older rock.

If the slope had been otherwise climbable—which, Parker concluded, it was not anyway—these smooth rock bulges would have stopped climbers when they were reached. "We can't go ahead," Parker told his companions, panting from the exertion of the difficult climb. "But let's try to work our way around the crater from here and see if there is any place where we can go up."

The two Relori agreed, and again all three were on the move. Their new mode of travel was a kind of crab-like sideways scrabble, constantly clutching for handholds on the top rank of treelets and shrubs, their eyes fixed upward and ahead seeking for some break, some route into or across the smooth lava wall that rose above them to the towering peak of Par'z.

They did not find it.

Daylight was still strong but the sun had disappeared behind the volcano's rim when the three searchers completed the circuit of the cone. They had struggled entirely around the upper edge of the island's vegetation but no path across the hardened lava had been located. Parker racked his brain.

Speaking aloud, but as much to himself as to the others, he asked: "What other entrance can there be? Probably natural gas vents and lava flows from beneath, but men could never live there long enough to get into the crater, or even if they could, there must be some surface entrance somewhere, that they got into the vent from. Could there be an opening on the mainland? Or on another island?"

Kaetha replied: "I know the mainland as far as the Wall of Teras. I am certain that there is no opening within many miles. In fact, I know of none on the mainland at all."

"Could it be beyond the Wall?" Parker asked.

"That would make a very long tunnel," Kaetha said. "And if it is . . . Broadarm, you know more of the Terasians than I, what do you think?"

"If there is an opening there, the Terasians do not know of its existence," the giant said. "I can swear to that. For some reason—I do not know what it is—the Terasians hate the Par'zians. They have only contempt for the Relori, but they truly hate Par'z. I am certain that if only they could get into Par'z they would send an army of destruction. But they cannot get over these walls any more than we can. If they knew of a tunnel entrance, they would surely use it.

"As for other islands," Broadarm continued, "I think we can rule out any known tunnels for the same reason. If they were known to the Terasians they would use them to enter Par'z and destroy the city. And if they were there, the Terasians would know about them. Founder knows, if the Terasians are anything, they are thorough. They control these waters. We can fish only at their sufferance, granted out of contempt. They have surely explored all the islands near the Country."

All three were silent for a time. Parker literally scratched his head trying to find a solution to the problem. Stupid habit, he thought, as if an idea were a head louse you could catch and crush into your skull. Yet, it sometimes produced results, as: "Look, friends, maybe we're making a mistake. We all assume that the Terasians are some kind of invincible supermen who could destroy Par'z in a day if only they could get in there, and since they haven't taken over Par'z, then they obviously haven't found the entrance.

"We had that problem at home sometimes. Sizing up the enemy. Sometimes we underestimated him and took a bloody nose for our reward. But then we would over-react and see him ten feet tall. He never was."

Broadarm and Kaetha squatted back on their heels, waiting for Parker to say more. He did: "I've never even seen a Terasian, but you tell me that they're human beings like anyone else. Your blood relatives, in fact. Maybe we've underestimated the Par'zians, too. If they're really the wonder-workers your tradition says—and that machine I saw says they are too—they may be perfectly capable of taking care of themselves. I'll bet a—damn, you don't have money, do you?—I'll warrant that there *is* an entrance, probably right on this island. And probably the Terasians know all about it, and they still can't get into Par'z if Par'z doesn't want them!"

When Parker finished speaking Kaetha said nothing. Broadarm hummed tunelessly for a moment, stroked his glossy mustache meditatively, looked speculatively up again at the steep lava wall, back to the woods and the sea beyond. "It could be," he finally said. "You argue well, Parker. You very nearly convince me, but—if there is an entrance as you say—find it!"

Parker made a woeful sound that even he had trouble identifying as an attempt at a laugh. "We might use several methods to search for an opening," he said. "We could brute-force it . . . try to divide the island into zones and then go over every zone until we had covered every square foot of surface. If we had Scenter with us he might be able to spot it better than any of us three. But we don't have Scenter."

He rubbed his chin this time instead of his scalp, then gave a vocal *whoop!* as a mental picture of himself drawn in simple comic book colors popped into his brain, the conventional light bulb of an idea burning brightly overhead. "Longa!" he almost shouted. "Set a cat to catch a mouse. I'm certain that if there's a hole she can find it. There never was a cat that couldn't find a hole with something live on the other side."

Broadarm looked puzzled, Kaetha dubious, at the suggestion. But: "It sounds worth trying," the Relori woman said.

Parker set up a call for the big calico and gave her a grateful hug after she responded by striding majestically up through the brush, treading heavily on Broadarm's toes, and seating herself at Parker's side. The American sat with the beast, his arms around her brindled neck, his face close to hers. The cat purred. Parker looked into the unnervingly intelligent eyes, then, feeling very foolish, he spoke to her.

"Longa, I can't even guess how much of what I say you understand. Maybe none of it. But look, we need a hole. A big, deep hole that goes very far into the ground." The cat purred, rubbed her face on Parker's face, her needle-sharp, inch-long incisors just a whisker from his nose and eyes. She looked into his eyes.

"Look, like this." Parker drew his friendmaker, gouged a pit into the soil a few feet below the point where it gave way to lava rock. Parker put away his weapon, patted the hole he had made, gave his hand to Longa to sniff. She sniffed his hand, then the hole, then butted him lightly, her damp cold nose pressed for a moment against his. "A big hole, Longa. Please, baby, find me a great big hole like this."

Broadarm said: "She's so pleased to get your attention, Parker, she'll probably *dig* you a hole."

The cat strode over to Broadarm, who still squatted on his heels. Longa turned her back on the giant. Parker watched as Broadarm, too, gazed curiously at the big cat. She seemed to buck forward onto her front paws, raise her hind quarters into the air. Her hind feet shot straight back, catching the giant on his chest, sent him sprawling on his back in a briar bush. Broadarm howled with rage and sprang to his feet, drawing his friendmaker as he rose, but before he could move to retaliate the cat had sprung onto the lava wall, coiled in an instant and with a final glance back over her patchwork shoulder vaulted again into the brush, out of sight.

Parker and Kaetha burst into delighted giggles as Broadarm fumed up and down.

"What a smart cat," Kaetha said.

"She's a good girl," Parker mimicked Broadarm's earlier words.

For a moment Broadarm looked as if he was going to seek vengeance on Parker and Kaetha now that Longa was out of reach, but he subsided, finally joined the laughter himself. "She is a smart cat," he conceded. "And she is a good girl, in her own way. I guess I wouldn't like to be thrown into a tree either."

They worked their way back down the hillside until the slope was gentler and the rough brush turned into comfortable trees. Waiting for some sign of Longa's success or failure they sat and sipped qrart, their backs against the trunks of trees. Kaetha sat with Parker, her hand in his and her head on his shoulder, quietly singing slow sad songs in an accent new to Parker. To his question she replied that the songs were old, and sung always in the old manner.

CHAPTER

9

They had not very long to wait before the wailing call of the big cat brought the three to their feet. "She's found it!" Parker said. "Let's go."

The two men and the Relori woman set off across the hillside at a trot, dodging among the trees, following the direction of the cry which came again and again. To Parker's ears the sound came as an eerie cross between an ordinary meow and a heartfelt cry for help; without being a word it still carried a full message.

Within a few minutes Parker, Broadarm and Kaetha drew up, half out of breath. Not far below the edge of hardened lava Parker saw a dark opening, largely hidden by undergrowth. At its mouth the calico danced nervously, pawing eagerly into the darkness, her tail twitching furiously while she gave out quavering, mewling cries of almost frantic eagerness. The American strode to the side of the cat, pulled her back from the opening and tried to sooth her with praise for her finding the hole, but the cat was hardly calmed.

Parker turned to Broadarm and Kaetha. "I'm certain that this is it," he told them. "Stand here and feel the air drawn upward. I don't know how this opening got here —whether it is an old gas vent, a dried underground stream bed, or . . . whatever it is—but that draw cannot lead to a dead end, and there's no place else for it to go but into the crater."

"We will come with you," Broadarm volunteered.

"No," Parker said. "This is for me alone. You are both

of Relore. I am . . ." He hesitated. "I must see. Wait
here if you will, until dusk. If I am not back, you go
back to the Country. You can surely reach the mainland
in the dark, even if we could not sail to this island without sunlight. I must do this alone, and you must go."

Broadarm seized the American, embraced him in huge
arms, released him with the wind crushed from his chest.
"Good luck to you, Parker," the giant said. "I will remember your words. And I believe we will see each other
again."

"Thank you," said Parker. "My love to Janna." Then
he took Kaetha once more to himself. They stood, holding each other. Parting words flew through Parker's
brain, none of them right. At last he let Kaetha go and
turned toward the tunnel.

"Okay, Longa, you go with Broadarm and Kaetha
now," Parker told the cat. She rubbed against his leg.
"Go on, kitty, they'll let you ride in the boat this time. In
the nice fishy smell." He took a few steps into the tunnel. The cat stayed at his side. "Go on, Longa," Parker
said. He pushed her gently back toward the tunnel
mouth. Parker took a few more steps into the tunnel, felt
a soft brush at his leg. "All right, Longa. You swam out
here, I guess you can swim back when the time comes.
Come along."

The tunnel was high enough for a man to walk in, broad
enough for him to hold his arms outstretched within the
lava walls. Before he had taken twenty paces Parker
cursed himself for not thinking to bring a torch. By
twenty-five he considered turning back to make one,
dreaded only the thought of turning back at all. If he
once did . . . Broadarm and Kaetha must still be on the
island. He could overtake them easily before they untied
the dugout and cast off for the Country again.

He could go with them, adopt Relore as his own place,
live there forever, happy with Kaetha—there was no
doubt in his mind that she would have him, although he
had never mentioned formal Relori marriage to her.
Their impromptu pledges by the stream-bank, he knew,
meant more than any public ceremony. And Trili, the
happy brown child, too would be his. And Broadarm and
Janna, his friends. A clean life, a good life it would be
in Relore and in the fields and the woods of the Country. But he would never rest, he knew he would never

achieve peace in Relore, unless he first made every effort to find the wonder men of Par'z, to learn if he ever could where he really was and whether there was any way to go home. And if he turned back now, Parker knew, by so much as a step, he would never return to Par'z.

With hands cold and sweating he moved ahead, took another step and then another deeper into the upward-trending tunnel. By the time he had taken thirty paces Parker wondered why the tunnel was not entirely dark. The light filtering in from the opening was negligible by this point, yet he could still see the rounded walls. By the time he had taken forty paces, Longa still at his side, pressing against his leg now and then as if for assurance, he could tell that the walls, the floor, the ceiling of the tunnel were lighted by streaks of faint luminescence, irregular, dim, a sickly shade of yellow-green, the streaks provided enough light to permit Parker and Longa to make their way.

Parker stepped sideways, felt the wall of the tunnel. It was cold and damp but had the feel of solid rock. At least a cave-in is unlikely, he thought. Whatever happens at the other end, I guess I won't be buried here. He put his fingers to the luminous material. It was dry and tended to crumble off if he rubbed it. The stuff had a musty odor and a powdery feel in his hand.

As the man and the cat went forward the tunnel changed its character. From the tall passageway wide enough for the man and the animal to stride abreast it narrowed, forcing them to switch to single file. To Parker's surprise, the big cat was as willing to lead the way as she was to follow. At points the passage broadened again but the ceiling dropped closer and closer to the floor until the man had first to crouch and finally to creep along, but the strong feel of walls and ceiling reassured him and the light streakings continued, even grew stronger.

The tunnel twisted, seemed at times to double back upon its own path, its floor at places running level, even descending, but always climbing again, leading generally upward toward what Parker was sure would be a final debouchement into the crater of the volcano. In the sickly glow of the tunnel, all sense of direction lost except for *forward*, all sense of time lost except for *now*, Parker stopped at last, nervously checked his weapons.

Longa stopped at his side, looked into his face intently. "Longa," Parker said, "this place is spooky. Plain spooky. I'm glad that you came along, friend cat. And I'm glad of another thing: I haven't seen any forks or side tunnels or we would be in bad, bad trouble." The cat continued to look into Parker's face.

Parker again felt foolish after talking to the cat. The sound of his own voice rang for a moment in his ears, echoing in the tunnel ahead and behind. From far, far back beyond the mouth of the tunnel Parker wondered if he could hear the sea which Kaetha and Broadarm might now be well across. He decided that he could not. There was a slight but constant flow of air in the tunnel, coming from its mouth behind him, drawn from the hillside outside the tunnel through the passageway and into the crater by some natural pressure. From the passageway ahead, far ahead, Parker wondered if he heard some slight sound, some rustling, slithering noise too faint to make more than a bare impression on the lowest level of the traveler's consciousness. Again, he decided that he heard nothing, that in the dead silence of the tunnel his mind was magnifying the least natural vibration, the sound of Longa's breathing and his own, the very sound of his blood rushing through arteries and veins, back to his heart to begin the cycle again, into a mysterious and frightening sign. He exhaled, realized that he had been unconsciously holding his breath in the silent tunnel. He began to walk forward again, listening to the sound of his own boots and the barely perceptible padding of Longa's soft-placed feet on the tunnel floor.

Again the luminescent streaks increased in number and brightness, and the tunnel widened and heightened into a room. Unhesitating, Parker stepped across the unmarked threshold. Just inside the still chamber he halted and surveyed the room. Its shape was irregular, vaguely globular, the floor running gradually into walls, walls into ceiling without clear differentiation. The yellowish streaks were everywhere, glowing, crumbling at the touch. The stale odor of ancient decay, long since turned to dryness and dust, pervaded the room despite the slight, steady draft of air entering behind Parker, from the direction that he unconsciously thought of as downhill although the tunnel was level here, and passing out of the chamber, drawn on through the passageway beyond, upward and into Par'z.

Parker looked at the wall, saw something that might be a rough drawing scratched into the solid lava, nearly covered by dry, crumbling luminosity. Beneath the crude carving lay a pitiful few bones. Parker quickly crossed the room to the relics, looked up to find Longa beside him, tail a-twitch, hair bristling along her spine. "They're human, Longa," Parker said. "And this . . ." He lifted an ancient artifact that lay beside the fingers of one skeleton hand. "And this was surely once a book."

The thing had covers of a hard substance that must once have been an artificial material, plastic perhaps, to have lasted through the untold years it had lain in the chamber. It opened to Parker's hand but within there remained only the dessicated scraps of whatever material had formed the pages. As Parker tried to find some trace of the content of the ancient record even these crumbled to dust. Of clothing, equipment, possessions, the only other remnant was a device about the size of an old-fashioned buccaneer's flintlock. It was made of the same enduring substance as the binding of the vanished book, covered with filigree, ornamental workings of vast complexity and symmetry in the surface of the dark, cool thing.

Parker examined the object, felt for a grip or handle, hefted its substantial weight, searched for a lever, a switch, a trigger, an opening. He found none. He laid it down again and returned to the cover of the book. It too was marked, not with meaningless ornament but with a clear, deep engraving that must be a title or label of some sort. The few flowing characters looked to Parker like something out of arabic or hindu, but meant nothing.

He dropped the ancient book where he had found it, looked again at the wall markings, but they were too few and too crude to be read as picture or word. "Whatever happened to you," Parker addressed the skeleton, "I only wish you could tell me. I only hope it doesn't happen to me." He put his arm around the neck of Longa for a moment, urged her to come along, and made his way, suddenly very cold, into the tunnel again, opposite the place where he had entered the room.

Again the tunnel wound its way, rising and falling,

turning, broadening and narrowing, but tending always upward, always hauntingly lighted by the sickly glow of the dried stuff on the surface of the lava, always filled with a dry, soft wind that stayed on Parker's back, giving him the direction when he ever became confused even of the way ahead and the way behind. And the tunnel was filled ever with the sounds of the man and the cat: breath, and the sound of boots, and the sound of soft placed pads. Parker still wondered whether he heard a wet sound far ahead.

After a long stretch of easy walking the tunnel's floor rose; so, too, did the roof, but less sharply. Parker and the cat found the opening now squeezed down so that the man had to drop to all fours and crawl ahead, upward, pushing with his booted feet and pulling himself onward with his hands. The shaft, though vertically close, was still broad enough for the cat Longa to creep, belly down, beside Parker.

The glow in the tunnel was becoming brighter and brighter, and as Parker reached ahead for a new grip on the tunnel floor he realized that the glowing stuff was no longer dried and crumbling, but moist, almost slimy to the feel. He stopped, rubbed some of the substance off the rock floor, looked at it on his hand. It gave back the same dull light that he had seen before. He looked again, saw that the brightness came from an increasing concentration and freshness of the yellow-green matter, rather than from any new source. He held his hand to his face, quickly pushed it back away at the sickening odor.

The slithering, rustling sound was renewed ahead, and Parker looked upward into the chute ahead of him. The glow increased to nearly daylight intensity and a quivering, jelly-like, slug-shaped thing, glowing a haunting yellow-green, seemed slowly to slither down the tunnel. Parker pulled back from it. It moved slowly forward. The man stared, sick fascination filling him. The slug slithered forward. Parker backed slowly down the chute, his eyes fixed on the thing, a cold hand gripping his bowels, cold sweat springing out on his face.

His trance was broken by the sound of Longa's furied hiss. He looked at the cat, saw her bristle as never before. Again she hissed at the advancing thing. Parker looked back from the cat, saw that the slug had been joined in the chute by another foot-long, slime-coated monstrosity. Behind the things, glowing yellow-green, slowly slithering downward toward the two invaders of the tunnel, the shaft was choked with quivering slugs.

Parker backed out of the chute, dropped to his feet again in the larger tunnel before the chute. The teeming slugs—drawn by the scent of himself and the cat carried through the tunnel by the constant wind, Parker thought —still slid forward while the great calico stood at bay, snarling and bristling at them. "Come out, Longa!" he shouted. The cat ignored him.

"Get back!" Parker screamed at the cat. He lunged forward again, seized her by the tail with his two hands, threw back all his weight to drag the cat, snarling and clawing, out of the chute. Parker transferred his hold from the cat's tail to her neck, grasping handfuls of the loose flesh there, pulled her frantically back along the tunnel for a score of yards. There he crouched, panting for breath, holding the cat who still half-strained to charge at the glowing slugs.

Parker calmed himself as best he could, looking back at the glow. The slugs were sliding slowly forward, still in the chute. At their rate of movement it would take many minutes for them to reach the two warmblooded invaders. If Parker and Longa retreated they could almost certainly outdistance the creeping slugs and escape to the outer hillside of Par'z. But Parker refused to take that course except as a last resort.

"Stay here, Longa!" he urged the cat. He pressed her downward with his hands. "Stay! Stay!" Squirming with impatience, the cat obeyed.

Parker drew his friendmaker; holding it before him he cautiously paced forward again, toward the glowing things. He reached toward them with his long knife, balanced to retreat instantly if need be. With the flat of the friendmaker's blade he shoved a slug sideways and toward himself, away from the other creatures. It made no sound and reacted only sluggishly—inside himself Parker repressed a giggle at the unconscious pun—to the touch of the metal.

He caught the thing on the hooked back edge of his curved blade, pulled it toward himself until he and it were several yards from the slowly advancing clutch of slugs. Gingerly he reached toward it with his naked hand, felt a yielding, cold, disgusting mockery of flesh; a

shudder passed through his frame and as the odor of the
thing now reaching his nostrils joined the touch of it he
retched, dizzied, felt the hot and sour sensation of his
last meal thrown back by revolting stomach muscles.

Parker pulled back his hand from the slug, steadied
himself to keep from falling to the floor of the cave. His
body shaking with waves of revulsion he lifted the great
sword-knife in two hands, brought it down laterally on
the slug's body. The thing split like a rotten melon. Behind Parker the big calico whined and yowled her eagerness. Parker used his blade again, this time as a tool,
sweeping half of the jelly-like mess toward Longa. He
watched the cat leap upon the quivering thing, heard
her utter a scream of rage such as he had never heard
from the throat of any living thing, watch the cat shred
the half-slug with claw and tooth in a fury unlike any he
had ever before witnessed.

Before the cat could spring forward to attack the remaining mass of slugs Parker had caught her and again
sat holding her, talking soothingly meaningless things in
her pointed twitching ear. All the while he was thinking.
The slugs seemed incapable of any but the slowest and
clumsiest of movement. He could retreat slowly from
them, dragging Longa with him until they had escaped
from the tunnel. But he would still be outside of Par'z.
Or he could try to advance through the slugs—another
shudder passed through him at the mental image of himself surrounded, packed in glowing, slimy, featureless . . .

To try to fight through the hundreds or thousands of
the things would lead only to suffocation. If only he had
scuba gear! Longa would surely help him—she seemed to
have an instinctive hatred of the slugs; probably only the
absence of the giant cats from the natural ecology of the
island kept the slugs from extinction—but even together,
Parker fighting with metal blade, Longa with tooth and
claw, they would be swarmed over by the things and die.
What had happened to the poor fellow whose skeleton
Parker had found? Maybe the slugs.

But . . . if the things could be drawn into a relatively
open area, even the room of the skeleton, things might
be different.

Parker forced himself to stride forward, slap at the
first few slugs with his bare hands. They had cleared the
chute now and were sliding through the straight tunnel

toward the two invaders. The close touch and smell of the man seemed to stimulate the slugs; their motion inceased although it was still—again, Parker held back a laugh that might turn to hysteria—little more than a snail's pace.

Retreating slowly, dragging the tense-muscled Longa with him, Parker retreated before the advancing slugs. Every now and again he would dash forward, slap at the glowing vanguard of slimy things, then jump back and lead them on again. Finally they reached the chamber of the skeleton.

Parker dragged Longa to the far side of the room, waited for the first slugs to creep through the entrance. When they did he again went through the routine, dancing forward, slapping at the things, pulling back, taunting, advancing, slapping, kicking, taunting. This time he was Carlos, the slugs were Parker, disgusting, cowardly weak things, offensive by their existence, creeping, shining, while he slapped and kicked, forward and slapped and kicked and back.

The floor was covered with the things now, Parker was holding Longa back from them while the cat howled and squirmed. Parker released her. "Okay, girl, go to work!" he shouted to the cat. He drew his friendmaker again, set to work killing the things to one side while Longa dispatched those to the other. Each slug took only one stroke of the heavy blade. Some Parker split the long way, others across, their jelly-like insides forming a flowing, stinking lake into which he vomited until his retches came dry, in which he waded killing, killing, sick, dizzied by the stench and sound, praying, praying in half-mad screams:

"Thank you, God, for my boots. Oh God, keep my feet clean of this filth. Thank you for my boots!"

At last he stood, leaning heavily against the lava wall, staring sickly about the chamber. There was no movement. The skeleton, the book, the decorated object were lost to sight, covered over in a pond of glowing yellow-green. Parker's breath came in gasps, heaves shook his frame; his one arm hung at his side, the weapon still held, the muscles of the arm exhausted from the slaughter. His other hand he held to his face, holding away the sight of horror in the room.

He felt the cat press against him, even her insane fury

sated, seemingly terrified by the killing that the two of them had done.

Now Parker forced himself to step through the horrible morass, make his way to the upper opening from the chamber. The cat trembling at his trembling side, he made his way forward, tracing yet again the passages to the chute. On the way there they passed a few of the glowing slugs, creeping blindly forward, stragglers that had missed their cues in the drama of mass killing. Neither Parker nor the cat harmed the things, but recoiled in horror and disgust as they moved past each other.

Slowly, well past the upward chute now empty of the glowing slugs, the tunnel's light grew less and less. The pathway continued to be a single one despite its turnings, despite its broadenings and narrowings. At last in near darkness, in another broad and high chamber like the place of the skeleton, Parker sat to rest. He spoke to the cat.

"How much more, kitty? This crater wall can't be much more than a half a mile through. We must have come—how many miles? I don't know. How long has it taken us? I don't know. And if it gets much darker we'll have to go back and spear one of those things . . ." At the thought, he made a sick sound. "Spear one for a torch.

"Well, come on."

They resumed their trek through the passageway. Finally it narrowed to another chute, unlighted, little thicker than a man's torso. Parker tried to urge the cat into the chute but she balked.

"Fair enough," Parker said. "I'll go first."

Friendmaker at his waist, bow slung, Parker reached ahead into the black funnel, drew himself in with his hands, then wriggled in until he was able to draw his legs up the least bit to gain purchase for a push. He straightened his legs, pushed forward, his arms extended ahead of him, then pressed outward on the walls of the chute with his hands, drew his body forward, drew up his legs again the slight amount that was possible, then pushed. Again he repeated the cycle, then again. The chute took a ninety-degree turn. Parker squirmed, got half his length through the turn, shoved his hands ahead and for a moment felt an emptiness about them. Suddenly a pressure was applied to his wrists, unyielding circlets closed on the flesh of his arms. Handcuffs, he thought frantically.

Two hands grasped Parker's wrists, pulled him from the chute. He stumbled, was pulled erect, stood confused. A voice spoke: "The distinguished personage will please honor me greatly by remaining still and silent, thus saving me the tragedy of taking his blood."

CHAPTER

10

Parker stood still, looking around quickly to take in his new situation. He had wanted to get into Par'z, now here he was—a prisoner again, his life threatened by the first person he met, if met was the right word.

One glance told Parker that it was night. Obviously darkness had fallen while he and Longa were making their way through the crater's wall. Longa herself was nowhere in evidence. Parker saw that he was high up on the inner edge of the crater. Far below the lights of a settlement flickered, many reflecting off the surface of what was obviously a body of water accumulated in the crater's cup.

Here on the high ground beside the tunnel opening he stood facing three men. All were armed with heavy-bladed instruments: one with a sort of battle-axe, the others with two-handed swords longer than Parker's own friendmaker. All three carried shorter knives as well. Almost immediately, as Parker watched, one of the three stationed himself beside the opening from which Parker had emerged.

"Please speak quickly, most welcome visitor. I hesitate to press you to haste but for the benefit of all including the residents of Par'z, you must condescend to inform us, are you alone?"

The American was startled by the intonation of the Par'zian even more than he was of his flowery words. It was almost exactly the archaic dialect of Kaetha's old songs—clearly understandable to Parker as the language of the Country, but a form which he had thought long obsolete. At least, it was in Relore. Parker managed to stammer an answer: "Yes. I am the only one. There was a cat with me in the tunnel, but she would not come through the last part of it. She must have turned back."

"I trust your word fully," was the reply, "as of course any Par'zman would give full faith to the veracity of an honored guest in our home place. Still, I pray you not to take offense, sir, that my companion colleague remains beside the tunnel entrance. Let us not permit the risk that you have been pursued, all unknowing one is assured, by some treacherous enemy who would work you harm.

"My good friend and brother will remain beside the opening to assure your safety from pursuit. Should another person put himself forth from the entryway he would quickly find his head welcomed by the cooling axe while the rest of him was entreated to wait a brief while in the mouth of the tunnel. And you, good sir, could I prevail upon your generosity to accompany my other kind compatriot and myself to our little guest house."

The Par'zman—if that's what they call themselves, thought Parker—made his way a dozen yards or so to a small structure. Parker followed closely, heard the third Par'zman follow behind him. Inside the building Parker was ushered to a wooden chair beside a plank-topped table. He sat down. It was too dark outside to tell many architectural details. Inside, the building was lighted by small lamps, slowly burning and casting a flickering light on the walls and the furniture.

To appearances the building was a simple wooden construction, not particularly like those in Relore but of an elementary design that might have fit into the Country without looking badly out of place. Parker looked at the two Par'zmen who stood in the room. Their brown skins, lank hair, and vaguely Asian features marked them as of the same racial stock as the Relori.

Parker looked at the closer Par'zman, put his hands conspicuously on the table as if to remind the others that they had first moved against him. He said, simply, "Well?"

"I crave your forgiveness," the Par'zman said. "I must make apologies for our binding your hands. Please allow me to explain who I am and why we are forced to visit this intolerable indignity upon your kind self."

"I am Inz Xa Tlocc Xi-Vrannannan, hereditary keeper of the Gate of Par'z through which you have recently entered our home place. The duty of the keeper of the Gate has been in my family for no fewer than three hundred seventy-nine generations, and so naturally . . ."

Parker did a quick mental calculation: that many generations at even twenty years per generation meant . . . well over seven thousand years! Longer than any civilization he knew of had ever survived. Had Par'z lived here in isolation for seven thousand years?

". . . we take pride in our faithful discharge of the municipal trust placed in us. Unlike our predecessors in the hereditary keepership who held the post for too many generations and grew weary of their burden and died out, we are still relatively new in the keepership and strive vigorously to prove worthy of our trust.

"Thus I must explain, sir, that the unprecedented arrival of two parties of newcomers to our home place in a short period of time arouses me and my good fellows to possibly offensive zeal which we feel nonetheless constrained to exercise rather than place the tranquility of Par'z which has so long been protected by dynasties of hereditary keepers of the Gate into any position which might suggest jeopardy. . . ."

The Par'zman droned on and on while Parker sat in growing amazement—and a mixed feeling of impatience and amusement—at the treatment he was given: A total stranger, dragged from the tunnel that was apparently the only entrance to the city in the crater, imprisoned, sat down and subjected to an interminable apology for that same treatment and a complete genealogy of his chief jailor's family for the last seven thousand years!

Finally the Par'zman paused for a breath. Parker seized the opportunity to interject: "Wait a minute!"

The Par'zman looked startled.

"Listen," Parker said, "I know you've got me pretty much at your mercy, handcuffed and outnumbered. But if this is some subtle kind of torture . . ."

"Absolutely not," the Par'zman replied. He sounded shocked and offended. "By the nine hundred ninety-nine gods of Par'z, Ashtra, Beshtra, Clostra, Destha, Ephthra . . ."

"No, no!" Parker interrupted. "Spare me the names of your nine hundred ninety-nine gods! Good grief, all I want to know is, what are you going to *do* with me!"

"But of course, sir," said the Par'zman. "You are unquestionably the most hurried person I have ever spoken with, if you do not mind my presumption in speaking so frankly of a new acquaintance. Even the others who arrived in Par'z were more patient, although they in their time seemed to be hurried in their conversation. I was merely starting to tell you who I am, sir, Inz Xa Tlocc Xi-Vrannannan, three hundred seventy-ninth hereditary keeper of the Gate, of my dynasty. If you do not wish to learn even the most elementary things about your host then I shall not even tell you of the previous three hundred seventy-eight keepers of this dynasty . . ."

"Thank God," Parker murmured.

". . . nor less of the prior dynasties of keepers of the Gate of Par'z. You may learn of the history of Par'z and her people some other time. You may tell me, then, who you are. Are you, too, of the sea people?"

"Who are the sea people?" Parker asked. Instantly he regretted asking any question of this long-winded, battle-harnessed Par'zman, but it was too late to stop a reply.

"The sea people come over the waters around Par'z. They say they have a great city on a great land across the water. The history of Par'z tells of ancient war with the sea people; indeed, it was war with the sea people that led to the establishment of the keepership of the Gate in the time of ancient Par'z. Par'z was then a greater nation than it is now; Par'zmen too went on the waters, but the sea people drove them from the waters and tried to destroy the city.

"But they could not enter they city. The only way in was through the tunnel and the Gate. The creatures of the tunnel did not exist then. They were created by the great Par'zman Clul Vyeh Ko Xi-Tatt, who at first meant them for captive pets, to light ladies' chambers at night and amuse children with their glow. Instead, Clul Vyeh bred them for size and loosed them in the tunnel, and they have kept out most interlopers ever since.

"Also, the Par'zmen of that time established the post of keeper of the Gate, which became hereditary in the time of Grag Lal Iyah Xi-Tlapatlat, was it not so, Ent Rrj Rir Xi-Alnalnaln?"

The other Par'zman, who had been silent to this point, said, "I am reluctant to dispute your recollection, InzXa, but was it not in the time of Ngg Va Mlaa Xi-Prpprappra that the keepership became hereditary? As I recall it was NggVa rather than GragLal who first insisted that the keepership not be handed about but kept within a single family as a continuing trust. . . ."

"Please!" Parker roared. The two Par'zmen looked at him. "Please," the airman said again, taking a tone as if he were speaking to children, "I am sure that the ancient history of your people is of great, great interest to you. And I would absolutely love to hear it all, some other time. But right now I wish you would set me free, or else decide what you're going to do with me."

The two Par'zmen nodded and *hmm'd*.

Before either of them could begin another lecture on Par'zian history, Parker asked, "Did these sea people call their home Teras?"

"Why, as I recall from the story of our people and the tale told by the ones who are with us now, why, *mmm,* they did say that the name of their own city was something like that, yes, I believe, Teras was it, do you recall it so, EntRrj?"

The second Par'zman nodded and made a vaguely positive sound but again before he could speak Parker asked, "And they are in Par'z now?"

"Yes," replied the keeper of the Gate, "they said that they had fled the tyranny of their own people and wished to come to live in Par'z, and since there were only three of them we permitted them to settle with us. They are in Par'z now."

"How did they get past the slugs in the tunnel?"

"They came on the mating day of the creatures. We asked them how they knew it was that day. Mating time is the only time when the creatures are harmless. They mate every hundred and eleven years."

"No," the other Par'zman interrupted him, "every eleven hundred years, is it not so, InzXa?"

"Ah, now you confuse me, EntRrj, is it one hundred eleven or eleven hundred? Let me see. Now in the time of Clul Vyeh Ko Xi-Tatt they bred far more frequently of course, but somehow over the years they have developed a longer life and slower breeding, so that . . ." He reached into a pouch on the harness from which his weapons hung and pulled out a few objects. ". . . let me see now, is it one hundred . . ."

The Par'zman offered one of the small objects to his companion, one to Parker, and put an end of the third to his own mouth. As Parker watched the keeper of the Gate bit off the thick end of the object and dropped the rest onto the table. It was a flat, longish thing, mottled brown and green, with green veins running through it. Parker looked at his own and realized that it was a seed-pod, very much like the winged pod of the maple that he had watched so often spin through the air like a miniature rotor.

"It is samra," the Par'zman said. "Very good. Will you not try one?"

Parker looked at the pod again. Yes, it was very much like a maple, only several times larger. With his still-cuffed hands he raised the samra to his mouth, bit off the swollen seed, and chewed it. A sweet, warming flavor seemed to flow from his mouth, filling his tongue, his body, his head with a glad relaxation. He chewed the seed more. It was the first food of any kind he had had since losing his breakfast of the past day in the tunnel.

"Now that we have shared samra and you know who we are, sir," the gatekeeper said, "at least to the small extent that you have permitted me to tell you who we are, would you be willing to share with us the tale of who you are and whence you come, whether from the sea people you call the people of Teras or from some other place."

Parker began to tell the Par'zmen who he was. By this time he had finished chewing the samra seed and swallowed the pulpy remains. He felt worlds better than he had, a warm euphoria creeping through him but his head clearer, if anything, than it usually was. "First of all," he said, "I am not from Teras. Not of the sea people you know.

"I did come across the sea with people of another land, called Relore, but I am not myself Relori either. My home is in a place we call America. It is far, far from here and I hope someone in Par'z will be able to help me find it again.

"Oh, and my name is Robert Leroy Parker," he concluded. No backwards officialese this time.

The gatekeeper repeated his name. It came out Rob Rtt Le Roi-Prrkerr.

"Good enough," the American smiled. "Call me Robert."

"Rob Rrt," the Par'zman said. "Thank you. You may call me InzXa, and my associate, EntRrj. I do not know of any land called Ammr-Car, but perhaps someone in Par'z will have heard of it. Now I suppose you are no enemy. What think you, EntRrj?"

"He seems no foe," said the second Par'zman.

The gatekeeper took Parker's handcuffs in his own hands, worked a complicated gadget in the middle, where they narrowed to hold the wrists together. The heavy wooden cuffs seemed to slip, parts moved and the Par'zman pulled them from Parker's hands.

"Now, Rob Rrt, you may go down into the city if you wish, but it is very dark and I would not suggest that you try it, not knowing the paths. The hillside is very steep. If you wish to sleep here, I will walk with you and show you the way in the morning, when my relief comes."

"Fine, fine," said Parker, his eyelids beginning to sag. "You people must have a pretty well-organized city to have guards and reliefs on a regular schedule."

"Organized? You mean like Teras as you call it—the city of the sea people?"

"Mmm," Parker assented.

"No, I think not. We Par'zmen are not organized. At least, if I truly understand what you mean. We know of such organization, from the tales of the old days. Leaders and authority and laws, commands and obedience, punishment for the disobedient.

"Why do we need that? We have no enemies. At least, none who can reach us. Except through the Gate. So we have the hereditary keepership of the Gate. And all other Par'zmen must take their turns assisting the keeper. They all understand the need for that. All Par'zmen serve in their turn. But that is all our organization."

Parker was nearly asleep by now. He tried to ask more. "Have you no government, no laws?" But he slid forward onto the polished table, sound asleep. Somehow through his subconscious he thought he half-heard some answer about a king, but it was quickly lost.

Parker awakened early. He found himself lying on a

straw pallet in the guardhouse where he had been brought the night before. The three Par'zmen were gone—guarding the Gate, Parker guessed—but a little stove stood in the building, unnoticed by the American the night before in his weariness. Several cups stood on the table; on the little stove a pot of something that smelled incredibly like fresh coffee was filling the vicinity with its ravishing odor. Parker looked around, hesitated a moment, then poured himself a cup of the hot stuff and sipped at it. It *tasted* incredibly like coffee, black and unsweetened, to be sure, but still with the incomparably right flavor for the first drink of the morning.

Holding the steaming cup in his two hands, Parker stepped outside the guardhouse and walked about on the heavily dewed grass. He looked downhill, but the cup of the crater was lost in blackness. Above the cup, the opposite rim of the crater was silhouetted black against the graying sky. Parker stared at the rim for a moment, and at the sky behind it in which the sun must soon rise.

But . . . if the sun rose in the east, and if he had approached the Island of Par'z from the east, and if the sun was shortly to rise behind the opposite rim of the crater from where he stood . . . then he was on the western side of the crater. The tunnel must worm its way from one side of the crater completely to the opposite side. No wonder the trip he and Longa had made in the tunnel seemed so long. They had not merely worked their way through the thickness of the crater wall, but had traveled halfway around the island, all in the tunnel!

He watched the rim, sitting on the grass, the cup of hot drink in his hands, oblivious of the dew. The grass inside the crater extended farther up than any vegetation outside, but there was no tree to break the black outline of the crater wall as a skyline. At last, as the sky lost its last tint of gray in favor of an overall blue, the edge of the sun climbed over the crater rim. Surrounded by a blaze of orange clouds hanging over the sea, the white brilliance of the sun seemed to spring over the crater rim, illuminating the upper portion of the opposite side.

Parker turned his back on the blazing orb, stood again and looked up at the rim above himself, saw it bathed in brilliance, blackish rock at the peak clearly lighted, the black shadow cast by the eastern rim below. The shadow dropped and dropped away as Parker watched. Now the grass line became illuminated, now more of the slope, now the aviator was startled by the appearance on the hillside before him of a human shadow until he realized that it was his own. He felt the warming rays of the sun on his back, looked about and after a few moments located the Gate. The three Par'zmen stood about it, whiling away the hours in endless, quietly convoluted discourse, undoubtedly on some abstruse point of Par'zian philosophy, history, or religion.

Olduncle said I'd find philosophers in Par'z, Parker told himself. He didn't know how right he was. Parker walked to where the three men were standing. They looked up only briefly at his approach. One was finishing a sentence with something to the effect that ". . . if the cosmic polyhedron is only finitely dimensional, you see, thereby requiring the adoption of a multiple-viewpoint consideration of the regenerative capacity of the criteria of absoluteness, then your belief that the universal precipitate of subpsychic emanations is patently untenable, if you will forgive my bluntness in expressing so unkind an opinion, but one which I must maintain is unavoidable in view of your own stated argument. If, on the other hand, you posit a cosmic polyhedron of infinite dimensionality this difficult problem is, if not absolutely solved, then more or less satisfactorily, one may suggest, circumvented, thereby avoiding the logically inconsistent and therefore rationally untenable argument that the cosmic geometric formulation of . . ."

"Professor!" Parker interrupted. As usual, the Par'zmen looked startled at the interjection of another voice into their discourse. "Uh, InzXa, you offered last night to show me the way down into the crater. I'd hate to take you away from your friends and your intellectual exercise here, but don't you go off duty soon anyway?"

The gatekeeper hesitated a moment, then he said, "Oh, ah, yes, certainly Rob Rrt, it is almost time indeed, ah . . ." His voice trailed off, then resumed. "My relief should be here very soon and then we shall head down into the city. I see you have availed yourself of a cup of . . ."—the word came out *coffee* in Parker's mind although he was sure that it had a different sound in the Par'zman's speech—". . . coffee. Very practical of you, and highly admirable, unless of course one holds to that school of thought which regards practicality as less than a leading virtue, as indeed some individuals do. On the other hand, were it not for the application of practical approaches to even impractical ends, even the impractical end would seldom be achieved, thus rendering impracticality an impractical approach to the life situation, while practicality is manifestly practical."

Parker dropped his cup on the soft grass where it lay unbroken beside his foot; he held his head in his two hands and giggled quietly at the Par'zman's new and apparently interminable stream of pointless ratiocination. The Par'zman took brief note, then ran on with his lecture: "I hope you are not feeling ill," he said. Then, after Parker's quick negative, "The problem which arises from proving practicality practical and impracticality impractical lies in the fact that this may be a mere redundancy, and therefore impractical in itself, a delight therefore to the school of impracticality but all in itself a rebuff to the school of practicality which, my being in essence a pragmatically oriented thinker, I find unpleasant to contemplate. Still . . . oh, my relief is here. Well, we shall have to continue this later."

"Swell," said Parker, "let's be sure to do that." He watched InzXa exchange a few words with the newest arrival, who disappeared into the guardhouse to emerge in seconds with a cup of coffee of his own. Parker wiped his own cup out with a handful of dew-wet grass, put it back on the table in the guardhouse, then started down the green slope with InzXa. Officer of the day going off duty, Parker thought.

As they started down the hillside Parker could see Par'z itself now fully lighted by the morning brightness. He sucked in a breath of sudden air at the sight before him. The water he had thought was at the bottom of the crater was there indeed: a sparkling lake, clear and deep and of the purest turquoise color he had ever seen. The rays of the sun glinted off its surface, blue sky and a few scattered clouds were reflected, and sails of a few small boats caught a gentle breeze that swept across the floor of the crater, a convection current, Parker thought, perhaps the same one that drew the air up the tunnel he had traveled.

The sails themselves were mostly triangular, the boats which they drew lightly across the water were all small, light craft. Although Parker looked from too high to see individual figures, it was clear that each boat could hold only a few persons. Still, the sails were what caught his attention, for if they were of uniform shape their colors were such as he had never seen before on water craft; there were golden cloths and crimson, purple, brilliant greens, blues of shades that blended with the water and blues of shades that stood in brilliant contrast with the water, pink sails and orange sails; Parker saw a gray that was not gray but shimmering silver, a black that was not the black of drabness but the deep, almost tangible black of the midnight void.

And built on the shores of the golden-glinting turquoise waters was Oz, was Baghdad, if not the literal sprawl of Arab squalor then the Baghdad of a thousand and one dreams, of the thousand and one nights.

It was a city of domes and spires of colors and shapes unendingly varied. Beside a gilded igloo rose a glinting enameled steeple, minarets and onion-shaped domes, buildings shaped like teepees, like pagodas, and as the American approached lower with his Par'zian guide he saw the variation too in finish: latticework on one building, abstract patterns worked into the surface of another, solids alternating with murals, pastels and brilliants, burnished tones and dull, worked materials and rough.

And opposite the city, across the glittering reflective waters of the lake, a miniature jungle, trees in nearly grove-like order, birds flying from limb to limb, and beside the trees an area of smaller growths, bushes, giving back a green to the bright sun of day.

Parker looked up, turned his gaze beyond the rim of the crater. He saw dark clouds in the direction of the Country, but clear sky over Par'z. So they are protected even from nasty weather, Parker thought. He wondered if the Par'zmen realized how well off they were. But he asked InzXa, "Doesn't it ever rain in Par'z?"

"Oh, yes," the keeper replied. "Enough to support our vegetation. And enough to keep up the level of the lake. Of course there are those who would rather . . ."

"No, please, no lecture," Parker pleaded. "Can't you just give me a little information?"

"Why certainly. I was merely attempting . . ."

"Right. I appreciate it. But, look, what happens if it

rains too much, doesn't the water level rise and flood the city and the woods?"

"Oh, no. The water never rises very much. I believe that there are natural openings that drain any excess from the lake, draining downward through our crater and emptying somewhere into an underground stream that reaches the sea."

Inz Xa Tlocc Xi-Vrannannan looked eager to go into another long discourse, this time on natural water drainage systems, but Parker headed him off with another question. "What do you do for food?"

"Ah, hmm," said the Par'zman, fumbling in a pouch attached to his harness. He extracted two more samrae, handed one to Parker and bit off the seed of the other. As he chewed he answered, "Mostly we eat food from the trees and bushes." He named a series of kinds of plants and their products, the words unfamiliar to Parker, but the American guessed, from the looks of the miniature grove, that they might be anything from berries to apples to citrus to bananas."

"And of course there are the creatures of the lake," InzXa went on. "There are those who argue that to take the life of these creatures for food is ethically indefensible. The interspecies transmigrationist, for instance, holds that to kill a fish or a lobster is the same act, morally speaking, as to kill a human, which is, of course, not done except in defense of the city. However, a transmigrationist who holds only with the intra-species migration of the soul would have no such objection. Thus, with regard to the soul, a human would be always a human, a bird a bird, or in the realm of the fish, a sole is a sole is a sole, if I may be permitted the small pun."

Parker felt mildly ill and bit down hard on his samra to counter the effect of the Par'zman's joke. "But there is no organized effort at raising food," the American said, half in observation, half in query. "No farming, no hunting, no organized fishing?"

"We have little need of organization, Rob Rrt, as I have told you. Why would we need it? If you are hungry, go to the trees for fruit. If you do not wish fruit, perhaps you will find eggs. If you wish meat, go to the water. It is full of fish. They are easily caught. Or slay a beast. If you wish coffee, pick berries and make some. If you wish samra, stand beneath the trees and it will come to you, or climb them and get your own. How should we work for food that is already there to take, Rob Rrt? Do you advocate irrationality as a mode of conduct? If so, you face grave logical discrepancies if you are to support your position rationally. It is not unlike the dispute over the relative practicality of impracticality, or . . ."

As usual, Parker had to cut into InzXa's discourse to get another question in. He asked, "Don't you have a population problem? No natural enemies, no danger of attack, plenty of food . . ."

"Our population is fairly stable," InzXa answered. "Life is long and easy, few die, few are born. They are balanced. Pantheists hold that this is the plan of the all-being to assure Man's place in the crater. If more were born we would eat up our food and face chaos. Fewer, and we would die out. In balance lies stability and freedom. However . . ."

"Fine," said Parker. "I see, thank you, please stop."

Looking puzzled as ever by the stranger's unwillingness to listen to his elongated logic, Inz Xa Tlocc Xi-Vrannannan remained silent until he and Parker reached the edge of the city. Then he said, "My home is very near here. My wife Nnan Vu Tlocc Xa-Ziritsar and our son Troi Xa Tlocc Xi-Daradavar will probably be upon the lake sailing now, but we can have some food. Then I will rest, but you may begin to see our city and perhaps find one who can answer your questions of how to reach your Ammr Car."

"Good. And remind me one time to ask you how your system of names works . . ." Parker saw the gatekeeper's eyes brighten at the suggestion. ". . . but not right now," the American added hastily.

They stopped at the first house they approached. Parker watched his guide closely to see if there were any special manners that must be observed, but the Par'zman entered directly. Parker watched him put down his weapons, did the same. He followed suit as InzXa wiped his hands on a cloth hanging in the room, thought that it would be good to get his own clothes off and give both the clothes and himself a thorough scrubbing as soon as he could.

The Par'zman produced a couple of fish from somewhere; they looked to Parker like fresh-caught trout.

Accompanying himself with a non-stop lecture on gastronomy and the proper preparation of gourmet dishes, Inz Xa Tlocc Xi-Vrannannan carefully cleaned and sautéd the two fish. He had Parker seat himself comfortably beside a low table, turned back and finished his cooking. Again from somewhere he produced steaming coffee, two peachlike fruit, and a small bowl of samrae.

He placed the dishes on the table, seated himself opposite Parker, and exclaimed, "By the nine hundred ninety-nine gods, now that is a suitable morning meal for two men!"

Parker fell to without further invitation. Only with his first taste of the fish did he realize how *hungry* he was. He had not eaten for twenty-hour hours—if the day is still twenty-four hours, he thought—and had lost even his breakfast of the previous day in the tunnel with Longa. No, thinking of it now, he *had* consumed one cup of Par'zian coffee at the Gate, and had chewed several of the samra seeds. But samra seemed to deaden hunger, for all its delicious taste and the warm euphoria it produced, rather than to satisfy it as nourishing food should.

He ate as he saw InzXa eating—without implements, but carefully, neither wasting food, despite its seeming abundance in Par'z, nor making a mess of the table or himself. Again a first meal in a new place, Parker thought. How unlike that rough, vigorous first dinner of venison and qrart in the woods of the Country, with four Relori hunters for his captors, conversing in their strange tongue about what to do with a captured madman. He was lucky, he realized, that they hadn't dispatched him on the spot, in view of what he'd later learned of Relori treatment of criminals and madmen.

And here he sat with Inz Xa Tlocc Xi-Vrannannan, three hundred seventy-ninth hereditary keeper of the Gate of Par'z, dining almost daintily on the white, flaky flesh of something that could pass for a trout or its twin, lovingly sautéed in something that tasted exactly like butter and lemon and a touch of curry powder. Parker shook his head wonderingly. Then, hungry for once for the Par'zman's voice, Parker said, "You speak of nine hundred ninety-nine gods. Then you speak of reincarnation. Then you speak of pantheism. What is the real religion of Par'z?"

The Par'zman looked up from his fish. "Real religion?

Real?" He looked strangely at the American. Puzzlement and indecision played on his face. "What an odd question! You ask so many odd questions, Rob Rrt, your land must be a strange one."

Parker grimaced impatiently.

"Well, then," Inza resumed, "I suppose one might reply that all religions are real, in that they exist. On the other hand, inasmuch as religion deals with the metaphysical nature of the universe, often with the supernatural, with the unseen and the unknown, with truths arrived at by philosophical or intuitive means, or occasionally by means of pure logic . . ."

Parker was learning how to deal with the Par'zian discourse by now. He finished his fish, slouched back with a piece of fruit in one hand and his steaming cup, freshly refilled, in the other, and let InzXa's running words pass over him. Somewhere along the line the gatekeeper would probably get around to answering the original question. Meanwhile, Parker quoted to himself, you might as well relax and enjoy it.

Inz Xa Tlocc Xi-Vrannannan rambled on. ". . . but in no case with the directly observed and objectively verifiable truth, as we think of truth in certain other modes of discourse, one might hold that all religions are equally unreal. My own adherence to the nine hundred ninety-nine gods is, frankly, more of a cultural tradition than a seriously held proposition concerning the existence of that many beings of supernatural mien. From the founding of the Xa Tlocc Xi dynasty of keepers of the Gate of Par'z, we keepers have held that nine hundred ninety-nine gods assure that nine hundred ninty-nine generations of the Xa Tlocc Xi dynasty will serve as the keeper of the Gate.

"Beyond that period, even tradition is unclear as to the fate of the Xa Tlocc Xi. Perhaps the dynasty will die out, perhaps the municipal trust will be lifted from our family, or perhaps the world will end."

Parker shifted position. "Enthralling, InzXa," he said, putting a peach pit back on his plate and taking a samra to chew. "Please don't stop."

"Ah, well," the gatekeeper replied, "I am delighted that you are showing an interest after all in the life of the mind. You know, I do need a rest but I will gladly stay up a bit longer to discuss this matter with you. You know, I did not realize what a religious man you are, Rob Rrt."

Parker said *mmm*.

InzXa went on. "Well, as I was saying, between the end of the dynasty, the relief of the municipal trust, and the end of the world, I personally rather incline toward the end of the world, but my father used to say that he thought that the tradition merely meant that the sea people—your Terasians—would cease their attempts to invade Par'z, and that the keepership would simply be abolished. This, you can see, is a subset of the second case, that of the termination of the municipal, trust. I ... did you want to ask another question, Rob Rrt?"

Parker was waggling his hand frantically, like a school child who had to make. "Yeah. Just, is there one dominant religion in Par'z?"

"Ah, Rob Rrt, there you go with organization again. I have heard that the sea people are all of one faith, but in Par'z each man follows that course which calls to him. The Xa Tlocc Xi traditionally observe the nine hundred ninety-nine gods. Others prefer fewer or more gods. There have even been Par'zmen, from time to time, who have held that there was one and only one god, but such beliefs have never gained many adherents. Too narrow, you see. If I meet a man who follows gods other than my own, why, perhaps there might be more than I know of. In the infinite universe of metaphysical speculation there is room for an infinity of gods. But a man who worships one god only . . . tends to be intolerant of the beliefs of others.

"Then of course there are those who believe that all existence is god—too diffuse a philosophy for me, I prefer my own Ashtra, Beshtra . . ."

"Yes, okay, great," Parker broke in. "I'm sure that you can reel off all nine hundred ninety-nine of them."

"Why, of course!" InzXa looked offended at the mere suggestion that he could not name his gods.

"Look, InzXa," Parker said, "I don't want you to feel unappreciated, right? I mean, you've been just fine to me, letting me past the Gate, putting me up a night, bringing me here and feeding me. And, uh, giving me the benefit of your great knowledge."

The Par'zman beamed.

"But, uh, I didn't come to Par'z just to visit."

Inz Xa Tlocc Xi-Vrannannan's face fell.

"I still hope I can find somebody who can help me get home. If I can find anybody who can really help me understand how I got here . . ."—his voice trailed off— . . . and then I'll have to get back out of here . . ."

This time it was the Par'zman who broke in. "No difficulty there. Right back out the tunnel. Did not you notice that the tunnel creatures came to your scent? The air flows always inward. If you go out, they will not know you are coming until you are past, and then you can move faster than a slug. Unless your own movements are very . . ."

"Don't say it," Parker warned, "I thought of the line myself."

"Oh." InzXa looked disappointed. "Well, you can see anyway that getting out is easy enough. Finding a Par'zman who can solve your other problem, though, that may not be so simple a matter."

"I'll have to risk it," Parker said. "Or if I can't get that help, I have another reason for getting back to the mainland. A personal reason. Meanwhile," the American went on, "there are a few slightly more pressing problems. Such as, where can I get a good wash and maybe some new clothes. These are about shot. And then I'd like to talk to those Terasians you said are here in Par'z. And then, does somebody in this place have a flying machine? That's my profession where I come from. I'd like to talk to that fellow!"

"Ah, Rob Rrt, you ask such delightful questions, I could speak for days on end about each of them. You are really the most stimulating person I have met in a very long time. Not like the three sea people who are here. They hardly speak to anyone but each other and not even to each other very much."

Parker made an impatient sound.

"Ah, but well, I suppose you want a one-word answer to each question," InzXa said sadly. Parker nodded. InzXa said, "I thought you would. Well, no one can be perfect, I suppose, although there are those who hold that human perfectability is possible. Well then. Ahem. Ah . . ."

"Where can I wash?" Parker asked.

"At the lake," the Par'zman answered sadly. He looked to Parker as if he was bursting with a ten thousand word treatise on laundry through the ages, but he got no chance to deliver it.

"And clothes?"

"At the bazaar."

"How can I get things at the bazaar? I have nothing to give in exchange."

"Rob Rrt, you are being silly again. No one in Par'z *needs* anything. All can live comfortably off their surroundings. Those whose inclination turns toward creativity take their products to the bazaar because they are proud of them, not to get other goods for them. If you see something you admire on display, tell the craftsman you would like to have it and he will be delighted to give it to you."

"Then the medium of exchange is just flattery?" Parker exclaimed.

"Not at all. Sincere appreciation, if you will. Hardly flattery. To flatter a craftsman with insincere praise is to patronize him. It is to shame him. Better the open insult, Rob Rrt, than the veiled insult of flattery!"

Parker pondered that one for a moment. Maybe the Par'zmen were not fools at all. They had a very different system from any he had seen before. Certainly far different from the Relori. But it was not nearly as simple as it appeared at first, any more than was Relore, and the depth of their values was something he had not recognized at first. "A good point, InzXa," he said. "I will remember that. But . . . I have more questions before I leave you. For instance, what about the man with the flying machine?"

"Ah, that would be Win Lao Draa Xi-Tretret. You will see him on the hillside most days."

"And the Terasians that you said are in Par'z?"

"They have built themselves a little shelter—I would not call it a house, properly—near the city."

"And where can I spend tonight?" Before Inz Xa Tlocc Xi-Vrannannan could answer, Parker added hastily, "I don't mean that I'm hinting for an invitation to stay here, InzXa. You've been kind enough already."

"Ah, but certainly, Rob Rrt. There is no need for concern. You may sleep here if you wish. You will find any house in Par'z is open to guests at night. Or you may wish to sleep out of doors. The grass is soft, and at the bottom of the crater here it is warm all night. Many

Par'zmen and Par'zwomen prefer sleeping outside. Among some, moonbathing is even a religious rite. Many others regard it merely as a pleasant pastime. You may do as you wish. That is the way of Par'z."

CHAPTER

11

Parker asked Inz Xa Tlocc Xi-Vrannannan for directions to the lakeside and to the bazaar. The Par'zman stood in the doorway of his house and detailed the steps and turns. Par'z was laid out in no grid or any other planned arrangement; instead, the houses stood helter-skelter, however they had happened to be laid out by their builders.

Few if any looked new to Parker. Not that they stood in disrepair—on the contrary, the people of Par'z obviously kept their homes in good repair, nor would the mild climate that prevailed in the crater do damage to buildings. But, Parker thought, with a stable population there was no need for new buildings, had probably not been for hundreds or thousands of years.

What stood already was preserved. Beyond that, the energy of Par'zmen went into decoration, embellishment, filigree; little cupolas protruded from the upper stories of many structures, ornamental bays and bowers, window nooks, half-doors, fretwork, stained glass, scrollery, every conceivable form of prettying was present. And in the open areas between the houses the dirt streets that twined and hooked, doubled and wound in random patterns, the dirt had been packed solid by hundreds of generations of feet of Par'zmen until a surface finer and firmer than pavement had been formed. And in the streets, the people.

Parker had never seen such variety in dress and appearance. In Relore the hard life dictated a near uniform of simple trousers and shirts of cloth, boots and moccasins, rawhide jackets and warm pelts for nights on the trail.

But here in Par'z, where survival was no struggle, where life was given to amusement, the human imagination had run riot in self-adornment.

Parker saw men in trousers, in togas, in cloaks, kilts, breeks, shorts, jackets. Some were barefoot while most wore sandals. And the women went even beyond the men. Again, every possible variety of adornment competed with bare flesh for the American's eye. Many of the Par'zwomen favored a sort of silken sari, worn draped over one shoulder and draped again at the waist, gathered there to flow softly over their legs. The colors would shame the brightests that Parker had ever seen before. Brilliant hues of all sorts, wild patterns: stripes, blendings, contrasts.

At last, dazzled more at the people of Par'z than the city itself, Parker found himself beside the sparkling, sail-dotted lake. It was larger than he had estimated from the hillside above the city. He found a quiet spot on the grassy shore, sat and watched the pleasure craft for a few minutes, musing again on his situation, then removed his boots and his Relori clothing and waded into the water.

The refreshing coolness of the lake drained the sore-ness and weariness of Parker's struggle in the tunnel. He floated, swam about watching the boats, rubbed himself off in the water. Then, feeling vastly better than he had since entering the hillside outside of Par'z, he swam lei-surely back toward the bank where he had left his cloth-ing. As he approached the shore he looked up.

A Par'zian girl sat beside his piled clothes and boots. Parker stood, the water up to his waist, and stared at her. Unlike most of the women he had seen in the city, she did not wear brilliant colors. She had on a single cloth of white material, draped over her left shoulder, leaving her other shoulder bare. The rich color of her skin stood in contrast to the pale cloth, bringing Parker's breath in a quiet gasp. The girl's single garment was clasped at her waist with a coppery band of metal, shaped into twining strands like gracefully sliding serpents.

Well, thought the American, nobody said there were no snakes in Par'z. I just haven't seen any.

The girl looked at Parker as he stood in the water. "I do not know you," she said.

"No, uh . . . ." he started to answer, halted, flustered. "I'm, ah, new in town." He watched the girl's eyes widen in surprise at meeting a stranger in Par'z. Parker said "InzXa the keeper of the Gate said I could bathe in the lake." The girl said nothing. Parker cursed himself for blathering like a schoolboy, but the scene was like a moment lifted from a grade B comedy: the naked bather, the passer-by sitting down at the water's edge near the bather's clothes. . . . Parker resolved to make another start:

"I am Robert Leroy Parker, called in Par'z Rob Rrt. I come from across the sea seeking wisdom." Oh God, that was even worse. *West of Pago-Pago* at the least.

The girl laughed aloud at his discomfiture. "I am Vou La Uax Xa Ruhjaruhj," she said. Parker stood silently. "You may call me VouLa," she said. Parker stood silently. "Why do you just stand there gaping?" VouLa asked.

All right, Parker said to himself, if I'm going to live some crazy movie scene and I've pulled straight man duty, I'll play the straight man. Aloud then: "You're sitting next to my clothes, miss."

"VouLa. And so, do you expect me to hand them to you?"

Without speaking again Parker strode from the water, straight toward the spot where VouLa sat with his boots and clothing. He bent over, picked up his Relori jeans, and pulled them on, hopping up and down on his right foot as he tugged at the left leg of the pants, then hopped on his bare left foot as he pulled on the right. With as much hauteur as he could muster against the girl's laughter, Parker strode away from the lakeside.

"Rob Rrt," she called, "you forgot your shirt and shoes. And what big heavy shoes they are! Why do you not use sandals?"

Parker stopped and turned. Partly, the girl was taunting him, no question of that. But she really seemed puzzled by his boots. The sheltered life, he thought. "I'm finished with them," he told her.

"But would you just leave them here?" she asked. "That would be very messy. You should put them away somewhere, or do something with them." She really seemed concerned, Parker thought. In a sealed-off environment, litterbugs must be a real menace, not just a nuisance.

"Thank you," Parker said sarcastically, returning to pick up his belongings. "Look, VouLa, do you just hang

around this place talking to strangers, don't you have anything better to do?"

"Oh, Rob Rrt," she answered, frowning, "now you do
sound like those other sea people. Of course I have nothing better to do than to talk with people. What should I
be doing, helping the trees to grow? Counting the fish in
the lake? But if you find me annoying, I will go away.
Or should I be praying? Are you some kind of religious
fanatic, Rob Rrt?"

"No, no, I'm not. And don't go away. I'm sorry. You
people really don't have much to do, do you? So you do
whatever you feel like, sail or stroll or make things to
give away at the bazaar." Besides, Parker thought, you're
really a very pretty girl, VouLa, and interesting in a
naïve sort of way. "I think I need some new Par'zian
clothes," he said. "Would you like to be my guide to the
bazaar?"

"What fun!" the girl exclaimed, springing to her feet.
"Come, I have never helped a man pick clothing before."
Before Parker knew what was happening VouLa's warm
arm was through his own and she was tugging him back
toward the city. He looked down at her as he permitted
himself to be coaxed along: the girl was unusually pretty,
he thought. Full-figured, smooth-faced, dark-eyed like
all the people he had met in this new world, she could
hardly have been past twenty. Her hair was long but worn
scooped over her head in a coif of fantastic strands and
curls. More evidence of leisure, Parker thought. That
must have taken hours of work—probably not only
VouLa's, either—but who cared, with nothing better to
do?

"Do you know what you will choose?" VouLa asked.
Her voice was as cheerful and pleasant as her appearance, Parker noted, for all that it lacked the maturity of
even the young Relori women he had come to know in his
weeks in the Country.

"Uh, no," Parker said. "A new pair of pants, I guess,
and a shirt. Do you think I'll need sandals?"

"Many do without," the girl replied.

"Mmm, well, maybe I will too. Say, maybe I should
find a place to leave my old things afterward. Do you
think InzXa would mind if I left them at his house?"

The girl said, "Probably he would not, but he lives on
the far side of town. You can just leave them at my

house. Maybe you can meet my parents when you come by to change."

"Okay," said Parker. They'll probably wonder what their daughter is doing picking up older men, he thought.

Parker and VouLa reached the bazaar by turning between a structure that looked at little bit like a Greek temple crossed with a resort cabana, and a building that must have come straight from Angkor Wat. The bazaar itself was a large open area, square and surrounded by roofed-over cubicles that obviously were shops. Not all were occupied.

Some were filled with finely worked pottery, others with small metal wares, a few implements and a good many satuettes of slim and wraithlike figures. Where did they get metal, Parker wondered. Have to ask somebody that, he thought. If I stick around here that long. One shop specialized in jewelry, rings and clasps and twined metal belts resembling VouLa's. Another had musical instruments, or what Parker took for musical instruments —he could only vaguely identify the unfamiliar shapes and functions of the things.

Halfway along the first row of shops Parker stopped suddenly. There was a booth of books, the shopkeeper poring over one of his own products, gazing lovingly at each page, tracing the drawings with his finger.

"Why do you stop?" asked VouLa.

"This shop," Parker replied, "the books! Maybe I can learn the answers to my problems from them. VouLa, what do I do here, what do I say to the shopkeeper?"

"That is easy. Walk in, introduce yourself, tell him what you want. He would not be here if he were not proud of his wares and eager to have people see them. And you can see that the shop is not busy. Although I thought we had come here for clothes, not books," the girl added.

Parker entered the shop somewhat hesitantly. "Uh, hello," he said. He thought, that's a clever opening.

"You wish to see my books?" the storekeeper asked.

Parker looked at the man for the first time—until now he had stared only at the books in the shop. The shopkeeper, really more a boy than a man, wore only a loincloth. His body was drawn, his shoulders pinched, his face narrow and pimply, his hair unkempt. Parker said, "What kind of books do you have?"

"The finest and the most books in all Par'z," the skinny boy boasted. "I have books on religion, nutrition, history, philosophy, music, poetry, art. And I have books of tales, those are the best, the treasurers." He reached out a bony brown arm and patted a stack of dust-covered volumes. "And the very best of all," he said, pausing for dramatic impact, ". . . the very, very best, I have written myself.

"Here," the boy said, rising and walking to a pile of identical-looking volumes, "here is *The Tale of the Golden Bolt,* written and illustrated entirely by me. I even cut the wood-blocks from which it is printed, myself, and with a friend made the paper and ink. It is a masterpiece, if I may venture a sincere self-evaluation."

"I'm sure it is," Parker said, "but I was thinking of something a little different."

"As you wish," said the boy, "but you can hardly do better than the works of Myk Jo Mocc Xi-Nrenren. Still, I have many others that I did not write myself. What sort of book did you wish?"

Parker thought for a moment before answering. If he was ever going to find out what place this really was, how he had got here, and whether he would ever have any way of getting himself—and Kaetha and Trili, if they would come—home again . . . What would he need? "A history," he said. "A history, a geography, and . . . I guess that's all for starters. Preferably with pictures," he added. He would have to have someone read the books to him, at least until he learned to decipher the writing used, and in either case, pictures would help him.

"All right," the young shopkeeper said. "I can supply one of each. But if you do not want a copy of *The Tale of the Golden Bolt,* how about *Selected Verses of Myk Jo Mocc Xi-Nrenren?* It is really very fine. When I published it it was called the major poetry event of the year."

Parker wondered who had called it that, offered himself a large wager that it was Myk Jo Mocc Xi-Nrenren, and turned down the bet as no contest. He kept himself from snickering at the boy's vanity—sincere admiration, InzXa had said, to patronize is to insult, and MykJo would probably refuse to part with the books Parker wanted if the American laughed at his own works. "That would be most generous of you," he said. "If I may take a history, a geography, and a *Selected Verses*. I am Robert Leroy Parker, called Rob Rrt. I will read the books carefully and comment to you in full. Especially on the *Verses*."

The boy handed over the three books with a huge grin on his face. Although Parker could not read the inscribed characters, he was certain that the slim book on top was the *Selected Verses*.

Parker and VouLa left the shop with the skinny shopkeeper re-immersed in his volume. "You did very well in the shop of MykJo," the girl said. "Now you must read the books and comment sincerely to him on them, even if your opinions are not all favorable."

"I will," Parker answered. "I'll have to find someone who can help me read them. This writing isn't like the writing I know, and I can't read it. Can you read, VouLa?"

"I can," the girl replied. "But I have never done very much. I would rather do more pleasant things than stick myself away with old books. I would rather sail, or swim, or lie in moonlight, or jump. Sometimes WinLao lets me use his jumper."

"Jumper? You mean the thing that goes into the air?" Parker asked.

"Yes," VouLa answered. "Win Lao Draa Xi-Tretret invented the machine himself. It is the only really new thing in Par'z in the memory of any living person. It is great, great fun, but WinLao says he is still working on the jumper so he will not give any to anyone else. He has only his own. But he has let me jump a few times. I do not go as high as WinLao does because it frightens me."

"I'd like to meet WinLao," Parker said, "and soon."

"I will take you," VouLa said.

"But first clothes, hey?" Parker said. The girl nodded enthusiastically. "All right," the American said. "Tomorrow, though, for sure, will you?"

"I will take you to meet WinLao tomorrow," VouLa promised.

Dealers in cloth and in finished clothing were scattered throughout the marketplace, and as he strolled from shop to shop Parker kept reminding himself that nothing was for sale, or even for barter in most cases. The craftsmen, whether jewelers, sculptors, wood carvers, weavers, tai-

lors or bookmen, were all in business for the love of what
they were doing. In Par'z there was no such thing as eco-
nomic need, and those who made things made them only
because they wanted to.

Finally Parker stopped at a shop featuring a shimmering, satin-like cloth made up in many forms and many
colors. The shopkeeper greeted him courteously. Parker
introduced himself, explained that he needed clothing,
one set only, please, for now. The American's taste ran
to plainer things than the shopkeeper offered, but at
VouLa's urging he finally settled on a pair of simple
black trousers and a gold-cloth blouse with broad collars
and blousy sleeves.

Parker was learning the strange workings of Par'zian
economics: he complimented the shopkeeper on the quality of the cloth, the color of the dies, the design and
workmanship of the clothing. With each word the shopkeeper seemed to swell from the quiet little man who had
met the aviator when he first came into the shop. By the
time Parker and VouLa left the shopkeeper was beaming
as broadly as had the skinny boy at the bookshop and
urging the American to come back any time for more
clothing, custom-designed if he liked.

Relori boots and shirt in one hand, Par'zian books in
the other, Parker allowed VouLa to steer him from the
bazaar, the girl carrying his new Par'zian clothing in her
arms. They made their way through the city, dodging
adults and children and a scattering of small domestic
animals, until a sudden turn in a tortuous alleyway
brought them to a dead end.

"This is my house," said VouLa.

Parker stared. The building was not very large: two
stories high it looked, built on a not very large plot of
land. A few trees—they were either palms or could pass
a quick inspection as such—grew near the door. The
house seemed to be built entirely of lace, a pale pinkish-
yellow pattern worked through the material giving it an
appearance somewhere between that of a Hollywood-
made harem and a little girl's birthday cake.

Parker reached out, felt the wall of the house. Not
lace, of course, nor pink cake icing, but a stone of some
sort. Parker thought of ivory, wondered how in the world
anyone had ever got enough ivory into Par'z to build a
house, decided that it must be some native stone rather

than tusks that had provided the building material. He felt VouLa take him by the hand and pull him into the house.

In a large room sat a Par'zman and Par'zwoman, he patiently working at a piece of miniature stone sculpture with a finely pointed tool, she sketching something—styles of some sort—with what looked like a shellacked charcoal stick. As the American and the Par'zian girl entered the room, the two middle-aged Par'zians looked up at them.

"Mommy and Daddy," Parker heard VouLa say to them, "this is Robert Leroy Parker." Well, she got the name right, he reflected. "I met him at the lake just today. If we have no special family plans for after dinner, I think I'll ask Rob Rrt to sleep with me tonight."

Parker choked, dropped his boots on the floor and became very busy trying to pick them up again. He kept his eyes on the floor and the boots as he scrabbled about, heard a voice—obviously that of the girl's mother—speak: "Oh, how nice, dear, he looks like a very nice young man, but this time do remember to take a blanket with you so you will not be chilly." Parker decided to keep quiet until he had his bearings better. He'd had a few cultural shocks in the Country, and the workings of Par'zian society were new again, but this was the prize-winner of them all!

VouLa had picked up the thread of conversation with her parents. "Rob Rrt is not a Par'zman. He came through the Gate yesterday. InzXa almost had his head off before he decided Rob Rrt was all right."

"How very nice," said her mother, still sketching. The girl's father continued to work at his sculpture.

"Uh, this is a very beautiful house you have," Parker ventured.

"This house, yes." It was the Par'zman speaking. "Been in the family from the year it was built. Grandfather hundreds of generations ago had the land by royal grant. Built the house. Been in the family ever since." He scraped away at his sculpture.

Parker brightened. Here was something he could talk about, he thought, without getting personal. And maybe learn something useful at the same time. "You mention a royal grant," he said. "Is there still a king in Par'z? Is there any government?"

The Par'zman seemed to consider a moment, then he

answered. "Think there is," he said. "Think there was a succession when I was a boy. Do not recall another. Must still be the old king, then. Nobody pays much attention, though. Doubt that he does himself."

Parker turned to the girl VouLa. He said, "If you're really going to be my guide in Par'z, add him to the list of people I want to meet, would you? That fellow who invented the jumping machine—"

"WinLao," the girl supplied the name.

"—and the Terasians, the sea people you say are in Par'z, and the king." Parker turned back to the girl's father. "Do you recall the king's name?"

What a question! the American thought, as soon as he asked it. But: "Will try to remember," the Par'zman said. "Was it Xaq Flao . . . no, he was . . . mmm . . . maybe Vah Imh Xi . . . no, no . . . ah! Got it! Rob Rrt, you find an old piper XaoQa. Maybe he forgets too who is king. You remind him. He is king."

Soon the Par'zwoman suggested that they go in to dinner. "I do hope it will be a nice meal," she told the others, "Esc Wou Jahh Xi-Cavava made it for me and he is just the finest chef in all of Par'z, and the last time he catered a meal for me the guests did not care for his seasoning and he was insulted and would not talk to me for such a long time. I just hope tonight's dinner will be nice or he will never do another for me." She swept from the room, her husband following, VouLa and Parker in the rear.

In another room—obviously the dining room, Parker thought—the four sat at a table covered with finely engraved patterns of scenes that—Parker looked closely at them, then looked away again, embarrassed. He would *have* to adjust to Par'z! After a first course of cold, juicy fruit slices a tall figure appeared in the doorway. Parker could barely see the man in the darkness of the passage from the next room; he held a huge glazed-clay pot before him, heavy wisps of vapor rising from it. As the man entered the room of the diners a whiff of the stuff reached Parker's nostrils. Whatever strange things people did in Par'z, they surely ate well! The odor was one of rich sea food mixed with spices, seasoning and vegetables and herbs into a rich, stew-like meal.

The chef placed the pot of bouillabaisse on the table

before the Par'zman and retired. The Par'zman began to
serve the food out to the others at the table.

"What about his dinner?" Parker asked. "Does he just
make the food and leave?"

"Esc Wou Jahh Xi-Cavava?" exclaimed the hostess,
"why, you saw what a tall, thin man he is. He hardly eats
at all. He tastes what he cooks, that is all. He will wait
now while we eat, and then we will give him our com-
ments on the dinner."

Parker went at the dish before him. If the food had
smelled good and looked better, its taste exceeded either
in perfection. Tiny bits of fillet floated in the hot, almost
buttery broth; chunks of pink and white lobster meat
dotted the stew; crisp bits of green vegetable—Parker tried
unsuccessfully to remember whether bouillabaisse aboard
ship had had vegetables in it—completed the spicy, warming dish.

And at the end of the meal, a cup of coffee. Parker
murmured a fervent phrase to InzXa's nine hundred
ninety-nine gods, thanking them for the Par'zian coffee.

There had been little conversation during dinner, that
given to small talk most of which meant nothing to the
American. There was some discussion of sailing after dinner—Parker asked if night sailing was a common Par'zian
sport and was told that it was—the talk resulting in
VouLa's promising to take the American for a sail while
her parents went about their own affairs.

After the meal the four filed into the kitchen. EscWou
awaited them. VouLa's mother told him that the bouillabaisse had been lovely, just lovely. The others joined her,
praising the fish, the heavy broth, the seasoning, the vegetables. No need for flattery here, Parker decided. Sincere
admiration, the curency of Par'z. Escc Wou had made a
good day's wages.

In the living room VouLa urged Parker to discard his
Relori trousers and put on his Par'zian clothes while she
went to her room and changed for sailing. She too had
new clothing to show off for her parents and Rob Rrt.
Parker borrowed a room, took his Relori boots and clothing and his Par'zian outfit there, removed the rough clothing of Relore, put on the satiny garments of Par'z. The
shining black trousers fit tightly but were not uncomfortable. They rode low on the American's hips, came snugly
to a point just below the knees—Parker saw a flash of a

picture of George Washington in knee britches—and
stopped.

The blouse was fitted to his torso, the collar opening
low and spreading to wide folds onto his chest. The
sleeves flared from the shoulders, were caught up again at
the wrists. He was barefoot. Parker stood before a tall,
burnished-metal mirror. Half he admired his own costume, half thought it was silly mummery. But when in
Par'z . . .

He returned to the living room. The man and woman
had returned to their work but the woman looked up as
he entered, said, "How marvelous, Rob Rrt, you must go
back and compliment your tailor. You do not look like a
sea person at all now, you look like a real Par'zman."

Parker made a polite sound in return, but he thought:
I'll bet I do! And that's what I have to watch out for. Life
here is too easy, too pleasant. If I don't watch out, I *will*
become a real Par'zman, and that will be the end of
Kaetha for me, and the end of ever getting home. So easy
to slide, when the sliding is so easy!

From above there was a swish and a rustle, then
VouLa's voice calling cheerfully, "Here I am." She stood
at the head of a staircase, looking down into the living
room. The others looked up at her. The girl had rear-
ranged her hair; the complex coif had become even higher
and more fantastic. From her ears glittering white-jewel
decorations fell almost to her shoulders. Held closely
about her she wore a long, full cloak of shimmering scarlet, reaching almost to the floor and her bare feet.

The girl rose to her toes, spun before the others, her
crimson cloak swirling about her shoulders, and as she
stopped she flung it back to reveal one shoulder and arm,
the brown flesh beneath the satin. Beneath the cloak she
wore a—Parker tried to recall the right word—a girdle,
perhaps, of the same glittering white jewels that made her
earrings, laid against a cloth of silver threads. The girdle
was slung upon her hips, dipping low beneath the navel,
falling in a straight, broad, glittering cascade almost to her
knees.

The cloak, the jeweled earrings, and the glittering,
broad girdle, were VouLa's costume.

For the—how many times?—Parker was struck speechless. He watched and listened in mute amazement as
VouLa's parents complimented her on her appearance,

then he permitted the elder Par'zians to shepherd himself and the girl out of the house, and let the Par'zian girl lead him once more toward the lake.

But I'm a married man, Parker thought. Of sorts.

CHAPTER

12

VouLa led Parker through the warm Par'zian night, weaving a twisted path through the patternless streets of the city. From windows of the city's buildings lights shone, flickering lamps and cressets. The streets themselves were lighted by cressets mounted on poles; their varied style told Parker that each was maintained by the nearest householder.

People made their ways through the streets by night as by day, moving at a leisurely pace. "Where is everybody going?" Parker asked the Par'zian girl at his side.

"Anywhere," she replied. "Visiting, or sailing, or home from sailing, or swimming, or to the bazaar, or home from the bazaar. Anywhere," she repeated.

"But I don't understand," Parker said. "Aren't there times set aside for different activities? Times when everyone attends to the same thing, like mealtimes? Or . . ." he stopped for VouLa's answer.

"Rob Rrt," she said, "everyone does whatever he wants, whenever he wants. You eat when you are hungry, rest when you are tired, do as you please, only respect the right of others to do the same. That is the way of Par'z."

"Don't you even have days of work and days of rest?" Parker asked.

VouLa laughed, a tinkling, carefree laugh. Parker compared the sound, in his mind, with the laughter of Kaetha. They were the sound of a crowing infant and a happy parent, by comparison. VouLa said, "Since no one works except by choice, why should we have days for work and days for rest? We schedule things out of consideration, or because we want to. We arrange to meet for a meal, or for sport, at the rising or the setting of the sun, or when the sun is halfway to its zenith, or at it, or halfway to its setting, or when the moon is high. But still, we do as we wish. Only Inz Xa Tlocc Xi-Vrannannan insists on comings and goings by schedule, but all men take their turn at the Gate, coming and going at the rise or the setting of the sun."

So, thought Parker, in this kind of society, it made sense. When every day was Sunday—or maybe Christmas, New Year's, and Fourth of July all in one—there was no need for a calendar.

They reached the edge of the lake, VouLa exchanging greetings with her friends and introducing Parker to each. Unlike the Relori, the people of Par'z seemed little interested in a strange face, despite their isolation from the outer world. Parker tried to estimate the population of Par'z, guessed at a few thousand but gave up at trying to be certain.

Parker and VouLa walked along the lake shore, the girl holding his hand and chattering happily about the friends they had met and the boat they would use. At last they reached it—a little craft, shorter than the Relori dugout but broader. The boat was built on a framework of bent wood covered with thin, waterproof fabric. A single mast held a simply-rigged fabric sail of vivid pink edged in deep gold.

From a compartment under the stern seat of the boat VouLa pulled a pair of shielded oil lamps, mounted them on waiting holders at bow and stern, and lighted both from flint sparkers built into the lamps themselves. She sat in the boat, pulling small cushions from the storage compartment for herself and Parker. The aviator pushed the boat away from the bank, jumped in and slid down beside the girl. He used a paddle removed from a mount inside the boat to get them farther onto the lake, then replaced it and leaned back, an arm over the boat's tiller, letting the constant gentle breeze of Par'z carry them across the water.

From other boats scattered on the lake pairs of lamps shone, casting strips and sparkles of light on the surface. Parker heard low voices, listened to distant exchanges of quiet, desultory conversation carried across the water. His revery was interrupted by VouLa. From somewhere she had produced an overflowing handful of samrae, offered one to Parker and took another for herself.

"Where did those come from?" he asked her.

"We keep some in the boat," she replied. Then: "Rob Rrt, is your country very much like Par'z?",

"No, VouLa," he told her. "My country is part of another world, far from Par'z and very different."

"I wish you would tell me about it," she said, leaning on his shoulder. "I often wonder what the world outside of Par'z is like. Is it as beautiful as Par'z? Do people live as we do?"

Parker sighed, thinking of an answer that would be as adequate as he could. Imagine a child, he thought, brought up in one set of surroundings, knowing nothing of the world beyond, barely aware that there *is* a world beyond, asking what it was like. Where do you start? "First," Parker said, "there is the world beyond Par'z. That's big enough for now. That's enough to understand." To a child who has never seen any world but jungle, any life but the primitive, in twenty-five words or less describe London. "That's the world I came from when I came into Par'z. Then there's the world I came from originally. I don't even know if that's the same planet as this one. Let's leave that for another time."

"Oh, I know about planets," VouLa exclaimed. "We will talk of them, then we will do more than talk of them. But for now. . . ."

"What do you mean?" Parker cut her off. But the girl would not say more. She demanded to be told of the world beyond Par'z. Parker told her of Relore, and what little he knew of Teras, and of the woods and the life of the Country.

She asked: "Is it as good as living in Par'z?"

"I don't think I can answer," Parker said. He took another samra from the girl, chewed it slowly while he thought. "Certainly your life here in Par'z is easier. Here you work if you wish, for fun. In Relore they must work or perish. Here you can do anything you feel like. The Relori are not bound by many laws, but they have to struggle for life. Their days are pretty well set for them. I don't know about Teras but the Relori surely dislike Teras.

"But of Par'z or Relore . . . I don't know." Parker made a gesture of indecision. "Their lives seem to mean something. You have more pleasures but . . . don't you ever get bored? Are you really satisfied?"

VouLa said, "I think so," but to Parker she did not seem certain. "Come," the girl said after a moment of silence, "swing us back to the shore. We will lie on the grass."

Well, Parker thought, this is it. I've never hesitated with women before. Kaetha came to his mind. Well I'll probably never see her again, Parker thought. He looked at VouLa beside him in the boat as they glided slowly back toward the edge of the lake. It wasn't my idea. Besides, when in Par'z, do as the Par'zmen do. But: damn, I'm no moralist and I've never been a saint. I've done my share of chasing around. I've killed men . . . why shrink from a beautiful girl on a beautiful night in a strange city?

Still he hesitated. Just go along and see what develops, Parker finally decided.

He leaped from the boat onto the grassy edge of the lake, helped the girl to put away the lamps and loosen the sail, brought the boat farther out of the water to keep it from drifting away.

Together, Parker and VouLa walked toward the edge of the woods near the lake. As they went, Parker noticed that she carried her large handful of samrae with her. She looked up at him, gave him a samra and chewed one. They walked on.

"I thought we needed a blanket," Parker said.

VouLa made a little shrug that Parker read as meaning half-annoyance, half-amusement. "That's just mother's idea," she said, "being silly worrying as if I were a baby. I sleep out lots of times and she always thinks I will be cold."

Parker had his arm about the girl's shoulders, felt hers about his own waist. He could think only that it was pleasant, languorous, to stroll that way on the soft, warm grass, barefoot, chewing samra, talking softly. There seemed no future, no past. In a little copse of trees they halted and Parker watched the girl remove her cloak and spread it on the ground. She sat near its edge, invited him to sit beside her. He did.

After a silence he said, "The planets . . . You know of the planets."

"Oh," she said. Parker watched the girl turn to him with a smile that he read as one of childish innocence.

"Well, anybody in Par'z knows what the planets are," she said. "We know that Par'z is an island, surrounded by a sea. We know that the sea is part of the world. The world is a ball falling around the sun, and the planets are other worlds like ours."

Parker was astounded. "How do you know all this?" he asked.

"It is in the books," VouLa said. "Do you doubt it? You can get a glass in the bazaar, and see that the planets are round. Par'zmen have made such glasses for . . . I suppose always."

"And everyone in Par'z understands the sun and the planets?" Parker persisted.

"Almost everyone," the girl replied. "I know one boy who says that he read a book that says that the world is a dish of water and Par'z floats in the middle of it. And that the dish is balanced on the back of a beast with an arm for a nose and sails for ears. And that the beast stands on the back of a giant turtle—there are turtles in the lake, you know—and that the turtle swims in a lake in a great city like Par'z, and the whole thing starts over. He says there is probably a turtle somewhere in our lake with a beast on its back with a dish on its back with a city in the dish.

"But I don't believe it. The planets are worlds."

"Are there people on the planets?" Parker asked. "Do you know if anyone from earth ever goes to other planets?"

"I think not," VouLa said. "Perhaps if WinLao's machine went even higher than it does. . . ."

"No," Parker said. "It would take a lot more than that."

Again there was silence. Then the Par'zian girl placed a number of samrae in Parker's hand. "Here," she told him, "chew these and it will be time to sleep."

Parker watched her put several of the seeds in her own mouth and chew them. He followed suit. His head was already light, his body suffused with a pleasant warmth from samrae. He had had . . . how many . . . on the boat, and while they walked, and while they sat and talked . . . Parker lost count. Now he chewed more, not rapidly but in succession, feeling the warmth creep to every corner of his body as he did so, feeling every part of his body with a clarity he had never felt before, feeling as if he could direct his consciousness to any point in his body, sense the outline and the structure of his own lungs, his brain; for a moment he became a corpuscle of his own blood, racing through dark, hot, busy channels, feeling the push of his distant heart, a thousand miles away, pumping, pushing him along to the far extreme of a hand or a foot.

He pulled back from the corpuscle, became himself again. He realized that he was lying flat on the satiny cloth that VouLa had spread on the grass. He opened his eyes, saw the girl lying beside him, her face filled with a tranquil ecstasy. He reached for her hand, intertwined his fingers with her own so that their hands rested between them, palm to palm, finger beside finger. He felt no sexual impulse toward the girl, no need to touch her further. They shared a contact with themselves, each other, the world outside themselves.

Parker saw VouLa open her eyes. They fluttered, opened slowly. She whispered to him. "Now we must leave here. Lie back, die a little death with me. We will see things together."

He lay back, facing upward, left his hand holding the girl's. He closed his eyes, felt himself growing smaller and smaller, drawing back into himself, leaving his body and its organs, abandoning feet and hands, legs and arms, he drew back, a cold now replacing the warmth that had so filled him, taking away awareness of his loins, his viscera, his eyes, his mouth. He maintained only a thread, passing somehow through his arm, to his hand, to the girl's hand. He felt as if he was sinking, somehow, yet at the same time rising, rising out of himself, out of his body, leaving the satin spread on the warm Par'zian grass, rising through the blackness of the Par'zian night, formless, bodiless, senseless and yet senselessly aware of the universe, of infinite distances and unmeasureable eternities of time that was timeless.

He had no body, no physical senses, yet he was aware of an immense blackness about him, no mere deprivation of sight but a phenomenon of separation from the physical universe by distances so inconceivably vast that the light blasted out by the explosion of the original primitive superatom in the creation of the cosmos had never reached this point, might never reach this point, but might flag in a kind of sheer inanimate fatigue and fall

back, back to the tame, tiny universe of suns and constellations, quasars and clouds of cosmic dust, puny and
ephemeral galaxies and pitiful clusters of galaxies.

He floated in non-space, never-time, a bodiless, dimensionless point, a quantum of self-awareness, pure,
uncontaminated by physical existence. For a timeless
time he remained suspended, a point, a nothing, an all.
Then he directed his consciousness back into the physical
universe to drift, inactive, observing, sensing only, an
awareness only. Of points of blackness that appeared
against the blackness, that grew, lightened, disintegrated,
became galaxies of stars and comets, planets and creatures, blind dumb unaware pieces of organic machinery
patiently feeding, growing, reproducing and dying, returning to soil, nourishing new life, becoming new life,
feeding, growing, dying, nourishing, growing in a cycle
that ended only when the suns went out, the galaxies collapsed, darkness returned, all fell back into formless
blobs of blackness against blackness, then were lost
again.

He approached closer, found an amusing little system
of multiple suns, red, blue and green, whose complex or-
bits had drawn a family of planets into endless gyrations
in ceaselessly varying gravitational flux. The planets did
not solidify but remained doughy, flexible things that
stretched and warped, grew and shrank as they wove
through the insane gyrations of their courses.

At another sun one planet gleamed and glittered
ceaselessly as Parker watched. He moved closer, somehow felt emanations of thought and communication from
the shining globe, but he was unable to comprehend the
messages or to return them in any way that brought a
response. Sadly he left the planet of intelligent crystal-
line life, sped through the interstellar blackness again,
felt himself pass through a group of pure energy vortices,
creatures of the black void, feeding off pure stellar radi-
ation in the deeps of space, but again he was not able
to make them aware of his presence, for all that he could
feel theirs.

In the solar system of a ruby-glowing star he saw creatures rise from the surface of a planet on huge wings.
They were almost human-like but gigantic, elongated
things, tall and thin, hollow-boned; on their gossamer
wings they rose from their world, flew the air currents

of its atmosphere to its very limits, their wings extending to greater and greater size, thining to little more than monomolecular films, until finally they thrust themselves with a final effort beyond the air, into the vacuum between their world and others, caught the solar wind of their ruby sun, became themselves glowing smoky-red jewels as they sailed to their moon on gossamer wings, circled it, sped to other planets of their sun and fled homeward in their turn.

Another solar system held only dead planets. Blackened to cinders ages past when their primary had flared into nova, they circled it now eternally as charred cinders, sterilized, disinfected of the life disease, while the sun itself had fallen back in its dying inner fires, formed a crust of its own solidifying ash, lit to a dismal glow by the husbanded energy of heat and light that remained within.

And even on the surface of that dying sun, that self-made, self-powering pseudo-planet, that world that had killed its offspring worlds, even there life had occurred. Great, dull beings, squashed flat by immense gravitational forces, spreading farther to cover the sun-earth beneath themselves, spread for miles, for leagues, huge things, pale and pasty as uncooked dough, covering the ground, sucking vampires drinking the heat and light of the dying star, holding in its radiance so that almost none could reach the dead cinders that circled it carrying the dead ash of ancient races.

Parker drew back from the vampire-smothered star, wished himself to return to Par'z. Before he could move a new idea struck—to return, instead, to his own time, his own earth, to learn what temporal and spatial relationship existed between his own world and the world of the Country. He hesitated, ready to move, realized chillingly that he knew neither where nor when he *was*, how to reach any point of known reference in time or space from the time and space where he had re-entered the physical cosmos, nor the time and place where he now held himself, a dimensionless point of consciousness, near the dying mother star of cinders.

A fear gripped him, fear that he was lost, lost now in a way far beyond any conceiving of what lost meant when he had been lost in the Antarctic snow, or lost in the forests of the Country. He was lost in a void of time and space, doomed to wander endlessly, a consciousness without physical being, an impotent omniscience floating forever, ever observing, never participating in the infinitely varied life of the universe, immortal perhaps, perishing only when the cosmos perished and returned to its primal atom, or surviving perhaps even then, to drift in eternal nothingness, a self not blind but sightless, not deaf but unhearing, for a time not merely beyond measuring but beyond time itself.

He felt a gentle tugging, a subtle sensation of the presence of another consciousness. His own perception was directed first one way, then another, but there was no sign of another presence except the gentle, barely noticed feeling that another essential awareness like himself floated in the void and attempted to draw him along, somewhere, with itself. Parker did not resist but willed himself, instead, to move with the other presence, to slide through the resistless coordinates of space-time with the other being.

Objects in the void seemed to move, to whirl, to shift their patterns in unfollowable ways. Parker felt himself move in space, in time, in incomprehensible dimensions, in fantastically paradoxical ways. He seemed to grow, to shrink, to become distorted—or perhaps he remained constant while the entire cosmos shifted its size and its shape. At last, guided still by the other presence, he felt himself readjust to a more normal perspective, saw that he was approaching—or at least that his viewpoint was approaching—a white-orange star that might be his own sun. Closer and closer he came, began to discern planets circling the luminary, but its glare became greater, its light and radiant heat increased as he approached until he lost sight of its planets, lost awareness of his cosmic orientation, lost consciousness of all except a white glare and a white heat that became greater, that seemed to swell him. He felt himself grow, grow, strain with a deep, mighty ache. His head felt as if it were bursting into white-hot chunks. He put his two hands to his head, covered his blinded eyes, then turned his face downward, opened his eyes to see his own black-trousered legs as he sat on the satin-covered grass.

"Whee," Parker groaned. "What a head!"

"Are you in pain?" came a voice from beside him.

Parker twisted his face toward the voice, looked ruefully at the girl VouLa. "If I'm lucky," he said, "I may die right now." He paused, then continued. "VouLa, what happened? Did you bring me back here from—somewhere else?" He looked up into the Par'zian sun, shining whitely in a crystal-like day.

"It was the samra trip, Rob Rrt," the girl said. "Sometime one awakens from it ill. Rest a little while here, then a swim and some food will make you well again. I do not believe that anyone has ever died of the illness after the samra trip."

"Nor of a hangover," Parker said, "but sometimes you wish you could." He looked earnestly at the girl. "But what *is* the samra trip? Was I really here all night? Was it just a dream? Or did I actually. . . ." He let his sentence trail off, hoping that the girl would supply the rest of it herself. She did.

"We never left this place," she told him. "At any rate, our bodies did not. As for what did happen, you may wish to discuss the samra trip with InzXa—" Parker indicated a negative and the girl continued "—There are many ideas of what the journey is. Some think it only a dream . . . but, Rob Rrt, can two persons share a dream? You held my hand last night and you took me on your journey. It was a good journey.

"Some samra travelers have gone into the heart of a flower, some into the mind of a lobster. I have done that once. Dark thoughts, the lobster thinks, slow and simple brutish thoughts. Some few have made journeys like yours. I thank you for taking me. I think I knew the way back because I have made the samra trip many times, and you never before. You would have found your way, I think, but your fear hurt me so I tried to show you the way."

Parker said, "Can't you use the samra to learn what the world is like? I wanted to learn if this is my own earth. I thought I could see all the world, and time, and learn what place and time this is against my world, but all I could see was glare when I came close to the solar system."

"So it has been for all who travel far from Par'z with samra. I do not know why. Somehow . . ." she hesitated, ". . . you can learn deep things with samra, like the mind of a lobster or the heart of a flower, or great and distant things, as we did   together. But not . . . not things of the world."

They were both silent for a time, then VouLa said, "Come on, we will both feel better after the water."

They walked slowly to the lake shore, Parker still in his new outfit of golden blouse and black trousers, VouLa with her scarlet cloak gathered about her again. At the lake edge they both removed their clothing, she laying her glittering jewelled girdle on her cloak, he placing his shirt and trousers beside them. They walked into the water together, slowly relaxing in the clean coolness of it.

Parker held the girl's two hands in his own, in the water, his mind returning fleetingly to another brown body in another place of water, with whom he had bathed—was it only days ago? He looked at the Par'zian girl with him, feeling nothing of the emotion that Kaetha aroused in him. With VouLa, instead, there was a different kind of intimacy. Her naked beauty pleased him but in a strangely unpassionate, sexless way. He felt like a brother, like a twin even.

He released her hands, then like a child splashed clear water onto her shoulders and face. She laughed, splashed back at him. They played that way, laughing together for a time, dodging and throwing handfuls of water at each other until the girl lunged at Parker, seized him as if to duck him in the water. He caught her around the back, his arms under her arms, lifted her half out of the water in an embrace, then dropped her back onto her feet in the water; they ran to the edge, Parker feeling totally refreshed, the samra hangover gone, leaving him feeling vigorous and hungry.

As they dressed again Parker watched the girl, somehow impersonally admiring the strong swelling of breast and hips, yet feeling no sense of arousal. Suddenly, more to himself than to VouLa, he said, "It's the samra! I should have known! This is a whole society of low-powered hopheads, chewing their samra all the time. A little bite acts like a low-grade narcotic. A good dose and you're off like an acid-head. No wonder there's no population problem here, everybody's a half-gone junkie."

"What are you saying?" VouLa asked.

"Only—" Parker looked at her "VouLa, when you

said last night that you wanted to sleep with me, you meant . . . ?"

She laughed, half puzzled. "I meant that I wanted to sleep with you. Was it not good, being together on the journey? Are you sorry you took me?"

"No, no," he said. "It isn't that. Only. . . ."

She waited.

"Only, in my country, VouLa. . . ." Now this is a hell of a time to get all embarrassed and tongue-tied, Parker told himself. "In my country, sleeping together is an expression we use when we really mean making love."

"Oh," VouLa said. She brightened. "But that is all right. You are very nice, Rob Rrt. I think I do love you. Is that all right?"

Parker groaned. "Uh, yes, that's perfectly fine. Uhh. . . ." Well, out with it. "But, uh, when I said we didn't just mean sleeping, but, uh, making love, I, ah, didn't mean exactly just that either. Uh, what I really mean was, uh, screwing. Um, didn't you ever hear of, uh, intercourse?" Parker was starting to feel like a dirty old man.

"Oh, you mean putting bodies together, a man and a woman?" VouLa asked.

"Yes," Parker whispered.

"Oh, why that's all right," VouLa replied. "We have to do that sometimes or there would be no children. It's kind of fun, I suppose. But people do not do it very much. There would be too many children if they did."

Out of the mouths, Parker said to himself. Aloud: "What about getting some breakfast?" he asked.

They returned to VouLa's home. Here, while the Par'zian girl changed her clothing, Parker checked his Relori boots and clothing and weapons and the books he had got in the bazaar of Par'z. All were safely stored. When VouLa reappeared she had exchanged her spectacular outfit of jewelled girdle and scarlet cloak for a simple sari, but one of many colors, a gold-orange background streaked with blues and greens, and golden colored sandals held by thongs wrapped about her lower legs.

She had abandoned the high coif of the previous night and knotted her long black hair in bunches, looking more like a school girl than ever.

She made a light breakfast of coffee and juice and a kind of light toasted loaf served with fruit. As she served the food a pang of homesick longing took Parker. The girl, the familiar breakfast, the relaxation at home, even the urban setting made this Par'zian household more like Parker's home than even the house of Broadarm and Janna had been, yet Parker found himself uncomfortable at the easygoing spirit in Par'z. It was the ideal life, he thought, in a way. No enemies, no struggle at all. The people lived in the closest thing to perfect freedom that Parker could conceive. And yet . . . they had no aim. Even the pursuit of pleasure seemed, from much of what he had seen, an unenthusiastic effort.

"VouLa," Parker said, "is there any challenge at all in your life? Anything that you feel you must do, any goal?"

"No," the girl answered. "We merely live. We take our pleasure as we wish, some by contemplation, some by creating art, some by playing and sailing, some with the samra. That is what our life is."

Parker sighed. "I suppose you like it."

"Yes."

"I don't think I ever could," Parker said. "I was born to another kind of life, VouLa. Not just different surroundings, but a different way of looking at things. In my world we work for possessions, we fight for our freedom. It's hard, but you keep at it. If you give up you're less than a man.

"In the Country across the sea from Par'z, even there it's pretty much the same way. But here," he made a gesture that took in all their surroundings, "I don't know, you get everything free. It's paradise, I guess. I don't think it could ever satisfy me."

"I do not understand you, Rob Rrt," VouLa said. "But you are a nice man. Where would you like to go today? I will take you."

Parker thought before he answered. He could drift through a dream-like time in Par'z. He had found a charming guide if he would settle for that. But he still had priorities. He still wanted to meet the helicopter man. He wanted to talk with the old king of Par'z in case the old man had any information for him. And it might still be a good idea to get to talk with the Terasians who were supposed to be in Par'z.

"I'd like to talk with the man with the flying device," Parker said.

"Oh, Win Lao Draa Xi-Tretret," the girl said. "He is

probably on the hillside jumping around already. We will go and look for him."

The girl rose from her place, Parker did likewise and they left the house. They worked their way through the streets of Par'z, pushed through a bustling crowd in the bazaar, and emerged on a side of the city where smooth grasses led gently away and up toward the hillside that formed the inner bowl of the crater of Par'z.

As the two advanced from the city's edge and crossed the grassy area the girl pointed into the sky, high above the lip of the volcano. She cried, "There he is, Rob Rrt, see him floating down!"

Parker thought that floating was not quite the right word, but still there was a human figure, silhouetted against the bright morning sky. Above his head a set of rotors spun, not holding him in the air but lowering him gently to the ground. As the figure dropped lower and lower Parker's hopes dropped too. What the man was using— he actually wore it, Parker now saw—was more like a toy than a flying machine. Parker tried to make out any source of power for the rotors but he could see none. If the blades merely windmilled then it must be an auto-gyro, he thought, rather than even the most elementary true helicopter. Well, go ahead. Maybe he would learn something worthwhile, and in any case it would be good to talk shop with a fellow aviator, however odd his stripe, once again.

The man had landed now, bouncing a couple of times on what looked like a kind of monopodal landing gear. He stopped, folded the shaft of the gear, then stepped out of the whole mechanical rig and walked toward the newly arrived pair.

"Hello, VouLa," he said, "how are you this morning, and who is your friend there? I do not think I know him."

VouLa introduced Parker—"Rob Rrt"—and WinLao, told the Par'zman that Rob Rrt was newly arrived in Par'z.

"Of the sea people, are you, Rob Rrt?" the Par'zman asked.

"No, I'm not," Parker told him. "I came here from a place called Relore. The Relori are not friends to the sea people." No need to go into his whole background again, Parker felt. Not now, anyway.

"That is as well," WinLao replied. "The sea people are

the ancient enemies of Par'z, you know. Inz Xa Tlocc Xi-Vrannannan let some in a little while ago and they have been bothering me."

Parker asked what WinLao meant.

"Why, they keep trying to get my machine from me. They have no patience. I am still working on it, learning from it and building another that will be better. Can you imagine the pleasure of drifting high in the air, Rob Rrt? Not in samra, mind you, but with your own body held aloft by a machine?"

"I can," Parker replied, "better than you would guess. But what of the Terasians— the sea people, WinLao?"

"They want me to build three of my machines for them. They have offered me wealth. How foolish! What can I want that I cannot get for myself, or make myself, or that someone in the bazaar cannot give me for my appreciation? And they offer me power over all Par'z. 'Wait until our people come,' they say, 'we will make you our ruler over all of Par'z.' Why would I want that? Why should I want Par'zmen to bow to me and do as I tell them, as the sea people offer me? I do not like them!"

Oh-oh, thought Parker. Reel three. The plot thickens. To WinLao he said, "What did you tell them, the Terasians?"

"At first I told them to wait. I said that I was building a second jumper that would be better than the first. I said that when I was satisfied that the machine was perfected, I would build many and give them away. Then they could have them."

"And their reaction?"

"They became very angry. They said they would harm me. That is unheard of! If a Par'zman does not like another he does not associate with that other. Why should any man harm another man? I told them to go away, and they did, and good riddance. I do not like Terasians. I am glad you are not a Terasian, Rob Rrt."

"Do you know why they wanted your machines, WinLao?" asked Parker.

The inventor said, "For pleasure, I suppose. They did not say. But what else is my jumper good for? It is really great fun to bound into the air, high and higher, and then to sail slowly downward. Would you like to try it?"

"Well, I would," Parker said. "But first," an idea was forming, "how high can your machine go?"

"I do not know. I have gone very high. It becomes very difficult, the higher you go, and dangerous I think."

VouLa chimed in. "WinLao has gone very high. I have seen him go much higher than I have the courage to go."

Parker asked, "But higher than the lip of the crater of Par'z?"

"Yes," WinLao said. "I have gone higher than the edge of the crater. It is a wonderful sight: the sea in all directions, and dark shapes, other lands I think, far off."

"As I thought," Parker said. "Look, WinLao, I know this will be hard for you to understand because Par'zmen are all . . . all non-agressive. You can afford it. Everybody has everything, God help you! The world outside Par'z is a hard place. In many ways, an ugly place. There are people in my world, WinLao—not the Country now, another world where I lived before I came to the Country—who think they know the only right way to live. They are so certain that their own way, their own system of religion or government or trade, is the only right one, that they want to make everyone else become like them.

"They hate anyone who differs from them. Your people and the Relori of the Country are different in many ways, but you have this much in common: you live in your own way, and you leave others alone. The Terasians, if they are like some people in my world, if they are as I'm starting to think they are, can't tolerate that. Teras may be the ancient enemy of Par'z, but I'm sure that Teras hates Par'z for another reason than that. Teras hates Par'z just because it exists, and its people are free, the Terasians can't stand that.

"How much do you think the sea people know of Par'z?"

WinLao stood silent for a moment before answering. "A few Par'zmen leave. Not many. But some are not satisfied with our arts and crafts, with sailing and with samra. Of course they are permitted to leave."

"How?"

"Why, through the Gate. If you came through the Gate, Rob Rrt, you must know how difficult it is to enter Par'z. But to leave is simple. The tunnel beasts cannot stop you. The keeper of the Gate will not stop you."

"Okay," Parker said, "that answers that. The Terasians patrol the waters between Par'z and the Country. They must land on the island occasionally and pick up any Par'zmen who are outside the crater. How they must burn when they hear about Par'zian freedom!

"WinLao, did you never think that your invention could be used to travel over the edge of this crater? That a few spies could use your jumpers to get out? Or a whole army use them to get *in?*"

The Par'zman looked at Parker in surprise and disbelief. "No," he said. "I've never thought of it."

"Well, don't feel too badly," Parker told him. "I don't suppose any Parzman would, except maybe InzXa. Look, WinLao, you have to stall these Terasians. I think you're safe as long as you have only one jumper done but they know you're working on more. They need more than one. If you finish three, you can be sure they'll act to get them from you and go over the edge with them. If you quit work you may force their hand in some other way . . . I don't know what they'll do then, but I'm pretty sure they'll act. But as long as you're working, or they think you are, you should be safe."

Parker turned to VouLa. "I want you to arrange a meeting with the Terasians for me," he told the girl. "It should be easy enough to do. Tell them that I'm an outsider too, that since we're the only outsiders in all Par'z, the Terasians and I, you thought we'd like to get together."

The girl looked seriously at Parker, her cheerful face sobered at the half-understood menace his words indicated.

Parker went on. "After I talk to them I'll want to see your king. Then possibly InzXa again. I can find InzXa myself easily enough—can you take care of the others for me?"

VouLa nodded her head, her mouth trembling. In the voice of a frightened child—for a moment Parker was struck by the thought that despite her voluptuous body and sophisticated use of samra, VouLa was somehow only a little girl—she said, "Yes, I am sure I can do it."

Parker touched the girl on her shoulder, urged her to sit and wait for him. Then he turned back to WinLao Draa Xi-Tretret. Before Parker spoke the inventor said "Would you like to try my machine? I am very proud of it."

Parker looked at the contraption that WinLao was now holding upright. The Par'zman had folded the rotor blades down, so that the whole machine stood on its one padded foot, its top some eight feet in the air above the men. The rotor blades—four of them, made of light, polished wood—looked a little bit like the blades of a slow-turning butcher-shop fan. For an instant Parker's mind flashed to the boyhood job as a butcher's boy that had earned him the nickname of Butchy.

The blades attached to a hollow cylindrical base, with catch-rods where they met their base to hold them rigid when they were extended. The hollow base for the rotors revolved freely on a polished track atop the main shaft of the jumper, a simple, straight wooden stick eight feet long.

Low on the main shaft were two foot pedals, almost stirrups, Parker saw, attached to the top of a heavy, very powerful looking spring that spiralled about the jumper shaft, rigidly attached near the bottom of the shaft, its top firmly connected with the stirrup-device.

Parker looked at the flimsy-appearing thing, tested the stirrups-and-spring with his hand, stepped back and looked at the thing again. "It's nothing but a damned pogo-stick!" he exclaimed. "A pogo-stick with a windmill rotor on the top of it. And you really got the altitude I saw with this thing, WinLao?"

The Par'zman said "I have never heard of a pogo, so I do not know what kind of stick you mean. The bouncing mechanism is my own invention."

"Oh-oh, I didn't mean to insult you," Parker reassured him. The one thing Par'zmen really value is ego-boost, Parker thought, the last thing I want to do is insult this guy. "I'm sure this is your own invention, WinLao. Only in my home there is a children's toy a little bit like it, that they bounce around on, called a pogo stick. But the revolving blades . . ." Now, how am I going to tell him about helicopters and autogyros without breaking his heart?

The Par'zian inventor said "I was inspired to build the rotors by watching samrae spiral through the air." From somewhere in his clothing the Par'zman produced a handfull of the ever-present winged seeds, threw a few of them into the air.

Together the two men and VouLa watched the samrae spin downward, the veined wings catching the clear Par'zian air, twirling gracefully downward as the samra seeds themselves gave their weight to pulling the light objects down to the gradually sloping grass. WinLao stooped and retrieved the narcotic seeds, put them back in his clothing.

"Now," he said, "watch this and then I will explain how the jumper works." He climbed onto the machine, balancing precariously on the machine's padded tip while he got his two feet firmly into the stirrups. He held the vertical shaft in his two hands, began jumping about on the grass, the machine somehow amplifying his jumps so that each bound was higher than the previous one.

"Did I say a pogo-stick?" Parker asked himself under his breath. "A super pogo-stick, maybe!"

He watched the Par'zman stop pumping, watched his bounces grow smaller and smaller until the inventor finally pulled a foot clear of its stirrup, used it to stop the action of the machine the next time he touched earth.

Panting slightly, the Par'zian inventor explained the device. "You see, Rob Rrt, when anyone jumps up in the air, he comes down with some force. You could calculate it by measuring his mass and speed when he lands. What happens to that force? Where does it go?"

Parker started to answer, stopped when he saw that WinLao was lecturing and did not really want an answer for his questions.

"Then energy is lost, dissipated," the Par'zman said. "Partly it is absorbed into the ground, but mostly into your own body. You bend your knees when you land, to absorb that energy, or else you feel it—as if someone had given you a good blow on the bottoms of your feet.

"The jumper works very simply. It does not create any energy, it simply *saves* energy, *captures* that energy from your jump, by storing it in the heavy spring as you land. By timing yourself, you can jump a second time just as the spring releases the energy saved from your first landing. That way, your second jump will take you higher because it will have the energy of your new jump plus the saved energy of your first landing.

"Your second landing will be harder than the first, but you will not be hurt if you land properly—again, the energy will be saved in the spring, so that your third jump will be higher still, and your fouth, and so on. If I could achieve absolute efficiency with my invention, there should be no theoretical limit to how high a man could jump, starting with just a hand's span and going a little higher each time. But the ground does absorb some energy with each landing, and there is air resistance both rising and falling, and the spring is not perfectly efficient anyway.

"But I can get quite high nonetheless. Higher than the walls of this crater."

"I know," said Parker, "I saw you from outside of Par'z."

The inventor beamed at the confirmation of his feat.

"But what about the other half of the machine?" Parker asked him, "what is the rotor for if you can land safely on the, uh, bouncer?"

The Par'zman's face told Parker that this was his moment of triumphant revelation. "That is the whole point of my invention," WinLao said. "For the real pleasure of the jumper, when you reach your highest point you want to drift down slowly, like a samra on the wing, not plummet like a thrown-up rock. When you reach the top of your highest leap, you flip up the rotors"—he demonstrated—"and come down slowly, looking about you, seeing wonderful sights perhaps, and enjoying a pleasant sensation of floating."

Parker said "I imagine you could control your descent by tilting your body and the jumper, and use it to travel with."

The Par'zian inventor considered for a moment, then said, "Yes I am sure you could. Where would you travel to?"

"Out of Par'z," Parker said. "Or into it!"

CHAPTER

13

Win Lao Draa Xi-Tretret held the jumper erect as Parker placed first one foot in a stirrup, then the other. The inventor said "I am making a special hand grip on my other model. It should make the jumper easier to use and give you greater altitude by losing less energy."

"Just don't work too fast," Parker said. Then: "Okay, here I go!" WinLao released his grip, Parker bent his knees slightly, then straightened fast, jumping a few inches off the grass, holding the jumper as he rose. As the single foot of the machine struck the grass again the aviator bent his knees. He felt the spring beneath his feet lower as it compressed, then rise again as it returned to its original shape. Parker straightened his knees as the stirrups rose. The downward thrust of the flier's feet offset the rising action of spring and the jumper stood still.

"Did it wrong, didn't I?" said Parker. He quickly pulled one foot from the stirrup and planted it on the grass to keep the Par'zian contraption from toppling onto its side.

From her position sitting on the grass nearby VouLa laughed.

WinLao said, "Most people do that the first time. You bent your knees too late and you straightened them much too late. This time, bend them before your impact—you might as well bend them as soon as you get off on your first jump, until you are getting much higher. When you land, as soon as the spring starts to compress, flex—straighten your legs and add that drive to the spring's compression. Then as you go up again hold your knees rigid—that is the most difficult part—or you will lose energy. Making the jumper work is merely a matter of using energy, not wasting it."

Parker climbed back into position on the jumper as WinLao again took a steadying grip on the machine. "After some practice you will not need help in starting, Rob Rrt," said the Par'zman.

Parker shouted "Okay," WinLao released the machine and Parker bounced it into the air again. This time as he landed he had his knees bent ahead of time, flexed them to drive the spring downward, felt a gratifying shove as the pole lifted into the air, still by a matter only of inches, but higher than Parker's own starting jump had carried him. The third time the pole left the ground it rose, Parker guessed, nearly a foot, but as it came down the landing was a little off vertical and Parker leaped aside, clutching the device to avoid a clattering crash.

Before he could speak WinLao said "Good for you. You will need some practice but you have the idea. I think I will go for a stroll at the bazaar. You keep working, Rob Rrt, I will be back in a while. VouLa, do you wish to come along?"

The girl said "I think I will stay and watch Rob Rrt."

WinLao disappeared. Parker asked the girl if she wanted to try the jumper but she said "No, you go on, I will watch. But I will help you start if you wish."

"Okay," Parker said, and set up for another practice run with the girl steadying the jumper.

Before long the aviator was getting higher into the air with each attempt, using the machine with increasing confidence although still, each time he plummeted to earth, he felt for a moment as if he were going to crash helplessly. There came to him the picture of a parachutist he had once seen, whose chute had failed to open. Miraculously the man had escaped with only two broken legs, and had lived to jump again—after three years in and out of military hospitals.

Still—Parker thought—if you don't panic, and if you use the jumper right, it takes the impact.

Finally, sweating heavily, half winded, he tried a last series of jumps, watching VouLa shrink from life size to child size as he rose, then grow back as he fell. A few bounds later, Parker looked down from his high point and the girl was the size of a doll. Then a figurine. The next time Parker rose, the jumper carrying him like a javelin hurled straight from the earth, he did not look down but turned his eyes eastward, back toward the volcano's inner wall and the sea and the Country beyond.

He had cleared the lip of the crater! Only for a moment was the sun-glittering sea beyond visible, and beyond it for a still briefer instant the black line of the Palmer Peninsula where lay both Relore and Teras, then he was dropping again, faster and faster, past the rim, past the naked rock within, past the first scrubby bushes and grass, to the green hillside from which he had risen. This time he reversed the timing of his actions, bending his knees when they should be held straight, flexing when they should be bent, and felt the offset as the mechanism of the jumper drove him into a much lower leap. A few repetitions and he stood once more on the grass.

He lowered the jumper to the ground as VouLa ran to him and took both his hands in hers. She danced once around him, pulling him in a circle so that he faced her, and chattered "That was marvelous, Rob Rrt, you have learned it in a morning better than I can do it with all my practice."

Parker looked at the girl's face and read something like hero worship there. You'd think I was Oscar Robertson, he said to himself.

He sat with VouLa and absently chewed a samra seed waiting for WinLao to return. When the Par'zian inventor did, he asked Parker how he had done. Parker told him and WinLao said "Then you are ready to use the rotors. Come, I will show you how they work."

He picked up the jumper, held it upright with one hand. "The mechanism is simple," he said. "When you reach your highest point you must raise the blades"—he flipped the four wooden vanes into their horizontal position—"and fix them in place"—he set the lock on the revolving hollow cylinder atop the jumper shaft—"quickly."

He dropped the rotors and raised them a few times while Parker watched. "You must get them up quickly and locked, because if you are already coming down fast before they are up and spinning, they will snap off. I know that," he said ruefully. "Come, try it," he said.

Parker stood beside the Par'zman, worked the rotor mechanism of the jumper. At first he could not get the catch set, then he caught on to the trick.

"Good," said WinLao. "Now, stand here and do it some times to get the feel of it. When you are fully ready, use the jumper to get high into the air, then set the blades. They will quickly catch the air and spin around so that you come down slowly. Do not try it from a low jump or the blades will not have time to take hold of the air."

Again Parker climbed into position on the jumper, took a small, tentative leap into the air with it, then bounded to a higher point, then higher and still higher until he caught once more the fleeting flash of seascape and distant land. He let himself fall, fall with alarming speed, he bent his knees, felt the heavy impact of the jumper and his own weight as they struck the ground, his knees flexing to add a final bit of energy to the tightening spring.

He saw the faces of VouLa and WinLao, the city and the lake of Par'z behind them in a momentary panorama of arrested unreality as he seemed to pause for the briefest fragment of a second on the ground. Then they blurred, flashed from vision, brown blobs against a blurred green and blue background as the whole valley sped from beneath Parker's feet. The jumper shoved, hurled him skyward; like a bronco-riding cowhand Robert Leroy Parker clutched the jumper waist-high with one hand, with the other grasped the rotor-mounting cylinder.

The edge of the volcano dropped beneath his feet, he could see clearly now, far across the blue sea that separated Par'z from the Country, could see clearly the land of the peninsula, caught even the suggestion of a black speck far to the north that might have been the Wall of Teras. He flipped the rotor blades into position, locked them in their place, dropped his hand to grasp the jumper pole now with both.

He felt a sudden tug upward, clutched tighter onto the machine, looked upward to see the four polished vanes windmilling above him, spinning first slowly, then faster and faster until they blurred, became merely a shining circular umbrella through which he could clearly see the sparkling blue sky above Par'z. Gracefully Parker drifted earthward. None of the dizzying rush of air and vision of the freely plummeting jumper this time.

Instead Parker felt a cool breeze as the air rippled his baggy-armed Par'zian shirt, now dirty and sweat-soaked, brushed his naked sweaty cheeks. Before his eyes the Country and the sea dropped beneath the black rock horizon of the crater lip, the rock and the brush and the grass passed again, slowly this time and with a strange dreamlike grace—Parker wondered if the effect was a lingering effect of samra—until he landed, not as gently as he had thought he might, but more gently than he had from previous long descents on the jumper with the rotors not raised.

Parker jumped from the machine and stood holding it. To him, WinLao said "That was perfect! Are you sure you have never used a device like this before?"

The flier considered a moment before answering "Well, never anything quite like your machine, WinLao." Then he added "If it's all right, I'd like to try one more, ah, flight. I want to try something a little different this time."

"What would that be?"

"I want to try steering as I come down. I think if the flier tilts his body he can travel laterally as he descends. Didn't you ever try that?"

"Never. But if you wish to, Rob Rrt, you may."

VouLa added "But be careful."

"I will," Parker told her. He climbed back into the stirrups of the machine, was soon bouncing with it higher and higher into the air. On a really hard-packed pad, this thing would perform even better, Parker told himself. Again he saw the rim of the volcano even with his face, again experienced the quick flashes of VouLa and WinLao, sun-bright buildings and glittering sail-dotted lake as he dropped back to the earth and rose again.

This time he made certain that he was well above the crater's lip, the seascape beyond clearly in sight, before he flipped the blades to their horizontal setting. Again there was the quick tug, again Parker tightened his grip on the jumper shaft as he began a slow descent. But this time he leaned forward slightly instead of holding his body and the tiny autogyro vertical. He felt the device pick up speed slightly in its descent as a little air was spilled off the ends of the broad, tilted rotor blades.

But Parker also felt the rush of air that told him that he was moving horizontally at the same time that he dropped toward the green base from which he had risen. He relaxed his arching muscles, felt himself and the jumper drop back to vertical, felt the quickened descent of the machine slow once again. Now he leaned backward, tilted the jumper shaft toward himself, felt again the increase in speed and, looking downward, traced his horizontal motion.

The jumper tipped farther, Parker felt a moment of fear, struggled to right it, succeeded nearly in tipping it completely on its side into a murderous plunge toward the ground, managed to bring it back to an upright position. Shaken, he allowed himself to drift to the ground beneath the windmilling blades without further aerobatics. But, he told himself, he had proven what he had set out to prove: that the jumper could be maneuvered in air, could be used to travel over obstacles and descend on the opposite side.

He was more firmly convinced than ever that it would make an effective invasion craft if it fell into the hands of Teras.

On the ground again Parker returned the jumper to WinLao Draa Xi-Tretret. He warned the Par'zman again to beware the three Terasians in the crater but WinLao, obviously enchanted with the new idea of travelling horizontally through the air, would speak of nothing but the greater sport it would provide through the Par'zian aeronautical community he hoped to found.

In despair, Parker asked VouLa to take him to the house of the three Terasians.

"I will do as you ask," the girl told him, taking the pilot by the hand. "But I do not think we will find them at home."

"Why not?" Parker asked, "Where will they be?"

"Beyond the orchards," the girl said, "they have started something they call a farm. No one in Par'z ever heard of such a thing before. They dig up the ground in straight rows and plant seeds. They say they are growing food. Why, people ask them. In Par'z there is plenty of food on the trees and in the lake. Par'zmen plant seeds only to grow beautiful flowers for their pleasure.

"The Terasians say all people must work. They try to make Par'zmen work but Par'zmen will not. They even threatened to harm some who would not work, and Inz Xa Tlocc Xi-Vrannannan and other men brought weapons to stop them. It was terrible. No one in Par'z remembers such an occurrence.

"So they leave Par'zmen alone now, except when they try to talk WinLao into building jumpers for them. The rest of the time they are either working on their silly farm or shouting at each other. They shout a great deal."

Parker said "A pretty sounding bunch. The more I hear about Teras and Terasians the more they sound like some people in my own world. And the less I like them!"

This time the path VouLa led Parker skirted around the edges of the glittering city of Par'z. At the side nearest the miniature jungle beside the lake—what VouLa called the orchards—stood a house that the girl pointed out as that of the Terasians. "They built that quickly when they came," the girl said. 'No one knew why they were in such haste. We would have taken them in. Perhaps a place could have been found for them to stay as long as they are in Par'z. If it could not, they could have made a beautiful house for themselves. Par'zmen would have helped to create beauty.

"But they would accept no help, and worked quickly. Their house is ugly but they stay by themselves in it."

Parker looked at the new house. His estimate agreed with that of the Par'zian girl. "It's ugly enough," he said. "But maybe they like privacy and don't plan to stay long. VouLa," he asked suddenly, "did the Terasians say why they wanted to come to Par'z?"

The girl stopped for a moment, obviously calling up a recollection. "Chacla did," VouLa told Parker. "Chacla is the woman, their leader. The others are men, Mocles and Stacles. Oh, I do not even like their names! I think Mocles is her husband and Stacles her brother, or maybe it is the other way around, I cannot even remember."

"Their reason," Parker reminded the Par'zian girl.

"Yes, yes," VouLa went on, "she said that they had fled from the sea people. She said that at first, that they did not like their own people and had run away to Par'z to live.

"But after they were here a little while they changed their story. Now Chacla says that Par'z should make peace with Teras. That we are foolish and wicked to waste our lives in pleasure. That we should help the Terasians to come to our home place, and teach us to work and be disciplined like them, and they will send us guides.

"And they do not like our many ways. They do not like our many kinds of houses, and clothing, and many different gods. They say that there is one right kind of building, one right kind of clothing, one true religion, one good way to live. They say that all people should be the same. Why? We ask why all the time, and Chacla and Mocles and Stacles answered for a long time, but no Par'zman was convinced. We kept asking why. Finally they stopped talking to us, and said that we would see some day, and be sorry, and now they stay by themselves in their ugly house and their silly farm."

"Okay," Parker said. "Maybe they'll talk to me. Is that them?" he asked, pointing to three figures near the trees.

The girl stopped in her tracks. "Yes." Her voice, strong and angry until now, was little more than a whisper. Parker looked down at her, saw that she was struggling not to show her fear of the three outlanders working nearby with rudely made tools.

"All right, VouLa," Parker said. "You've brought me here and you've told me plenty. Why don't you go home or to the bazaar or someplace, you've done enough."

The look of gratitude in the girl's face made her, for Parker, more childlike than ever. His sister, his twin? No, more like a baby sister now, this strange girl so experienced and still so innocent. "Go ahead," Parker said. He hugged her as he would have hugged Trili, gave her a kiss on the forehead, then released her.

"Thank you, Rob Rrt," she said. "I will go home and change clothes, then meet you at the book shop in the bazaar. MykJo is my friend, I will go there and he will read his poetry to me. He loves to read his poetry when he can get someone to listen, or sometimes even when he cannot."

Parker looked after the girl briefly, watching her carry her ripe woman's body with a gawky adolescent's manner, then turned again to the three figures working in the field. They continued to work, ignoring him. Parker approached them, walking carefully between planted rows to avoid damaging their work. Maybe agriculture in Par'z was superfluous, but let each man do as he wishes, Parker quoted to himself.

A few yards from the three figures he halted. They still did not look at him. "My name is Robert Leroy Parker," he said loudly.

Three brown faces turned toward him. They were so alike that he had to stare for a moment to tell that the

closest to him was the face of a woman. All three wore
their hair chopped off straight across at the base of the
skull. They wore identical long-sleeved jackets of dark
cloth, hanging loose over the tops of identical heavy trousers of the same dark color and material. All wore heavy
work shoes. They still did not speak.

"You are from Teras?" Parker asked. "You are
Chacla"—he looked straight at the woman—"and Mocles
and Stacles?"

"What do you want?" the woman asked him.

"Look," Parker said, "I'm a stranger here myself."

The three Terasians looked at Parker now. They stood
silent for a long moment, then the woman spoke again:
"Explain what you mean!"

Oh-oh, Parker thought, this babe is bad news. Still, if
he was to see his plan through, to learn what he could
in Par'z and then go on to decide what came next, he'd
best learn what he could of Teras as well. And if these
three beauties were agents of Teras rather than refugees
—where did that leave Parker? He was neither Par'zman
nor Terasian, the struggle was not his struggle.

But, he told himself, this was no classic-style war nor
was he able to hold himself neutral and aloof while the
childlike and inoffensive Par'zians were enslaved.

"What I mean, Chacla—"

She cut him off: "In the compeerage of Teras you
would address me as Chacla-sib. In time all the children
of God will be of the compeerage. You will use the
proper form of address."

Damn! Some people won't let you even try to be
friendly. Parker tried again: "What I started to say was,
I'm not a Par'zman." Before he could say any more, the
Terasian woman interrupted again.

"You are not a Par'zman, eh? You are certainly no
Terasian, I can tell that."

Parker wondered if his accent sounded strange to
Chacla—hers did to him, although the Terasian speech
was closer to the Relori in its sound than was the
Par'zian.

"Are you a Relori, then?" the woman asked with a
sneer.

"What's wrong with the Relori?" Parker asked her.
"Aren't they children of God too?"

"Vermin!" the woman raged, "Scum and vermin, that

is what the Relori are. By living they blaspheme. They are the surplus infants of Teras, given by God and intended to be given back to him. Those scavengers steal the offerings of Teras, and our rulers let them live. But a day will come, a day will come after Par'z is taken. You will see if still you live, all men will be of the compeerage but there will be no Relore!

"And you, I can tell you are no Relori. Simple hunters and fishermen, the Relori. Who are you, tell me!"

"Okay," said Parker, "I'm an American. I came from a place far from the Country, far across the sea." At least I think that's the truth, he said to himself. "I'm trying to find a way to get home."

"How did you get here?" she demanded.

Parker looked more closely at the three hard faces of the Terasians. In the face of Chacla he saw a mixture of ugly emotions: suspicion, fanaticism, hatred of all that differed from her own idea of righteousness. She fingered the hilt of a foot-long dagger, broad based, tapering to a stilleto-like point.

You'd use it, too, without much hesitation, Parker thought. In the faces of the other Terasians he saw . . . something similar to the expression of the woman, but not identical. A dull look, of numb obedience rather than fanatical dedication. A blankness toward the stranger, and—perhaps—the merest hint of dubiety.

The men were armed like the woman, but carried farm tools too, one a hoe, the other a crude wooden stick such as Parker had seen in King's Ferry, used for poking seed-holes in turned soil. They watched dumbly as Parker talked with Chacla—or Chacla-sib.

"I got here," Parker said, "by a ship, and then by a"—there was no local word for helicopter—"by a machine something like WinLao's jumper. Only much larger and more powerful."

"Where is your machine now?"

"Long gone, Chac-" he stopped himself from using her name, avoided the problem of adopting Terasian custom of starting another argument, "my machine is long gone, a total wreck, and the wreckage completely lost. I have no idea where it is."

"We will see about that," the woman snapped. "But if you are from a far country that has such powerful machines, you may be able to make a contribution to the compeerage. Teras would not be ungrateful to one who helped bring the ways of rightousness to the rest of the Country. The fool WinLao will not work with us, he will regret that if he still lives. But if you are able to help, Parker-sib. . . ."

As the Terasian woman spoke, she attempted an ingratiating smile. To Parker's horror, he realized that the woman's face, set in a stern expression, at least looked natural. When she tried to play coy, he did not know whether to recoil in disgust or burst into laughter. Instead of either he restrained himself and said "We can see about that later on. But I don't understand why you hate the Par'zmen. If you don't like their way of life—hell, I don't exactly agree with all play and no work myself, but so what? They're sealed off in here, they don't even try to get out. What harm can they do to Teras, or to anybody?"

"Ah, Parker-sib, you may yet be trained to obey that which is right, but you clearly do not understand. Par'z *exists*. It is *here*. The life of these frivolous, undisciplined fools is an abomination. No decent person can rest until they are brought to heel. Can you not grasp the obvious morality of that? The righteous cannot permit the wicked to sin, just because the sinners leave the righteous alone. To permit sin is to condone sin, to condone sin is to sin."

Oh boy, Parker thought. "And the Par'zmen are all sinners," he filled in for the Terasian woman.

"Yes! They waste their lives in useless pleasure. They dress in gaudy and ostentatious clothing—I see that foul shirt of yours, Parker-sib, but I am glad to see that it is stained with the sweat of decent labor."

Parker looked down at his shirt of golden satin, mourned the mess he had made of it and wondered if the Par'zian tailor would be offended if he showed up in it looking for another.

"And they have no sound religion," Chacla ranted on, "some of them are godless and some have many gods and even those who have only one god have no decent concept of guilt, or shame, or the need for labor. Wicked fools! You would have us tolerate such viciousness, Parker-sib? You will learn better than that!"

"Uh, yes, well, ah, maybe so," Parker said. "Maybe I will at that. But what I was wondering was, umm, what you three plan to do."

The look of suspicion came back into Chacla's eyes. "They plan nothing," she said, indicating her two companions. "I am the senior member of the compeerage present, I am the commander. What I plan to do is work for the good of the compeerage."

"Well, yes," Parker agreed. "I'm sure you are. But I wondered if you were planning to leave Par'z any time soon, or just stick around and try to convert the ignorant natives, that s all."

She looked at him strangely. "Convert the natives? You mean bring them to understand the will of God? Do not be as naïve as they are, Parker-sib, if you would have a role in the new day of the compeerage. We will convert them when we come with heavy sticks. If we could get our land-cars into Par'z we would roll over them in a day. Armed soldiers will take longer, but we will conquer. We will destroy the edifices of sin. We will bloody and shame the sinners. We will kill those who resist, and more, as a lesson to the rest. Then . . . those who survive will convert themselves.

"Will you be with us?"

Parker tried not to show his disgust. What was the difference between Hitler and Stalin, he thought, and Teras. Conquest called liberation. Murder called justice. Tyranny called morality. "Give me a while to think about it," he said. He looked into the three faces. He turned around and walked back along the row of turned, rich soil, halfplanted with a crop that no one needed. Potatoes, I'll bet, was what he told himself. They would be growing potatoes.

Near the end of the row, stepping carefully to avoid the Terasians' plantings, he turned and looked back. The two men had bent to work, Chacla standing over them watching every move. One of the men raised his head for a moment and looked in Parker s direction. Parker saw Chacla move her mouth, speaking to the man, and gesture harshly. He dropped his head and returned quickly to his work.

Parker wondered whether it had been Stacles or Mocles who had looked after him at the cost of a reprimand from Chacla-sib. With a tiny shock the American realized that he did not even know which of the two Terasian men *was* Stacles, which Mocles. Not that it matters, Parker told himself. Those Terasians all look the same to me. Even the woman.

He skirted the end of the field, gave the Terasians' rude shelter a careful berth, and headed for the city of Par'z. Its shining colored roofs and wildly varied architecture brought a small, trembling thrill to him as he looked momentarily at the Terasian structure again. Always, he thought, always the victim and always the bully. He thought for a moment of Carlos, dead now for seventeen years. Seventeen million years?

Parker headed for Par'z and the bazaar, for Vou La Uax Xu-Ruhjaruhj at the book shop of Myk Jo Mocc Xi-Nrenren. When the Terasians came, if VouLa and MykJo survived, they would receive nice short functional sib-names, and VouLa would probably do all right in baggy brown clothes hoeing a field. MykJo would surely die.

MykJo would be the more fortunate of the two.

Parker found the bazaar himself, shouldered his way through crowds of Par'zmen shopping and chattering, men and women examining trinkets and clothing, sandals and small works of art, choosing carefully before spending precious appreciation with eager shopkeepers.

Parker looked around in the open area about which the many shops were crowded. He let his eye wander from pleasure to pleasure, from slim girl to rounded woman to well-formed man, from colorful sari to toga to blouse and trousers to kilt, from glowing warm tones of orange and maroon and gold to nearly incandescent reds and blues, and striking pure white and deepest black setting off smooth brown skins and lustrous black hair. And for a moment, across the throng, a glimpse of a drab brown, baggy jacket that disappeared all but instantaneously into the colors of the crowd.

Parker worked his way from the center of the bazaar to the edge, where storefronts pressed against the open square and Par'zman traded with Par'zman. He passed bright, colorful shops and dingy ones, crowded shops and quiet. At last he reached the book shop of MykJo Mocc Xi-Nrenren, slipped quietly in.

The thin-bodied, sallow-faced poet sat on a table wearing only a grimy loincloth that had once been white and a skullcap streaked with bands of reflective color. In his lap an open book lay. He read aloud from it in a reedy, cracking voice, his head nodding and bobbing as he read, the glossy cap catching the flickering light of a greasy oil lamp even in the daytime, throwing back its light in streaks and blurs that made the cap look like a spinning, twirling, whirring disk, that made Parker, as he watched the play of light, think of bright sunlight reflected through the whirling blades of a propeller.

At the poet's feet, sitting in identical cross-legged posture, Parker saw VouLa. She had obviously been home and changed her clothing again, to a crimson skirtlet that fell in pleats nearly to her knees. She wore silvery slippers and about her neck and shoulders a filigreed ornament of spidery silver that fell away to tinsel-like stalactites that traced glittering lines of reflected fire across her bosom.

She looked up at Parker as he entered the shop, gestured him to silence. The poet continued his reading of strange verse, incomprehensible to the American but obviously holding an almost hypnotic enchantment for the girl. Maybe it's better on samra, Parker thought.

At last MykJo closed the book and looked up. He acknowledged the presence of the pilot with a tiny nod, then said to VouLa "That is all I have done of Garm Forty Four. I am not entirely satisfied with the meter yet, and I would like to find a better rhyme for transmute. But it seems to be coming along."

"Oh, yes," VouLa said in a half-breathless voice, "I think it will be one of your very best, MykJo. Do you not agree, Rob Rrt?"

"Well, I do not know MykJo's other works," Parker replied, "so I can't really compare. But I can tell you that I have heard no better poetry since arriving in Par'z."

"I can tell that you are very perceptive of literary values," MykJo said to Parker. "Even if you do not know Par'zian verse as yet, you seem to have an instinctive grasp of that which is truly fine." MykJo slid his feet from under him, dropped them to the floor beside his table and stood facing Parker. VouLa also stood. "Have you come to discuss books?" MykJo asked hopefully.

"I'm afraid not," Parker told him. The poet's face fell. "But I would like to return and discuss books some time," Parker said. "The only thing is, just now, VouLa promised to take me to meet someone and I have to discuss things with him very urgently."

MykJo said "Oh," sadly.

"But another time," Parker told MykJo. He turned to the Par'zian girl. "Are you ready, VouLa?"

The girl nodded quickly, took Parker's arm and moved with him to the door of the shop. As they reached the door that led back to the open area of the bazaar, Parker caught a glimpse of a brown-jacketed figure scurrying away. He thought to pursue but VouLa had pulled back into the book shop by a step, said "Thank you, MykJo, I will come back to hear more."

By the time the girl returned to his side—a matter of seconds only—Parker had lost sight of the brown-clothed figure.

"We'll go now to see the king of Par'z, all right?" Parker said to the girl.

"Yes, Rob Rrt," she replied. "That is, I am fairly certain that he is the king. He is a very nice old man, and comes and plays a tune at the house where each newborn child lies in Par'z, and does the same each time there is a death. Yes, king is what we call him. But most of the time people just call him by his name, XaoQa."

They had crossed the full width of the bazaar now, passed from the busy marketplace and turned a short distance down a less crowded street. They halted outside a house of unprepossessing size, but one covered with an incredible mosaic of multicolored carven stone, each stone a different shade from its neighbors, each formed to a different musical instrument, some of obvious function, others of a nature enigmatic to Parker.

There were clearly horns, and drums, bells, cymbals, gongs, harplike things and other stringed instruments, containerlike shapes that might be sounding boxes or even rattles. They came in all sizes, from something that looked like a bull-balalaikda to tiny triangular plates that might be finger cymbals, from a giant curving thing that could pass as an alphorn to tiny, tiny cylinders that might be soprano oboes of nearly supersonic pitch.

From within the house, floating through the grille-work of the variegated walls to reach Parker's ears came a sound as of a small choir singing a haunting, wordless, refrain, an *a capella obligato* of tones that rose and sank, blended and wove in intricate harmony that called vaguely to Parker's recollection archaic religious music that he had once heard and found of no interest.

Taking the hand of the girl at his side, feeling himself like a child, Parker stepped softly, awe-struck, into the carven house. A single room opened before him, with arches of byzantine complexity leading to others beyond. The walls were polished and decorated, the ceiling painted as a midnight sky, the floor of reflecting, veined marble.

On a mat in the room sat a man. There was no choir. The seated figure looked old, by far the oldest person Parker had seen in Par'z—or, as he thought back, in the Country either. His pate was wholly without hair, his face not so much wrinkled as drawn tight by the years and the slowing processes of life. A few white hairs straggled from his chin. He was entirely naked, his wasted, hairless body a mocking caricature of that of a small and undernourished child.

The sound that sounded like a choir came from a fantastic wind instrument played by the wizened brown man. It stood on a single spindly leg, as thin and unsteady-looking as was the musician himself, but that held the thing up. The instrument had a single mouthpiece leading to a close-sewn leather sack; to this extent, Parker thought, it resembled a bagpipe.

At the other side of the sack finely carved cylinders protruded, each with a jumble of stops and slides. As the old man sat at the strange instrument his hands flew over the cylinders, opening stops, closing them, changing the position of slides; each cylinder gave a different tone, each movement of the old man's hands changed one of the tones, producing an effect uncannily like that of many human voices blending in wordless song.

At last the music ended. VouLa made a brief sweeping motion of her arms and waist, something that to Parker's eye could have passed for an impromptu version of a curtsy. "That was lovely, XaoQa," she said, "I have never heard that music before."

A smile creased the ancient brown face, spreading a tracery of lines from the corners of the old man's mouth and eyes. He extended a shrunken brown hand to the girl, who took it in hers and helped the old man to rise.

"Thank you," he said, "and thank you for your compliment. I was playing a polyphonic motet of Lassus that I learned in a samra journey. I think I am getting it as the composer intended, although he did not quite think that it would be played as I play."

"This is Robert Leroy Parker," VouLa told him. "Rob Rrt is from a far land beyond even the Country. He wishes to speak with you, XaoQa."

For the moment Parker did not know how to address the old man—royal etiquette was out of his line. He considered the military rule: junior officer sends his respect, senior officer sends his compliments. He rejected that, tried a deep nod of his head that nearly slopped over into a bow and said "I'm honored to meet you, sir."

The old man returned the nod. Well, that must at least have been acceptable, then. The old man asked, "Have you a birth or a death to celebrate?"

Parker answered, "No, I'm afraid you don't understand why I'm here." The old man looked puzzled. "You are the king of Par'z, aren't you?" he asked.

The old man's voice, thin and quavering, came: "I am XaoQa the piper. Are you not here about piping? That is my occupation. It is the duty of my family. Soon I will be gone and another Qa piper will celebrate for me."

Parker felt distress and embarrassment for the old man and wondered what he could say. If the old fellow was king of Par'z, he had obviously forgotten it in his dotage. To Parker's immense relief, VouLa spoke.

"Come, XaoQa, sit down. The motet was beautifully piped, but it has tired you." She led the old man to a chair and helped him to sit, then knelt at his feet and took his hand in hers as Parker watched. "XaoQa," the girl said, "you must remember your full name and tell it to Rob Rrt. He wants to learn things, and you know more than any man in Par'z, if you will remember them for him."

The old man sat silent for a long time. To Parker it seemed that he was lost in senile reverie. The flier expected the old man to say nothing, or at best to ramble of ancient inconsequentialities. But to the aviator's surprise when the old man spoke it was with a confidence and authority that belied the weakness of his voice.

"I am Xao Qa Fltt Xi-Pikikik the seventeenth the one hundred twenty third, Qa Fltt Xi king of Par'z, emperor of the far lands, ruler in abeyance of the salt seas, lord teacher and sacred piper of life and death. You have a petition?"

Parker shot a covert glance at VouLa. Her eyes did not

leave the face of XaoQa; her face held an expression that told Parker clearly she took the old man's claim seriously.

Parker said, "I, uh, do not know what place this is, Par'z and the Country. I do not know what happened to my own world, nor how I came here. I do not know what race of people you are, who inhabit Par'z and Relore and Teras. Do you know the answers to any of these, XaoQa?"

The old man rose from his chair, tottered wordlessly from the room. Parker whispered hurriedly to VouLa the only question he could frame: "Is this all for real?"

"He is very wise," the girl whispered back, "but sometimes he forgets. If he remembers all he knows he can tell you much."

The old man reappeared in the archway through which he had disappeared. He carried with him a thick, dust-covered book, brought it to his seat and once again lowered himself into the chair. He put the book in his lap and turned it so that Parker could see the spine and cover. It was a copy of the same geography that MykJo had given the flier; without being able to read the Par'zian script he could recognize that much of the marking. He cursed himself for a fool for not taking the time to study at least the pictures in the book when he had it at VouLa's house.

The old man opened the book, slowly turned pages as if seeking one in particular, stopped at last with the book open flat on his knees, said to Parker, "Does this picture mean anything to you?"

It was a map of the earth!

Parker knelt beside VouLa to get a closer look at the ancient map. The projection was an unfamiliar one and the ready guides of latitude and longitude, the compass rose and declination diagram of military maps were missing, the conventional symbols were different, the colors unfamiliar, the legend in the unreadable Par'zian script, but it was still, unquestionably, the earth.

He said, "It is the world."

"Yes," XaoQa said. "It is the world, as known by our ancestors before our enemies forced us to retreat to Par'z. We knew all the world, once. Now, few Par'zmen know that we ever knew of the world beyond our home place." Parker looked at VouLa, thought of her questions about the world beyond the crater.

"Do you see where you are?" the old man asked.

Parker looked for Antarctica, found it in a surprising position on the page. There was the continent, the Palmer Peninsula; he traced the islands from the Robert English Coast: big Alexander, then smaller Adelaide, then tiny Biscoe. He pointed to Biscoe Island, said to XaoQa, "This is Par'z."

"Very good," the old man grinned, "very good, Rob Rrt, few Par'zmen could find their own home on this map. Yes, here is Par'z, and here is the Country," he said, moving his dry finger across the narrow strait on the page, "here is Teras and here is Relore."

Parker traced a mental line from Biscoe Island back to McMurdo Sound, moved his imaginary marker eastward half a thousand miles and pointed to a remembered point. "Is this the location of the South Pole?" he asked, pointing. Before XaoQa could answer Parker raced ahead: "You do know what the Poles are," he half-asked, "you do know the shape of the earth, and that it turns on a canted axis?"

The old man smiled more broadly at Parker. "Better, better," he said. "I think not twenty men in Par'z understand that, Rob Rrt. Of course there is a South Pole, but why do you think it so near? It is about here." He pointed his finger at the map. Parker looked, his eyes goggling from his head. The old man was pointing at a spot near Wyndham, Australia!

"XaoQa," Parker said, "this map shows the world—the world I knew before whatever happened to me—but the Poles were here"—again he pointed to the spot near McMurdo, and with his other hand to the remembered region beyond Hudson's Bay—"and here."

The two men, the young man and the parched ancient, stared at each other. "Are you certain that the South Pole is where you showed me?" Parker asked.

"Quite sure," the old man told him. "If it were here"— McMurdo—"we could not live warmly as we do. Do you not know that the earth's poles are frozen, barren?"

"All too well," Parker said. He rubbed his jaw, staring at the map in the book held by the old man, trying to grasp the implications of what the map told him. Then: "If the poles are in new places," he said, "then the whole axis of the earth must have changed position. How could that be?"

The old man did not answer.

Parker went on: "Or the whole crust of the earth slipped." Was that any less incredible? Geologists spoke of continental drift, but that was a process that took tens of millions of years. Impossible! But if I really was frozen, Parker thought, how do I know how long I was out of things? If I was frozen really solid, if every body clock was stopped—completely—then time meant nothing. I could have been out for a couple of weeks or a couple of years . . . or a million centuries!"

Kneeling before the old man, staring at the familiar but distorted map on the ancient knees, Parker trembled at the thought. A million centuries. The empires of the earth were utterly gone. Not merely fallen but gone into dust and ashes, the dust returned to the earth, the ashes blown away. His world was forgotten. More than forgotten, totally effaced, gone as if it had never been. And he, a sport of the wildest improbability, lived again in another world, earth still, yes, but for all that, another world as much as if it had been the dying planet-sun of the energy vampires he had seen in the samra dream.

Return home? He dismissed the very thought now. Home had never existed, now.

Parker looked into the face of XaoQa, the ancient husk of a man a hundred million years younger than he. He asked, "And the people . . . the race of Man, are they all the same, in all the world?"

"I think so," XaoQa said. "We no longer know the men of far distant lands. But I think all men resemble one another. Was it not so in your time?"

Parker said, "No. There were brown men, yellow, black and white."

For the first time since the map had been produced, VouLa entered the conversation. "How nice that must have been," she said. "What interesting patterns they could make in dance. They could use colors differently in clothing themselves and in decorating their bodies!"

Parker had to laugh at that. "It wasn't always so simple, VouLa. There were some problems too."

"I cannot see why," the girl said.

"Well, never mind that now. They are all gone." He looked to XaoQa again. "The question is, where did they all go? And where did your race come from?"

XaoQa looked down at the map again. Pointing his finger at different lands he asked "Were the men of different colors separated in parts of the world? Were they of equal numbers?" He looked closely into Parker's face. "If they were to breed together, what was the result?"

Parker put his hand to his forehead and rubbed his head. "Let me see," he said. "Well, they were separate at one time, I guess, but in most of history there was commerce and travel between different lands and different races. And, uh—there is no word in your language for something else. Oh, men sometimes could own other men, and often they would capture men of different races for that."

"How strange," VouLa interjected.

XaoQa said nothing.

"Uh, I guess there was always some interbreeding," Parker said. "The children would share some of the characteristics of each race when that happened. In my own age transportation was becoming easier and easier, and armies travelled to foreign continents too. There must have been more crossing than ever."

"Ah," XaoQa nodded, "we are beginning to understand, are we not, Rob Rrt? And the number of people of the different colors?"

Again Parker stopped to think, trying to remember bits of data he had once come across, tossed aside as of no use, but maybe retained somewhere in the back of his brain. "Let's see," he said. "My country was mostly of the white race."

XaoQa and VouLa both looked at him questioningly. Parker felt a rush of blood to his face. "My ancestors were the . . . men who belonged to other men, that I told you about. They were brought from a different land.

"There must have been about two hundred million white people in my country." He looked at XaoQa to see if the number meant anything, but the old man only looked interested. "And about twenty million, uh, we brown and black people were called Negroes.

"Europe"—he pointed at the map on XaoQa's knees, indicating each continent with his finger as he spoke— "two hundred million more, mostly white. Russia, two hundred million more."

He pointed to India. "Five hundred million black and brown people." Africa. "Three hundred million, most of them black." China. "Seven hundred million, yellow."

Japan, southeast Asia, Indonesia. "Close to four hundred million more."

When Parker finished enumerating to his best recollection, XaoQa said, "I think your world was mostly brown or black or yellow people. In a passing of many years, is it not obvious what happened?"

CHAPTER

14

From behind Parker a voice, harsh yet restrained, almost to a whisper, an accent that grated on the flier's ears yet was not wholly new to him: he whirled and saw one of the Terasian men standing in the doorway of XaoQa's house. The man's whole posture spoke of a cowering, beaten soul while his face held hopeless entreaty.

"Parker-sib," the man said, "I am Mocles of Teras. Please, I must talk with you. I am sure the others are after me, please, you will help me. . . ."

The man's pleading voice was cut off as another brown-clad figure appeared behind him, lunged, pulled back and fled into the daylit Par'zian street. Mocles hung in the portal of XaoQa's house for seconds, his two hands convulsed on the pillars that flanked the opening, the expression of entreaty on his face giving way to an awful amalgam of terror and shock. He fell forward onto the marble floor, limp as a thrown dummy.

Parker did not stop to examine the man but vaulted over his prone figure, through the doorway and into the street beyond. The passageway leading away from the bazaar was deserted, the opposite direction Parker took, but a few running paces brought him to the milling market crowd. Pursuit was hopeless. The second figure—the second brown-clad Terasian, Parker was certain—was beyond overtaking.

Yet, the American thought, exit from the crater was limited to the Gate guarded by Inz Xa Tlocc Xi-Vrannannan or the jumper of WinLao. The gatekeeper would question a fleeing alien—Parker was certain that for all his philosophical flights, InzXa was competent enough a guardian. And Win Lao Draa Xi-Tretret was already alerted against the sea people.

Parker ran back to the piper's house. Within its portal the limp form of Mocles lay untouched. The aged monarch-musician had not yet been able to rise from his seat. VouLa stood beside XaoQa, her expression one of horrified surprise. And no wonder, Parker told himself, at the sudden introduction of murder into this most peaceful and free-wheeling of societies!

He knelt beside the Terasian, hurriedly dredging military first aid lessons from long closed chambers of memory. There was a wound in the man's back, not wide but deep, deep. There was almost no bleeding now but a red stain marked widely down the man's back and brown cloth covered left buttock, showing that a single great spurt of blood had followed the withdrawal of the weapon after its single murderous plunge into the Terasian's back.

Parker took his wrist, felt for a pulse and of course found none. No pulse at the throat or temple, no sign of breathing, the eyes wide and staring in horror and despair. Parker reached and closed them with one hand, acting from no respect for the dead but for the small peace of mind that might be salvaged for the three living still in the marble-floored room.

He looked at the wound in the man's back. Well, no surprise there either, except at the skill of the assassin. A single violent thrust. Presumably, Parker thought, with a Terasian dirk such as he had seen at the farm of the three foreigners. One thrust, passing between the ribs of the victim Mocles, severing the great vital muscles of the heart, severing the vital chambers of the heart, then the weapon withdrawn, no sound from the victim, no struggle, only one gout of red from the targetted back, and death in an instant.

Parker looked at XaoQa and VouLa. He said "I guess he really did want to get away from Teras. Maybe he ran away from the others, or maybe they sent him to spy on me and then Chacla sent Stacles to spy on him. Thus Teras treats her turncoats, anyway."

XaoQa had left the room. VouLa sat half collapsed in his chair, weeping and shuddering and cringing away from the corpse. In a moment the old man reappeared carrying a thick, curving horn. He stepped gingerly over the body of Mocles, lifted the unfamiliar instrument to his lips and sounded a piercing, wailing note. A handful of Par'zmen drifted over from the bazaar, stood silently watching the ritual of the dried old man and the dead young one.

The ancient Par'zmen lowered his mouthpiece, called in a high thin voice that matched closely the last wailing note "I am Xao Qa Fltt Xi-Pikikik the seventeenth the one hundred twenty third, Qa Fltt king of Par'z, emperor of the far lands, ruler in abeyance of the salt seas, lord teacher and sacred piper of life and death. All present hear me pipe the dirge of Mocles the Terasian, now dead in this place."

A response rumbled from the standing Par'zmen, indistinct to Parker's ears but obviously part of a ritual long memorized and half forgotten by the chanters.

Then XaoQa again lifted the curving, carven horn to his lips; it was a black horn, black as blackest midnight, polished and reflecting the Par'zian sun, a working of fine silver figures covering much of the smooth black instrument. From the ancient's withered lips came wind of surprising power, from the slivered black horn came a music like none Parker had ever heard. Low and sad it was, slow tempoed and crying loss, calling of ineffable distance, incredible remoteness and unknowable homes as far beyond the cosmic fastness of Parker's samra journey as that journey was beyond ordinary distance.

The sound rose and wailed, fell and throbbed, rose again in question that was half a promise and promise that was nothing but question.

The piping stopped. "Set's over" XaoQa sang.

"S'over" the witness chanted in response.

XaoQa turned back into his house, VouLa helped him to step over the body of Mocles. The old man disappeared with his black silver horn.

"Will he come back?" Parker asked VouLa.

She said yes, and very soon the old man returned from his inner chamber and sat again in his chair as if nothing had happened at all. Parker turned toward the doorway. The body of Mocles was gone, and with it any sign that the man of Teras had ever been in the doorway of the house.

Parker looked toward the old man once again. "XaoQa,"

he asked, "Mocles was killed by one of his Terasian companions. Have you any law in Par'z, any method of dealing with this?"

"I am XaoQa the piper," the old man said. "Is it a birth or a death that calls for my piping?"

"Nothing, nothing, XaoQa," Parker said. "We had merely come to visit you and to hear you play. Thank you, XaoQa, it was fine music."

Parker drew the girl VouLa to her feet. The old man too reached up a hand for help. Parker and VouLa assisted him to his feet. He smiled his thanks, tottered to his floor mat and took up his Par'zian baghorn again. Parker and the girl slipped from the house as XaoQa, clearly oblivious to their leaving, returned to his music.

In the narrow street outside Parker asked the girl if XaoQa was often like this.

She said simply "He is very old. He is a good man and everyone loves him. When he remembers he is Qa Fltt king of Par'z he is also very wise. When he forgets and is just XaoQa the piper. . . ." she ended her speech with a shrug of brown shoulders, glittering silver.

"The killing must have shocked him," Parker said. "I hope he'll remember himself. But, VouLa, I still must know, what is the result, in Par'z of murder?" At least there's a word for murder, Parker thought. If they have the word, maybe they understand the thing and have an answer.

"I do not know," the girl replied. "One man killing another . . . has it ever happened in Par'z? We know what war was. And the keeper of the Gate killed many men in ancient times, before the creatures that guard the tunnel were made. But this is no war. I do not understand this killing. Is there something we should do?"

"Anywhere else . . ." Parker started to say. Anywhere else he had ever heard of, there was murder enough and assault, rape and robbery and all the ugly rest, to lead to a complex criminal code. Even in Relore, as Broadarm had described things, there was a code, although a simpler one than Parker had known before. But in Par'z there had been no crime for—how long?—before today. "You have no way of . . ." Parker tried again, ". . . you don't know what to do about violence?"

The girl only looked frightened and puzzled.

"No one knows?" Parker asked.

"Maybe InzXa," VouLa said.

"Good idea," Parker said. "Do you want to come with me to see him?"

Again VouLa was weeping, more quietly now. He wanted to help her somehow, but knew of no way. He reached for her arms, drew her to him in the street. The girl buried her face in his shirt while his strong hands steadied her shaking body. Like a heart-broken youngster the brownskinned child-woman held the broad collar of Parker's splendid golden shirt, wiped her tear-wetted eyes.

She leaned back, still held by the aviator. "Thank you, Rob Rrt," she said, managed a weak smile for him. "Please, I would rather go home now and rest. You need not take me. InzXa would almost certainly be at the Gate now. Go and talk to him if you must."

"All right," Parker said.

"Please come back to me later, Rob Rrt," said the girl.

He said "I will," and released her. He watched her disappear into the bazaar. He turned around, trying to get his bearings, finally located the western wall of the crater and set off to reach the little guard house and Inz Xa Tlocc Xi Vrannannan, the hereditary keeper of the Gate.

Parker made his way through the twisting streets of the city, at last broke through to grassy hillside and climbed toward the Gate of Par'z. At a distance of some hundred yards he called and waved but the gatekeeper and his two assistants were immersed in conversation and none looked up at the approach of the aviator.

He came closer until he stood beside the three Par'z-men. They still continued to talk. Parker waited for a break in the conversation, finally gave up and interrupted. "InzXa," he said loudly. The Par'zmen continued to talk. "InzXa, listen to me!" Parker said.

The gatekeeper looked at Parker. "Oh, hello, Rob Rrt. I did not know that you were interested in the quasirealistic coordinates of interior theoretical hypergeometry. What a nice surprise. Here, join our little discussion group. This is. . . ."

"No!" Parker cut him off. "I am not interested in theoretical anything! Listen to me, InzXa, something terrible has happened in Par'z and nobody seems to be doing anything about it. XaoQa is practically in a state of shock and nobody else even seems to care."

"What, what has happened?" the Par'zman asked.

"Murder!" Parker said.

The Par'zman only repeated the word, his voice indicating more of puzzlement than any other reaction.

"Murder," Parker said again. "One of your three Terasian self-styled refugees, Mocles, is dead. One of the others killed him, stabbed him from behind, in the heart. I think it was the other man, Stacles. Stabbed him in the back, between two ribs, right through the lung into the heart."

"Remarkable," InzXa said. He turned to one of the other Par'zmen with him and began "EntRrj, this may have considerable bearing upon our recent discussion of the higher religio-philosophical implications . . ."

"InzXa!" Parker roared.

"Eh?"

Parker tried to control himself, to speak calmly. "InzXa," he said again, "try to forget about theories and abstractions for a minute, can't you?"

The gatekeeper looked blankly at the fiier.

"A man has been killed in Par'z," Parker said. "Murdered. Stabbed in the back by another man." Parker stared at the Par'zman's face, struggled desperately to hold his attention on the reality of the moment. "InzXa, do you understand what I'm telling you?"

The Par'zman nodded yes.

"Okay," said Parker. "Now, you seem to be the closest thing in this crater to any kind of . . ."—the words were missing, Parker did his best to find approximations that would mean something to the Par'zman—". . . sheriff or lawman of any kind. XaoQa can't help us. There's no such thing here as . . . dammit, there isn't even a word!" He had to use the English, *police.*

"InzXa, this is serious." Oh, Christ, Parker thought, I used one English word and I'm losing 'this guy again! "InzXa, you have to come down into the city and do something. I'll help you. I'll go by VouLa's house and get my friendmaker and we'll get the Terasians."

The Par'zman looked soberly at Parker. "Oh, I fear I could never do a thing like that," he said calmly.

"Why the hell not?"

"Oh, well, you see I am the three hundred seventy-ninth hereditary keeper of the Gate of Par'z. I defend the city against invasion."

"Yes, yes," Parker blurted. "Sure you do. So what!"

"Oh," the Par'zman smiled innocently, "I could never interfere with the internal affairs of Par'z. My charge is to defend the Gate. That is my sole official capacity. Within the city, I am a private citizen. I could never go charging about with my weapon bared, frightening people and avenging things that you say happen.

"At that, Rob Rrt, I must say that you yourself have even less official standing in Par'z. At least I am a resident, you are merely a visitor."

Parker threw back his head and sought aid from the blue sky. None came. He made a final attempt. "InzXa, please." The gatekeeper looked calmly at Parker but showed no sign of changing his attitude. Parker looked at InzXa's two assistants. They looked even less interested in doing anything. "Any of you," Parker said, "do you know what I'm saying? Murder! In Par'z. Aren't you going to do anything at all?'

The two assistants stood silently. InzXa looked down and said, as if he were chagrined at some minor social error, "Perhaps I should not have let the three sea people enter the Gate. I did not expect them to behave in an unruly manner. I am sorry about it. But now they are in Par'z, I cannot pursue them."

Then the Par'zman's face lighted as he made everything right again. "I will not admit any more sea people," he said.

Parker gave up. "Okay," he said. "Don't let any more in. And do me one more favor, InzXa, don't let the others out either. Will you promise me that? Especially if they're carrying something that looks like WinLao's jumping machine. Hold them here and get word to me, will you?"

"Oh, anyone may leave Par'z," the gatekeeper said. "But I will not let them take the machine until you get here."

In despair and disgust, Parker spun and headed back downhill. He stopped at the house of VouLa and her family and found the girl alone, reclining on a luxurious pallet of silks and furs. He wondered where furs came from in Par'z: other than a few domestic animals in the city, he had seen no fur-bearing creatures within the crater. In the miniature jungle beside the lake, that Par'zmen called the orchards? Wild beasts? Well, perhaps, unlikely though it seemed. Still, InzXa had mentioned meat from beasts.

Parker squatted beside VouLa and touched her gently upon one arm. She looked at him and said, "What happened at the Gate? Will InzXa help?"

Parker shook his head, no.

"He was your only hope, Rob Rrt. In our home place we all live at peace. Little children learn to leave others to go their ways. If even the keeper of the Gate cannot help, no one in Par'z can."

"I expected as much," Parker told her. "I'm tempted to take on the other Terasians alone, damn it, but they're rough characters, the women as bad as the man, maybe worse. And if you Par'zman won't lift a finger to save yourselves . . ." He looked at VouLa. She merely returned his look, an expression of puzzled fright in her face.

"I don't know," Parker resumed. "I don't think you're stupid. You're just . . . innocent. This whole place, your little country, your little city, your little jungle, your little lake, it's like a child's dream. Par'z is just one great big kindergarten, and you're all like children."

Still VouLa watched him, leaning now on one elbow, not speaking.

"I can't just adopt a whole miniature nation as if they were—you were orphans. Do I look like the welfare department?"

Again the girl began to cry softly. She said, "Rob Rrt, what should we do? InzXa should never have let the sea people in, but he did. What can we do now?"

Parker said "Okay, you can do this much, keep Win-Lao from finishing his second jumper. It would be better if he took apart the one that is finished, let's say for modifications, and didn't get it put back."

VouLa nodded her head. She said, "I will go to Win-Lao. He has always been my good friend. I will tell him."

"Good," Parker said, "he didn't seem too impressed when I told him this morning. Will you go to him now, while I go to the Terasians again?"

The girl nodded assent to this too.

"All right. You go see WinLao. Try to make him understand what I couldn't get him to see, that not only his safety and his invention but the whole city of Par'z is in danger if those two get hold of two jumpers.

"I'll get out to the Terasians' farm and see if I can do any good there. I don't know what. And you'd better get my friendmaker—the sword-knife I left here before— for me. I don't want to visit those two again unarmed. We can walk together as far as the farm. Then you go on to see WinLao. Afterwards will you meet me at the lake again?"

When the girl agreed Parker added "When you leave WinLao you circle around to the lakeshore. I'll meet you by the water where your parents keep their boat."

The girl rose and left the room, returned quickly with Parker's friendmaker. He slit a carrying loop for the weapon in his trouser leg, slid the sword-knife into the loop, and told VouLa that he was ready to go. The girl threw a cloak around her shoulders and went with him.

On the way through the city to the Terasians' farm Parker asked VouLa what had happened to Mocles' body after the piping of the dirge.

"Didn't you see?" she asked in return.

"No, I was more concerned with XaoQa. When I looked back to the doorway, the corpse was gone."

"The other Terasians took the body," VouLa said. "The Par'zmen who had listened to the piping would have taken the body, but before they could take it. the sea people came and took it. Rob Rrt," she asked, "what will happen to Par'z? What will the Terasians do to us?"

Parker thought for a while before answering, as they continued to advance through the streets of the city. Finally he said "If they can get jumpers and get out, they'll head for home, I think. If their people haven't invaded Par'z in all these years they've hated you so, it must be because they just don't have anything like the jumper to carry them over the walls. Once they get a couple, if they can make hundreds and thousands of copies, Par'z will be finished.

"If they can't get jumpers . . . I don't know. I'm sure those two would like to set up a little dictatorship for themselves in Par'z, but I wonder if they could. There's no government machinery here to seize, so they can't just take over an existing system. I wonder if they could build up a force for themselves. Maybe they just wouldn't be able to get any henchmen to work for them. They could murder and terrorize individuals but if there's no structure to control, then maybe they just couldn't ever really run the place.

"Still, I wouldn't want to risk it if I could help it."

They had reached the edge of the city now. The ugly shelter of the Terasians was nearby. Beyond it, in their newly plowed field, Parker could see the two surviving sea people. Beside them a dark mass lay unmoving on the earth. The sun was at the western rim of the crater of Par'z, about to drop below and throw the interior of the volcanic cup into a long shadowed dusk before true night descended.

"You go ahead to WinLao," Parker said to VouLa. "Remember what to tell him, and when you leave him, go the long way around. Don't come by here again."

The girl clutched her cloak tightly about her shoulders and arms, turned and ran off toward the inventor's home near his testing field. Parker felt for his sword, assured himself that it was handy and as sharp as it had to be. He squared his shoulders and started across the plowed land to the Terasians.

As he approached he heard the voices of Chacla and Stacles, hers pushing out strong and harsh, his no less unpleasant but less loud, with a beaten spiritlessness to it that set Parker to shuddering for a moment before he regained control of his body.

As Parker approached the Terasians he called to them "Listen, I want to talk to you. I. . . ."

Chacla interrupted him. "You will be still. This is the funeral service of Mocles. You will respect our practice, Parker-sib, if I may call you as one of the compeerage. You will wait quietly."

Parker drew up. Even the Terasians. . . . "I'm sorry," he started to say, "I didn't realize that. . . ."

"Wait quietly!" Chacla shouted at him.

He stood watching and listening to the two Terasians then, until their ceremony was over. He watched Chacla. She held a little book in her two hands, squinting to read it in the fast-falling shadow of Par'zian dusk. The man Stacles held an identical volume.

The Book of Common Prayer? Parker wondered. Or *The Thoughts of Chairman Mao?* Or did it matter with people like the people of Teras?

Chacla said loudly, half as if to Stacles and Parker, half in prayer to a slightly-hard-of-hearing deity, "All life is given to serve the compeerage. All who live, live to work for the strength of the compeerage. All deeds are for the compeerage. All words are for the compeerage. All thoughts are for the compeerage.

"Is it not so?"

The weak voice of Stacles responded "It is so."

Parker saw Chacla fix her countryman with a gimlet stare. The Terasian's eyes widened, his mouth trembled. More loudly than before, with a crack in his voice, Stacles repeated "It is so."

"There is no rest in life," Chacla resumed. She seemed hardly to look at her book now, seemed to Parker to know the words by heart. "There is no joy in life. There is no pleasure in life but the strength of the compeerage. Is it not so?"

Stacles answered quickly this time, and loudly, "It is so."

"In death there is no life. In death there is no joy. Even in death there is service to the strength of the compeerage."

"Service to the strength of the compeerage," Stacles read loudly.

"Life becomes death," Chacla resumed, "death becomes putrefaction, putrefaction becomes strength for the compeerage."

"For the compeerage," Stacles howled.

Chacla bent, Stacles bent. They shoved the dark form on the ground into a shallow trench dug between rows of turned earth. Both stood. Stacles lifted a tool from the ground and began to cover the trench with Par'zian dirt.

Chacla strode to where Parker stood, horrified at the Terasian funeral service. "At the end Mocles would have been a traitor to the compeerage," Chacla said. "Instead, he is now fertilizer for our crops."

Parker said nothing.

"You have come to say that you will join us, foreigner?" asked the Terasian woman.

"No."

"Fool," Chacla spat. "The Par'zmen will be slaughtered. The survivors will become our slaves. You could have been a satrap. You. . . ."

"I thought your precious compeerage meant brotherhood," Parker interrupted. "I thought you believed in equal work for all, equal reward for all. Now you're talking like plain conquerors."

"Of course all are equal in the compeerage," Chacla snapped. "Is it not so, Stacles-sib?" She faced the Terasian man.

"Oh, it is so, Chacla-sib," he murmured.

"But," Chacla went on, "virtue is rewarded and wickedness is punished. These Par'zian sybarrites must be taught a lesson."

"Uh-*huh*," Parker grunted. "And I suppose that virtue means submission to the compeerage and conforming to all your commands."

"Yes," Chacla rejoined. "Obedience to the will of the compeerage, for the good of the compeerage, is required conduct."

"And anyone who has different ideas?"

"We are not merciless, Parker-sib. If at all possible, sinners are permitted to repent, to serve the compeerage as reparation for former sins. In short, to remain alive. Only those who remain in defiance of the right must pay with their lives. Or a few who must die for reasons of state and virtue. Or those who must be taught a lesson like the Par'zmen. Or vermin whom we will exterminate in our own good time, like the Relori."

"In other words, knuckle under or die, is that it, Chacla?"

"Chacla-sib. I have told you, Parker-sib. I do not like to repeat. And I have told you, obedience is virtue, defiance of the will of the compeerage is not tolerated."

"And who decides the will of the compeerage?"

"Parker-sib," the woman dropped her voice, again assumed the disgusting, ingratiating air of their earlier conversation, "I tell you this now one time only. There are those whose duty it is to lead, those whose duty is to follow. Those to command, those to obey. Here, I command for the compeerage. Stacles obeys and lives to work. Mocles defied and is now acting in place of dung for our potato crop."

Parker laughed under his breath. Right about the potatoes anyway, he told himself. And Teras had a word for slave! To Chacla he quoted a line that popped into his mind from some long-forgotten source. "Some animals are more equal than others."

"Do not blabber nonsense," Chacla returned to her

overbearing way of speech. "You are a strong and clever man, Parker-sib. And I think you might know much that would be of value to the compeerage. I offer you a final opportunity to save yourself from death or slavery."

Parker's eyes popped at the last word.

"Do not be shocked, Parker-sib," Chacla said. "After we take Par'z there will be only two classes of persons, the members of the compeerage . . . and the slaves of the compeerage."

Parker quietly rested his hand on the hilt of his friend-maker. The carved and polished handle felt good in his palm, the bulk and reassuring firmness of the heavy-bladed weapon pressed against the outside of his leg. He measured Chacla and her acolyte Stacles with his eye, deciding what to do next.

Attack the two Terasians, here and now, fight them to the finish as a sort of preventive warfare? The idea did not appeal. Declare himself a sort of one-man committee of vigilance and avenge Mocles' death? Parker was nei-ther Terasian nor Par'zman—how could he give himself that jurisdiction, even in his own mind? Besides, with odds of two to one against him, he ran a good chance of winding up like Mocles. He did not want to die. But also —at least, so Parker told himself—if he should die the Terasians would be totally unchecked. With himself alive, at least there was somebody working against them.

Parker began slowly to back across the field, widening the space between himself and the two Terasians. He was far from certain that he was doing the right thing, but he had tried. There was obviously no chance of talking the Terasians out of their planned conquest. He quoted to himself again from some forgotten source: decide what's right, then go ahead.

But if you can't decide?

"You will regret your treachery, Parker!" Chacla shouted after him. She omitted the formal ending now. "You will probably die," she called. "If you become our slave you will wish you had died."

All Parker could think of to call in return was a Har-lem epithet that surely meant nothing to Chacla. But it made Parker feel better.

Parker got well out of range of a thrown Terasian knife or any quick silent rush before he turned his back on the two sea people. When he was past their crude home he turned and headed through the city again toward the edge of the lake. The city was becoming lighted now. The color and variety of its architecture and the wide ranging manner and dress of the people buoyed Parker's spirits, depressed by his confrontation with the Terasians and doubts about his own actions.

When he reached the lake Par'z was completely in the shadow of the lip of its volcanic crater but the sky above still held the azure brightness of afternoon. Parker wondered at the effect, decided that the sun must still be above the horizon of the western sea, lighting the waters of the Bellinghausen and the other cone of Biscoe—Par'z.

On the lake pleasure boats were already carrying lighted oil lamps at bow and stern. Par'zian music floated across the water. Tinny transistors on the Central Park boat lake, Parker told himself. He stood for a moment with his eyes closed, trying to recapture the feelings of familiarity. Dirty, noisy, crowded, and always with the man to worry about, still home was home. No loud commercials, no frantic announcers interrupted this music. At last Parker laughed and opened his eyes.

VouLa stood looking straight at him. She asked why he laughed.

"I'm afraid you wouldn't understand," he replied. "I just thought of Chacla selling bad breath on the radio."

"Chacla?" the girl asked. "What is radio? What do you mean?"

Parker said "Never mind, let's take a walk."

"Oh, yes," VouLa said, "but don't you want to look at me first? I went home and changed for you."

Parker looked at the girl.

"I feel much better now than I did," she said.

"You look lovely, VouLa," he said. He did look at her. She had painted her face, or had it painted by some artisan of Par'z. One entire side of her face was covered by the image of a fantastically plumaged bird, colors flashing from each closely delineated feather. The girl's eye, when she opened it, was the bird's. When she shut it, the bird shut his. A long, brightly colored beak crossed above her forehead against a background of painted blossoms, seemed poised a fraction of an inch above her other eye. When she shut that eye, the bird seemed to peck at a glinting jewel painted on the eyelid. The tail plumage of the creature swept around the girl's throat be-

hind her head and upward, sweeping up, her hair meta-
morphosed into gorgeous streaming feathers punctuated
with open blossoms and sparkling gems.

Parker gasped at the girl's outré beauty.

"Do you not want to see the rest of me?" VouLa asked.

"Sure," Parker said. To himself: this place may be
conquered and enslaved, and all she wants to do is hold
a fashion show. Well. . .

The girl spun once, gracefully, her blue-and-silver cape
floated high about her. She opened the catch that held
the cape at her throat and it slipped to the ground at her
side as she stopped her turning, again facing Parker.

Now he looked at her as he had not before. The girl
was entirely nude, but painted over all her body were
fantastic lines, pictures and abstract patterns in all colors.
Birds of incredible plumage flew from her shoulders,
jewelled filigree covered her arms. On her chest and as
far down as her ribs was a blossoming profusion of flowers from which the birds above had seemingly emerged,
the flowers seemed to cup and nestle her generous breasts,
bloom covering every inch of flesh, the very nipples tinted
as fragrant blossoms. Over her abdomen, her pelvis and
thighs and legs, the motif recurred, flowers and jewels and
birds, half realistic and half abstract, twining and blossoming, climbing and glittering in a dazzle of color.

"I apologize, VouLa," Parker said. "I told you a moment ago that you looked lovely. I was just being polite
to you. Now I see you, you are truly lovely. I have never
seen such a sight as you. I'm sure, I never will again."

The girl said only "Rob Rrt," and stepped forward toward him. In his nostrils a perfume came from her, a perfume of the flowers that covered her flesh.

Parker stepped close to the girl, looked down into her
wetly glittering eyes, the only part of her not covered
with fantastic decoration. He held her, felt the texture of
her flesh against him, naked beneath the painted fan-
tasies; he bent to her and kissed her upon her lips, at first
softly, the scent of her perfume rising through him as
they touched.

"VouLa," Parker said, "we have much that's important
to discuss, and serious."

She dropped her face, whispered almost inaudibly,
"Yes."

"In the morning," said Parker.

CHAPTER

15

Parker rolled over and blinked his eyes, then sat up in the Par'zian morning. Beside him lay the girl VouLa still asleep, her body a garden of blossoms and jewels, her face appearing as innocent as ever. Parker rose quietly, covered the sleeping girl with her own cloak and walked slowly to a stand of fruit trees to pick breakfast for the two of them. Sleeping with VouLa, he thought, could develop very easily into a habit.

He stood beneath a fruit tree for a few minutes watching a dawn mist rise slowly from the water. He looked upward to the fast lightening sky. The sun was not yet visible but its rays as it climbed from the Weddell Sea beyond the Country had already turned the eastern lip of the crater into a glowing cinder of red-orange. The mist around Parker held a scent of damp freshness; all of Par'z was silent. The world seemed freshly created, hushed for the imminent coming of life; today, Parker told himself, I must leave Par'z, or I will never go.

He reached up quickly, picked two large peach-like fruit from the nearest tree and walked back to the spot where VouLa lay. He knelt beside the girl in damp grass and watched her in silence for a time, marveling anew at the unreal beauty of her body, at the incredible experience of lying with this girl through a night of sensations that seemed halluncinatory even as they were truly taking place.

At last Parker touched the girl gently, on her lips, and spoke her name softly, repeatedly.

She held her eyes shut but took his hand in her two and placed it on her body. She said "Rob Rrt, has the day come?"

Parker did not answer the question, but placed the fruit he had brought on the grass and slid his now freed hand beneath the girl's shoulder blade. He dropped his own weight back on his heels and drew the girl upward so that they embraced, her cheek resting on his own, his one hand holding her upright while she held his other hand with her two hands, to her body between her breasts.

"I spoke with WinLao as you said to, Rob Rrt," she told him very softly.

Parker said nothing.

"WinLao said he would not finish his second jumper yet, but I think he will soon."

Parker said "Soon or late he will. He's too much of an engineer not to, and too proud of his invention. God help you all."

VouLa released Parker's hand with one of hers and picked up a peach. She held it to his mouth until he took a bite, then she did the same, taking the juice where he had broken the perfection of the fruit. In a moment she said "What will you do, Rob Rrt?"

"I will leave Par'z today," he said.

The girl showed no surprise. She said "You must, I suppose. You are a good man, Rob Rrt. I will be sad when you are gone, but I can see that you are not like us. The sea people are not like us either, but they are not good."

"I'm not just deserting Par'z," the aviator said. "If your people can handle Chacla and Stacles, they'll be safe here. But if the Terasians get hold of WinLao's jumper they'll build copies. I can show the Relori how to build jumpers too. Maybe we can save Par'z. If only your people would do something. But they're so innocent they won't even. . . ." he stopped. VouLa was smiling at him and offering another bite of peach.

After the two had finished their breakfast of fruit by the lake side they bathed, VouLa removing the paint from her body with Parker's help, then walked slowly through the now-light streets of the city, arms about each other, Parker, at least, loath to reach the girl's home, but at last they did, and walked through the house until they reached her own room, on the second storey, where Parker's Relori bow and boots and clothing were. VouLa lay upon the pallet of silks and furs while Parker removed his Par'zian shirt and trousers. Then he went to her, and lay with her; moving softly he kissed her upon every part of her body, and she him upon every part of his body, and at last they kissed each other again on the lips, and

Parker rose again and dressed in his Relori trousers and shirt, and fixed his sword at his waistband on one side and his quiver of arrows on the other, and drew his Relori bow down over one shoulder so he could carry it with his hands still free, and walked from the house.

He strode past Par'zman and Par'zwoman in toga and sari, past pagoda and igloo and XaoQa's house carved all of musical instruments, and passed the edge of the city and walked up the grassy hillside toward the Gate. At the Gate he met the accustomed three guardsmen. InzXa was not present but Parker recognized one of the other guards as a man he had met before.

"EntRrj, I am leaving Par'z," the American said.

"As you wish," the guard replied. "By our belief, you will find the trip out of Par'z more easy than that coming in. But remember, once you leave, you will almost surely never come back."

"I understand," said Parker.

The guard stood aside. Parker moved to the opening in the crater wall that was the Gate of Par'z. For an instant he hesitated, thinking of VouLa and of XaoQa, of WinLao the inventor and MykJo the bookman. Damn, Parker said to himself, I've lost the books I had from MykJo. Well, little matter. With the knowledge of the aged XaoQa there was little doubt that he was truly in the distant future, that there was little chance or none at all of ever reaching his home world again.

He regretted not bringing a fistful of samra seeds too, but if Parker once walked down the hillside again, he knew he would stay in Par'z forever. The life there was too pleasant, too easy, and there was VouLa, already like a child to Parker, and a sister, a mistress and a priestess, herself his Gate to worlds of dreaming pleasure in the samra journey and worlds of beauty and joy with her own flesh.

Parker drew his bow from over his shoulder, hurled it savagely ahead of him into the Gate of Par'z, dived headlong after it and began the tortuous wriggle through the same last passageway that he had taken into the dreaming world of Par'z less than three days and more than that many lifetimes ago.

He struggled through the end passage, out into the first room of the tunnel on his way from the crater. The breeze from the outside world still blew, gently and as steadily as it had when Parker had headed the other way, but now it carried a stench of rotting animal material that turned the pilot's stomach.

He worked his way from room to tunnel, from tunnel to chute to funnel to room, lighted always by the familiar yellow-green phosphorescence that meant the presence, at some time, of the tunnel slugs. When Parker first saw one of the creatures lying motionless on the floor of a chute he realized the source of the stench that pervaded the entire hollow passageway: it was the stink of the decomposing thousands of slugs that he and Longa had slain days before in the room of the ancient skeleton. Parker managed to squirm past the slug without touching it, nor did it show any sign of awareness of his presence until he was past it and the steady breeze brought his own odor to the thing.

Then it moved slowly after him, but Parker soon distanced the slug. As Parker continued through the tunnel the very sparsity of the slugs made him more and more impressed with the terrible slaughter that he and the great cat had committed on the things. He felt no guilt at the recollection of the act: surely the slugs would have killed Longa and the man had the two outsiders not practiced their tactic of temporary retreat to the skeleton chamber followed by murderous counter-attack.

Still the amount of killing he had done, assisted by the cat, turned Parker cold with recollection. And if the luminescent creatures bred as infrequently as InzXa thought, the tunnel would be lightly guarded within for many years to come. The Par'zian Gate guardsmen had better be alert.

By the time Parker reached the slaughter room the tunnel was rank with the smell of decay and bright with the recent excrecences of the glowing horde that had filled the tunnel only days ago. The chamber itself was lit almost brilliantly by the jelly-like foul-odored mess that covered its floor to a depth of many inches. Parker drew back at the entrance, had to force himself to step forward, to set foot into the yielding, sucking substance of gleaming corruption.

He crooked one arm across his face, pinching off his nostrils in the corner of his elbow; he forced the flesh of his forearm down over his mouth, breathing through the rough Relori cloth of his shirt so that each gasp of air before reaching his mouth was at least filtered through the layers of woven fiber. He made it across the room as quickly as he could and bolted again into the tunnelway, retching at first and then sucking in welcome lungfuls of the relatively fresh air that moved through the tunnel from the outer face of the volcano.

Again the series of chambers, passages, chutes, all now dimly lighted by far fewer and older traces of slugs, and a rare single slug that lay totally dormant until Parker had passed it, then pursued the intruder briefly before ceasing once more to move.

Again it was late when Parker emerged from the tunnel, this time not the full night into which he had emerged from the Gate of Par'z, but dusk. Parker emerged from the tunnel head first, stood and stretched, looked at the sky for the first time in many hours. It was a dark gray; the cone of Par'z cut off any last rays of the setting sun while, looking eastward across the sea toward the Country, Parker was unable to distinguish the dark bulk of land that he sought.

Three days, Parker thought, is it only three days since I saw Kaetha and Broadarm here? A day with Longa in the tunnel, a night in InzXa's guard shed . . . a day in the city and a night, that night with VouLa in the samra journey . . . another day with WinLao the inventor, and the Terasians, with the piper-king, and then the night when VouLa had come to him as blossoms and jewels and winged things . . . and then this day in the tunnel again.

Only three days, Parker thought, and now InzXa and VouLa and XaoQa, WinLao and MykJo the earnest, skeletal would-be literary man, and all the fairy city and sail-dotted water of Par'z were less than a mile away and yet as distant as seaports in the moon.

Parker heaved a sigh and started down the outer cone of Par'z, into the wooded hill land between the naked lava and the sea. In the quickly descending darkness he looked for some dinner, found a few fruit-bearing trees. He studiously avoided the kumquat-like growth, watching a few of the huge yelow-trimmed black butterflies benignly perched on the fruit, moving their great wings slowly, gently in the falling night.

The American finally plucked a few pieces of fruit, found a comfortable spot beneath a bush, and crawled in. He carefully checked his bow and friendmaker, loosened his boots, and leaned back to dine at his leisure. His thoughts drifted to Kaetha and Broadarm. Three days. By now they would not even have reached Relore. If I'd known that I could get into and out of Par'z so fast, I'd have asked them to wait here for me. Well, too late. They're well into the Country by now, the dugout is on the wrong side of the water, Longa is . . . Parker wondered. Probably she had gone back through the tunnel slaughtering more slugs, Parker thought, unless she too had grown sick at the sight of the things.

Back through the tunnel, and down the hillside and into the sea. She swam from the Country to Par'z, she could make it back the same way. Parker wondered if she had even overtaken Broadarm and Kaetha in the dugout as she had overtaken the three paddlers on their way from the Country to the island.

I'll have to get orgainzed tomorrow, Parker told himself. A good night's rest and some breakfast and then to scout up some way of getting back to the mainland myself. My chance to play Robinson Crusoe. Not even Friday. He lay back and started to drift into slumber. Some kind of crude craft shouldn't be too tough, then back to the mainland and see my buddy Broadarm again, and Kaetha. He closed his eyes and tried to call up the Relori woman's slim, handsome-featured face, and succeeded fairly well, except that the face kept looking rounder than it should, the eyes more ironically innocent, less mature than they somehow ought to be.

In the morning Parker woke refreshed. A little stiffness from sleeping on the ground passed quickly with a walk around Parker's sleeping area. He tied his boots up, breakfasted on fruit again—growing weary of the diet—and climbed back toward the vegetation line once more. This time when he looked to the east the bulk of the Country was clearly visible beneath the dawning rays of the sun.

Crouching in the dewy morning Parker felt a chill run through his frame. He wished he'd made a camp fire the night before, settled by gathering some loose twigs and leaves and building a small blaze to warm himself now. He squatted by the fire, held his hands over it, then got up and found some good sized branches, long dead and well dried, and threw them on. The fire blazed up nicely, rivalled the equally bright, distant sunlight piercing the cool air, made the flier more content to sit again and get the morning into his lungs.

He breathed deeply, wished he'd brought some of the Par'zian equivalent of coffee through the tunnel with him. He looked steadily toward the east.

To the aviator's surprise he felt a pang of homesickness as he gazed across the sparkling sea toward the Country and toward Relore. No great welling up of feeling in the chest, no held back tears, but still a real pang. Somehow Relore was becoming home now, not as much home as the home of his boyhood but certainly as much as King's Ferry had ever been; far, far more home than McMurdo had been or any other duty station.

Far to the left—to the north toward Patagonia, Parker thought—he could make out a black speck on the edge of less black land. The Wall of Teras. Something there was that made walls, that made Man make walls, from the Wall of China to the Wall of Berlin to the Wall of Teras. But . . . was the Relori palisade different?

He looked outward and down to the sea, lying calm and a gray-green itself beneath the gray-blue sky. The water was quiet, cold-looking; Parker thought he could smell the familiar odor of the salt sea, wondered if he was fooling himself. He scanned the water from the south, far off in the direction of Relore, all up along the coastline to the spot opposite the island where he stood and then farther northward toward the Wall of Teras.

Not far offshore, northeast of the island, a black object lay quietly on the face of the sea. Parker looked, looked a second time, then began jumping and waving his arms, shouting "Relori, hey you Relori, I'm stranded here, come ashore!" There was no visible reaction from the black object. Of course not, beyond voice range and they wouldn't see me jumping unless they were looking straight at me. Maybe not even then if they don't have a glass of some kind to bring things close.

He stood still, made an eyeshade for himself with his hands and squinted at the thing on the water. It's a boat or a ship all right, Parker whispered half-aloud. It's a boat. But it's a hell of a lot bigger than the dugout Broadarm and Kaetha and I came in. Bigger and different, too. Broader. And with room for rowers, all along both sides. And—Parker squinted again, trying to be certain—sails? There seemed to be a simple structure of masts, no sails were raised but they might still be there, furled.

If so, the ship had probably been there for some time, most likely anchored overnight at the least. And—Parker was almost certain that it couldn't be Relori without his at least having heard that the forest people had sailing craft as well as their little dugout fishing craft. It all seemed to say that the ship was . . . Parker refused briefly to admit it to himself, still the flier almost *had* to conclude that the ship was from Teras.

For a moment he stood motionless, his head light, his body stiff at the shock. Then he dropped to a half-sitting, half-squatting position. He scuttled down to the edge of tall trees, cursing himself, knowing that if the Terasians had a watch ship at the island they had probably seen him by now. His mind caromed from his own situation to Kaetha and Broadarm, hoping that they had got away from the island and reached the mainland again before the Terasian craft had anchored off Par'z.

Still, was this a routine reconnoitre of Par'z by her ancient, her incredibly ancient enemies the sea people, the Terasians? Or was the ship there for some special reason? For a moment Parker wondered, then he felt the third shock he had in a matter of minutes: sighting the ship, realizing that it was not Relori but Terasian, and thinking now of Chacla and her two companions. Well, one companion now that Mocles was dead, but—if the three had been plants rather than refugees, as was certainly the case—this ship must mean either reinforcements or the return of a ferry to pick up the agents!

Parker saw a smaller speck detach itself from the anchored boat and begin to move slowly away from it toward the shore of the island. Damn! he said under his breath. Wave like an idiot and you'll get seen. He spun, meaning to get farther away from the point where the landing party would make shore, ran his eye once up the cone of the volcano and saw above it, spurting into the air over the crater rim, a black-silhouetted figure, then another.

As Parker watched, the first figure reached its zenith, dropped back below the rim; then the second did the same. The first reappeared in seconds, climbed even higher; rotors snapped into place and the figure began floating slowly downward, tilting and sliding horizontally as it did so, over the rim and toward the shoreline. Again the second figure followed, above the first now, and farther from Parker and the shore.

Chacla! Parker thought . . . and following her, Stacles. WinLao must have gone ahead and finished his second jumper after all . . . and if the two surviving Terasians had the machines and were escaping the city in them it meant, almost certainly, that WinLao the inventor was dead. Parker's mind raced: Terasians were landing on the island, Terasian agents were escaping from Par'z with the jumpers. If the machines were taken to Teras and studied they would be duplicated by the thousands, an army would vault over the volcanic rim. Par'z would fall to the compeerage exactly as Chacla had predicted.

Parker slipped his bow from his back, drew an arrow from his waistquiver, knelt and sighted at Chacla. By now she was almost over him, still high, high above Parker's position. He drew back, released the shaft. The arrow flew straight, barely missed the woman who jerked back in startlement at the attack.

Quickly Parker drew a second arrow, nocked it and sped it upward at the Terasian woman. She was controlling her jumper with one hand now, had pulled her own dagger. As the arrow reached her altitude she batted at it contemptuously with the dagger, knocking the Relori shaft sideways. No matter, the American thought, at her height the arrows have spent all their force anyhow. They couldn't do any harm to anyone.

Parker jumped up, ran frantically to a group of fruit trees. He looked up, saw that Chacla had passed overhead, was still moving slowly, slowly down the slope beneath the windmilling blades of her jumper. Parker looked at a tree bearing peachlike fruit, another, one with something that looked like bluish-purple apples, then a kumquat tree. He held an arrow in his hand, plunged its shaft through a kumquat, then through another, nocked the arrow, sighed and drew, let fly.

The arrow sped toward the airborne Chacla. A few drops of the kumquat juice sprayed back on Parker's hand. He ran, terrified at the recollection of the butterfly kiss he had received in the Country, ran as fast as he could and plunged his juice-tainted hand into his morning campfire. The still blazing flames seared his hand,

sent waves of pain and nausea to his head but still he
held his hand in the flames, still, counting aloud to force
himself to hold his flame-tortured flesh in the fire.

After agonized moments he could stand no more,
pulled back his charred hand. A few of the deadly butterflies circled him indecisively, then drifted away.

Parker looked skyward again. His shaft had achieved
its purpose. Chacla must have batted it again, as she had
the previous arrow, and caused the kumquat's fatal juice
to spray onto herself. Parker saw a peppering of black
dots rising from the forest, then a cloud of yellow-
trimmed, black fluttering shapes. Through a haze of insects Parker saw the Terasian woman gesturing, wiping
frantically at herself as she realized what had happened,
what she had done to herself. Parker heard her voice
rise once in a half-scream half-shout of command to the
hovering Stacles.

The Terasian man obeyed, slipped his rotor sideways,
edging toward Chacla to try in some hopeless unimag-
ined way to help her. To Parker's eyes the cloud of fluttering blackness became too thick, he could no longer
see the two Terasians; he heard a splintering crash as
their wooden rotors locked, shattered each other. For a
brief moment the two sea people became visible again as
black, wavering parodies of themselves, flutter-edged sil-
houettes that writhed and screamed and screamed and
plummeted to the earth not fifty yards downslope from
the American.

Parker ran down the side of the crater, dodging trees,
leaping small bushes to reach the spot where Chacla and
Stacles had fallen. Parker had lost sight of the Terasian
ship and its landing party, knew only vaguely the direction that the two falling bodies had taken. In a matter of
minutes, breathless, his burned hand sending a steady
stream of pain messages to his brain, Parker found
Chacla and Stacles.

The two Terasians lay locked in a final insane embrace, their bodies and faces bloated beyond distinguish-
ing one from the other, their posture, however—the one
seeming still to grasp frantically at the other, the second
to struggle at the last to escape from the first—told the
American which was the commanding woman, which
the servile male. Huge black and yellow wings of butterflies that had been crushed in the struggle of the crash of

the Terasians protruded from beneath the two bodies. A few others lay about them on the ground, dead or struggling feebly in their death throes. Those insects that had been unhurt in the fall were gone now, disappointed, Parker mused, at scenting kumquat and finding only useless flesh. Parker hoped that no inadvertent meal of the sort ever would give the butterflies a preference for hot blood.

The jumpers of the two spies were smashed hopelessly but still Parker hauled them clear of the corpses, with his good hand hung one over the elbow of the burned arm and with that reasonably secure picked up the other jumper in his unburned hand. He started back up the hill-side carrying one jumper, dragging the other. The climb was very different from the hasty descent of minutes before, working back uphill, dragging the two wooden machines.

At last Parker reached his campfire again. He stood over it, threw in the shattered jumper that he held in his good hand. Then he used that hand to grasp the second jumper from his other arm, to lift it and hurl it into the flames. He watched the two jumpers quickly burning, turning from broken machines that would not work but that might be analyzed and copied, into unrecognizable ashes.

The jumpers were too large to fit into the fire at once. Parker started to draw his friendmaker, realized that his knife hand was the seared one, and clumsily drew the weapon instead with his good hand. He looked at the clean blade, shrugged, and used it to poke the last stray chunks of the burning jumpers into the embers of his camp fire.

As Parker drew back, dirty, exhausted, in pain from his burn but bitterly satisfied that the secret of the jumper was safe for Par'z, he looked about him and saw a ring of human figures. Brown-clad, grim-faced, dumpy figures in baggy trousers and jackets that made it impossible even to distinguish sex, one of them spoke. "Do not move or speak or you will be killed instantly!" the Terasian said. The accent was familiar now, the harsh delivery. Apparently this leader was a man.

Parker stood as ordered, holding his sword-knife clumsily in the wrong hand, feeling weak and sick again from his burn. The Terasian spoke to his comrades: "He is the one who must be responsible for the killing of two compeers."

Then, to Parker: "You, foreigner! Drop your weapon. We are all armed. You cannot fight us."

Parker looked at the Terasians. Each was armed with the broadbased, fast-tapering Terasian dagger. Several, including the leader, had long, heavy sticks tied to their backs. They seemed to be pointed at one end, useful for spears at a distance or jousting-sticks in close combat.

"Now! Quickly!" the harsh voice came.

Parker looked down at his friendmaker. If I could handle it properly, he thought, I might take on the bunch of them. He counted the Terasians. Almost a dozen. Rotten odds, but if he could break through, make a run. . . . For where? Not off the island. It's not big enough to offer much of a hide-and-seek place. Maybe back to the tunnel. No, with his burned hand he was operating at half efficiency, he'd never make it through to the Gate or anywhere near before they had him.

He spit once in the fire, dropped a single epithet and threw his friendmaker too into the flames.

The Terasian leader said "You will come with us. You will be taken to our ship and questioned by our captain. You will answer all questions."

"You really so sure of that?" Parker asked.

The Terasian chuckled before he said anything more. Finally he said "You will answer the captain's questions. Unless you would rather tell me all that has happened, who you are, where our third compeer is. . . ."

Parker shook his head no.

"Very well," the Terasian said. "When Captain Byeryas questions you, you will wish you had chosen to give your answers to me instead."

Parker stood staring at the Terasian leader. He felt another of the sea people tugging at his bow; Parker shrugged it over his shoulder and turned to watch it added to the fire.

"Now," said the Terasian who had spoken, "you will come along."

Parker was shoved violently from the rear, stumbled forward and caught himself with his good hand. The Terasians had kept their roughly ring-shaped formation around him, holding to a distance that prevented his striking one of them from the rear and breaking the circle to escape. They worked their way downhill, Parker getting a prod with a Terasian weapon-stick whenever he slackened his pace.

Parker kept an eye out for any opportunity to break away as they moved toward the sea, but none arose. They passed near the bloated corpses of Chacla and Stacles but none spoke as they moved past, the bodies quickly dropping out of their vision. Not even a burial party, the American thought as they moved past the bodies. They'll go for carrion if anything can eat that poisoned meat, otherwise just lie there till they rot.

When they reached the shore the party halted. Parker looked at the Terasians' landing craft, a little skiff that would hold only a few men at a time. It must have taken several trips to land all the Terasians, surely it would take two, more probably three to get them all out to their ship.

"Into the skiff!" a Terasian ordered harshly. Simultaneously Parker felt a shove that was almost a blow from a fighting stick. He stumbled toward the little boat, turned and cursed the man who had struck him, but climbed obediently into the boat and sat. Four Terasians took seats and oars, facing the rear of the craft. Parker was seated in the bow, also facing the rear. The Terasian leader sat in the stern, a spear in his hand pointed directly at Parker's chest.

"Row!" the Terasian ordered his men. They began to lean into their oars, drawing the open craft toward its parent ship. Parker tried his luck by half-turning to look at the ship for which they were headed, wondering what retaliation the move would bring from the spearman, but there was none—apparently he was free to look around, at least, as long as he made no move to escape.

The Terasian ship looked larger from the viewpoint of the closing skiff than it had from high on the crater of Par'z. Thirty feet long, the American estimated, and ten or twelve' wide, the Terasian ship was build of a blackened, glossy wood. It rose to a carved prow front and rear, a heavy sweep reaching from the rear deck into the water. The sweep was unmanned as the ship lay at anchor, from its looks Parker guessed that it would take at least two men to handle it.

A dozen places for oarsmen lined each side of the

ship, its hull an open shell in which the rowers would sit, planked over to make a single deck. A curved roof rose over the center of the ship, covering an area that Parker's eye measured at only eight or ten feet in length, less in width to permit oar positions beside it.

A mast rose at either end of the roofed portion, double crossbars showing where sails were to be square-rigged. All it needed, Parker told himself, was Burt Lancaster swinging from a halyard with a dagger in his teeth.

The skiff bumped alongside the sailing craft. The Terasian in the stern of the skiff ordered Parker to climb onto the ship. He reached up with his unburned hand, found a good grip on the railing of the larger ship and pulled himself up, stood on the wooden deck of the Terasian ship and looked about. From Parker's position he could see the remaining crew assembled in the bow of the ship, seated on rowers' benches or on the rough floor of the ship. A Terasian stood before them, familiar book in hand, shaking his other fist and haranguing the men from the pages he held. Parker could not make out his words, but could hear an occasional loud word followed by a response from the assembled sailors. Religion and politics he thought, married to produce this.

Again Parker was prodded from behind. He looked over his shoulder, saw the leader of the Terasian landing party gesture him to walk, not toward the assembled sailors but toward the shaded cabin of the ship. Parker obeyed, stepping over benches, climbing from plank to plank of the ship's deck. At the edge of the roofed section he stopped, bent over to bring his eye level below that of the roofing and peered within. In the darkness he could see nothing.

"Go on," the Terasian said, his voice much quieter now than before, but filled, Parker thought, with malicious anticipation. "Go on," the Terasian almost hissed, "now you will meet Captain Byeryas."

Parker held the edge of the roof with his good hand, swung gingerly beneath it and found a level piece of planking for his feet. Within the sheltered cabin he smelled a sour, stale odor. He looked into the darkness, his eyes becoming accustomed to it, providing more vision as irises opened to night wideness.

The cabin of the ship was set out in stained and ancient

plush, a wild contrast with the spruce appearance of the ship itself. Parker had trouble telling the color of anything in the thick darkness of the cabin; everything seemed a dark brown-red, shading off into russet on some objects, red-black on others. There were cushioned stools in the cabin, and a thick, grimy rug covered most of the floor beyond where Parker stood. A single porthole on either side of the room was closed, its round frame filled with a substance so nearly opaque that the shape was barely visible even in the bright day.

Parker stepped forward, the Terasian behind keeping the point of his spear in the aviator's back. From deep in the cabin, low, low in the ship's hull Parker heard a wheezing sound, a steady, pulsing wheezing as the breath of an asthmatic.

He stepped forward farther, peered deeper in the direction of the wheezing. There, sitting crouched down in the bottom of the ship, flesh covered with grimy rags that had clearly been splendid trappings at some ancient date, sat a huge creature, incredibly obese, its pate utterly bald and giving back an occasional ray of light that chanced to struggle into the shadowed cabin. Its flesh seemed an amorphous mass greater than the distended hide could contain, the face round, dark eyes lost in pits of fat, the nose a barely visible protuberance through which breaths whistled spasmodically, the mouth a black hole in the flesh of the face.

And the body—Parker was trapped between fascination and revulsion. The flesh seemed to pour down the creature, leaving visible no neck, great softly rounded shoulders, huge rounded breasts—Parker could not even tell whether the thing was a man or a woman, the great masses of hanging flesh mammaries or simply fat. The belly was so great that it rested on the thing's own lap, while tiny feet and hands, incredibly small and delicate appearing on the gross creature, lay motionless.

Beside Parker he heard the Terasian accent of his captor: "Byeryas-sib, I have returned and brought this captive."

For a long moment there was silence broken only by the regular shuddering breath of the obese creature. Parker stared again at it, seeing in the parody of a human form some mad gigantic version of the slugs he had killed in the tunnel of Par'z. Finally the huge thing spoke in a horrible croaking whisper. "Lincar-sib, where are our agents? And what is this thing you bring me?"

The Terasian's voice quivered as with fear as he answered. "Byeryas-sib, only two of our siblings came from Par'z. The third must be lost within the crater. The two who emerged succeeded in obtaining the flying things that we have seen over the crater, and we would have them aboard ship now, but for this foreign thing." He struck Parker.

"This foreigner shot the two down, I do not know how. We saw them flying as we started up the hillside. Somehow he knocked them down. They were dead when we found them. Their bodies were swollen and black. He also had stolen the flying things from them, and destroyed them."

Again the great sluglike thing spoke. "That is all you know, Lincar-sib?"

The man whispered, "Yes, Byeryas-sib."

"Then report yourself to the chaplain, Lincar-sib. You have failed the compeerage. He will prescribe penance for you."

The man beside Parker fell to his knees, pleading with the huge creature slouched in darkness. "No, Byeryas-sib, I was blameless, I did not fail the compeerage. It was this foreigner's doing. He must be chastised, not I!"

"To the chaplain, Lincar-sib!" the croak repeated.

"No, I will not die!" the man shouted. He rose, held his spear before him in two hands. Parker jumped back and watched the man lunge forward, only to be met himself by two spears, one on either side of the sitting monster. Two figures, black hooded, black clothed, arose from the darkness on either side of Byeryas. They seized the bleeding form of Lincar between them and dragged it backwards from the cabin.

In a few minutes Parker heard a voice from outside, chanted responses, a splash. Two black forms passed beside him in the darkness of the cabin, and disappeared to the two sides of the huge Byeryas.

"That was some penance," Parker said.

"The compeerage expects efficiency as well as fidelity from its siblings," Byeryas croaked. "Whether Lincar's failure was the result of treason or of mere incompetence is of no moment. One regrets his foolishness in attacking the captain of this ship, however. Had he confessed to the chaplain and done public penance instead of dying on the spears of my own children, it would have been more instructive for the crew."

The delicate hands, so inappropriate at the ends of the bloated arms, moved sideways, seemed to caress empty blackness where Parker knew the two killers of Lincar crouched now beside Byeryas.

"What do you want of me?" Parker demanded.

"Do not demand so, foreigner," the monstrous creature said. "Remember that you are aboard my ship the Bakhid, and that I am captain, lord master of the ship. What was done to the unfortunate Lincar can happen to you."

"You could kill me now, Byeryas," Parker returned. "If you let me live you must want something. What is it? And what do I get for it?"

"You do not cringe, at least," Byeryas said.

Not so you can see it, Parker thought in reply. He waited for the huge Terasian to continue.

"Very well," Byeryas offered. "You will tell me who you are, from whence you come, all that you know of Chacla, Mocles and Stacles. That will do for a beginning. Then we will see what follows."

"No deal," the flier said. "That's all one sided. If you want information you have to give something in return."

Byeryas was silent. From outside the cabin Parker could hear men stirring, walking about. He looked over his shoulder toward the prayer meeting and saw that it had ended; the men were taking places at the oars and masts of the Bakhid. Parker saw Byeryas incline that huge hairless head to one side, heard the croaking voice whisper a command to an invisible black figure in the dark. The darkness stirred, brushed past the American.

In a moment there were voices outside the cabin. The black shape returned, again brushed past Parker to reach its place beside the swollen captain. No one spoke in the cabin as the activity continued outside; Parker caught fragmentary sounds and glimpses of men scrambling to climb the masts and raise the ship's square sails while others hoisted her anchor. Finally a chorus of voices drifted into the cabin, its burden half a hymn of grim tones, half a work chant. Parker heard oars begin to creak, felt the ship begin to move through the water.

For minutes there had been silence in the cabin. Now

Byeryas broke it, croaking "We are headed for Teras. You are right that I want your information or you would be with Lincar now. Tell me what I wish, cooperate with the compeerage and you will be treated well aboard the Bakhid. And when we reach Teras, rely upon it that my voice is heard in the highest circles. Your treatment there will depend upon my good will."

"How do I know?" Parker asked.

"Eh?" the monster croaked. "What do you mean?"

Parker said "I mean, I spill it all for you and then you tell your goons to skewer me and throw me to the fish. Or we get to Teras and I'm a slave. How do I know you'll keep any promise, once I tell you what you want?"

Byeryas said "Ah, I understand. Well, at least your name, foreigner, that can do you no ill."

"My name is Parker."

"Well, well, Parker-sib. You see, I call you my sibling even though you withold that courtesy from me, and I bear you no grudge for the affront. Parker-sib, let us say this. If you refuse to cooperate with me, I will have you tortured." The Terasian paused for what Parker assumed was dramatic effect. The American did not react. Byeryas resumed "I will have you tortured until you change your mind and cooperate." Another pause. "Or until you die."

Still Parker stood silently.

Byeryas went on "But if you cooperate you will be at least comfortable. You may even wish to hold back somewhat, eh?"

In the cabin's murk Parker thought he could see a grin through the rolling fat of Byeryas' cheeks, surprisingly tiny teeth glinting whitely in the black room.

"Yes," Byeryas said softly, "you hold back a small bit if you wish. As long as you cooperate, you will be comfortable. By the time you have told all, you may wish to join us. Otherwise . . . well, Parker-sib, let us discuss otherwise another time." Byeryas raised a tiny, almost effeminate hand in a gesture toward Parker.

Why, you'd almost think he was really trying to be friends, the American thought. And what can I do? Break and I'm dead. Defy this fat thing and they torture me till I'm dead anyway. Or till I'm beaten. I don't know how good they are at torture but I must have a limit and if they can reach it without killing me, I'll talk. And—what can I tell them anyhow, that can harm anyone? Par'z is

safe as long as the Gate is guarded, as long as the Terasians don't know how to build jumpers. I can't let them get
that data. And Relore . . . there's nothing to tell about
Relore they probably don't know already.

Parker said "Okay, Byeryas. No, I won't call you Byeryas-sib, but Captain Byeryas if you like a title." Again in
the darkness Parker saw the fat ship master's teeth. "What
do you want, eh? I'll tell you what, one more thing and
I'll talk to you."

The Terasian now kept silence.

"Give me a knife," Parker said. "You don't have to
worry, I can hardly take over your whole ship with one
knife. Maybe I'll use it on myself if the mood grabs me."
He laughed sourly. "A knife, and you get answers."

The huge head inclined its bald scalp again, murmured
to a black-clad acolyte. The black figure rose, moved, returned, slipped an object into Parker's unburned hand.
The American held the blade up, looked closely at it in
the little light available, tested it with a finger, then slid it
into his waistband.

"Good," he said. "Now, where did I come from? Par'z.
And what happened to your three, uh, siblings?"

Byeryas nodded for Parker to answer.

"All three dead. Two of them killed the third in Par'z.
He changed his mind about working for you and wanted
to get out. The others stabbed him."

To Parker's surprise Byeryas asked "What did they do
with the body?"

"Buried him for fertilizer in a potato patch," Parker
said.

"Good," Byeryas croaked. "They did well, and I think
you speak truly, Parker-sib. And the other two. You killed
them, Lincar said. Perhaps we should have kept him alive
longer to test your story. Well, done is done. How did you
kill the others? And which died first?"

"Mocles first," Parker said.

Byeryas nodded and made an inarticulate croaking
noise.

"The others I killed outside the crater."

"They flew," Byeryas interrupted. "How did you kill
them if they flew? Lincar saw them up a-high."

"Bow and arrow," Parker said.

"But the bodies? Lincar said they were swollen, dis-
colored. How did you do that?"

"They were poisoned before they ever left Par'z. They would have died soon anyway. I only shot them down to stop them from reaching you with the machines they stole in Par'z."

"And you then burned the machines," Byeryas supplied.

"Yes," Parker said.

"Do you know how the machines were made?" the Terasian asked.

"No."

"Very pretty, Par'zman. We will see later on whether you are as ignorant as you claim. Meanwhile, you confess to murdering two siblings of the compeerage of Teras."

Again Parker said "No."

The Terasian echoed the word, vocal inflection turning it to a question. Then: "You admit you killed them, yet deny it too?"

"I killed Chacla and Stacles," Parker said, "because they were thieves fleeing with stolen goods. That's not murder in my book!"

"Ah," the Terasian answered, "I see where we stand now. Very well, Parker, ah, Parker-sib—you see, I still give you courtesy. Well, done is done. We will reach Teras in two days. You will be free on the Bakhid until then. Make no trouble and we will see how matters turn. But I warn you, make no trouble."

One of the dark-clad shapes rose from beside Byeryas and took Parker by the arm. The aviator felt himself spun around and half-shoved half-guided through the murky cabin and back to the deck of the Bakhid. He climbed onto the planking, blinded by the daylight after becoming accustomed to the cabin's darkness.

He stood outside the cabin surveying the ship and its surroundings. The Bakhid stood well off Par'z, the green slopes and blackened lava peak of the island reduced to a toylike appearance by steadily widening distance. In the other direction the Country was visible only as a dark line separating sea and sky. From the lower elevation of the water's surface, the Wall of Teras was no longer visible as it had been from the high slopes of Par'z.

The water itself was still smooth, the sky above shone brightly as the strong sun penetrated a thin gray layer of cloud. Parker watched the sky, wondering whether the sun or the clouds would triumph. If this was the rainy season in this region then peculiar air currents over Par'z had won that city blue skies for the first few days of rain; still, Par'z could hardly be immune to rainfall and yet keep up the level of its lake and the vegetation in the crater.

Aboard the Bakhid Terasians manned the dozen oarsman's posts on either side of the hull, stroking steadily to move the ship along, sailing northward along the coast, needing only a slight angling to her course to reach the shore once she passed the Wall of Teras. The men worked to a chant led by a priest or underpriest of some sort—Parker stared at the leader, tried to identify him as chaplain or chaplain's assistant. As usual for Teras, Parker found the sea people's chanty a paean to work and obedience for the sake of the compeerage. The Terasian religion was the grimmest he'd ever come across.

Parker walked to the bow of the ship, stepping over benches, dodging scattered crewmen as he went. The Bakhid carried many more men than it took to handle her oars, enough, Parker estimated, to run shifts around the clock when the captain wanted to make time on the water. He looked aloft, saw that the ship's sails were also stretched, catching what breeze there was to add to her speed.

The Terasians who were not rowing sat on the benches the ship provided, or stood in small knots talking in low tones, not interfering with the chant of the priest and the rowers. When Parker approached any group of sailors their conversation ceased, their faces were turned from him. Parker wondered whether they were acting under orders or just playing safe by not talking to strangers. He decided to test them.

He walked up to a small group of the brown-clad men, was greeted by silence. "You fellows all regular navy?" he asked.

No answer.

"I'm navy myself," Parker tried again. "In for eleven years. Decided to make a career of it."

None of the Terasians spoke although Parker thought he detected a stir among them.

"Too bad about Lincar," he tried. "A friend of any of yours?" Whoops, that was a bad shot, Parker told himself. There they go. He watched as the knot of Terasians broke up, one brown figure joining another undertoning group, two more moving quickly to another part of the ship to resume their conversation, a fourth walking a few paces by himself and sitting on the bench.

Parker followed the last man, sat beside him. The man rose and walked away again. This time Parker walked past him until the flier reached the bow of the Bakhid and stood there, his elbows resting on the wooden rail of the ship, his burned hand on the wood, his chin held between thumb and forefinger of his good hand as he stared far, far across the sea toward Cape Horn, the fresh salt breeze of the sea in his nostrils, land far behind, far ahead and to the east.

It was a time to take stock, Parker told himself. Especially since there's nothing to do for me, and nobody even to talk to.

So here I am, he said to himself. Aboard a little ship, practically a prisoner despite being on partial parole and even having a knife in my belt. And how I got to this world, I'll never know for certain. Not by any miracle of InzXa's fourth dimension or any other wild occurrence that might be reversed. Just frozen after the crash and cold-storaged for too long to imagine. And revived, thawed, I should have been just so much preserved meat; somehow, by some crazy quirk I came out of it. So.

And now what? Par'z was a lot of fun but I wouldn't want to live there, Parker told himself. I'd have a great time for a while but I'd go stir crazy in time, I couldn't just spend my life playing with hobbies like WinLao or MykJo or that fancy chef whatever his name was. Cross it off.

The Relori, though. A tough people, vigorous, open, free. They might yet go somewhere. And Kaetha is a Relori. I want her wherever I wind up. And Trili. And the good guys in Relore: Broadarm and Janna, and Fletcher. And more.

Teras? Forget it. Last thing I need is a bunch of authoritarian militarists who mix a crummy religion with a crummy government and come up with a nation of slaves. See the world as nine-tenths slaves and one-tenth slave drivers and take your pick which you'll be. Count me out, Parker said under his breath.

He sucked in a great lungful of the tangy, bracing sea air and looked at the sky to see that the morning's clouds had grown thicker and darker, holding back much of the sun's radiance and turning the day from one of brightness to one of gloom. The wind too had freshened from a pleasant breeze to something less pleasant. Then the first drops of rain began to fall, damping Parker's skin and clothing and spotting the wooden rail where he stood.

He turned to see what steps the Terasians took when the rain fell. Some of the crew had already clambered up the ship's twin masts and were busily furling the sails to keep them from being torn loose by the strengthening wind. To Parker's surprise, other than that there was no visible reaction to the storm. The priest still chanted, more loudly now to be heard over the wind. The oarsmen still responded, still leaned rhythmically into their oars, leaning backward to draw the Bakhid ahead through the water, then sitting erect as they recovered from the stroke, raising the wooden blades, moving them horizontally above the water, plunging them downward into the brine and then drawing them once more through the water.

The other Terasians who dotted the benches and planking of the Bakhid remained in position, talking, resting, moving about on occasion but with no more urgency in the falling rain and rising wind than they had any earlier.

A huge bolt of jagged lightning streaked between sea and cloud far ahead of the ship, writhed for a fraction of a second yellowish-white against the blue-gray darkness of the distant horizon, then ceased. A seemingly interminable period of silence followed before the thunder of the release reached the ship and Parker, a monstrous booming, growling sound that struck with the suddenness of a great explosion, grew, held, then faded slowly so that it was difficult to tell through ringing ears when the sound had ended.

The rain was falling heavily now, in drops that came larger and more closely together, then in sheets. The sea, from its level self of the journey's beginning, had turned now into a heaving monster of swells and troughs, walls of water that broke across the bow of the ship, sprayed her interior heavily with chilling brine, then moved on. Parker no longer stood at the rail but sat between two benches, his legs and buttocks flat on the plank flooring between the seats, his arms around the bench on either side of him. He was no longer able to see the sailors, the oarsmen, the priest. If any chanting continued it was totally lost in the roaring of wind and sea; if any rowing continued Parker could not see it.

With a start he thought of the men at the sweep, standing in the stern of the ship, holding her pointed into the waves. As long as the Bakhid held her prow into the waves she would survive; if she turned side-on to the towering water walls she would surely be swamped, very likely turn turtle. For an instinct Parker had a great urge to do something to help the Bakhid. But there was nothing he could do so he clung to two benches and waited for the end of the storm.

It passed gradually, the waves and the wind slackening first, lightning and thunder occurring less and less frequently, the rain itself coming less heavily, and less, until at last it was over. Briefly the clouds remained thick and dark, then Parker watched a point of brightness appear and enlarge until the sun was visible through a rent in the cloud cover. Its position showed that noon had passed and it was a lowering sun that lighted the sea and the Bakhid.

Parker stood watching the crew recover from the storm. First a roll-call was made; to the American's surprise a number of Terasians had apparently been lost overboard during the storm. To his greater surprise there was little reaction to the loss. The priest-foreman and his assistant—Parker saw now that there were several assistant chaplains on deck, acting as petty officers—made assignments of Terasians who had formerly sat and talked, to replace lost oarsmen. Beyond that, no one seemed to care that lives were lost.

If that was the Terasian attitude toward people!

With the storm over rowing recommenced, an underchaplain calling out the stroke to the tune of another work-hymn. Another gang was pressed into service clearing out the water left behind by rain and waves with simple pumps. Parker walked over to the priest-officer in charge of the pumping crew and volunteered his help. He was ignored.

"Okay," he shrugged, and walked back to the ship's railing. At this rate, he thought, getting back to Relore might not be any easy proposition. His status aboard the Bakhid, despite his truce with Byeryas and his parole, was still at least as much prisoner as passenger. He did not doubt that there would be further interrogation before the Bakhid docked at Teras.

Going to Teras was itself both an attractive and a repellant prospect. Attractive because Parker had found himself, almost from the moment of his awakening in the Country, in the middle of a complex, three-cornered relationship among the city-states of the region.

Relore had started, according to her own tradition, as an outgrowth—no, more an unwanted excrescence—of Teras. Relying still on Teras for part of her population, still Relore hated her own parent-people the Terasians. And when Relore's population periodically grew beyond her ability to support and contain, she herself sent off colonizing expeditions into the otherwise unexplored high country to the south of the, uh, capital-C Country.

Teras in turn largely ignored Relore, tolerating the activities of the Relori in rescuing abandoned Terasian children and even permitting Relori fishermen to take fish in the sea that was well controlled by Teras. Still, by the testimony of the late, unlamented Chacla, not all Terasians subscribed to the official policy of toleration toward Relore, for all that official Teras regarded Relori as vermin and Relore as unworthy of being granted even the status of enemy.

But Teras concentrated her wrath on her ancient enemy Par'z. How long ago had Par'z and Teras warred, and Teras defeated her enemy, deprived her of her lands, swept her ships from the salt seas, pushed her people back into the single remaining bastion of their island city? And yet the Terasians still held their grudge, still circled Par'z like hounds with a treed raccoon, and still would like to invade the enemy citadel and deal her the final crushing blow. With the mission of Chacla and Mocles and Stacles, Teras had nearly succeeded.

And as for Par'z herself, unaware of Relore, remembering Teras only in dusty tradition and in a single, almost vestigial public office, the Par'zmen slumbered on. They sailed their little shells and engaged in endless, inconclusive philosophies, and made their clothes and their foods, and painted themselves, and chewed their samrae and dreamed and dreamed in a kind of innocent lifelong childhood.

And here was he, Robert Leroy Parker. An exile of the centuries. He had seen Relore, he had seen Par'z, and it looked as if he was going to see Teras in another day. The alternative . . . He looked over the ship's railing into the sea. No place to swim to from here, and Parker was no one to commit suicide.

Parker lay down on one of the Bakhid's benches, found that the ship's rolling made it impossible to get comfortable. He stood up, walked to the rear of the ship, watched the steersmen at their sweep for a while, then walked back to the bow. He watched the rowers, listened to their chant with the chaplain, scanned the horizon for any sight of land. Par'z was lost to sight. If Par'z was really Biscoe—Parker was almost certain that it was —then Anvers and Brabrant islands should be coming in sight to port before very long, but they were not yet visible.

To starboard, still a mere line on the horizon which the Bakhid paralleled, lay the darkness of the Country. Shadows were lengthening, the sun nearing the horizon far across the sea to port.

Parker lay down again, this time between two benches. The plank deck of the Bakhid might not have been designed for comfort, but if her crew could sleep there Parker could as well. He found a shaded spot for his eyes, threw an arm over his forehead and managed to fall asleep.

He was wakened by a stirring on the deck. Sounds and unmistakable odors told him that it was dinner time for the crew. The non-rowing Terasians had all been served from a galley somewhere—Parker sought the service line in vain—and were sitting or standing around holding semi-circular dishes of something edible. From its odor Parker deduced that it was fish stew, not the most delicately aromatic nor perhaps the most elegantly served, but nourishing sea-fare. Many of the men also held tough-looking chunks of bread which they tore with their teeth and used to sop up their stew.

Parker's salivary glands began working but he could find no one to give him food. The Terasians still refused to answer his questions, moved off across the deck of the Bakhid when he persisted.

By the time the meal was over Parker was pacing the deck of the Bakhid in impatience and disgust. The freshly-fed Terasians moved at a command from the priest-overseer, handed their empty bowls to the rowers and took over their oars. The priest-overseer, too, was replaced by another of his trade who took up a new rhythmic prayer of labor. The new crew of oarsmen took up the rhythm, stroked the ship forward with a surge of renewed energy that quickly fell into a regular pace.

The sails—Parker glanced upward at the ship's twin masts for a look—had been re-hoisted after the rainstorm. The sun had now dropped beneath the horizon.

Parker watched the relieved oarsmen—the day-shift, his mind labelled them—stretching and yawning, slapping one another's arms and backs, and making for a lineup near the steering sweep at the rear of the ship. From a huge kettle—Parker had not seen it before but he told himself that it must have been there all along—another priest of some sort. Parker labelled him a very junior clergyman, was ladling the fish stew into the sailors bowls.

Parker unobtrusively added himself to the end of the sailors' line, moved up patiently toward the stew cauldron. Maybe nobody will talk to me, he told himself, but they have to feed me at least. They didn't spare me a violent death and turn me loose aboardship to starve to death. Did they?

He reached the head of the line at last. The young priest looked at him in puzzlement. Why, he's nothing but a pimple-faced kid, Parker thought. "How's about some chow?" the American asked.

The priest stared at him.

"Hey, I'm hungry."

This time the priest answered. "None for you."

"Why not?"

"My orders are to feed the crew. First the shift going on. Then the shift coming off. You are not one of the crew. You are a prisoner."

"Well," Parker said, "I won't argue about that. But look, prisoner or not, what am I supposed to do about getting some chow?"

"Ask not this humble priest, foreigner. I serve the compeerage obediently. I have been ordered to serve the compeerage and all its siblings aboard the Bakhid. You are not of the crew. You are not of the compeerage."

"You smug bureaucrat," Parker sneered. "I know your kind. Give you anything not covered in the regs and you're at a complete loss."

The priest looked flustered. He started to speak, stumbled over some inarticulate syllables, then brightened as he looked past Parker.

Parker turned to see what pleased the priest. One of the dark-clad figures from the captain's cabin was moving quickly across the deck toward where they stood. The priest said "A child of Captain Byeryas comes. You will be taken to the captain. You will be told what to do. I will have nothing to do with you."

The dark figure, hooded and cloaked in dull black, stood for a moment before Parker. A gesture, then. The figure turned, moved once more toward the cabin. Parker followed uneasily.

CHAPTER

16

Ahead of Parker the black-clad form disappeared into the captain's cabin. Parker paused for a moment outside the covered area and looked briefly at the sky, clear now of clouds, dotted with uncountable points of brilliance. The sea, too, seemed to have a phosphorescent quality, as of marine life-forms that generated their own light at night or in deep waters .

Parker ducked his head to move beneath the overhang of the cabin roof. As he swung into the captain's quarters his hand brushed the floor for a moment; to Parker's surprise it was dry. Then there must be some way to seal off the cabin during storms. Again the American was impressed by the capabilities of the peoples of the Country . . . for all their seeming lack of advances, these were not primitive peoples.

Within the cabin the black figure had disappeared— back to the side of the captain, Parker surmised. A single oil lamp beside the obese form of the Terasian commander lent a flickering orange illumination to the room. Parker stood looking at the bald figure of rolling flesh until the captain said "Come near to me, Parker-sib. Will you not join me for dinner?"

Parker advanced across the cabin and sat, facing Byeryas, on a thick carpet. Between them were ranged ornate dishes of beaten metal that gave back dull reflections of the wavering lamplight. Each dish held a different kind of food, some of which Parker recognized, others of which he could only guess about. He suppressed a comment about its being time for a genie to appear and carry him off to see his beautiful princess.

The Terasian captain spoke. "Try some of the sweetmeats," the croaking voice said, "or a cold vegetable to begin your meal." A dainty hand at the end of a gross arm indicated dishes as Byeryas spoke.

Parker watched the Terasian eat, lifting each small dish in turn, taking morsels with tapering fingers, returning the dish and moving to another. The American followed suit. He still could not erase the Arabian nights image from his brain. "This is very good," he said, "I was getting pretty hungry up on deck and I couldn't get any food."

The Terasian chuckled. "My apologies, Parker-sib. I did not intend you to be kept hungry."

Parker took a good mouthful of something that tasted like beef strips in onion and chewed happily.

"But I did not wish you to settle for rough sailor's fare either." The Terasian reached for a hanging jug with one hand, lifted a cup—no, dammit, it was a goblet and there was no other word—and extended the vessel toward Parker. "A little wine to go with the repast?" the Terasian offered.

For an instant Parker worried about drugged wine, then decided that if Byeryas meant him harm there was no need for treason. Odds of a shipload of men against one required no treachery, especially when the lone man had originally been unarmed. Silently he reached for the offered goblet, held it before him while the Terasian poured a wine so dark that in the ill-illumined cabin it flowed like a stream of pure liquified blackness, catching the light of the oil lamp and throwing it back in glimmers and flashes of gold.

Parker sipped the fluid. Its flavor matched its appearance perfectly: dark, powerful, without any suggestion of sweetness but yet giving brilliant flashes of flavor that froze and burned at once. He drained his cup. The Terasian refilled it, said "Careful, Parker-sib, this is not the mild qrart that Relori drink."

The meal progressed accompanied only by small talk of the food and the wine. Parker asked Byeryas if the variation in fare was part of the teachings of the compeerage. The Terasian laughed cynically, croaked a reply: "I am the master of this ship. Aboard the Bakhid my word is the will of the compeerage. If you knew Teras better you would see why men are eager to sail with me."

By the end of the meal Parker felt sated with food, relaxed with the black rich wine that Byeryas served. Almost invisibly one of the dark figures, the children of Byeryas—Parker wondered at that!—cleared the remains of the meal. The goblets were gone, replaced by smaller vessels of polished wood and fine metal-work, the wine had given way, to Parker's immense wonder, to something that could pass muster for excellent brandy.

Parker leaned on one elbow, watching the obese figure opposite himself. The black-clad "children," if they were present in the cabin, were as usual silent and unseen. A warmth pervaded the American, and a weariness that he attributed as much to the meal and drink as to the activities of the day.

He finally said "Captain Byeryas, your hospitality is outstanding." Parker saw the Terasian smile thinly. "I thank you for it," Parker went on. "But I have a feeling that you have something else in mind than just a social evening."

The Terasian laughed loudly. "Most perceptive of you, Parker-sib."

"Rather obvious, I thought," Parker answered.

"Well, then, in any case you are right. As I told you before, we make Teras tomorrow. In fact, we could be there early tomorrow, but I have given orders to make such speed as will get us there well after dark."

Now it was Parker's turn to wait for the other. He sipped his brandy.

"You have been well treated aboard the Bakhid, Parker-sib."

Parker nodded.

"You have been questioned, but only gently," the Terasian went on. "I do not believe all the answers you gave, but let it pass. There is something else to discuss." The huge form shifted position, rolls of flesh seemed to heave and slide as Byeryas moved. "What do you think will happen to you after we reach Teras?" the captain asked.

Parker wondered about that himself. He had no idea what would happen to him—or, being more honest with himself, too many ideas of what might happen, all different and none pleasant. Finally he settled for "You tell me, Captain. You're the Terasian, I've never been there."

"So be it, Par'zman," said Byeryas. "If that is what you really are, which I doubt."

Parker said nothing, waiting for Byeryas to continue.

The Terasian did. "You will be taken from my ship, turned over to the night-priest and his acolytes. You will no longer have that knife at your waist, of course."

Parker felt the blade, waited for more words.

"You will be taken to a chamber high over the city, and there you will receive a visitor, the holy voice of God, Nissral. You will tell Nissral all he asks, Parker-sib. You will not die resisting his questions. Nissral is too skillful for that. You will wish to die, but you will live. You will never forget your visit from Nissral."

The words of Byeryas reached Parker like pounding fists, pounding him awake, pounding him out of the relaxed half-stupor of the heavy meal and the drinking. "What's the idea of telling me, Byeryas? Part of the softening up?" he demanded.

The Terasian stared at Parker out of heavily lidded eyes, eyes buried deep in a face innocent of hair. The very hairlessness of the Terasian officer added to the impression of obscenity in every quivering fold of flesh. "I will tell you an anecdote, foreigner."

Parker waited, now fully alert.

"I was not always as you see me today," the croaking voice went on. "I was once . . . well, very different from the thing you see here squatting in eternal darkness. I lived in Teras then. I was regarded as a promising acolyte, a future priest who would someday wield great power in Teras.

"I was also . . . shall I say, far more attractive to look upon than is this Byeryas you see in shadow.

"Another under-priest was also growing in favor and power. One of the opposite sex. There was a great attraction toward me, but I did not return the interest. Finally I was pressed. I spurned the other, I was betrayed by false accusations. I was taken to the high room, and there met the predecessor of Nissral. My innocence was proved only when I reached the extreme torture. I told all. All, Parker-sib, as you will tell all. And there was no guilt.

"But I was left to become as I am now. The false accusation was overlooked as an unfortunate error. The captaincy of the Bakhid was given to me as a sinecure. For thirty years I have not left this ship, nor will I ever. I seldom leave my cabin."

Parker was shaken by the story. He stammered "But . . . but who was the other priest? Or . . . she must have been a priestess, that is. I . . ."

"You do not understand," Byeryas sighed. "Here, give me your hand." A huge arm reached toward Parker, the slim hand at the end of it took his own, pulled it toward the great fleshy being with surprising force.

For a moment Parker resisted, then let Byeryas place his hand on the inside of one great swollen thigh. The Terasian pulled Parker's hand to the top of the bloated limb. There Parker felt his hand held to quivering, hairless flesh. He felt a pubic fold. After a moment Byeryas released his hand. Parker drew back, aghast.

"You are a woman!" he exclaimed.

"I was a woman," Byeryas corrected him, the croaking voice low. "I was the most beautiful woman in Teras. What was done to be because of Nissral made me this thing that I am now." The hoarse voice fell still more, until Parker had to strain to hear the Terasian speak. "Before they were through with me they let Nissral have me. It would not have mattered to me, by then I cared about nothing. But then, after they let me go, after I had become captain of this ship, I found that I was with child.

"Yes, these are my children." The bloated figure moved its hands, made petting motions in the blackness by its sides. "These two were got on my body, by Nissral. They are the only Terasian spawn not counted by the compeerage in centuries, the only ones not carefully included in the plans of the state. If you could see them, Parker-sib, unhooded. . . . Well, best you do not.

"Does my story charm you, foreigner?"

Parker hesitated, collected his wits as best he could.

"Uh, Captain Byeryas," he said. "This is . . . what you told me, ah. . . ."

"It is horrifying, Parker-sib, you agree?"

Parker nodded.

"But you wonder what it has to do with you. Rest assured, I do not tell the story merely to entertain guests aboard the Bakhid. In truth, it is a story no one has heard before tonight, from my lips at least. In Teras . . . I have not been in Teras in thirty years. Perhaps Nissral tells it in whispers. Likely it is the secret of a few priests and will die with them."

Byeryas reached toward Parker with a slim hand. The Terasian touched him lightly with it, almost caressing the American. "You are in the company of a monster, foreigner, I know what I am. Tomorrow night you will be in the power of a greater monster. You will be given to Nissral. Unless you would rather kill yourself first. But I know you already. You would not do that now. Later on you would, but you will not be able to do it.

"I will offer you an opportunity for freedom or death, Parker-sib. I know you will prefer freedom, but believe me, death too is preferable to the tender ministry of Nissral. What say you?"

Parker asked only "What do I have to do?"

"Avenge me," Byeryas replied. "I will turn you over to the night-priest and acolytes in your own clothing and booths. I will certify to them that you are unarmed."

"And then?" Parker asked.

"The interrogation chamber—I have not seen it for three decades but I know every stone and seam there, and I have kept in contact, I know it has not been changed —the chamber is high in a tower overlooking the harbor of Teras. There is a single window, barred, but with a strong knife I believe you could loosen one or two bars. You could never make your way out through the city, but you could leap from the tower into the water. You might be killed. You must take that risk.

"The Bakhid will stand by. If you leap, my men will pick you up. They are all loyal to me, no one else. We will sail downcoast again and put you ashore where you wish. Par'z? Relore?"

"What if I refuse?" Parker asked.

"You will be disarmed and turned over anyway."

"How can I smuggle in a weapon?"

"It can be hidden."

"How do you know . . ." Parker hesitated. "Byeryas, how do you know I won't take your deal and then betray you to Nissral?"

The Terasian looked seriously at Parker. The she croaked at him "That would be your great error, Parker-sib. Bad enough to go to Nissral at all. Let him suspect treachery and you will curse your own cleverness. Believe me, if you will not work with me, then I have no stake in your destiny. For your own good, if you will not work with me, draw your knife and lunge now. My children will end your pain before your touch can reach me. That is the best you can hope for."

Parker considered the offer in silence. Then he asked one more question: "What if I take your bargain but just escape without killing Nissral? You'll never know the difference, Byeryas."

"I will," the Terasian said. "You bring Nissral's heart with you steaming from his chest when you leap from the tower. I tell you I will have it for dinner! Fail to bring it and we will turn you over to the acolytes again, an escaping prisoner.

"You have only these choices, man. Do my bidding, or die now, or go to Nissral. If you choose Nissral you will wish you had not. Death is the safe choice, Parker-sib. I am the risky one. Nissral is the choice of madness, of hell on earth."

"All right," Parker said. "I'll take it. I'll kill him or die trying."

"You will succeed, Parker-sib. But if you fail, you had best die trying, yes. Do not survive failure. Death is not the worst alternative before you."

Parker rose from the carpet before Byeryas, made his way carefully to the entrance of the captain's cabin and climbed back onto the deck of the Bakhid. He started automatically to walk toward the bow of the ship, then turned and walked instead to the stern. For once, he thought, I'm more interested in where I'm coming from than in where I'm going.

He stood by the rail, listening to the rhythmic chanting of the under-priest on duty and the oarsmen as they drew the ship slowly through the night. Some clouds were now in the sky but they were still few. Stars uncounted sparkled against the utter blackness of the night; a nearly full moon threw light on the Bakhid and long reflections on the dark sea.

The air was cool, salty, the sound of water lapping at the ship's hull filled in the background for the chanting oarsmen; a slight breeze crossed the deck of the ship but her sails were furled. Parker wondered whether the Terasians failed to understand tacking, or whether this was simply part of Captain Byeryas' timing in order to bring the ship to Teras the next night instead of during the day.

Well, no way of telling that, short of asking, and Parker had had enough of silence from the deck-hands. And he was certainly in no mood to return to the captain's quarters and ask there.

He gazed into the sea, looking for luminosities. There were a few, but not the spectacular show he had thought might appear. Still, the night was beautiful. A lovely girl, Parker thought, that's what I need. A lovely girl and an orchestra, the night. I could be William Holden.

He lay on the deck and gazed up at the stars. What men walked other planets, he wondered. The samra journey had shown him other forms of life, other worlds, but no men. Did that mean that mankind had missed his chance at the universe? He thought of the strivings of his own day, the first feeble steps that would lead mankind from its tiny mudball world to the infinite universe, of the struggle and the sacrifices, the deaths and the fights. Spend it on schools, spend it on arms, spend it on medicine. Space is one big boondoggle. Can't afford it. Some other time. What good is the moon anyhow? Explore the sea. Develop the atom. Wipe out poverty. Conquer pain. Feed the world.

Maybe there *were* men out there somewhere. Somehow William Holden and spacemen got mixed up in Parker's mind, swirled, blended, faded and he slept.

He woke up surprised at having been able to sleep at all. The sky was light already, the sun edging into view over the distant Country. Parker clambered to his feet wondering about breakfast. Sure enough, there was a chow line going. From the looks of the rowers and the tone of their unending chant, they were still the night shift, waiting for their relief to finish a meal and take over so that they could have breakfast and rest.

Might as well give it another try, Parker told himself, and attached himself to the end of the line waiting for

food. As the queue inched along he had time to inspect
his burned hand. The skin was tender, partly blackened
and partly an angry, blistered red. But the pain was not
great, and Parker found that he could move his wrist and
his fingers gingerly. He decided not to try too much at
the risk of cracking the dried skin. Anyway, the hand did
not throb as he feared it might, and there seemed no infection in it.

When he reached the head of the line there was a different under-priest handing out the food. Parker prepared for another argument but apparently Byeryas had
sent word and he received a piece of fruit and a hard
roll. He made his way to a bench and sat down to eat
while the rowers changed shifts.

No black-clad messenger of Byeryas appeared to sum-
mon Parker to the captain's cabin and Parker did not
volunteer to visit the Terasian again. Instead, he spent
the day on deck, dozing at times, watching the sailors and
listening to their chanting, gazing across salt water to the
dark line of the Country and savoring the smell of sea
air.

It rained again late in the morning; the storm this time
held none of the violence of the previous day's weather
and the Terasians ignored their drenching, letting the
sun that followed the clouds dry their clothing as they
worked. By mid-afternoon the Wall of Teras was visible,
a dark divider cutting across the Country to the very
edge of the sea, and if the Relori were right, crossing the
entire Palmer Peninsula, from Bellinghausen to Weddell.

From the rail of the Bakhid Parker gazed at the Country, trying to discern any features beyond the dark mass
he had observed ever since leaving the tunnel from Par'z.
The Bakhid was not quite coasting: the Palmer shoreline fell away to the eastward as the peninsula stabbed
toward Patagonia to the north. To keep the Country in
sight—there was no evidence so far that the Terasians
used maps or any instrument to navigate by, and Parker
guessed that they would keep within seeing distance of
the shore most of the time—the men at the sweep of the
Bakhid must be holding to a course east of north. During
the day they had edged closer to the land as well as moving up the coastline.

Now Parker could see the Palmer Peninsula clearly.
To the right—south of the Wall—the Country showed

dark green and irregular, a sub-tropical growth of trees that made the word forest an understatement, yet stopped somewhere slightly short of jungle. The countryside looked like virgin growth: thick, hardy, vigorous, apparently untouched except by occasional hunting parties since the remote era when the Aantarctic ice cap had begun to melt and the forest growth to appear.

Then the Wall.

Then Teras. First, immediately north of the Wall, there was nothing, not even green but in its place the dull brown of bare earth, earth that looked as if the tall growth had all been destroyed long ago and not even grass permitted to grow in its place. Then the flat tints that spoke of tilled fields, too far off for human forms to be visible if there were any at work.

Then the city. Black, black as the Wall of Teras, dull black, low, flat, squared off with the precision of a military fortress. Parker tried to recognize the tower where he was to be taken, saw only one projection rising from the city along the water. It was not as high as he'd expected, only . . . Parker's eye measured the black tower . . . about three, at most four storeys above sea level. Still a hell of a jump. Enough to kill you if you hit the water wrong. But it could be done with a good dive.

Parker walked about the Bakhid again, stood near the sweep for a while watching the steersmen at their work. Suddenly the two days he'd spent aboard the Terasian ship became dear to Parker. At the thought that he would soon be in Teras, pledged to murder a total stranger at the price of his own escape from torture and mutilation, yesterday—this morning—even right now became the good old days, to be held to mentally as long as possible.

Parker stood, watching the Terasian sailors, dreaming for a moment of his own days, how long forgotten, as an enlisted sailor handling routine tasks aboard a small craft. Nothing quite like the Bakhid in the United States navy. He'd have quite a tale to spin out if he ever got back. But no, he knew that he would never get back. Well, someday when he was an old, old man, Trili's children or grandchildren could gather at his feet in a house in Relore, and he would tell them of the great adventure he had had, once upon a time, in the land of Par'z and behind the Wall of Teras. Suitably expurgated, of course.

Parker watched the sun reach the western horizon, falling into the arms of the far distant sea. He turned from the Terasian sailors he had been watching and started for Byeryas' cabin, met one of the black-clad children—thirty-year-old children—emerging. "Coming for me?" Parker asked. The dark figure did not reply but turned back into the cabin, gestured for Parker to follow, and moved ahead.

As he had before, Parker swung down into the covered area where Byeryas stayed with her—Parker could hardly use the word despite his Thomasian certainty of Byeryas' sex—her children. The huge figure sat, as ever, barely visible in the thick darkness of the room. At Parker's entry Byeryas' voice croaked out "It is time now to prepare you for Nissral. I offer you a final opportunity to avoid that by dying here, quickly and without pain."

Parker answered "If I chose death, Byeryas, I would have gone over the rail before now."

The obese captain nodded in satisfaction. "Good Parkersib. Hand back your knife to my child and sit you down. You will be made ready."

Parker complied, slipping the Terasian dagger from his waistband, holding it hilt-forward to the black shape that rose from the darkness beside Captain Byeryas. Parker sat on the carpeted floor of the cabin, waiting to see what the children of Byeryas would do. In a moment he felt hands taking his burned arm, spreading salve on it, then wrapping the injured arm and hand in light bandages that appeared miraculously from some corner of the captain's room.

Without speech the two dark forms moved about Parker, leaving his burned hand, going to the foot of the opposite leg and removing his Relori boot. From beyond the two working figures Byeryas' voice came, thick with irony yet demanding no reply. "Strange, Par'zman, that your clothing and your boots are of Relori style. The result of much commerce between Relore and your own city, one would imagine."

Parker's boot was off now. He watched the two dark Terasians working over his leg, rubbing it with some stinging fluid that left the skin puffy and inflamed as would a burn. This accomplished the Terasians applied the same salve they had placed on his real burns, then began applying bandages loosely to the simulated injury.

They completed a layer, then one of the workers placed the Terasian weapon that Parker was to use upon the bandage. Another layer of wrappings and Parker could feel the dagger pressing against his leg, yet saw only a vague bulge beneath the bandaging.

His boot was replaced, laced over the bandages. The wrappings extended above the top of the boot, the discoloration above the top of the bandages.

"Very neat," said Parker. "That should get the knife past even a pretty thorough check." It was a good thing, though, that none of these people had gadgets like metal detectors.

"Still, I would not put it past our people to rip open bandages," Byeryas said. "That is one reason for bringing the Bakhid—and you—into port at night. When you are turned over to the acolytes, if it is late enough at night, they will likely make only a quick check of you before throwing you in prison.

"But if I know Nissral—and, Parker-sib, believe that I know Nissral—he will not wait for morning to visit you. When he hears of a prisoner sent by Byeryas, he will come from anywhere, whatever he is doing. Then you must act, Parker-sib. Do not fail, Parker-sib. If you fail me you fail yourself as well. Gain the vengeance I seek and you gain your freedom also!"

Parker tried to sound unconcerned. "I'll do it, Byeryas. Once I lay hands on Nissral, I'll be right back." A sudden problem rose in Parker's mind: "How will I recognize Nissral?"

Byeryas laughed quietly. Then the huge Terasian said "Do not worry about that, Parker-sib. There is only one chief inquisitor in Teras, and that is Nissral. You will know him. If nothing else, he will tell you who he is. He never tires of telling who he is."

"Okay," Parker said. He sat there on Byeryas' carpet, his stomach tense, his hands feeling cold and wet, trying to think of more to say.

"We will land in a few hours," Byeryas said. "Now it is time for dinner. Will you join me, Parker-sib? You really should have some food before your mission. And it will help if your bandaged hand does not look too fresh."

Parker looked dumbly at the fresh wrapping that covered his burn, then back at Byeryas. After a long silence he decided that the one thing he did not want, now, was to be alone on the Bakhid's deck. And for all the presence there of priests and crewmen, being on deck, for Parker, meant being alone.

He looked at the gross figure opposite, opened his mouth and finally managed to say "All right, Captain Byeryas. I'm not very hungry but I'll be glad for the company."

Byeryras waved a huge arm tipped with a dainty hand. The two dark children moved about in the dark room. In a few minutes dinner was again laid out between captain and prisoner, the finely worked dishes holding a fresh variety of fruits and condiments, sauces and meats. Again Byeryas put two goblets on the carpeting and reached for a wicker-coated bottle that hung behind her bloated form.

CHAPTER

17

Parker stood on the black dock at the Terasian waterfront, a child of Byeryas gripping him at either arm, the American's eyes turned momentarily back to the unlighted bulk of the Bakhid standing beside the dock, the black water of the port lapping at her hull with a low sound that said *chop, chop, chop* to Parker's brain. He turned his head away from the ship and looked ahead into the city of Teras.

A mist filtered through the night air throwing a hush over any sounds that might have drifted through straight, broad streets, turning regularly spaced torches into haloed points of brightness in the night. Parker could see little of the city between darkness and mist, but what was visible confirmed the view from the Bakhid: uniformity, regularity, an overriding sameness in all of Teras's structures.

In the night there seemed to be a single building material used for every structure, for the streets and even for the quays and piers that projected into the lapping salt water: a dull-surfaced black stone, coated now with condensation of the evening mist to make little beads of moisture here and there, tiny rivulets running down walls where drops combined, an occasional glimmer of reflection where the angle of a wall, a torch, an eye combined with proper precision.

After a moment a priest and two crewmen of the Bakhid climbed onto the dock beside Parker and the children of Byeryas. Without a word the priest took position at the head of the little party. Parker remained the focus of the group, a black-garbed figure at either side, the Bakhid sailors—Parker threw a glance over one shoulder—in the rear, their thick Terasian jousting spears levelled at his back like javelins. Were they and the priest in on Byeryas's treachery and Parker's role in the plot? Probably not, Parker thought, the old principle of security applied here, and Byeryas was clearly possessed of the intelligence and experience to apply it. The fewer people who knew a secret, the less chance of somebody's blowing it to the enemy.

At a signal from the leading priest the party began to move forward, along the wharf where the Bakhid had tied up and toward the city of Teras itself. The remainder of the crew were kept on board. For a moment Parker wondered how Byeryas had arranged that: maybe Terasian discipline said they could not be dismissed until next day after tying up.

Before Parker and his escort had reached the beginning of the dock they were challenged by a guard. The priest from the Bakhid answered, the guard demanded more facts, the priest spoke more. Soon the guard called for assistance. Parker quoted to himself: give the alarm in case of fire or disorder . . . call the corporal of the guard in any situation not covered. . . .

In a moment another guard had joined the first, then another. These must be the acolytes, Parker told himself. And next we'll see. . . . Right, the night duty officer, uh, priest. Almost on cue another Terasian, this one lacking the arms carried by the acolytes, strode up. His clothing was identical to that of the guards, or for that matter of the sailors from the Bakhid. So far, Parker had seen only Byeryas and her two children to dress differently from the other Terasians in their brown uniform of baggy trousers and jacket.

Still, the newcomer carried himself with an unmistakable air of authority, brushing past the assembled acolytes with a gesture of accustomed command, approaching the priest who headed Parker's group and exchanging a mumbo-jumbo greeting straight out of the ceremonial of the Mystic Knights of the Sea. It could be no other than the secret exchange of the Terasian priesthood.

For a few minutes the two priests, one night guard commander for Teras, the other commanding the one-prisoner detail from the Bakhid, stood aside exchanging words too quietly for Parker to understand. He looked at his escort and at the acolytes, saw them eyeing each other with suspicion. Aha, the sea-swabbies and the shore patrol. See 'em love each other. The men around Parker stirred. The acolytes facing them stood quietly, each holding a jousting spear, its shaft of the smoothest polished blackness, its metallic point shining as if buffed for inspection before its owner went on duty. Which was almost certainly the case, Parker concluded.

At last the two priests separated. The man from the Bakhid returned to his party and gestured to the two children of Byeryas. They hustled Parker to the new guards, deposited him in the middle of a group where he was immediately surrounded by spears. Parker thought: I don't know why the Terasians never tie anybody up, but I'm sure glad they don't, and if they never heard of it I'm not going to give them any hint.

He stood his ground, staring straight ahead. At a command from the night-priest the party moved off, away from the Bakhid party and into Teras proper. Parker had little chance to see the city. Within a hundred yards they halted. The priest gave more commands. An acolyte spoke to a guard inside a doorway and shortly Parker was hustled forward again, into the stone entrance of a huge, depressing-looking structure of the ubiquitous black stone. A pile, Parker thought. I never knew why a building was sometimes called a pile but this one tells me exactly why.

The night-priest disappeared. Wordlessly acolytes hustled Parker through a huge torch-lit hall, up black stone stairways, along dismal and ill-lighted corridors, up more stairways. At last they stood before a solid black stone wall. Two acolytes dragged open a massive stone door —even now Parker could not help noticing its solid thickness and obvious weight.

He felt a violent prod in the back, leaped from the javelin-point, found himself in a half-ring, forced inside the newly opened room. It was dank, lighted by a single smoking torch near the ceiling. Parker wondered crazily who pulled the duty of changing the torch every day and lighting it every night, or whether it was reserved for special occasions and lighted now only when word reached the guards that the chamber was to have an occupant.

Parker was thrust onto the floor by acolytes, felt an agony in his burned arm and hand as both hands were pulled behind his back. Now they were tied. Parker cursed aloud. I must have given 'em the idea by telepathy, he told himself bitterly. Now his boots were opened and pulled roughly from his feet. He simulated a cry of pain as the boot was dragged from his supposedly burned leg. Within himself Parker praised Byeryas' foresight and the skill of her children in bandaging his real burn and faking the leg injury to conceal a weapon rather than merely leaving it in his boot.

The acolytes tied his ankles together also, left him wordlessly, lying in the corner of the room. Parker watched them retreat, still facing him. A different acolyte carried each boot. As they closed the massive cell door behind them Parker wondered if his boots would become the acolytes' booty, or whether such freebooting was forbidden by Terasian law. He giggled half-hysterically, squirmed to a sitting position in the corner of the stone room and set to work.

If Byeryas was right, Nissral would be turning up to question him. But how soon? It might depend on how far away Nissral was, what he was doing, how long it would take word of the prisoner to reach him. Even, Parker thought, whether Nissral wanted to start his interrogation immediately or preferred to let his victim stew for a while first.

There was nothing to do but assume the worst—that Nissral would be coming through the heavy door at any time—and prepare for him as quickly as possible. First priority was to get out of the ropes that bound him hand and foot: Parker had to figure out a way to get the knife that lay concealed in his leg bandages. Sitting propped in the corner his hands were tied behind his back, his legs stretched on the floor before him. To reach the bandages and the knife was impossible.

Try another position. Parker flopped onto his side, his eyes for a moment scanning the walls of the room. They seemed innocent of peepholes. But no matter, if there was one he would have to chance being caught; to wait passively for Nissral would be fatal. Parker tried to swing his arms over his head, to bring his hands in front of himself. He got them level with his shoulder blades fairly easily, ducked his chin onto his chest and strained. No good. Unless I can develop free-wheeling shoulder joints, he thought, that will never work.

Maybe he could stretch downward, though, get his hands behind his ankles, raise his knees and work his hands around beneath his feet. That worked a little better than the over-the-head plan, in fact it came agonizingly close to success, but it didn't quite succeed. Parker lay on his stomach now, his chest raised off the floor as his hands strained downward, his heels pulled back and up raising even his knees off the cold stone. He could almost work his tied wrists over his heels. Almost, almost —then he hooked straining fingers under the edge of the bandage covering his bogus leg burns, tugged, the wrapping loosened, an end came away in his hand and the knife clattered to the floor with a sound that must have been audible for hundreds of miles.

Parker lay motionless, praying that the noise of metal striking stone had not been heard. There was no sign that it had. He waited still, determined to count silently to a hundred before moving again. Before he'd reached thirty the tension was too great. He scrambled around, belly-down, until he saw the Terasian knife, dully visible on the dull stone floor. He edged over until he lay beside it, then rolled once more onto his back so that he lay on the knife, felt its hilt digging into his back.

He pressed down with the back of his head and his shoulders, pushed against the floor with his now bare feet until his lower back was a fraction of an inch off the stone. He felt rapidly with his tied hands until they had located the knife. With his unburned hand he grasped it tightly by the hilt. He let himself down from his flexed position and rolled halfway over so that he lay again on his side, his back against the wall, his hands tied behind his back and the knife clutched in one hand, his eyes fixed on the stone door of the room.

He struggled with his good hand to work the sharp Terasian knife back and forth over the rope binding his wrists together, to shred away strand after strand until his hands would be free. That didn't work either. A few strands gave way but Parker just could not get the leverage he needed to cut through his bonds. Turning the hilt carefully in cold fingers he reversed the knife so that the sharp double-edged blade pointed downward toward his heels instead of up toward his wrists. He tried the back-arch again and was able to reach the rope that held his ankles together, but again the position was not firm enough for him to bring the pressure he needed.

Wait a minute, one more try. Holding the knife still with its blade toward his feet, he wrenched himself sideways, twisted again, leaned one shoulder against the cold wall and squirmed to a kneeling position, his knees on the floor before him, feet under his buttocks, his back and upper arms pressed against the wall, hands wedged between the wall and the light rope that held his ankles together.

That worked.

By using the wall as a brace he was able to slide the sharp blade up and down against the ropes hard enough to make good progress through them. Soon his ankles were free. Still he knelt with his hands tied behind him, holding the knife. He reversed the hilt again and tried to cut through his wrist bonds using the same method he had in freeing his ankles. Still the progress was agonizingly slow. After what seemed like perspiration-soaked hours Parker stopped sawing at the ropes.

He lay on his side again, extended his hands as far down as he could, tried to work a free foot up and between his forearms. It still did not work. He rolled over onto his back, worked his hands to a point below his buttocks, found to his delight that he was now able to slide them along the backs of his thighs toward his feet. Next he lifted both feet off the floor, held one straight up, doubled the other leg at the knee and was able to wriggle a foot over his tied wrists, between his forearms and down again. In a moment he'd done the same with his other foot and sat with his tied hands in his lap, still holding the knife.

If I had put the knife down before I did all the gymnastics, Parker told himself, that would all have been a lot easier. Have to file that away for next time, under a suitable heading. Let's see, *bonds, wrist and ankle, cutting of with smuggled knife.* Yeah, my information retrieval system will bring up something about clipping coupons every quarter.

Quickly now he had his wrists cut free and the knife again concealed in rewrapped bandages on his leg. What to do next? Damn, if Nissral wanted a prisoner to stew, he was stewing all right. No point in trying to escape immediately. If he could open the door it would only let him into a nest of Terasian acolytes who would promptly recapture, re-search, retie and reimprison him. And they wouldn't miss the knife again.

If he made it out the window and survived the leap into the sea, Byeryas' men would have him. And without the gory relic of Nissral to prove completion of his assignment in Byeryas' behalf, he would still wind up back in the jug.

All right, he would have to wait for Nissral and carry out Byeryas' bloody mission against the priest. Okay, better feign still being tied when Nissral arrived, that way there might be a chance that the interrogator would allow himself to be in the chamber alone with Parker and give the American better odds. All unintentionally, of course. Then what?

Plan ahead. Parker saw himself in the room now with the dead Nissral at his feet. If he was lucky there would be no other guards in the room, no alarm would have been given. Still, what now? He stood in the center of the room, turned in a complete circle. The window! Right, that was Byeryas' plan for him, and there was the window as the ship's captain had described it. Mean, rather high in the wall but not above reach for a tall man. Barred.

Parker threw a glance over his shoulder at the stone door. It stood closed, as if it had never been used and would never swing open until the very stone of the building crumbled away. I know better than that, Parker thought. But I have to risk this.

He stood beside the high window, examining the bars.

Byeryas had said that he could chip away at the material holding the bars in place, loosen one and clamber through. Parker looked more closely. Bad news, that was Byeryas' mistake but likely to cost Parker his life. The bars were not cemented in in any way, but set, like pegs, in holes in the heavy stones above and below the opening in the wall. The stone must have been drilled out before the room was ever constructed, the lower stone set in place, the bars stood in the holes, then the top stone slipped over them and fixed.

Parker cursed under his breath. There would be no getting those bars out of the window. He stood staring at the bars, the stones that held them in place, the wall that the stones made a part of. Wait a minute! If he couldn't take the bars out of the window, maybe he could take the whole window right out of the wall!

How were the stones held in place? Parker looked more closely than ever, ran his fingers carefully over the seams between the stones. They seemed carefully fitted, held in place by the weight of the stones above, even here on the top floor of the building. But the barred window . . . let's see . . . it had presented a special problem because of the bars themselves. They could not sustain the weight that solid rock carved to shape could. So the weight of the building—Parker leaned heavily on stone after stone trying to test out his ideas—the weight of the building seemed to have been distributed carefully *around* the window. The window itself was installed as a unit and—carefully, Parker even touched the tip of his tongue to the wall to confirm his idea by *tasting* the difference—the whole window, top stone, bottom stone and bars, was cemented in place!

Parker was debating whether to try chipping away at the cement with his knife when the door began to move inward. The aviator flung himself onto the floor, lay with his back concealed where the wall met the floor. The remains of the ropes around his ankles should still pass muster if not inspected too closely; if they were examined . . . well, too late to worry about that now. And the severed bonds at his wrists were behind his back again.

The door opened fully. Parker watched a single figure silhouetted in the doorway for a moment, tall and slender, in a flowing cloak. Then the newcomer entered the room, walked to its center, gestured impatiently at someone in the door without turning to look back. The door was drawn shut. So far—perfect!

The tall figure advanced to stand above Parker, looked down at him from a sallow face beneath a shaven skull, a lank mustache turning downward at the corners of his mouth, a thin beard falling straight to a point beneath his chin. The newcomer and Parker exchanged stares, then the tall figure spoke: "You made a mistake in coming here."

That was quick enough, thought Parker. Before he could answer the tall man continued. "You will answer all questions truthfully and completely. Your pain will be less that way, and over more quickly."

Parker said "What do you want to know, Ming?"

"Ming?" the tall figure repeated. "You will not mistake me for any other. I am Nissral, high priest and chief inquisitor of Teras. Now, you will tell me who you are."

"A friend of Byeryas's," Parker said.

Nissral took two steps forward, raised a foot covered with a stiff-pointed slipper, drove it into Parker's groin and stepped quickly back as the American doubled forward, barely able to hold his hands concealed behind his back.

Parker gasped at the kick and lay still.

"Name," Nissral asked.

"Hopalong Cassidy," Parker replied.

This time he moved before Nissral's kick arrived, managed to catch the blow on tensed stomach muscles. Nissral followed it with a second kick, landed on Parker's cheek. As the Terasian stepped back Parker felt blood begin to flow where the flesh had torn beneath his eye. This guy didn't kid around.

The American volunteered "Parker."

He saw Nissral nod at that. "Good," Nissral said, "now you are doing better. How came you here?"

Parker looked at the Terasian, said "Byeryas sent me."

"And what were you doing aboard the Bakhid?"

"Just a pleasure cruise with a beautiful girl," Parker said.

For a moment Nissral looked enraged, seemed about to move forward to punish Parker further, then backed instead until he stood again in the center of the room. "Enough banter," he said. "Had you given me the answers

I required you might have died quickly and without too great suffering, Parker."

No sib nonsense, Parker told himself.

Nissral resumed, "But you would make yourself obnoxious with remarks. Very well." The Terasian removed his cloak and lay it on the floor, the outer side of the material against the stone floor of the room. He moved to the far side of the cloak, wearing beneath it what looked to Parker like a carefully tailored silken version of the usual baggy Terasian garb.

Nissral knelt beside the cloak, began to make motions on it with his hands. He looked up at Parker for a moment, said "Our mutual friend Byeryas remains aboard the Bakhid when it is in port. From the captain's cabin she will hear your cries. But do not worry. When I am questioning, cries are often heard." He resumed whatever it was he had been doing on the cape.

Parker craned his neck, trying to see what Nissral was up to without giving away the freedom of his limbs. The Terasian's cloak clearly had pockets and loops distributed on its inner surface. Nissral was running his hands over many of the objects attached to the cloak, letting a finger rest for a moment on one, then pulling back, testing the edge of another. He's good, Parker had to concede silently. Kind of crude, but he has a psychological touch too.

He saw the Terasian stop again, draw an instrument from a loop in the cape and began to rise. Okay now, Parker thought. Any doubts I had about killing a stranger, they're gone. And if his prisoners are usually noisy, that means I don't have to keep him all quiet, that's a break.

Nissral walked around his cloak, slowly approached Parker, dropped to one knee just beyond the range that a bound man might reach in one desperate lunge with his feet. This guy *is* good, Parker thought. Well, he should be with thirty years of practice under his belt.

Nissral held up a metalic object. It looked like a simple band, perhaps three quarters of an inch in width, thin enough to be flexible and closed into a loop the better part of a foot in diameter. Where the metal band closed with itself to form the loop there was a small attachment that looked like a gripper and small butterfly nut.

"I want you to understand all that is happening," Nissral said. "I intend to let you feel this fool's crown in a moment. Then you will tell me all the circumstances that led to your capture by Byeryas' soldiers and your imprisonment on the Bakhid."

Parker started to speak to Nissral but the Terasian shushed him. "No point in answering now," he told Parker, "you will feel the crown in any case. Save your answer until I ask for it."

Nissral scuttled around until he was squatted beside the wall beyond Parker's head, perfectly safe from any attempt by a man in Parker's position with hands and feet bound. Come on, Parker thought, straining his neck back and rolling his eyes upward to see what the Terasian would do. Come on, it's almost time, you're almost in the right spot.

The Terasian reached forward with the metallic band, slipped it over the American's head until it was resting above his ears, the band circling forehead, temples, and the back of his skull. Nissral held the band in place with one hand, suddenly struck Parker on the forehead with his other fist so the prisoner's skull snapped back and struck the floor. Nissral leaned forward, steadying the band with one hand, with the other grasped the butterfly nut and began to tighten. An excruciating pain filled Parker's head, sparks began to swirl before his eyes. He gasped, cried aloud, jerked one hand from beneath him and struck sideways at the Terasian bending over him.

Nissral was driven sideways by the blow. Off balance, his hands were jerked from the torture instrument, unintentionally dragging it from Parker's head, tearing the flier's flesh again, this time drawing a gout of blood from the American's forehead. As Nissral toppled backwards Parker sprang from the floor to a crouching position, blood streaming now from both forehead and cheek, lunged forward at the startled inquisitor.

He got both hands onto Nissral's throat, squeezed with both, his unburned hand tight on the Terasian's jugular, the other, injured hand doing duty an inch above, its muscles obeying Parker's commands, the charred flesh ignored in the struggle. Through his own streaming blood Parker saw Nissral's expression of surprise and terror, saw the Terasian open his mouth to cry for assistance. All that came was a rasping noise, accompanied by Parker's quiet, breathless laugh. He gripped and wrenched at the Terasian's throat, felt a sudden crumble within, then felt himself lifted surprisingly and thrown by Nissral's convulsive reaction.

Parker landed yards away, hard. He staggered to his feet, felt an impact from behind and landed on the floor again. He scrambled, twisted, saw Nissral leaping toward his cloak to get some weapon. Parker was after the Terasian, dived in a football tackle, failed to grasp Nissral firmly but managed to knock him half-sideways, away from his object. Parker sprang to his feet again, stood on guard between Nissral and the cloak with its implements. Nissral opened his mouth again as if to cry for aid, but again there was no sound.

Quietly Parker said "Crushed voice box, Terasian!" He began to edge cautiously forward, wished that he had Byeryas' knife in his hand but dared not bend to open his leg bandage and retrieve it. Parker saw Nissral move to one side as if to dodge past him, lunged to stop the Terasian. Instead Nissral moved the other way. Off balance, Parker was barely able to twist, kick at the wiry figure moving past him. He connected with Nissral, deflected the Terasian from his cloak once again.

Nissral turned, Parker threw a long punch at his face, felt his hand connect but at the same time felt a jab from Nissral's bony fingers plunge into his solar plexus, barely missing a fatal rupture of the sternum. Parker rabbit-punched at the Terasian's neck, missed his target and landed glancingly on Nissral's ear. A hand sped toward Parker's face, gouged at one eye already half-blinded with blood from the flier's torn forehead. Parker felt Nissral's grasping fingers slip on the flowing blood.

He jerked backward from the sharp nails, shot one foot forward and upward at Nissral, saw him in turn double over, clutching at his groin. Parker leaped at the other, threw an arm around his back, one hand in the Terasian's armpit, the other holding him by the chin, ran with him once, with every bit of remaining strength, brought up violently at the stone wall, fell gasping onto the floor with Nissral still in his arms.

Parker disengaged himself from the limp Terasian, stood over him and looked down. Nissral appeared strangly foreshortened. In the half light cast by the room's flickering torch Parker could not tell for certain whether Nissral's neck was broken or his skull crushed by his impact against the wall, or both. Parker turned from the body and staggered to the barred window of the room.

He carefully removed the dagger from his leg bandage and began to chip at the cement holding the stone blocks of the window into the wall of the building. By the time he had badly blunted the point of the dagger he was convinced that he could not get the cement cleared that way. For a moment his mind was a complete, hopeless blank. Then he turned once again, stood with his back propped against the stone wall, and surveyed the room.

The door opposite was still closed, thank God for that, and by Nissral's earlier words, Parker thought, the door was likely to stay closed until some signal was given by Nissral. Which, of course, would never happen. Otherwise, Parker guessed, he was reasonably safe in the room until ... oh, at least the following dawn.

Parker walked to the place where Nissral's body lay, stood over the unmoving form and gazed at the Terasian's clothing. He might get into the Terasian's brown garb, for all that the trousers and jacket of the thinner man would be strained by Parker's dimensions. The cape that lay in the middle of the room would help also. Let's see, Parker thought, if I even put on the cloak I might make it past someone in the darkness. I could call for the door to be opened, leave Nissral huddled in the corner and before they realized that they had the wrong corpse . . . risky, but a chance.

Except for calling the acolytes to open the door. I don't know what jargon Nissral would use, and a man in his position would almost surely use some kind of distinctive speech. Damn!

Okay, an alternate. Wait for the day shift to come on and open the door, then try the same stunt. But then I lose the advantage of the darkness. In daylight I wouldn't last five minutes.

Parker strode angrily up and down in the room, walked to the window again and tugged futilely at the bars, retraced his steps to stand over the corpse once more, silently cursing Nissral for not offering any help. Parker strode to the Terasian's cape, kicked angrily at it as Nissral's torture instruments threw back the faint, flickering light of the torch that lit the room. When Parker kicked at the cape the instruments clanked.

He dropped to one knee in an instant, began to inspect

the tools that Nissral had brought in the pockets and loops of the long garment. One bore an uncanny resemblance to a giant corkscrew. Parker shuddered at the possibilities the tool suggested, imagining Nissral happily at work using it on a bound prisoner who screamed and begged and screamed and was Robert Leroy Parker.

He pulled the corkscrew from its holder in the Terasian's cape, carried it to the window and tried gouging out the stone around one of the stone bars. It did not work. He shifted his attack to the seam where window stone was cemented to wall stone. The cement was carefully applied, making a surface flush with the two adjacent planes of stone. Parker began scraping away at the cement, found gratefully that it yielded to the hard, sharp point of the tool.

Parker worked until he had gouged a miniature trench completely around the window stones, upper and lower. If they would go he could follow easily. But the curve of the metal stopped it from following deeply between the stones. Parker placed the corkscrew on the floor, gently—no need to call attention now, with needless sounds . . . or would silence be more suspicious than noise? He retrieved the corkscrew, threw it against the stone door of the room, let go a loud moan that took no special effort.

He felt better then. Okay, Butchy, he told himself. Let's not be haphazard about this. The corkscrew was the first thing that caught our eye, fine, but let's see what else Nissral was kind enough to furnish for our convenience.

Parker returned to the cape, squatted beside it and began more carefully to examine the Terasian instruments it contained. The purpose of some he could only guess at, that of others was all too clear. A kind of iron glove . . . a long thin instrument, hmm, too flexible for scraping cement . . . a. . . . Parker stopped, lifted the thing to get a better look at it. A hypodermic needle?

He examined the hollow tube, the syringe-like container to which it was attached, the plunger that made the thing work. The syringe was empty, apparently. Parker held the needle before his face, pointed it upward and slightly away from himself, worked the plunger in and out several times. Nothing seemed to come out. He pointed it downward, worked the plunger again. Still nothing. He pointed it toward his hand, tried again, felt a miniature breeze as air was pushed through the needle. No question about what it was, and that it was in good working order.

But why did Nissral have it? And was Terasian science that far advanced? From what Parker had seen aboard the Bakhid and since his arrival in the city, little though that was, he could still form an opinion of Terasian technology, and it was not on the level of a society that used injected medicines. Unless . . . it was *not* representative of Terasian development any more than WinLao's autogyro was typical of Par'zian science. Unless Nissral's hypo; like WinLao's aerial machine, was a sport, an isolated development, almost an accident.

And what was it used for? Swiftly Parker scanned over the remaining objects inside Nissral's cloak, found what he was looking for: several bottles of glazed clay, their mouths stoppered with some stuff resembling paraffin. He set one on the floor, carefully scraped away the seal with the still-razorlike edge of his Terasian dagger. He laid the dagger on the floor, raised the bottle and looked in. He caught only a glint of torchlight reflected from a liquid surface.

He held the bottle to his nose, sniffed. No odor. Holding the bottle in one hand, gingerly able to get some use of his burned arm and hand, he picked up the long flexible instrument from Nissral's cape with his other hand, dipped its end into the bottle, brought it out with a drop of clear liquid on it. He held the stuff before his eyes. It looked like water, but that seemed unlikely. He deposited the drop on the cloth of Nissral's cape still at his feet.

In an instant a tiny wisp of smoke rose from the spot where he had placed the drop. The smoke dissipated into the atmosphere in the room. Parker looked at the cloak where he had placed the liquid. A neat hole had appeared. He lifted the edge of the cloak, examined the floor beneath it. There was a small pit beneath the spot where the liquid had been placed.

Some stain remover *that* stuff would make, Parker mused. If he'd spilled something on the cloak that marred even the floor beneath it, the fluid would remove even the second stain. What was it? Parker rubbed his head in puzzlement, quickly stopped when a fresh flow of blood from his torn forehead began. Still, the stuff's action did not seem wholly new. It was like . . . the acid from the kissers! Either Teras was synthesizing organic chemicals, or . . . no, that was impossible! If *not*, then Nissral or his people were somehow harvesting the acid like ants milking aphids.

That didn't seem very likely either, but it made more sense than a highly-developed chemical industry in this otherwise non-technological country. Okay, so Nissral used a hypodermic needle and an organic acid for torture and murder. What good did that do Parker?

He placed the bottle carefully on the floor, lowered the tip of Nissral's hypodermic into the fluid, drew out the plunger. Careful to avoid any contact with the acid he carried the needle to the window, held the needle almost flat against the stone and pushed gently on the plunger, releasing a small volume of the liquid. A line etched itself in the stone. Parker moved the needle away, looked closely at the new mark he had made in the wall. Promising but far too slow.

He held the needle to the cement at the bottom of the trench he had dug around the window, repeated the experiment. The cement crumbled away like so much wet sand. Holding the hypodermic in his hand Parker jumped once, began dancing around the prison room in relieved delight. "Oh, Christ," he keened, "oh Christ, oh Moses, oh Buddha, oh Mohammed, oh oh oh oh I wish I knew the names of InzXa's nine hundred gods, oh God I'm gonna get out of here alive!"

He danced back to the cloak of the dead Nissral, knelt and carefully filled the hypodermic syringe to its capacity, moved back to the window and began working his way around the stone, carefully squirting the acid onto the cement, watching it crumble away, squirting again. After a little while he retrieved Nissral's long thin tool and used it to brush and scrape away at the crumbled cement.

When the work was nearly half done the bottle was empty. Parker counted the remaining bottles from the Terasian's cloak. There were plenty—if they all held the kisser fluid or something equally useful.

Parker did not stop to speculate. He opened a second bottle, filled his hypodermic, returned to the window and resumed work, tentatively trying one shot of the stuff to see if it still worked. It did. Before very long he was able to feel some give in the whole window unit when he strained at the bars. More work. Parker looked outside through the bars. It was still black out. He wondered how long it would be till morning, realized that he had no notion at all, went back to squirting acid at cement and clearing away crumbled remains.

Suddenly the window unit shifted by itself. Just the slightest bit, but enough. It was loose. Parker put the needle aside, tugged at the bars, felt a little more give, planted his feet beneath the window and shoved on the bars. They yielded, leaned away from Parker's fingers, pulled irresistably out of his grasp. The whole unit, stone, bars, stone toppled away from Parker, disappeared leaving a gaping hole as wide and as high as Parker's arm was long, in the middle of the black stone wall.

After what seemed like a long time there was a huge crash from below the tower. Parker leaned out the newly enlarged window and looked down. He could see nothing, but by the sound of its landing the stone assemblage had struck not water but some solid object. A projection of the building itself? A dock? There was supposed to be water below. Parker was supposed to dive and be picked up by Byeryas' men. But if there was something solid there . . . was this the right room? Did Byeryas have her recollection of the building's layout twisted? Was there water only a few feet beyond where the stone had struck, or had Parker been betrayed?

He stood back into the room. Everything had looked as if it was working out, for a moment. Now . . . now it was all a question again.

From below, both within the building and without, Parker heard shouts and the sounds of running feet. Someone would surely be here in a minute to investigate. He looked outside again, still saw nothing, heard footsteps and voices growing closer in the building. Parker climbed on the new-made, lower window sill, balanced himself to jump, then stopped, frozen. He had killed Nissral at Byeryas' bidding. His only hope now was to be saved by Byeryas. He needed the grisly souvenir that Byeryas demanded of the deed!

Parker dropped back into the room, grasped his knife, ran to the corpse of the Terasian inquisitor. He hesitated for a moment, averted his eyes, then looked back, plunged the partially-blunted tip of the weapon into Nissral's flesh below the left lowermost rib, drew it horizontally until the Terasian's organs lay exposed.

He looked up as the door to the room began to open.

Parker dropped his knife, seized two of the remaining bottles of kisser acid, threw them in quick succession. One sailed high as a brown-clad Terasian acolyte entered the doorway. The liquid rained upon him. For an instant he stood framed in the opening, then staggered back writhing and screaming. The second bottle struck short of the door, spraying its contents onto two more acolytes who pushed past their retreating comrade. They collapsed, their legs suddenly porous-looking to Parker, who watched them clawing at themselves and heard their screams.

Before more guards could arrive Parker returned to his bloody work. He thrust his good hand into the chest cavity behind Nissral's ribs, felt around, discovered a roundish, fleshy object. He closed his fingers around it, put one knee on Nissral's chest above to hold the corpse in place, heaved backward and upward. With a wet squishing noise the thing came out in his hand.

Clutching the bloody prize Parker ran across the room, hurled himself from window to get as far from the wall of the building as he could, arched over into a serviceable imitation of a diver's jack-knife, and headed down, he hoped, into water.

CHAPTER

18

Parker sat once more in the darkened cabin of Byeryas, captain of the Terasian ship Bakhid. The sunlight from outside the cabin, intensified by its reflection upon sea water, penetrated the two covered portholes of the cabin only enough to provide a gloomy twilight in the room. Opposite Parker squatted the grotesque parody of woman that commanded the ship. At either side of the captain Parker could barely discern a darkly garbed form that blended almost unnoticeably into the darkness of the room.

"You fill me with astonishment and admiration," Byer-yas told Parker.

He asked why.

"You succeeded in a task I thought impossible, for-eigner. You not only freed yourself of Nissral's captivity and actually slew him in naked combat—I hoped all along that you might succeed in that—but you tore open the building itself to escape. Truly remarkable!"

Parker shifted his position on the carpet. "You lied to me about the window bars, Byeryas."

"I did not," the monster returned. "Truly I did not lie." She lifted both her swollen arms, fluttered her tiny hands placatingly. "They must have remade the window since I last saw it, Parker-sib. When I was in that room"—she paused, resumed in a lower voice—"When I was in that room last, long ago, the bars were cemented to the blocks above and below the window. It was remade and I did not know it."

"Well, no matter," Parker said. "I got out. I was lucky to clear the dock with my jump and land in the water. If the stones hadn't gone first I might have dropped straight down and wound up with broken feet or worse. That would have been a bad old joke on me!" He did not laugh. Neither, to Parker's pleasure, did Byeryas.

She said "I am glad that your new wounds are no more serious than your burn. In your bandages you look a dying man."

Parker grinned and raised a bandaged hand to a band-aged cheek, then to the head wrappings that held a clean pad and salve over his torn forehead. He said "Yes, well, it was the knife in the leg bandages that saved me. Now that I've kept my half of the bargain, Captain Byeryas, what about your keeping yours?"

Byeryas grinned back. "One question only. Once you found that you could not remove the bars from the win-dow, how did you succeed in tearing that hole in the wall? Teras will probably think they have held a superman imprisoned, and fortunate to be rid of him at the cost of only four lives."

"I'm kind of sorry about those other three. A little time with the late Nissral, Captain Byeryas, and I under-stood how you could want his heart ripped out. But I guess those three guards, uh, acolytes, were just ordinary soldiers on guard doing their duty. Well, you go in the soldier business, you take your chances on that. It's too bad."

"The window, Parker-sib."

"Oh, yes, the window. Captain Byeryas, do you think those acolytes were volunteers or conscripts?"

"In Teras no such distinction is drawn, Parker-sib. Clearly you do not understand Teras. Every Terasian is a soldier of the state and a soldier of God and virtue. Work, prayer, fighting when necessary, all are the duty of every citizen. All wear the brown of Teras, all are organized into disciplined units, march to work or to prayer or to battle. The three guards you killed were neither conscripted nor persuaded to serve. The very question of whether they would serve or not was never raised. They were Terasians, that sufficed.

"How did you burst the window?" she added.

"What if I won't tell you?" asked Parker.

The huge Terasian woman grinned at Parker, hesitated as if toying with possible answers. Parker felt the room grow suddenly close and unpleasantly warm. He tried not to squirm. At last Byeryas said "You have brought me revenge I have longed for for thirty years, Parker-sib. For thirty years have I served Teras faithfully and well, but never from a sense of duty, believe me.

"I do not hate Par'z, hopelessly sealed within a dead volcano. I do not care about Relori fishermen. On orders I stop one now and then, harass a little, turn most loose, kill a few, it matters little or nothing to me. Only did I bide my time. Only did I pray that both Nissral and I should live and not go to fertilize Terasian crops.

"I waited only for the opportunity to have him killed, to have him killed with pain and degradation, and to hold in my hand the trophy of his murder.

"You brought me this, Parker-sib. Oh, I savor the thought of Nissral's fears when you cast off the crown and seized him. What art to wait, to let him tease you first, to accept the blows of his foot, to let him settle to his foul torture and then to attack! Oh, lovely, Parker-sib. And to die under your bare hands, broken like an egg upon a wall, it is too beautiful! And the heart, the very heart, torn still hot and bloody from his new-dead body and brought to me as if from the sky!" With the last words, Byeryas' voice rose ecstatically until Parker feared she would become hysterical, but she stopped speaking suddenly, sat panting in her never-changing position.

Parker watched Byeryas reach one dainty hand forward, her gross body bending and straining with the effort. She patted him fondly on the cheek that did not bear a wound. "You don't want to tell me how you opened the window, Parker-sib? So don't tell me. So what," she said.

Parker realized suddenly that he had been holding his breath through Byeryas' dizzy speech. He let out a lungful of air, drew in another, repeated his question. "Will you keep your half of the bargain? Will you take me where I wish to go and then leave me?"

Byeryas nodded. Then she said "Where?"

Parker said "I want to go to Relore."

"I thought as much," Byeryas answered. "I thought you were no Par'zman, for all that my men found you on the island of Par'z. You are Relori, then?"

Now Parker held silent for a moment, deciding what to tell the Terasian captain. The truth, he decided, no need to lie now to Byeryas. But—what was the truth? Finally he said "Yes, I am a Relori."

Byeryas grinned once again, said "You took long to answer so simple a question. Would you deceive me? I think you are not a Par'zman and I am quite certain you are no Terasian, you could not fool me to that degree. So by elimination—and also by your boots—I thought you a Relori from the start. If not. . . ."

"You could say that I'm an adopted Relori," Parker said.

"Then where is your original home?"

"Just someplace far away," Parker said. "A place very far away, and I have been gone from there for a time so long that your thirty years of exile from Teras is to it, as a flickering instant must be to a long lifetime."

"Perhaps you do not wish to return to your home," Byeryas said. "I mean to your home in Relore. I have no further interest in Teras, Parker-sib. I am avenged against Nissral. For me, Teras is a dead place.

"The crew of my ship are loyal to me. Teras to them is only a place of loathing anyway, work and oppression, mating by command and by schedule, their children selected or abandoned by the state so they are strangers to their parents even if they survive. They will sail with me if I command it. Or even ask it.

"Shall we sail for your distant country, Parker-sib?"

Parker's head spun at the prospect. Home, Byeryas offered to take him home. Away from the Country, away from Relore in the woods, away from sleeping Par'z, away from black Teras. Could the Bakhid cross an ocean? Parker consulted a mental geography. The ship would not really have to cross an ocean at that. She could sail northward to the tip of the Palmer Peninsula, then sprint across blue water where the Bellinghausen blended into the Pacific and the Pacific into the Atlantic.

That would be the only really tough part. Less then a thousand miles of open water to Cape Horn. Then they could sail up either coast, past Chile and Peru to California or along Argentina, round the corner where Brazil poked toward Africa, cross the Caribbean and then either into the Gulf or up the Atlantic coast again.

What would be there? Certainly no United States of America. Not after *millions* of years. Would there be any trace of the old civilization, or only savagery . . . or some new society with a culture and science of its own?

Parker held his hands to his head, trying to squeeze a decision out of himself. Then he said "Byeryas, I must go first to Relore. There are others . . . I have promised."

Byeryas asked "A woman?"

"And a child," Parker said, "also adopted, if they will have me. Let me return there and speak with them. Then I will decide."

Byeryas sighed. "I had hoped," she paused, "I had hoped to go—*now*, without hesitation, without debate. But you are right. I will order my crew to stop the first Relori fishing craft they see. You will be transferred to that craft. Go on to Relore and your woman and your child."

She gestured to one of the figures beside her. It rose, took Parker firmly by a shoulder and guided him from the cabin. Dazzled again by the brightness on deck, Parker sat shading his eyes with his hands and watching the child of Byeryas confer with the under-priest on deck. The under-priest nodded agreement, looking at Parker; then returned to his chanting while the child of Byeryas disappeared into the cabin once more.

Today it did not rain, although at mid-morning clouds turned the sky a dark gray and a cold gale swept the Bakhid. Parker watched the dark clouds slide across the sky, the masts of the ship silhouetted against their movement. By afternoon the same wind that had chilled the bandaged passenger had also swept away the clouds, leaving a sun that shone brightly in a crystal day.

Parker plodded from the ship's bow to its stern, sat, managed to doze briefly but awoke unrefreshed, made his way back again, gazed listlessly at the unchanging sea, then at the unchanging oarsmen of the Bakhid, their figures rising and bending and rising again as they stroked the ship now southward under the steady chanting of a sub-priest, their reliefs scattered about the deck planks and benches of the ship chatting in small groups, dozing, moving about.

From the under-priest directing the rowers came a new call, a changed chant. Parker ran to the very prow of the ship, his interest renewed by the priest's cry.

Ahead he could see a tiny speck upon the water, bobbing with the low swells that went all but unnoticed on the larger Bakhid. The priest had picked up the tempo of his chant. Whether by some signal or pre-arrangement off-duty sailors rapidly took up positions alongside perspiring rowers. Parker turned his gaze down one side of the Bakhid, back along the other. Every oar was now manned by at least two Terasians, some by three.

The pace of the Bakhid picked up perceptibly. Parker counted oar-strokes, watched the surface of the water now boiling past the wooded hull of the ship, trying unsuccessfully to calculate her speed. But when he again looked ahead to the speck the Bakhid pursued it was clear that she was gaining rapidly on her prey.

Soon Parker could make out the object ahead. It was a dugout identical to the one he and Broadarm and Kaetha had used to travel from the Country to Par'z, perhaps the very one. He strained his eyes to make out the paddlers aboard. Again there were three; Parker could not make out their identities—the dugout had her stern to the Bakhid and was moving straight ahead as fast as six arms could move the simple craft, Parker could tell. But the garb of the three in the dugout plus the nature of their craft told Parker that they were Relori.

When the Bakhid had come within fifty yards of the dugout the three men in the tiny craft shipped their paddles and turned toward the onrushing Terasian ship.

All three held Relori longbows, arrows nocked, pointed defiantly at the pursuing ship.

Parker climbed onto the prow of the Bakhid, held precariously to a wooded projection with his good hand while he waved the burned one in the air. "Hold on!" he shouted at the Relori. "We're not raiders. We won't harm you."

For a moment there was a consultation aboard the dugout. Then the Relori in the stern of the canoe, closest to the larger ship, cupped his hands to his mouth, his previously nocked arrow still held in one hand. "Who are you?" he shouted. "What do you want?"

Parker listened to the Relori's voice as much as to his words. The intonation was familiar, the face . . . he squinted at the Relori. . . . "Is that you, Scenter?" he shouted back.

The man looked startled. He called up to the ship "Yes. I ask you again, who are *you?*"

"I'm Parker," the aviator called back, "don't you recognize me? Robert Leroy Parker." He watched the Relori as he looked up, puzzlement giving way to recognition.

At last Scenter asked "What happened to you, you are all bandages! Are you a prisoner?"

"No," Parker started to shout. Then "Well, yes, I was. Scenter, I'll explain later. The Terasians have agreed to set me free, will you just take me aboard?"

Again the Relori looked puzzled. Then, to Parker's relief, he said "All right, we will approach you."

Parker turned to relay Scenter's message to the chanting under-priest, found that the priest had been listening to his exchange and that the Bakhid's sailors were already holding the ship steady with their oars rather than propelling it through the water.

"Tell the Relori that I'm coming with them, I'll be right back," Parker called to the priest on deck. He raced past rows of Terasian oarsmen, reached the darkened cabin of the Bakhid's commander, swung under the overhanging deck planks and into the darkened room. His eyes still dilated by the deck's brightness of sun and sky and water, Parker felt the cabin's darkness thicker and blacker than he ever before had. He stumbled forward in the darkness, called out "Byeryas, the Relori are here. I will go now, with them. I have come. . . ." He stopped in mid-sentence. Something was wrong in the cabin, something missing.

Parker stood for a moment in the darkness, in the silence, suddenly disoriented. He put his hand to his forehead, tried to think, to imagine what was wrong. "Byeryas," he began again. Then he knew what was wrong. From the first time he had entered this cabin until this time the rhythmic wheeze of the gross officer's tortured breathing had filled his ears. The first time he had heard it the sound had filled his consciousness with chilling speculation about its source. Later he had grown accustomed, practically ceased to notice the sound, but always, in Byeryas' cabin, there had been the sound of Byeryas' breathing.

Now the sound was absent.

Parker made his way to the side of the room, burst open a porthole. Light streamed into the room, more light now than ever Parker had seen in the place. He turned back to the captain's never-changing position. She sat there as ever, hairless pate lolling forward, her great fleshy torso seeming only a hung mound of boneless, soft flesh; great, pendulous breasts resting on roll and roll of fat, grossly bloated limbs in repose.

From between the gigantic mammaries there projected the hilt of a Terasian dagger, its handle bloody. Parker walked closer to the gigantic corpse, looked down at it, saw that the hands, too, were bloody. To either side of Byeryas lay a dark shrouded shape, blood on each chest.

The American gave way to impulse, laid one hand on the dead flesh of the Terasian captain, with his hand bracing the body in place he pulled the bloody-hilted dagger from her bosom. A fresh gout of blood followed the weapon from between the mammoth breasts. Parker looked closely at the dagger, then tossed it down on the carpeting of the room.

He turned back to the exit of the cabin, climbed onto the deck of the Bakhid. He walked quickly to the bow of the ship and spoke to the priest standing there. "I have made my farewells to Captain Byeryas," he said. "I will go with the fishermen now."

The priest nodded assent. Parker crossed to the gunwale of the Bakhid, looked over the side to see that the Relori dugout was being held alongside by her three crewmen who steadied their little craft by holding onto Terasian oars. Parker clambered over the gunwale and down into the dugout where he sat in front of Scenter.

Parker spoke to Scenter in as low a voice as he could muster. "Don't delay," he said. "Don't seem to be running off or they'll pursue us, but get away fast and get to shore fast!"

He looked back up at the deck of the Bakhid from which he had just climbed down. The under-priest was still at the gunwale looking over, the ship's oars were still held unmoving. Parker smiled at the priest and waved a hand. "Good-bye," he called. "Thanks for all the good food, and have a good trip."

The priest did not answer but remained gazing down at the canoe and Parker. Again Parker said softly to Scenter, "Let's go!"

The Relori laid his bow on the floor of the dugout, took up his paddle and began to stroke with it. Quickly the other Relori followed suit. Before they had gone a hundred yards Scenter asked Parker what had happened, and why the hurry to paddle to land now that they were away from the Terasian ship.

"Their captain is dead," Parker said, "but they don't know it. It was suicide but when they find the body they'll think I did it!"

The Relori paddled rapidly away from the Bakhid, at first on a southerly course but quickly swinging to the southeast and then almost due east, heading for the mainland shore. Parker cast glances behind them repeatedly but the Terasian ship, once distanced, did not appear again. Did that mean that the priests had not discovered the corpses in Byeryas' cabin—or that they had chosen not to pursue the smaller craft—or simply that the tiny Relori dugout had lost the Terasian vessel? Parker wondered, but not for long. What mattered was that Scenter and he and the other Relori now had clear travelling to the shore.

They made land before sundown, beached the canoe, then secured it as Parker had first seen the canoe Broadarm and Kaetha had used to get him to Par'z. No giant to do the task this time—the three Relori strained to lift the wooden hull; Parker found himself drafted to lend an extra set of muscles in getting the dugout raised and secured in the lower branches of a bonewood. Bottom up, no rainwater would accumulate in the dugout to rot out its bottom.

They quickly found their camp, game hanging over a slowly smouldering fire, light packs hung nearby. Parker looked at the smoky little fire, admired the efficiency of it—the hanging meat was smoked and at the same time scavengers were held off by the same fire. Smokey the bear might not like the idea, but this wasn't his forest.

When the fishermen began to sprawl about the camp Parker asked Scenter if they wouldn't be safer moving on before they slept.

"The Terasians do not know where our camp is," Scenter said. "The smoke is so little they will not see it. We should be safe here until morning at least, and then we will be gone."

Parker shrugged. "I guess you know your business," he said. "I'm kind of worried, but if you're sure. . . ."

Scenter said he was.

Parker said, "Okay, but then, uh. . . ."

Scenter jerked his sharp-featured face up, looked at Parker. "Then what?" he demanded.

"Then, uh, if you'll introduce me to your friends, and, um, Scenter, it seems that every time you come across me in the boondocks I'm barefooted. I'll have to borrow another pair of moccasins if anybody has some with him."

Scenter laughed, introduced Parker and the two other fishermen. One of them had moccasins in his pack, offered them to Parker. Parker tried the shoes, found he could wear them, thanked the Relori.

"Now," Scenter said, "we have to decide what to do. Parker, you and Broadarm and Kaetha left Relore together some . . . let me see . . . about ten or twelve days past."

"Right," Parker replied. "I've lost track of the exact time."

"Broadarm and Kaetha returned. . . ."

"They're both all right?" Parker interrupted.

"Yes, both well. They said they left you on the island of the wizards. Now you are given back to us by a ship of Teras. What happened?"

Parker rubbed his bandaged head with his bandaged hand, wondered what he could tell Scenter and the others without staying up all night talking. Finally he said "Look,

Scenter, I'm not keeping secrets from you or anything like that . . ."

The Relori nodded.

". . . but so damned much happened in a few days, and I know Olduncle will want a full version . . ."

Scenter nodded again.

". . . but okay, briefly then. After Broadarm and Kaetha left me I got into Par'z. What happened in Par'z—" Parker's brain whirled with recollections "— well, a lot happened there, but what matters is that when I got back out I ran into some Terasians. I got mixed up in, uh, I guess you could call it an old Terasian political squabble. Strictly involuntarily.

"But I had to clear out of there fast. The same side that I had to do some dirty work for also paid off by freeing me. That's how come they picked you fellows up today, Scenter. That's about it."

Parker sat quietly, holding close the knowledge that Kaetha had returned safely to Relore, was there now waiting for him, and he was on his way back to her. To his friends, too, Broadarm . . . Broadarm, and the warm, gregarious Janna, and little Trili.

Scenter interrupted his pleased musings with another question. "But the dead captain of that ship," he wanted to know, "what is that all about? And what kind of dirty work did you do in Teras?"

"Oh, the captain of the ship, well. She was a horrible old woman," Parker said. "I think she was, anyway, or maybe it was just a long obsession with revenge that made her act. . . ." Parker stopped talking for a moment, stared into the fire thinking about all he had killed or, even un-intending, caused to be killed. Strange, a military man in his old life, yet he had never killed in a war. Only Carlos, when he was a boy, and that only in desperation. And now, in the span of a couple of days. . . . These were peo-ple, not paper targets or leering demons, even the worst of them. Chacla at her worst had apparently acted from a sense of duty, however fanatical. Even Nissral . . . well, Nissral clearly enjoyed his work. If there was a leering monster among them, it was Nissral. But what had made him as he was?

"The captain," Scenter prompted.

Parker abandoned his musings. "I'm sorry," he said. "I was a captive on the Bakhid. The captain took me to

Teras to give me to their chief inquisitor. It meant death by torture."

He looked at the three impassive faces of his listeners. There was a moment of silence, then Parker went on. "Before they turned me over to the torturer, though, the captain said that she had an old score to settle with him. She gave me a knife. It was a question of die under torture or kill the torturer and escape. I don't think I have to defend my choice between the two."

Parker looked at the others. Scenter shrugged at the implied question. He said "But the captain?"

"I got back to the ship," Parker said. "I even brought the torturer's heart with me, ripped from his body." He shuddered now at the recollection of the stone room, the silent corpse, the slit he had made below the ribs. . . . "The captain was pleased. She had her revenge at last. But," Parker sighed, "Once she had her revenge, she had nothing left to interest her. She had two grown children on the ship with her. She killed them both and then herself."

"And you think the Terasians will hold you responsible for her suicide?" asked Scenter.

"I don't think they'll think it was suicide. I think they'll decide that I killed her."

Scenter rubbed his jaw. "By the Founder, Parker, they'll be after you for four murders then, the torturer, the ship captain, and the two children."

Parker sighed again. "More than that," he said. "They had three agents in Par'z. Two of them killed the third, and later I killed the other two to keep them from setting up an invasion. I guess one more or less won't really matter, but the Terasians will probably blame me for all three deaths. And the torturer I killed, some guards bought theirs too. I couldn't help that. There were three of them. Then Byeryas—that was the captain's name— and her two children. That makes, uh, ten murders that they'll blame me for." He shuddered again at the number of lives taken within twenty-four hours. Well, counting the spies, a little longer. Mmmff, so what.

"I really did kill, uh, six Terasians." He looked at the Relori sitting around him. Their faces held neither condemnation nor approval. "I don't think any were murder. Only Nissral—the torturer—was premeditated, but even then if I hadn't got him first he would have killed me under torture."

"We cannot judge you," Scenter said. "My concern is only with what Teras will do now. I think we had best all return to Relore as quickly as we can. We will forget about fishing now. In the morning we will set out and make the best speed we can. We should have enough food for the trip. If we happen to come across game as we travel, all right, but not hunting parties as such.

"Parker, when we reach Relore you will tell Olduncle all you have told us, I hope, and give him more information. You seem to be only a victim of . . ." Parker saw Scenter shrug, visibly grope for words ". . . of happenstance," the Relori resumed. "But I fear this may be a very serious matter for all of Relore."

Parker stood and walked about the little camp. "I'm afraid you're right, Scenter," he said. "But I don't see what I could have done any different." Let Par'z go under? he thought. That was the crucial point, and Par'z meant nothing to the Relori.

"We cannot judge you," Scenter said again. "We must get back to Relore and help Olduncle determine what must be done, that is all."

CHAPTER

19

They reached Relore in less than three days of forced marches, long trail sessions, short rests, torzzi watches at night, early starts and late stops. They reached the palisade exhausted and hungry; Parker in particular finding that his burned hand and torn face, although apparently healing without infection, still took his strength.

Once inside the settlement Parker headed for the house Kaetha and Trili shared with Fleet. He felt a hand on his arm, turned and saw Scenter looking earnestly at him. "Did you not agree to give Olduncle a full account of these days?" the Relori asked.

Parker hesitated, torn in two directions. After a moment he took Scenter's hand in his own and pulled it from his arm. "You go ahead to Olduncle's cabin," he said. "I'll meet you there right away. If he can't wait for me, you can start filling him in."

Scenter looked at Parker doubtfully.

"I'll be there," Parker said, "don't worry."

Scenter turned away and headed for the village leader's home. Parker watched him for a few steps, saw the other fishermen headed away, then turned once more toward Kaetha's house. He walked quickly, looked for a moment at the sky as he walked. The sun was low; by this time the day's work should be over, Kaetha should be home. Parker made his way between the log buildings of Relore, ignoring the stares that his bandages won for him. For the last few dozen yards he ran.

Inside the cabin Parker saw Kaetha giving dinner to her daughter while Fleet sat nearby sharpening a friendmaker. Parker stopped for the briefest moment in the doorway of the cabin. He watched Kaetha as she saw him there, put down the child's dishes and stood; to Parker it seemed that the woman rose with dreamlike slowness and grace. He heard her gasp a single word, his name, saw her run across the room toward him as he ran toward her, caught her in his arms and stood in the center of the room holding her, saying her name and kissing her lips.

When he released her he laughed with sheer pleasure of reunion, watched her own expression of joy mixed with concern. "What happened?" Kaetha said, touching his bandaged face.

"Nothing," Parker said. "Well, not nothing, but I'm okay, I'll tell you all about it later on, I needed to see you first, Kaetha." He turned to the others in the room. "Hello, Fleet," he said, "hello, Trili, was Janna good to you while your mother was away?"

The little girl answered "Janna let me stay up late and she told me stories every night."

Parker said "Good." Fleet said nothing. Parker put his arm about Paetha's waist, said to the other man "Fleet, Kaetha and I want to step outside for a little while. Will you watch Trili?"

For a moment there was silence, then Kaetha said "Please, Fleet."

The hunter grumbled assent. Kaetha said "Trili, you eat. I will ask Fleet when I get back."

Outside the cabin Parker walked a short distance with Kaetha in silence, then stopped, held her with her back against the wall of a cabin, ill-lighted. He looked into her face, felt his heart thumping as it had not since he was a thrilled and frightened adolescent. He kissed Kaetha once again, warmly, held her, their mouths together, hands pressing at each other's backs. When Parker took his mouth from her, half breathless, he said "Kaetha, these days apart . . . I know now, I want you for my wife. "Will you . . ." He paused.

The Relori woman said "Could you doubt since that morning?"

"And Trili," Parker said.

"You will be good to her," Kaetha said. "Fleet is not, you will be. But your face, and your arm," she said, concern in her voice.

"I just burned my hand," Parker said, "it's all right. And I got a couple of cuts on my face. I'll tell you all about it, but I have to report to Olduncle, he's waiting now probably. I'll come back for you later, Kaetha, you go back to Trili. I only wanted to see you before Olduncle."

He walked back to the cabin with Kaetha, embraced her again for an instant and turned his steps in the now full night of Relore, to the town plaza and the house of Olduncle. He walked quickly, feeling buoyed by the few minutes with Kaetha. Somehow, Parker felt, he had settled things for himself and for the future. He had been long in giving up hope of ever getting back to his own time and place in the world. Even the session with XaoQa in Par'z had been only the capper on a conviction he had already reached, that whatever quirk of nature it was that had brought him from a twentieth-century deep-freeze to this distant time of blended race and traded climates would never be undone. That the trip he had taken was strictly one-way.

But even then he had felt himself adrift in this new world, a stranger in a strange land, a stranded visitor surrounded by aliens and unable to make his way home. Now there was no longer any doubt in his mind. He would take Kaetha for his wife, Trili for his own child. He even let himself think of more children, his and Kae-

tha's, and a future in Relore. Parker's experiences in Par'z
and Teras only convinced him the more that he wanted
to live with the Relori.

In the village leader's cabin Olduncle sat with Scenter.
From somewhere Fletcher had also come, and the three
looked at Parker as he entered the building. Olduncle
motioned Parker to sit also, brought out his eternal qrart
jug and passed it; the swigs were brief tokens only, the
meeting was obviously going to be strictly business, and
serious.

"Parker," Olduncle opened, "I am told that you have
visited Par'z, then Teras, killed several Terasians and
escaped or been expelled from Teras."

Parker said only "Yes," waited for Olduncle to continue.

He did: "When you were here before I asked if you
wished to stay with us, become one of us. When you left
here you said you still hoped to find your own home.
Now you are back. I assume you have decided to accept
our offer since you have returned."

Again, "Yes."

Olduncle said "Very well. I am not certain that we can
still make the offer we once did. You must tell me all
that has happened that involves Teras in particular. You
know that our relationship with Teras is precarious at
best, that they are a powerful nation. You know also that
we do not turn criminals loose, we want no outlaw bands
ambushing our own hunters. But since you are not Relori
to start with. . . ." He looked straight at Parker; Parker
stared back. Olduncle finished, "I do not know what we
are going to do.

"You tell us what happened, then we will try to decide."

Parker told his story, very much as he had told it to
Scenter and the other fishermen their first night in the
woods. He gave more detail on Par'z, especially on
Mocles and Stacles and Chacla, told of killing the two
spies as they fled Par'z using jumpers, and of burning the
machines before they could be taken back to Teras. He
told of Byeryas and Nissral, of his own involvement under duress in their ancient hatred, his escape from the
Terasian interrogation chamber, the death of Byeryas'
two children and the captain's suicide.

He concluded: "So if the Terasians want to push it, they can accuse me of ten murders. And I did kill six but I'd hardly call them murders."

Parker watched Olduncle's face as he finished speaking. The village leader showed no sign of his reaction to the story. Olduncle said "Fletcher, you know Parker. You are a respected man in Relore. What do you think?"

The hunter did not reply immediately. He looked from Olduncle to Parker, then back. "I wish Parker had never gone to Par'z," he said at last. "If he had never involved himself with their ancient war we would have no problem now. But once he was involved, I think he did what was proper."

"Yes, yes," Olduncle said impatiently, "I am not interested in moralizing. What do we do now? What do we do if Teras demands Parker?"

"I say, we keep him. You know what Teras is, Olduncle. If they leave us in peace, fine. But we cannot bow to them."

"Why not? If they regard us as vermin, let them. Only let them leave us alone."

"Olduncle," Fletcher said, "you must be growing old and timid. As long as we are men and Teras wishes to think us vermin, let them. Yes. But if we begin to act like vermin, we give their foul regard for us truth. They humiliate our hunters, they harass our fishermen. Soon or late they will turn upon us. I do not believe they will wipe us out, I do not think they can. But if we must die, let us die as men fighting, not as roaches."

Parker watched Olduncle as he listened to Fletcher's speech. The older man turned to Scenter now, said "And you? What is your opinion, Scenter?"

The diminutive scout spoke, his mobile features expressing emotion that Parker read as Scenter's words came excitedly: "Fletcher is right," he said, "I too know the Terasians. I think they will destroy us some day. I would not have Relore attack Teras, but if war comes we must resist them. I saw the Terasians free Parker. If they demand him back we must refuse. Let them send one to argue before you if they wish."

"So," Olduncle said softly, looking from Fletcher to Scenter, from Scenter to Fletcher. "So it shall be." He reached behind him, brought out qrart and began to pass it around.

"Is that all?" Parker asked. "Three men vote and that's it? I'm glad you, uh, decided what you did, but. . . ." He stopped, looking at Olduncle.

"We did not vote," the Relori said. "I am the leader of Relore, the decision was mine alone, Parker. I asked Fletcher and Scenter for their opinions only to help me to form my own. You may stay."

Parker could only sit for a moment. When Scenter handed him the leader's jug he wet his tongue, barely, then passed the jug to Fletcher and rose, feeling suddenly exhausted, his nerves at the limit of their endurance, his head light. He turned, left the leader's cabin.

Outside the doorway, almost before he could reach the plaza, Parker saw Fleet standing. Fleet's face held an expression of fury. "I heard," he hissed at Parker. "You have brought nothing but trouble, first upon me alone, now upon all of Relore. Go back, Parker. Tell Olduncle that you will return to Teras. Then go to Teras. I will even take you."

Parker started to brush past the Relori. Fleet held an arm before him, grasped Parker's shirt when he tried to continue. "Do it!" he said loudly. "Do you want to destroy Relore?"

"You heard us all?" Parker asked him. "You know what happened, then. You heard Scenter and Fletcher and Olduncle. Why didn't you burst in and argue with them?"

Before Fleet made any answer Parker saw two figures emerge from the cabin of Olduncle. They were Fletcher and Scenter. They stood watching Parker and Fleet.

Fleet released Parker's shirt, dropped his blocking arm. "Go to Kaetha then, you foreign scum! Tell her not to expect me back if she has made her choice!" Fleet spat at Parker's feet, stalked angrily away. Fletcher and Scenter remained.

"I think we are in for real trouble, Parker," the bigger Relori said.

Parker answered "Fletcher, Scenter, how can I tell you . . . Look, Relore is like my home now. I have friends here now. I want to marry a Relori woman, stay with you. But maybe Fleet is right. Can I cause a war between Teras and Relore? Maybe I should go to the Terasians myself."

"No," Fletcher said. "Fleet is wrong. He is bitter

against you, you know that. And he may have a touch
of the coward in him too. Scenter was right, inside. If
Teras is out to destroy us, let them try, and let Relore
resist to her utmost. At least, no degrading surrender."

Parker said, simply, "Thank you, Fletcher. And you,
Scenter. All I can do now is become a Relori. And if the
Terasians come, I will stand against them."

Fletcher and Scenter went away, Parker following with
his eyes as the two headed from the plaza, now empty
in the full Relori night. Then Parker too went, slowly and
feeling drained, to the house of Kaetha. When he arrived
there she rose from a spot before the cabin, took his hand.
"Trili is sleeping," Kaetha said.

"Can you leave her?" Parker asked. Kaetha nodded.

Parker led Kaetha by the hand, found a grassy bank
near the stream that ran through the village. They sat together, their shoulders and arms pressing side by side,
talking quietly. Parker told Kaetha of the session with
Olduncle and the others, pausing now and then as he
spoke, but Kaetha did not add any words until he had
finished. Then she said "And Fleet?"

"Fleet wants me to give myself up to the Terasians,"
Parker said.

Kaetha said "No."

"You may not feel that way if war comes, Kaetha. Or
if you do, others may feel differently."

"You do not know Relore as well as you think," the
woman said. "We may not have a city like Teras, Parker,
but we are independent and we dislike bowing. No Relori
likes the way Teras treats our people when they find them
in the woods or on the sea, but the Terasians always stop
short of war with us. If it comes to war now, then it must."

"All right," said Parker. "All right. I'm sorry, Kaetha.
I'm at my limit now. I have to rest. He drew one leg up,
started to rise but half fell, catching Kaetha's shoulder and
steadying himself. The woman stood, drew his arm
around her shoulder to help him stand. "Every time I get
in trouble, you help me out of it, Kaetha." Parker mum-
bled the words, half unconscious from the drain of his
wounds and from sheer exhaustion. "You're my good
friend," he rambled on, "even if I love you, you're my
friend."

He managed to make his legs work, wobbling along,
Kaetha helping him, through Relore, to the simple build-

ing. He started to slip down, lost consciousness on the way.

Parker opened his eyes again to see that the sun stood high over the Country. He was in the house of Kaetha and Trili and Fleet but no other person was in the house. He sat up, steadying himself with his hands until his head stopped its spinning, looked down to see that he still wore his loosened clothes of the night before. Someone—surely it had been Kaetha—had removed his borrowed moccasins.

He stood carefully, feeling like a feeble old man, afraid to lose his balance and crash helplessly to the floor of the room, made his way to a cupboard and found some food. He was able to eat a piece of fruit and some already cooked meat, sitting propped against the wall, then rested again until Kaetha and Trili returned late in the afternoon.

Trili came to where Parker had propped himself up and stood looking at him. Parker returned her look, then raised his eyes to Kaetha watching the child from the doorway of the room. She smiled. Trili said "Are you better, Parker? Mother said you were sick."

Parker said "Much better, thank you. I hope you don't mind me in your house." He put out his good hand to the child who stared at it, then slowly put her own hand in Parker's.

She said "Fleet is very mean. If you will be nice you can stay in my house and live with us."

"I promise to try and be nice," Parker said to the child.

Kaetha had advanced into the room until she stood over Trili. She said quietly to Parker "You can stay, you know. By our custom I was Fleet's responsibility when my husband was killed. But the house is mine, not Fleet's. If you really want to stay. . . ."

Without taking his hand from Trili's, Parker reached up with his other despite its bandage, and took Kaetha's. "Oh yes," he said, "for good." He managed to rise and embrace Kaetha briefly. Then he said "I don't feel sick. Weak, though. I guess the burn and then bleeding just knocked me down for a while. But what's for dinner?"

Kaetha served a meal of fresh meat brought by hunters, vegetables and rough bread and qrart. Afterward Parker felt stronger and sat up in the cabin while Kaetha prepared Trili for sleep. He volunteered to tell her a story before she slept, felt better than he had for so long when the offer was accepted. He stuck to familiar tales of his own childhood.

The next day he was stronger, felt able to leave the cabin in the morning and walk. That night, with Kaetha and Trili, he visited Broadarm and Janna for a reunion that ended early when exhaustion again overcame Parker. Still, day by day he regained strength. Soon the bandages were gone from his arm and face, leaving behind scars that began only slowly to grow faint. Still, he was able to use the burned hand fully—more important, Parker thought, than the fact that it carried the mark of the flames from his campfire outside of Par'z.

He acquired new clothing and boots and weapons, began working again in the fields beyond the city, felt that soon he might be ready to leave the village and hunt again. Before he had any chance, the Terasians arrived.

"Just we three," the leader of the group explained. Parker was present in the village square before the home of Olduncle. Most of the hunters and fishermen were there, many older men, and women too, Parker saw as he looked at the crowd, sitting and standing around Olduncle and the three brown-garbed strangers.

The Terasian spoke again. "Just we three are here representing the compeerage of Teras. The ship that brought us waits a march away off the coastline. If we do not return Teras will attack Relore. You will be totally destroyed."

Olduncle answered the Terasian. "You see I have called many of my people here, Terasian. Now tell us what you want of us. Any Relori will be free to speak. We will answer you here, this day."

"You harbor one here who has sinned against the compeerage. He has taken the lives of ten servants of the compeerage." The Terasian scanned the plaza with his eye, stopped, gestured angrily. "I see the killer," he shouted, pointing at Parker. "You will give him to us. He will pay the penalty he owes to the compeerage!"

"And what else, Terasian?" asked Olduncle.

"You will give him to us now and we will permit you to exist in our shadow. In any case, Teras has been too soft for too long. One good performed by this man—" again he gestured at Parker"—was to dispose of the weakling Nissral. Under our new leaders there will be no more abandonment of infants. The compeerage will have other uses for surplus infants.

"Further, you will be forbidden the use of the sea. Relori fishermen will be disposed of. And your hunting must be held to the area south of your puny village. You will not venture in the direction of Teras under severe penalty."

Parker heard a low rumble pass through the crowd of Relori. Olduncle turned to the crowd. He said "Would any here bow to such terms?"

For a moment there was a silence punctuated with angry half-aloud cries of "No," "Never," "Fight first." Then a voice familiar to Parker shouted "What is our choice?" Parker looked for the speaker but could not see him. He did see Olduncle look at the Terasian as if passing along the question.

"You have no choice, vermin!" the Terasian grated. "Yield and you survive a while longer, while it pleases us. Resist and we will roll over you now."

"Give him the man!" a voice shouted from the crowd. Again Parker tried to locate its source, to identify its owner. "Relori, do you know who the murderer is? He is not even one of us, he is the foreigner, the usurper of our rights, that man!" Parker saw the speaker now, recognized face and voice in an instant. Facing him, pointing from across the Relori crowd, stood Fleet.

Parker stood looking at the crowd of familiar and half-familiar Relori faces, the men with whom he had hunted, the women he had seen in their fields with their husbands, a few even of the children he had seen at their play. People he had hoped to become one of. He saw them all, following Fleet's pointing finger, staring at him. "I am the man," he said. "When I was found in the forest Relori took me and cared for me. Relori has been good to me. Its people have been generous. If you will let me, I will become a Relori. But if I am to cause war, I will go to Teras."

For a moment Parker thought he saw doubt in many faces, wonder at whether this man, still alien to many of them, should be shielded at such risk. Parker saw neighbor nudge neighbor, head bend to head to exchange low words. Then a voice: "Go, go, foreigner. Go to Teras and leave Relore forever!" The voice was Fleet's. The words seemed to galvanize the crowd, to decide the doubtful.

Shouts of "No, do not yield!" came. A huge figure seemed to grow out of the crowd, rising to the height of a man, a very tall, broad-shouldered man. "I brand *you* coward and traitor," Broadarm's huge voice rumbled. "You, Fleet, alone in Relore would bow to these shameful demands. If you love Teras so, you return with her emissaries. Parker will stay, and I will stand with him."

"And I." It was Fletcher.

"And I." Scenter.

Again a rumble spread through the crowd, a rumble of agreement and affirmation. Parker saw Olduncle turn toward the Terasians. "You have heard our people speak," the leader said. "I could argue with them but I will not. I agree with them. Their decision is mine.

"Relore does not wish war with Teras. Leave us in peace, we will leave you in peace. If you will not give us your unwanted children, that must be your own affair, for all that we deplore your practice. If you wish, we can meet and discuss hunting and fishing rights. And we will not give you Parker."

The Terasian spokesman pulled himself up to a greater height. "We do not discuss terms with filth. We offer you survival not by right but by our sufferance. We do not negotiate. We command!"

Parker held his breath, waiting for Olduncle's angry reply. It did not come. Instead, the Relori said quietly "We will discuss your requests gladly. But you cannot command us. If you will not reason with us, you must do whatever you think right to do."

The three Terasians turned and marched toward the gate in Relore's palisade. As Parker followed them with his eyes he saw another move after them through the crowd.

CHAPTER

20

Oh boy, Parker thought. Now it's really going to hit the fan!

"What now?" The questioner was Fletcher. He looked at Parker expectantly.

"You mean, in my world? Hah!" Parker rubbed his chin thoughtfully. "I guess this is about as close as we can come, around here, to some kind of diplomatic ultimatum. We turned 'em down. I'm grateful for that, Fletcher, Olduncle. But unless I'm mistaken, they'll be back. Probably with an army in tow. And you folks haven't ever fought a war, have you?"

"We've never had to. We have no enemies. Well, we've known the Terasians were hostile to us. But they've always been willing to leave us pretty much alone."

"Yeah. Till I arrived. Well, if Relore has never fought a war, neither has Teras. Or at least not since they drove the Par'zians into their retreat. So that should more or less—"

He was interrupted by a burst of shouting and the sound of running feet coming from outside the palisade. The shouting drew closer. Three Relori struggled through the gate, one on either side helping to sustain the third who was being half-dragged between them.

"What's happened?" Olduncle rose, spun to face the newcomers.

"Terasians!" one of them gasped. "Hundreds of them! We were just headed out for a hunt, and we came upon them on the trail. They fired without warning!"

The two Relori lowered their companion to the ground. A shaft protruded from between his shoulder-blades. It was clearly of a different sort from the Relori arrows, the product of a different society.

"Get the gates shut!" Olduncle roared.

The gatekeepers leaped to obey his command. They

264

swung the heavy wooden gates, grunting with effort. Old-uncle shouted for more men and women to help them, and figures sprang toward the gates, adding their muscles to the effort.

From outside the sounds of heavy rumbling wheels and marching feet were heard. There was a series of thuds as arrows slammed into the wooden palisade and the gates.

Parker ran from the place where they had been conversing and threw his weight into the effort. Through the narrowing crack between the gates he could see a Terasian column, broad and nearly square like a Roman phalanx, filling the clearing between the palisade and the nearest woods. Advancing through the center of the Terasian force was a heavy battering ram. It was mounted on metal-shod wheels. Its tip was pointed, apparently by careful axe-strokes, so that it looked almost like a gargantuan pencil.

The ram was within twenty yards of the gates. Terasian soldiers raced ahead of it, struggled to press through the narrowing space. A few managed to get their arms or legs through the gate; one man in the familiar baggy clothing of the Terasian compeerage managed to squeeze through just before the gates met with a heavy thump.

Moans and howls emerged from the Terasians whose limbs had been caught in the closing gates. The lone Terasian who had got through before the gates shut hefted a kind of bladed spear. Without waiting for words he set himself, charged at the nearest group of Relori.

A man in rough Relori garb sprang aside, blood spouting from a long, shallow gash. The Terasian howled in triumph, sprang again to the attack. A second Relori drew his friendmaker, slashed at the Terasian's arm.

"Just disable him!" Olduncle was moving toward the scene of battle, but before he arrived the Relori's blade thunked into the invader's flesh. He had aimed for the Terasian's arm, but the latter, twisting and ducking to avoid the blow, had inadvertently brought his shoulder in line with the flashing blade. The friendmaker went deep into the muscles up the Terasian's upper shoulder. His head tilted crazily as he fell, dropping his weapon.

Parker ran to his side and dropped to one knee. The Terasian glared at him briefly, moved his lips silently, and died.

"Damn!" Parker hissed. "We might have learned a lot

from him. Even so . . ." He looked up, saw Fletcher standing over him, watching.

"Look at this guy's clothing," Parker said. "Look at his boots." He tapped the Terasian's footgear. "Look at that. These folks have had a long walk through the woods. I'd have thought that they'd come here by sea, but I guess they had to march to get their ram through. And their boots aren't suited for long tramps through the countryside, they're city boots. This guy isn't in such hot shape!"

"That's good news," Fletcher nodded. "Do all wars start as suddenly as this one?"

Before Parker could get his answer out there was a crash from the direction of the gates. "There goes the ram," he growled. "There's going to be no mobilization period for this war. I just hope Relore is ready to fight, because that gate isn't going to hold for more than a few minutes."

Relori were scurrying about, oldsters herding small children to the questionable security of wooden buildings in the center of the village. Everyone else, from pre-adolescents to middle-aged, were seizing weapons and heading for the village square near the gate in the palisade.

"I can't stay with you," Fletcher shouted at Parker. "I have to work with the archers!" He sprinted away, began shouting to the men and women, armed with long-bows, who were assembling themselves. In seconds they were forming ranks, drawing arrows, preparing to decimate at least the first wave of the enemy who might penetrate an opening in the wooden barrier.

The palisade shook and the sound of the battering ram striking the wooden gates reverberated throughout the village.

Parker felt a hand on his shoulder, turned to face Olduncle. "You've cast your lot," the elderly man said. "You are with us now, whether you choose to be or not, Parker."

"That was decided before now," Parker said.

Olduncle nodded, moved away, speaking quietly to this person and that.

Parker moved forward, scanning the array of Relori who faced the city's gates, preparing to meet the Terasian force. That wasn't how Parker would have advised them to face this enemy, he thought. It was a textbook case of the woodsmen against the overorganized, over-equipped, overdisciplined invading force. The right tactics had defeated that kind of invader in every war from the American Revolution to Vietnam.

But there wasn't time for a retreat to the woods, for the Relori to arrange themselves to pick off Terasian stragglers, to cut their supply lines, to sabotage their outguards and gradually chip away at the invaders until they were demoralized and halfway decimated, ready to pull out and abandon their enterprise, not because they had been beaten but because they could never consolidate their position.

There was a cracking sound and the whole section of palisade enclosing the gates shuddered visibly.

To either side of the Relori archers were ranged detachments of warriors—yes, for these hunters and fisher-folk and farmers were now fighting for the survival of their society—armed with friendmakers, spears and knives. Once the hail of Relori arrows had taken their toll, these squads would close with the enemy and fight it out, hand-to-hand, to the death.

With a shudder and a long, slow creaking that resembled a single sustained scream, the main gates of the Relori town yielded. They opened and closed from both sides, like shutters; now the one of them, smashed by the Terasian battering ram, folded like an ill-conditioned boxer taking a hard belly punch. The ram was pulled back on its metal-shod wheels, shoved forward again even as the broken gate continued its collapse.

Now the second gate gave way, its upper hinge torn bodily from the wooden post of the palisade wall. The sound of the hinge being ripped from its place came like a shot. The lower hinge remained connected, acting like a fulcrum. The door toppled inward, looking like the wall of a dynamited building in a slow-motion news-reel. It struck the ground with a thud that shook Parker, nearly knocking him from his feet.

A cloud of dust rose from the bare ground where the door fell. A light breeze was sweeping through the village, running, at this point, parallel to the inner wall of the palisade. It carried the dust rapidly away.

Through the now open gates, the Terasian battering ram extended into the village. Scores of Terasians clustered around it. A row of them ranged along either side of the massive wooden ram, still clinging to handles driven into its sides like pitons in the face of a cliff; thus they had propelled it forward to perform its destructive work.

Now masses of Terasian soldiers, clustered around and behind the ram, launched themselves forward, pouring through the opening in the palisade wall. They wore the uniform drab brown garments of Teras; all carried short, heavy javelins. And all of them carried curved shields; from Parker's perspective they seemed to be fabricated of heavy, woven wicker.

Relori arrows, Parker thought, would have an advantage over Terasian javelins except at close range; but if the Relori fired at once, their bows might not give enough power to pierce the invaders' shields, and if they waited for the Terasians to close the distance between them, they would lose their advantage to the javelins.

Parker watched the Relori archers. Fletcher stood in command of them, one arm raised, signaling them to hold their fire.

The Terasians remained in a massed formation, ignoring the squads of Relori swordsmen and advancing at a trot toward the archers. Many of the invaders, Parker noted with satisfaction, moved at an uncomfortable, limping pace—clearly the penalty of tramping through the woods in heavy, stiff boots. That would distract them, possibly enough to effect their combat efficiency.

The Terasians closed the distance to the Relori archers —thirty yards, twenty-five, twenty. One of their officers —Parker couldn't see who—shouted a command. The Terasians hefted their javelins.

Parker heard Fletcher shout an order to his archers. To a man—and woman—they nocked arrows, drew on their bows.

Standing with the other Relori swordsman, Parker had the mad, fleeting notion that he was a spectator at some sort of wild west rodeo show, that all of this wasn't quite real but a cleverly staged simulation of some historic battle, and that there was no way that he—a paying customer—could possibly be called on to take any risk.

The illusion was shattered as Fletcher issued the command to his archers to fire. Simultaneously the unseen Terasian officer shouted an order to the massed phalanx of javelin-bearers.

The front row of the Terasian phalanx hurled their javelins, dropped to one knee as the second rank took position to throw their own javelins over the heads of the first rank.

At the same moment the Relori archers—ranged in a shallow formation that permitted maximum firepower at the instant of Fletcher's command—released a flight of arrows.

The simultaneous flights of arrows and javelins passed through each other like interpenetrating ranks of marchers in a carefully choreographed band formation. The sounds of their release provided a background for the sight: grunt of effort, rattle of javelin, twang of bowstring, swish of missiles in clear air. And then the *thwack!* of iron-tipped arrows penetrating wicker shields; the two forces had been close enough at the moment of release for the flashing arrows to do their work.

Some, true, were deflected. Some struck and were held harmlessly in the Terasian's shields. But the greatest number struck the invading warriors and sent them tumbling to the ground.

And from Parker's left came the sickening sounds of Terasian javelins plunging home in Relori bodies. The defenders carried no shields. Their defense in combat was keyed to stealth and mobility, to lightness and litheness of movement, the quick and accurate attack, and when an enemy javelin struck there was only thin cloth or soft leather between its metal-shod tip and Relori flesh.

Fletcher shouted commands, and a second flight of arrows followed the first, while flights of javelins from succeeding ranks of the Terasian phalanx flew toward the Relori.

From farther back in the Terasian phalanx the javelins had less effect and less accuracy than those thrown in the initial exchange. The weary Terasians, fighting after their long march from their walled city, were in a reduced state of combat effectiveness. But the Relori arrows, also having to reach a greater distance now, were arriving with reduced force and accuracy; their flight an increasingly high arc, they arrived with more of their force expended and rattled harmlessly off Terasian shields.

"Now!"

The voice came from the party of Relori on the far side of the gate from Parker, but still it carried to him with force. He could pick out the man who had shouted, a giant whose massive shoulders as much as his towering height would make him visible in any crowd.

Broadarm!

And beside him, nearly as gigantic, and fully as visible in the cluster of fighting men and women, Janna!

Parker, accustomed to fighting thousands of miles from home while families waiting for word remained in distant America, realized with an agonizing twist in his gut, that he had lost track of the whereabouts of Kaetha. Trili, he knew, had been safely hustled off to shelter with the other children and oldsters of the village. But where was Kaetha?

But there was no time now to search or even to wonder. Again, Broadarm's voice echoed, and Parker and those around him, friendmakers drawn, charged at the flanks of the Terasian phalanx. The opposing flights of arrows and of javelins had ceased to cross the open area. The broad, thin line of Relori archers, their bows discarded where they had stood, were charging, drawing bladed weapons as they ran.

The invading Terasians, forced from the attack onto the defense, had drawn bladed weapons of their own. They were surrounded on three sides by counterattacking Relori. Friendmakers flashed in the bright sunlight, Terasian weapons jabbed in reply, blood spouted from wounds.

The wicker shields of the Terasians proved both an advantage to them and a handicap. The shields could not stop the attack of a hard-swung Relori friendmaker landing blade-edge downward atop the wicker implement, nor could a Terasian shield stop a friendmaker driven head-on with the full weight of a Relori defender behind it.

But a partially-spent blow or a glancing slash or off-center jab could be deflected, saving the Terasian shield-bearer from a serious wound. But at the same time the shields limited the movement of the Terasians who carried them. A warrior's mobility, his ability to twist to avoid a blow or to strike one, was reduced by the weight and bulk of the clumsy shield. All the while, his ability to slash or jab with his own weapon was restricted by the presence of the wicker defense.

Parker was among the Relori charging from the right side of the village's smashed gates, into the phalanx of invaders. The first foe he encountered was a squarely built man whose eye caught Parker's as they closed. A message seemed to pass between them, as if they exchanged a challenge and an agreement that only one of the two would survive the encounter.

The Terasian was a shorter man than Parker. He fought in a cautious style, his knees bent and his feet spread, his shield held high so that he barely peered over its upper rim.

Parker feinted a high jab with his friendmaker, as if poking at the man's eyes. The Terasian dodged skillfully, shot his weapon-bearing hand around one edge of his shield and poked at Parker. The Terasian's blade caught Parker on the upper arm, then was gone. Parker looked down and saw a small spot of blood on his sleeve. He had been pinked. He laughed ruefully. The wound was trivial but his opponent was not the easy mark he'd appeared.

Parker lunged forward, putting his good shoulder and as much of his body weight into the lunge as he could.

The Terasian dodged skillfully, turning in place rather than stepping away.

Parker's blade struck the Terasian's shield, glanced off the curving wicker harmlessly. The Terasian raised his own blade and swung downward. If the blow struck, Parker stood to lose his sword arm from just below the elbow. Desperately he jerked his body backward.

His friendmaker scraped the edge of the Terasian's shield. The hooked tip of Parker's weapon, completely without intention on his part, caught at the edge of the Terasian's shield and, as Parker's weight tugged it backward, the shield came around and toward him. The Terasian, his shield-arm hooked thrugh a pair of grommets on the back of the shield, was also tugged around so he stood with his back three-quarters toward Parker.

Instead of trying to recover his position, the Terasian continued to swing around, making a complete circle so as to face his opponent again. But as he completed his spin he realized—too late to make a correction—that he had made a fatal mistake. Parker, his friendmaker freed from the Terasian's shield as the wicker rim slipped from the weapon's hook, was slashing toward his belly.

The Terasian realized in the instant that Parker had made a small, counter-clockwise swing of his weapon and was now propelling it through a backhand arc. If the Terasian had had his shield in its normal position, he could easily have deflected the off-speed slash. But his shield was on the wrong side of his body as he came through his spin. Parker's blade caught him squarely in the side, just below the ribs, and ripped into his flesh.

Parker tugged his friendmaker back toward himself, felt its blade hesitate momentarily, then slide from the Terasian's body as the latter slipped to the ground. Parker flirted for a fraction of a second with the idea of taking the fallen Terasian's shield—but he abandoned the thought. Unskilled in its use, he would hardly benefit from it.

And he had no time for further thought as he heard a Relori's voice shout a warning to him. Instinctively he crouched and spun, felt the wind as a Terasian weapon swept over his head, a weapon that would have caught him in the neck or upper chest and surely put him out of the battle save for the warning shout.

He found himself joining a struggle already under way, one Relori—Parker recognized small, agile Scenter—against two Terasians. One of the latter, the one closer to Parker, was a tall, fleshless soldier with a thin, sneering expression plastered on his face. The other was shorter and broader in build.

Scenter had been holding off the two Terasians, using his natural agility and the greater freedom of his unencumbered condition to dance away from and around his opponents. But the Terasians, their shields overlapping to make a wall impregnable to Scenter's attack, were clearly wearing down their foe.

Parker struck at the man opposite him, aiming his weapon at the towering enemy's thighs beneath the edge of his shield. The Terasian batted downward with his shield, at the same time swinging a blow downward with his blade.

Instantly, Parker realized his peril.

He used the downward force that the Terasian's shield had imparted to his friendmaker to swing the blade into an upward arc, simultaneously dropping into a crouch as he moved his friendmaker into a horizontal posture. It caught the Terasian's descending blow, barely in time. The colliding metal blades rang out, and Parker felt a jolt vibrate from his fingertips to his shoulder. He very nearly dropped his sword but managed to hold it and to recover his position.

At his side, out of the tail of his eye, he caught sight of Scenter, now having a somewhat better time against a single foe instead of two. The Terasians had been forced to unlock their shields as their two opponents maneuvered, lest one Relori sprint behind them as they held the other at bay. They were nearly back-to-back now, each confident that his rear was protected by his companion. Parker wondered if an attacker might not be behind him, but he resisted the impulse to turn and look.

Better the risk of a surprise attack, than the certain death that would result from turning his back on the towering Terasian foe.

He parried a lunge by his opponent, countered with a short lunge of his own, missed, recovered, tried a sideways slash that was deflected by the Terasian's shield. The Terasian was holding his shield high as Parker jabbed at his face like a boxer keeping an opponent off balance. Now Parker struck at the man's legs again, swinging his blade in a fast arc that would land at the kneecaps if not countered.

The Terasian swung his shield downward again, this time also propelling himself backward, knowing that the force of Parker's swing might pierce the wicker shielding.

Suddenly Parker saw the Terasian rise, as if striving to leap into the air. An expression of ineffable shock appeared on the Terasian's face. Convulsively he swung his arms sideways, the wicker shield to his left, his glittering blade arcing away to the right, propelled by involuntarily flexing fingers.

The hooked tip of a friendmaker protruded from his body just below the sternum. Startled, Parker realized what had happened. Scenter, fighting for his life against the Terasian's partner, had made a desperate lunge. His opponent had dodged, and the blade had encountered the back of Parker's opponent. The latter, propelled backward by his own effort to avoid Parker's slash, had impaled himself fatally on Scenter's blade.

Parker shouted a word of thanks at the smaller Relori. He saw a look of pleasure on Scenter's face, but in the instant of the expression's appearance, it disappeared again. Scenter tugged desperately at his friendmaker, striving to pull it from the body of Parker's now-defunct foe. Realizing that he could not get his blade free, Secnter sprang away, disarmed.

But his own foe was after him, and before Scenter could take evasive action he was impaled on the Terasian's blade.

Parker followed up the act, now having the Terasian at a total disadvantage. The Terasian tried to tug his blade from Scenter's body, but Scenter, blood gouting from his belly and his mouth, clearly dying, still thrashed and pounded on the earth. Parker offered the Terasian no more mercy than the Terasian had given to Scenter. As the invader tugged at the handle of his weapon, Parker brought his friendmaker forward from the hip as if it were a gravity knife. It slipped through the Terasian's brown garment and into his flesh.

Parker jerked back on the weapon.

The Terasian spun away, tumbling onto the now-unmoving Scenter. Both bodies twitched, an unspeakable parody of wrestlers struggling desperately for a grip on each other, and then lay still.

The battle was moving, the arrangement of the two forces altering as the Relori pressed in on the invading Terasian unit. The Relori flanking forces were heavier and denser than the former archery line. The flanking forces had pressed in on the phalanx, squeezing its original square configuration into an elongated rectangle that stretched from the gates of the village and pointed like a dagger at its center.

The former archers were spread too thinly to hold the advancing tip of the Terasian salient and were gradually bent into a vee, its angle established by the Terasian advance, its arms closing to an ever tighter acute angle as the warriors spread themselves along the edges of the salient.

Even so, the advance was no sign of success for the intruding force. The Terasians had attacked at the end of a difficult overland march and were fatigued and partially disabled. The Relori warriors were fresh and strong. It was the Battle of Hastings revisited, but with the roles of invader and defender reversed. This time it was Harold's Britons who were fresh and healthy, the Normans of William the Bastard who were exhausted from the outset.

And it was the fresh Relori who won the day.

The defending flankers closed behind the Terasian force, cutting off any possibility of retreat through the smashed palisade. Not that there was any thought of retreat on the part of the Terasians. Whatever their faults, their courage and their discipline never wavered. They fought to the last soldier. Only a single figure, in the noise and confusion of the carnage, broke and disappeared into the village.

The ground lay littered with bodies, muddied with gore. The Terasians, failing to take account of the difficulty of the overland march and arrogant in their strength and discipline and in the contempt with which they regarded Relore, had taken on more of a task than they could perform.

But they neither complained, nor surrendered, nor ran. As several of the Relori leaders were later to remark, it would have been better to take prisoners than to exterminate the invading force to the last soldier. But again, the battle had been conducted on so impromptu a basis, there had been no time for a session of tactical planning and the issuance of orders. It was only the long-term cohesion of the Relori society and the constant companionship and *de facto* training effect of their hunting parties that had enabled them to meet the challenge when it came.

Now Relori wandered among the scattered forms, searching for friends and brothers and sisters, seeking wounded among the dead. No Terasian had survived the battle; none had permitted himself to survive. But a number of Relori wounded were found, and carried tenderly from the place of battle to be ministered to with the nature medicines of their people.

Parker found a familiar, graceful form lying in a pool of gore, blood still oozing from a hideous gash in her skull. He fell to his knees, found Kaetha still breathing. The only injury she had sustained was a terrible blow to the skull. If it had hit with the narrow edge of a blade, it would surely have been fatal on the moment. But she had been struck by the flat edge of a hard-swung weapon.

The impact had knocked her unconscious and had torn her scalp for half the distance from ear to forehead, producing a spectacular flow of blood that would give the appearance of an injury far more serious than that actually sustained.

She would recover.

She would take nursing and rest, and would carry a terrible scar only partly covered by her hair, for the rest of her life. But she would recover.

There was a single shout, then the murmur of voices, then the sound of a man's voice raised in menace and command. Parker looked up from the slim form he still held in his arms.

It was Fleet!

Fleet, who had left Relore with the earlier Terasian emissary, who had changed his soft Relori clothing for the baggy brown uniform of the Terasians and returned with the invading phalanx.

He stood now, growling commands. In his left arm he held the still, terrified form of Trili. In his right hand, his Relori friendmaker, its back-blade pressed to the child's throat, its hooked tip digging into her soft flesh just where the jawbone curves to meet the ear.

"You're a pack of fools," he hissed at the assembled villagers. "You should have turned this foreigner over to the Terasians while there was still time. Now it's too late. Keep him or send him away, it's up to you. But I'm going to Teras, and this child dies if anyone tries to stop me!"

He stepped from the shadow of a wooden building, into the slowly declining sunlight.

"Teras will be back," Fleet resumed. "Relore is finished." A half-hysterical laugh escaped his throat. "The only way—the only chance you have—turn over Parker to the Terasians. Send him under guard. Or"—again the mad giggle—"kill him now, and send his head to Teras on the end of one of their javelins."

"Let the child go!" Parker shouted.

"Are you crazy?" Fleet glared wildly in all directions. "How long would I last if I let Trili down? You're all against me. Only the Terasians are my friends. You people all sided with this foreigner against me. Kaetha wouldn't have me, but she'll lie with that filth! Let me pass, or the child dies!"

He drew the friendmaker a fraction of an inch to the

side. Its hooked point drew a bead of blood from Trili's neck. The child whimpered and squirmed briefly in Fleet's arms.

"Will you let her go if I go with you?" Parker held his own friendmaker away from his body, ready to drop it to the ground if Fleet accepted his offer.

Fleet took another step away from the wooden building, another step nearer to the village gates.

"Maybe that would do. Maybe it would do. You! You!" He shouted across the clearing to Broadarm. "Come over here."

The giant exchanged glances with his wife, Janna, with Olduncle, with Parker himself. No word was spoken. Hesitantly, the heel of his hand resting on the pommel of his own weapon, he crossed the space that separated him from the renegade Fleet.

"That's close enough!" Fleet barked.

Broadarm halted, looking around unobtrusively.

"Now you!" Fleet gestured to Parker. Fleet managed to convey his message with the movement of one elbow, keeping his other hands around Trili and his weapon. His gesture to Parker spoke clearly: *drop your friendmaker.*

Parker complied.

"Now, over here! Kneel! You, Broadarm, if you want to spare Trili's life, here is your chance. You can play executioner. Take off this interloper's head and bring it to me on the tip of a javelin!"

"Fleet! Come to your senses, man! Nobody turned against you. Kaetha chose Parker. That can't be helped. She's free to make her choice. Put down the child, stay here in Relore. We need everyone now."

Fleet drew the blade across Trili's neck. A thin ribbon of red appeared. A drop from it rolled toward the child's chest. She began to cry softly, less in pain than in mortal terror.

"Drop her, Fleet! For your own—"

Broadarm got no farther.

The lithe, particolored form rose from its place atop the building behind Fleet and launched itself into the air with a single graceful motion. It was the giant cat Longa.

Fleet might have heard a slight sound, might somehow have sensed that he had delayed too long, drawn out the drama too far, for the delicious sense of vengeance and omnipotence it gave him. Now it was too late for him to evade the flying creature.

Longa crashed into Fleet's back, her legs flexed, her claws extended. The man was knocked to the ground, his friendmaker flying through the air to clatter harmlessly onto packed earth, the child Trili landing on all fours, rising to her feet and turning desperately in search of a familiar pair of arms. Janna found her and nestled the terrified child against her body.

No one else could move more than to watch the brief, foreordained struggle between Fleet and Longa. The man could do no more than try to curl into foetal position, to cover the soft, vulnerable organs of his face and throat, his belly and his genitals, from the savage attack of the big calico. The only effect of Fleet's efforts was to delay the inevitable, and that by a matter of mere seconds.

The sound of the great cat's snarls echoed off the still-standing palisade. The snarling was punctuated by a single cry of terror and of pain from the turncoat Relori, then by a groan.

Then the cat gave her victim a single mighty shake, the way a terrier shakes a weasel to snap its neck, and then she dropped the gore-spattered remains of Fleet and stalked from the village. No one approached her as she strode to the nearest trees and disappeared among them.

Later—many hours later—Parker and Kaetha were together in Kaetha's home. No lamp flickered, but bright moonlight poured through a large window, filling the room with soft, cool illumination. The soft sound of Trili's breathing came from the next room, and the shuffle and call of sentries floated through the village.

Kaetha had slept deeply; now she wished to talk.

"You're going to stay, then? You've given up hope of returning to your homeland?"

Parker nodded. "I was lost in time as well as space. I might find the place where my home once was. Some-day—someday, I think, I'd like to try. To try and find what's going on in the rest of the world. The Country isn't a very big place after all. But Relore is my real home, now. I'm at home here, Kaetha, with you."

She moved gingerly, favoring her wounded scalp and her other bruises. "Then this terrible battle is over. We can go back to our old ways." There was more hope in her voice than there was conviction.

"I wish you could. *We* could," Parker amended. "But the old ways are finished, Kaetha. It's my fault, I suppose. I—well, I didn't make the change, but I was the catalyst that provoked it. Teras lost a raiding party, but Teras is still there. They'll be back, and they'll be ready for a tougher battle than they were this time. They thought it would be a breeze for them to conquer a bunch of disorganized farmers. Next time it will be a tougher proposition.

"No." He shook his head. "And I don't think we can start from scratch and build a force that can stand against Teras. If we can shake Par'z out of its happy dream. Damn it, everything around here was pretty comfortable till I arrived. Now—"

"You did nothing wrong," Kaetha said.

"I didn't intend to. In I walked like Mister Big Dummy and started knocking things out of kilter."

"What's done cannot be undone," Kaetha insisted. "And if we cannot have our old ways back . . ."

In the cool semi-darkness, Parker nodded. "Things are going to hum around here. We'll be inventing technology. Reinventing it. Remembering and rebuilding it. Like it or not, we'll wind up exploring the rest of the world, and who knows what we'll find! Someday I suppose we'll have aircraft again. And someday maybe even spaceships again."

He laughed then, in part at himself, in part in irony.

"You and I will never see it, Kaetha, but Trili or her children or their children might. Someday, if we're lucky, people will go to the stars. They may have done it before, somewhere between my time—my first time—and now. They may still be up there somewhere. And someday we'll go and look for them!"

AUTHOR'S NOTE

One Million Centuries first appeared in the fall of 1967. It was my first professionally published work of fiction. I had been trying for some years to sell short stories, but without success. My good friend James Blish suggested that I try a novel. I dragged my heels for a while, then produced an outline and a few sample chapters, and Larry Shaw of the old Lancer Books offered me a contract on the strength of that material.

I signed it, and the commitment was made.

In due course the book appeared. Larry was enthusiastic, and, boy, was I ever excited and proud! I expected the world to sit up and take notice.

It did not.

I continued to be able to ride the subway unrecognized. My face did not appear on the cover of *Time* magazine. NBC did not telephone to ask me to visit the *Tonight* show and chat with Johnny Carson. Among the literary prizes which I did not win were the Hugo, the Nebula, the National Book Award, the Pulitzer, and the Nobel.

In fact, I was astonished at the *lack* of reactions to my masterpiece. There were a few reviews, mostly friendly, mostly in the science fiction fan press but also in such papers as the New York *Post* and Hartford *Courant*. And at least one science fiction fan, Fred Patten (bless his heart!), did mention the book as a *possible* Hugo *contender*. Even that equivocal endorsement was balm to my aching ego.

In due course the book went out of print, Lancer Books went out of business, *One Million Centuries* became a minor collector's item, and I turned my attention to other projects.

Now David Hartwell of Pocket Books has offered me several weeks' worth of grocery money for the right to reissue *One Million Centuries,* and I am grateful both for the shekels and for the opportunity to get my first novel back in print. I have made a few changes for this edition, and readers may be interested in just where they occur.

The original edition of the book opened with a chapter set in the Twentieth Century, wherein Robert Leroy Parker, a helicopter pilot, is involved in a crash while on a rescue mission in Antarctica. Parker's co-pilot, Harry Logan, is killed. Parker is frozen alive, to recover in the remote future where the remainder of the novel is set.

James Blish read the book in manuscript and commented, "You ought to drop this framing sequence. Start the book where your real story starts, with Parker's reawakening." I was too close to my own prose at the time to realize that Blish was right (he almost always was—there was a man, and I miss him!) but for this new edition, I have belatedly heeded his good advice, and simply dropped the frame.

In discussing the new edition, David Hartwell pointed out that the original closing chapter was both overlong and rather weak. The story rather fizzled out than ended. I have consequently tossed out the old final chapter, and written a new one, both shorter and (I hope) more emphatic.

These are the only major changes in the book. I have made a few other, minor, fixes.

Rereading *One Million Centuries* for the first time in nearly fifteen years, I found it neither as bad a book as I'd feared, nor as good a one as I'd hoped. I think I've learned a good deal about the craft of fiction since 1966–67; I know I've still a lot to learn, and if God lets me stay on this planet and keep working for some more years (I'm not sure how many it will take) I still hope to become a first-class writer.

Now, two final notes on the matter of verisimilitude.

In *One Million Centuries*, Robert Parker learns the rudiments of a new language in just three days. And he becomes thoroughly fluent, if never quite eloquent, in a short time more. This time is not specified, but it appears to be a mere few weeks.

It has been pointed out to me that this is an achievement unlikely in the extreme. I concede the point, and ask the reader to accept Parker's linguistic feat as a "given."

On the other hand, when I invented my acid-generating, fruit-pulp-sucking butterflies in 1966, there was no corresponding species known in nature. Less than a year later, such a species was discovered to exist. Not only do these creatures secrete a caustic chemical just as my "kissers" do, but they *use* this secretion for just the purpose I had guessed they would, i.e., to dissolve spots on the rind of thick-skinned tropical fruit, following which the butterflies take their nourishment through a proboscis inserted into the fruit.

Richard A. Lupoff
1980